NO GREATER LOVE

Dara Viane

No Greater Love
Copyright © 2010 Dara Viane
Published by BookBelle, LLC

All rights reserved. No part of this book may be reproduced (except for inclusion in reviews), disseminated or utilized in any form or by any means, electronic or mechanical, including photocopying, recording, or in any information storage and retrieval system, or the Internet/World Wide Web without written permission from the author or publisher.

For more information please contact www.daraviane.com

Book design by:
Arbor Books, Inc.
www.arborbooks.com

Printed in the United States of America

No Greater Love
Dara Viane

1. Title 2. Author 3. Historical Fiction/Romance

Library of Congress Control Number: 2009911192

ISBN 10: 0615331335
ISBN 13: 978-0-615-33133-1

Dedicated to Jesus…the author and finisher of our faith, who for the joy that was set before him endured the cross, despising the shame, and is set down at the right hand of the throne of God.
Hebrews 12:2

*Greater love hath no man than this,
that a man lay down his life for his friends.*
John 15:13

I

Fleeing the vindictive wrath of Caesar's son, the young couple fought their way through the flourishing summer vegetation, running as swiftly as their sandal clad feet would carry them across the verdant countryside, hoping against hope; they could escape the Roman soldiers who were in relentless pursuit.

"Leave me!" Tamar cried out, stopping to catch her breath.

"I will not leave thee!" declared Josiah, halting in his steps, his alert brown eyes anxiously scanning the horizon for soldiers.

"Josiah, I beg thee…leave me! I can go no farther! Save thyself!"

"There is no time to spare, Tamar! The soldiers are gaining on us! Come," urged Josiah, taking her by the hand and leading her onward.

Striving to keep pace with Josiah, Tamar forced one foot in front of the other, mustering what little strength she had left in her body, but her effort was futile for she did not have his physical stamina. Her weary legs soon gave way beneath her and she stumbled, falling face down in the grassy terrain, hearing as she fell the thunderous sound of approaching horses.

Overtaking the female fugitive, the Roman officer descended from his horse with lightening speed and planted his dirty hobnailed boots on her coarse homespun dress, pinning his fair prey where she had fallen. "Over here," yelled the Prefect of the Praetorian Guard, his black, malevolent eyes fastened on Josiah, who stood a few yards from him, motionless with fear.

"Run! Run, Josiah! Run!" shrieked Tamar as two mounted soldiers galloped onto the scene.

"After him!" ordered the Prefect, putting his right boot down on Tamar's back, mercilessly pressing her against the earth.

Fearing for his life, Josiah darted into a densely wooded area and quickly disappeared from sight. Familiar with the lay of the land, he took refuge in a nearby shallow ditch, outwitting the soldiers who presumed he would run farther into the woods. Hiding under the cover of assorted vegetation, Josiah waited in the trench until his pursuers tired of the hunt. When the coast was clear, he crept back to where Tamar was being held, coming as near to her as he could without being spotted by the soldiers. His heart and mind racing, Josiah scaled a tall, stately oak, and concealed himself amongst the tree's foliage, keeping watch over Tamar from his lofty vantage point.

Unable to track down Josiah in the untamed brush, the soldiers called off their search and returned to their commander empty-handed.

"Where is he?" growled the Prefect, staring at his men.

"He cannot travel far on foot! We shall flush him out," assured one of the soldiers, joined thereafter by the other. "The Jew will not escape us! We will find him! He will not esc…"

"Silence!" snapped the Prefect, casting a sinister eye on the young woman at his feet, a slow fiendish smile coming over his fierce countenance. "Since ye incompetent fools hath failed to apprehend the Jew, we shall use his pretty, little dove to lure him."

Understanding their commander's intent, the unscrupulous soldiers descended from their horses and closed in on the defenseless maid.

Grabbing Tamar up by the arm, the Prefect forced her onto her feet. "Hold her!" he barked at the soldier, who bore a nasty six inch scar on the left side of his battle hardened aspect.

Terrified, Tamar struggled wildly, flailing and kicking as the Prefect handed her over to the scarred warrior, but she was no match for their collective strength. Taking possession of her, the soldier brutally yanked her arms behind her back and held them in an excruciating vise. The second soldier, desirous of the maid, stripped her of her cloak and cast it to the ground.

Finding herself in the clutches of evil men with no way of escape, Tamar bowed her head, conceding defeat.

Determined to gaze upon the damsel's face for he knew well the measure of her beauty, the Prefect seized her by her long, wavy, dark brown hair and jerked her head back, enabling his soldiers to get a look at their attractive prisoner. In the flower of her youth, Tamar's sweet countenance was one of fair skin and delicate features. A rosy hue colored her shapely lips and cheeks. Gracefully arched brows accented her thick lashed, large, dark eyes. Gentle of spirit, Tamar's uncommon beauty was more than skin deep, but the soldiers had no interest in her spirit.

Leering at her, the Prefect exclaimed, "I swear by the gods of Rome…she is as lovely as Venus herself! Is she not?"

"Truly, she is!" the soldiers agreed wholeheartedly, feasting their hungry eyes upon the vision of loveliness before them. Spellbound by the maid's good looks and comely form, nothing about her person escaped their unholy inspection.

Josiah's heart sank at the soldier's discovery. Tamar was too beautiful to hide under the drape of a cloak and far too beautiful to unveil in the presence of uncivilized men. He knew he would have to sacrifice himself in order to save her and even then, his sacrifice would not guarantee her safety, but it was a risk he would take for he loved Tamar too much to forsake her in her time of need.

Bearing her captor's scrutiny, Tamar prayed for the courage to suffer what she must at the hands of the ruthless soldiers.

"What shall we do with her?" asked the scar faced soldier, wantonly surveying the captive in his custody.

"We shall return her to Drusus…but first, we must teach her a lesson," answered the Prefect, his beady, black eyes flashing dangerously. "She must be punished for trying to escape."

The two soldiers snickered, each having their own warped brand of punishment in mind.

Releasing his grip on Tamar's dark mane, the Prefect ran his stubby, calloused fingers ever so slowly across her pink lips, tracing the outline of her mouth as he uttered a vulgar, blow by blow description of the evil he intended to perpetrate upon her.

Assaulted by the Prefect's unwelcome touch and foul communication, Tamar endured the indignity in silence, fearing if she cried out she would aid the soldiers in their diabolical scheme to ensnare Josiah. Frightened out of her wits and compelled to do something to defend herself, she unleashed the only available weapon she had in her arsenal. Attacking her Roman tormentor, she sunk her teeth into his hand, biting his distasteful flesh as hard as she could.

Caught off guard, the Prefect cursed as he hastily drew back his throbbing hand, not nearly as amused as were his soldiers, who howled with laughter. "She is spirited…like a wild cat," snarled the Prefect, holding his bitten appendage.

"Leave her alone!" shouted Josiah, courageously stepping out into the open. "I am the one ye seek!"

Hearing Josiah, the Prefect turned about and regarded the male fugitive, his black orbs narrowing with malice. "Hast thou returned to save thy little dove?" he hissed.

"Release her!" demanded Josiah, standing before the soldiers, who made no move to apprehend him. "I am the one ye want."

"We would much rather have her," taunted the Prefect, smiling ominously.

"Run, Josiah! Save thyself!"

"Hold thy tongue, little dove. He shall not run for he fears what may befall thee...as well he should."

"Do her no harm, Prefect!" voiced Josiah sharply, eyeing his adversary. "Drusus shall surely learn of thy wicked deed and it shall not go well with thee!"

Impressed more by the young man's bravado than his words, the Prefect questioned, "Jew, what is her relation to thee?"

Fearing the truth would further endanger Tamar, Josiah swallowed hard, hesitant to reply to the Roman officer.

"Answer me, Jew!"

"She is my...my...sister."

"Art thou prepared to die for thy sister?"

"Do to me what ye will...but let her go," stated Josiah gravely, surrendering to the soldiers. "I am to blame for her escape."

"No, Josiah! No!"

"Seize him," ordered the Prefect.

Handing over the maid to the Prefect for safekeeping, the scar faced soldier joined forces with his fellow warrior. Obeying their commander's directive, the soldiers took custody of Josiah, who was their willing prisoner for the sake of Tamar.

"Kill the Jew!" commanded the Prefect savagely, tightening his grip on Tamar.

Hearing his fate, Josiah began praying aloud to the God of his forefathers.

"No!" screamed Tamar, struggling frantically to break free from the Prefect. "He is innocent! Innocent...I tell thee!"

"Put him to the sword!"

"I beg ye...do not kill him!" Tamar pleaded tearfully as the most horrifying moment of her life loomed before her. "Hath mercy...I beg thee...hath mercy! Do not kill him!"

Following orders, the callous soldiers knocked Josiah to the ground and violently drove their sharp, lethal swords deep within the young man's unarmored chest, ignoring his emotional plea for clemency.

"Josiah!" shrieked Tamar with blood curdling finality.

Satisfied Drusus' royal dictate had been carried out; the Prefect released the maid and summoned his soldiers for further instruction.

Loosed from the Prefect's restraint, Tamar ran to Josiah and sank to her knees beside him. Raising his bloodied torso from the ground, she pulled him close and tenderly cradled him within her arms, crying, "Oh...Josiah... what hath they done unto thee?"

"Tamar..." uttered Josiah weakly.

"I cannot live without thee," moaned Tamar, gazing into the gentle, brown eyes of her beloved.

"Thou must..."

"I cannot," she sobbed, tears streaming down her face.

"Be strong..."

"No! Josiah...do not leave me! I cannot bear to live without thee!"

"God...shall provide...someone...to care for...thee," he gasped, trying to hold onto life a moment longer.

"Josiah...why? Why didst thou return?"

"...because I...love thee..." and having breathed his last words, Josiah's spirit left him.

"Farewell...my love," cried Tamar, her tears falling on Josiah as she passed her trembling hand over his lifeless eyes and closed them. Heartbroken, she drew Josiah's bloodied corpse into a final embrace and clung to him, weeping bitterly.

"Fetch the woman," ordered the Prefect, returning to his horse to get a rope from his saddlebag.

Obeying their superior, the soldiers headed toward the grief stricken maid, but were hindered from their duty when Tiberius Marcius Maximus came riding into their midst on a majestic, black stallion and blocked their access to her. Exuding an air of confidence, the centurion saluted his commander as was customary.

Irritated by the centurion's untimely arrival, the Prefect masked his hostility and conducted himself according to military decorum, returning the salute. The soldiers did likewise.

Possessing the heart of a warrior, Tiberius Marcius was a centurion of distinguished valor. Highly regarded by his fellow Romans, he was particularly revered by those who had served alongside of him in battle. He had a reputation for being fearless in the face of death, a reputation he had indeed earned. Formidable in deed and appearance, his tall stature and fit, muscular physique were unrivaled. Handsomely featured, it seemed as if his magnificent face and body had been masterfully sculpted for he had the look of a Greek god. His chiseled features were strong and distinct. Swarthy of complexion, his wavy hair and piercing eyes were black as polished onyx.

His physical characteristics were so striking and his military persona so daunting; he commanded the attention of all who saw him.

But not everyone thought well of the centurion or appreciated his fine physical attributes. The Prefect hated Tiberius Marcius Maximus in the purest sense of the emotion. Envious of his exemplary military career and the accolades he had garnered from the esteemed members of the Senate, the Prefect considered Tiberius a dangerous political enemy. Neither did he like the fact the centurion had attained the coveted favor of Caesar and his son, Drusus.

Under the ever watchful eye of his commander, the centurion took note of the grieving woman. Mindful of his assignment, he dismounted his steed and walked over to the Prefect, encountering him face to face.

"For whom doth the maid weep?" Tiberius inquired, studying his enemy's aspect.

"Her brother," the Prefect answered, meeting the centurion's steely gaze.

"What hath befallen him?"

"Drusus decreed his death," replied the Prefect haughtily, not in the habit of answering to a lower ranked officer.

"Is she the one we seek?"

"We?" questioned the Prefect, testily.

"Drusus hath ordered me to escort the maid back to the palace. Prefect, I ask thee again. Is she the one we seek?"

"See for thyself," retorted the Prefect, loathing both the message and the messenger.

Sensing his commander was extremely agitated; Tiberius Marcius held his tongue as he was not interested in a confrontation with a soldier not his equal. Turning on his heels, he made his way toward the bereaved maid.

Drawing near the young woman, the centurion stooped down and gingerly pried the deceased from her mournful embrace, laying him to rest on the blood soaked ground. "Come, let us depart from here," said the centurion, gently taking Tamar by the arm.

Overcome with grief, Tamar rose to her feet with the soldier's assistance, her head bowed in sorrow, her long, dark hair shielding her tearful countenance from sight.

The centurion had seen countless women weep over men who had met with death under Roman law, yet he had not grown altogether indifferent to their anguish. "Woman…look at me," he demanded, viewing the latest casualty with compassion.

Fearing the soldier would harm her if she did not obey him; Tamar lifted her head and met the centurion's gaze.

Beholding the maid he had been sent to retrieve, Tiberius Marcius was struck by her beauty and moved by the heartrending sadness in her large, dark eyes. Despite her disheveled hair, her tear streaked face, her blood stained dress and hands; he found the young woman extraordinarily beautiful.

"Bring some water," ordered the centurion, glancing at the soldiers, who then looked to their commander for his consent before making a move.

With a curt nod of his head, the Prefect approved the request and a water pouch was brought to the centurion.

"Woman, stretch out thine hands," directed Tiberius, opening the pouch.

Doing as she was told, Tamar put forth her bloodied hands, numbly watching as the centurion poured water over them, washing away the crimson stain of Josiah's blood, but not the indelible stain of guilt she felt over his death. Emotionally distraught, she could not even begin to fathom the centurion's act of kindness.

"Drink," he said, offering her the container.

"No," she refused tearfully.

"Drink," he insisted.

Yielding to his demand, Tamar took the pouch from the centurion and sipped a little water to appease him.

When she had finished drinking, Tiberius passed the container back to the soldier standing near, catching sight of his superior, who was observing him. Accustomed to operating under the Prefect's surveillance, he proceeded to interrogate the young woman before him. "Art thou the one called Tamar?" the centurion inquired, regarding the maid intently.

"I am," she answered meekly, casting her teary eyes downward.

"Who aided thee in thy escape?"

"Josiah."

"Is that him?" asked the centurion, pointing to the dead man.

Tamar nodded affirmatively, drawing a ragged breath.

"Were there any others who aided thee?"

"No."

"Woman, come with me," stated the centurion, laying hold of Tamar's arm.

Stiffening at his touch, Tamar looked on Josiah's lifeless body and speaking in a voice barely audible, she asked timidly, "Am I to die by the sword?"

Moved by the enormity of the maid's fear, Tiberius declared, "Woman, I give thee my word…no harm shall befall thee. Thou shall not die this day by the sword or any other means."

Hearing his vow, Tamar raised her dark eyes to his. There was something reassuring in the centurion's voice. He did not conduct himself like the others. He seemed a cut above them, set apart somehow. But how could that be? Were not all Romans the same? Overwrought with grief and unable to comprehend the possibility the Roman soldier was any different from his cohorts; Tamar let the thought slip from her mind. It was enough to know he did not intend to do her violence.

Escorting Tamar past the Prefect and his men, the centurion came upon a cloak lying on the ground. Surmising it belonged to the maid, he bent down to retrieve it.

Seizing the moment, Tamar broke away from the centurion and ran back to the Prefect. Hurling the might of her small frame at his armored chest, she angrily beat her fists against him. "Murderer! Filthy Roman pig! Murderer!" she screamed, assailing the Prefect verbally and physically. "If I were a man…I would make thee pay with thy life for what thou hast done!"

"Sadly for thee, fair maid, thou art not a man," grunted the Prefect, callously shoving her to the ground.

Finding the spectacle quite entertaining, the Prefect's soldiers laughed at the distraught woman and cruelly mocked her.

"Prefect, I remind thee of our orders! She is not to be handled roughly," asserted Tiberius, reclaiming the maid.

"Centurion, thou hast not properly handled her thyself! Here…take this…thou wilt need it," growled the Prefect, hurling his rope at the feet of Tiberius, who noted it, but did not pick it up.

"Murderers! Pigs!"

"Silence, woman!" rebuked the centurion, lifting the maid onto her feet and leading her away from the soldiers. Reaching his equine, he handed Tamar her dusty cloak and she accepted it with fearful expectation, bracing herself for the wrath of the centurion, but to her amazement, he held his temper. "Woman, wait here…and do not run. Provoke them no more…lest they do thee greater violence," he cautioned and then walked off, confident she could not escape on his steed for none but he could ride solo on the prized stallion.

Tamar heeded his warning for she was too afraid to put his words to the test, having seen the soldiers' penchant for violence firsthand. At the mercy of her circumstances, she could do little else but watch the centurion as he spoke with his commander.

A heated discussion ensued between the two men. A stickler for military protocol, the Prefect greatly objected to his authority being subverted and voiced his displeasure in no uncertain terms to the centurion, who by virtue of imperial order had the upper hand over his commander.

Generally, all Roman soldiers, no matter their rank had the upper hand over those they ruled. Whatever they said, one had to obey and whatever they wanted was forfeited, including one's life. Their tyranny knew no bounds and no atrocity seemed beyond their capability. They had murdered untold numbers of men, women and children in the name of Rome. And now they had murdered Josiah in cold blood. Tamar hated the soldiers for what they had done. Yet, she could not bring herself to hate the mysterious Roman who had come to her rescue, but neither did she trust him.

His contentious dialogue with the Prefect ended, Tiberius returned to his steed and stepped into the saddle. Mounted, he leaned down, extended his strong arm to the maid and pulled her up onto his horse, seating her behind him.

Looking back at Josiah's corpse, Tamar bid him a silent farewell, unaware the soldier's hungry eyes were devouring every inch of her.

"He desires her for himself," remarked the Prefect snidely. "Did ye not notice how gently Tiberius Marcius handled the Jewess?"

"Gentle or not…he shall find her no more willing than we," replied the scarred soldier, mocking the centurion which elicited laughter from his cohorts.

"I cared not whether she was willing," said the other soldier, smacking his lips.

The centurion heard the crude comments as he was within earshot, but he ignored the soldiers, deeming them of little importance. He was, however, concerned about the Prefect for he had not taken well the usurping of his authority.

Leaving the soldiers behind, Tiberius rode off toward the city with the woman he had been assigned to retrieve. Holding the reins in his left hand and resting his right on the hilt of his fine sword, he pondered the predicament of his fair passenger, uttering not a word to her as he maneuvered his horse through the narrow, bustling streets of Rome. Experience had taught him to maintain silence with those who crossed his path in the line of duty, lest by some means emotion cloud his judgment. Having adhered to his personal practice, he drew to a halt at the well protected entrance of Caesar's palatial estate which was manned by the Praetorian Guard. A member of the elite military branch, the centurion was met by a royal stable attendant, who dutifully assisted the maid from the stallion and having set her upon the ground, he then took control of the reins, steadying the animal as the officer dismounted. Leaving his steed in the care of the attendant, Tiberius turned toward the maid.

Realizing she was about to face Drusus, Tamar fixed her dark eyes on the centurion and pleaded, "Soldier, hath mercy upon me…I beg thee! Do not deliver me to Drusus for he is a cruel man!"

"Woman, what is that to me?" queried Tiberius, concealing his personal feelings behind a stoic countenance.

Disheartened by the centurion's seeming indifference to her plight, Tamar turned away from the soldier, covered her face with her palms and cried afresh.

"Woman, be not afraid," voiced Tiberius, placing his strong hands lightly upon her small shoulders.

But Tamar did not hear the soldier. She heard instead the words of Josiah echoing within her soul. "God shall provide someone to care for thee." Strengthened by her beloved's words, she brushed aside her tears, drew a deep breath and turned to the centurion, who sensing her unspoken resignation, took her by the arm and led her into the Emperor's palace.

Having been informed of their arrival, Drusus was standing before the ornately carved seat of power, looking quite regal in his finery when the centurion entered the grand throne room with Tamar. Seeing Caesar's son, Tiberius struck his breast in deference and salutation, paying him homage. The royal heir acknowledged the centurion with a cursory glance in his direction, his eyes irresistibly drawn to the object of his desire.

Next in line to rule Rome, Drusus was a powerful man and he used his power more often than not for his own benefit. Indulging in all manner of pleasure, his noble status afforded him the time and wherewithal to gratify his every whim. He denied himself nothing. The son of Caesar was accustomed to having what he wanted, when he wanted it. No one dared to deny him…no one except Tamar.

"Bring her forth," directed Drusus, marveling that the maid's beauty was no less captivating, despite her unsightly, bloodied raiment.

Obeying the royal command, Tiberius escorted Tamar across the length of the ivory colored marble floor, placing her before Drusus and the imperial throne. Stepping back, the centurion withdrew from her a few paces.

Feeling the penetrating gaze of Drusus upon her, Tamar did not dare lift her eyes to his for she knew them to be the eyes of lust.

"Tiberius Marcius, thou art to be commended for finding the maid," declared Drusus, tearing his gaze from Tamar and looking to the centurion.

"It was not I, but Sejanus that found her, Your Highness," replied the centurion, giving the Prefect his rightful due.

"It is admirable of thee to be so forthright, my friend. I doubt Sejanus would hath granted thee the same courtesy," remarked Drusus, well acquainted with the questionable character of the Prefect. "Tell me…did he follow my orders explicitly?"

"He did as thou commanded."

Visibly pleased with the answer, Drusus turned to Tamar and said, "Woman, if thou had done my bidding, Josiah thy kinsman would still be among the living. Alas, thou did not and he hath perished. His death is upon thy head. Mighty are the gods that hath seen fit to deliver thee into my hands. Thou art now mine!" he proclaimed, relishing the factuality of his words.

Staring blankly at the floor, tears welled up in Tamar's eyes. She could not bear to hear the precious name of her beloved spoken by the one who had ordered his execution. Suppressing the urge to verbally lash out at Drusus, she held her peace, standing as quiet and lifeless as the large stone statues which adorned the throne room.

"Woman, bow in the presence of thy lord and master!" roared Drusus, basking in his power.

Refusing to acknowledge his sovereignty, Tamar remained standing. She did not move one muscle to obey him, nor did she intend to as long as there was breath left in her body. Drusus would never be her master, no matter how long she lived in his palace. She would see to that.

"Woman, bow down in the presence of thy lord…or suffer his wrath!"

stormed Drusus, galled by the maid's blatant disrespect for his exalted position.

In spite of his threat, Tamar would not pay homage to Drusus, deeming it preferable to endure his fury rather than give him the satisfaction of her obedience.

Observing the battle of wills been waged before him, Tiberius was astounded by the maid's courage. He had seen valiant men cower before Drusus, but never had he seen a woman with a will as strong as a legion of soldiers, defy one so powerful.

Infuriated by Tamar's insubordination, Drusus flew at the maid, raising his ring adorned hand to strike her.

Moving swiftly, Tiberius came to the maid's defense, seizing Drusus' wrist in mid air.

"Unhand me, centurion!" Drusus demanded, enraged by Tiberius' intervention.

Startled, Tamar looked up and what she saw made her fear for the soldier. Seeing the men locked in a struggle; she wondered what had possessed the centurion to act on her behalf. Did he not know Drusus could destroy his life? Did he not care? Why was he willing to risk himself for her?

"The maid hath suffered sufficiently for one day, Your Highness," asserted Tiberius boldly, exerting painful pressure on Drusus' wrist.

Yielding to Tiberius' formidable physical strength, Drusus relented and lowered his arm, saying, "Tiberius Marcius, if thou wert not a mighty man of valor and a loyal friend, I would summon the guards and hath thee put to death this very hour!"

"I would expect no less of thee, my noble friend," said Tiberius with a grin, making light of the threat.

"It is like thee to laugh in the face of death," remarked Drusus sternly, rubbing his aching wrist. "Tiberius Marcius, thou art either completely mad or brave beyond measure! Be warned, my courageous friend, I will not tolerate interference from thee again! Next time, I shall not be so magnanimous!"

"Consider thy loyal subject duly warned," said Tiberius, reverently bowing his head to the Emperor's son.

Placated by the centurion's response, Drusus fastened his eyes on Tamar. Drawing unnervingly close to her, he commanded, "Prostrate thyself before me, woman."

Physically and emotionally depleted, Tamar could no longer withstand the ordeal and began sobbing uncontrollably in front of Drusus, who derived perverse pleasure from her tears. Laying his regal hand a top her head, Drusus exerted downward pressure, forcing her to her knees and she tearfully surrendered to his sovereign will.

"Drusus, noble heir to the throne, hear me," petitioned the centurion, fixing his black eyes on Caesar's son.

"I will hear thee," said Drusus smugly, regarding the soldier.

"Your Highness, I call to thy remembrance the oath thou swore unto me in Pannonia."

Some years earlier, the legions in Pannonia had mutinied and Drusus had been sent to subdue the revolt, a task he eagerly assumed. Determined to earn his father's hard won approval and attain a much desired triumph, the royal heir was not deterred by the awful weather or the eclipse, the latter of which, he took to be a good omen and so it was for his undertaking was successful. Upon his return to Rome, Caesar granted him a triumph and Drusus generously rewarded all those who had contributed to his momentous achievement. But when it came to the centurion who had saved him from the dagger of an assassin, Drusus had sworn an oath. An oath, Tiberius Marcius now called to his remembrance.

"Thy timing hath me puzzled, my fearless friend. What dost thou desire of me that thou should remind me this day of my oath?"

"I desire the maid, Tamar," replied Tiberius coolly.

Drusus' face fell. The very thought of giving up the lovely maid was more than he cared to consider. "Would thou hath me pledge thee so little," questioned Drusus in disbelief, his heavy hand still weighing upon the crown of Tamar's head. "She is but a woman…and a Jewess at that! Thou knowest it is within my power to give thee gold and kingdoms, yet thou ask of me a woman! Truly, thou hast been on the battlefield too long!"

"I desire the maid," repeated Tiberius.

"Thou doth desire a maid when I can offer thee riches untold! Surely, thou jest!"

"Thou swore on thine honor and all that is sacred thou wouldest grant me whatsoever I requested of thee," reminded Tiberius, steadily holding Drusus' gaze. "Is not the Emperor's son bound by the pledge he swears to another?"

"I shall not grant her to thee!" bellowed Drusus angrily, withdrawing his hand from the whimpering maid. "Ask anything of me and I shall grant it, save her!"

"What is this I hear, my son," interjected the Emperor, making his presence in the room known.

Paying homage to Tiberius Caesar, the Emperor of Rome, the centurion knelt down on one knee, struck his breast with a closed fist and declared his allegiance. "Hail, Caesar!"

Terrified, Tamar bowed her face to the cold marble floor, abasing herself before the Emperor. She would not risk incurring his displeasure as she had his son's for Caesar's hatred of the Jews was not to be taken lightly.

"Son, would thou deny the Roman citizen who saved thy life, the pledge thou swore unto him? Hath the pledges of Caesar's house become worthless?"

"No, Pater," Drusus answered, humbled by the tactful rebuke.

"Grant Tiberius Marcius whatsoever he asks of thee. Honor thy pledge, my son. Do what is noble in the sight of Rome."

"Pater, I am willing to honor my pledge…withholding only the maid," argued Drusus, stealing a look at Tamar, who lay prostrate before the royal family, quivering with fear.

"Drusus, the interest thou hast in this particular maid greatly displeases me! It is not prudent to pursue this Jewess! She believeth in but one God! Wilt thou provoke the gods of Rome to anger on account of her? No…thou wilt not!" thundered the Emperor with righteous indignation, his pudgy face reddening. "I shall not permit thee to offend the great and mighty gods of Rome! Once again, thou dost owe Tiberius Marcius a debt of gratitude for by his request he hath saved thee from destruction! Need I appoint him thy personal guardian?"

When Caesar's words ceased reverberating off the palace walls, a silence fell upon the stately throne room. Not even Drusus, whose inflated ego was battered from the reprimand dared to speak to Caesar. He knew as well as the others to bridle his tongue.

"Tiberius Marcius Maximus, thou art a soldier of remarkable courage. Thou hast served Rome valiantly," proclaimed Caesar, dispelling the terrible silence he had created. "Thy distinguished feats of bravery are well known among the people, but of all thy deeds, saving the life of my son exceeds all thou hast done thus far. Therefore, I, Caesar, shall grant thee thy petition. The Jewess is thine. Her life is in thy hands. See that she doth remain in thy custody. If she doth not and I per chance lay eyes on her again, I shall unleash my wrath on her as I hath upon her miserable people. Be it known, I shall not waver from this judgment."

"Thy will be done, Sire," said Tiberius, accepting the royal decree.

"Centurion, take the maid and depart," commanded the Emperor, dismissing his faithful subject with an imperious wave of his hand.

After performing the customary obeisance to Caesar, Tiberius Marcius carried out his bidding and ushered Tamar from the palace.

II

Brokenhearted, Tamar suffered the midday trek in silence, seated behind Tiberius upon his black stallion, her slender arms wrapped about the centurion's armored waist. Close physical contact with a Roman soldier was repugnant to her, but as she was powerless to change the dreadful circumstance in which she found herself, she held onto him lest she fall from the horse. Grieving the death of Josiah, quiet tears slipped from Tamar's eyes as her sorrow gave birth to despair.

Traveling Rome's narrow, cobbled streets, his sure footed steed carrying him ever nearer to his home, the centurion was distracted from his usual military contemplations. He tried to think on something other than the fair maid he had taken from Drusus, but he could not get her off of his mind. Although he knew very little about her, what he did know intrigued him, namely, her courageous spirit. She had attempted to go toe to toe with Drusus and though she had failed to withstand the Emperor's son, Tiberius had found her courage remarkable. Not one to meddle in the personal affairs of others, particularly those of the royal house, he had thrown caution to the wind and rescued the maid from her powerful enemy. It was a dangerous thing to come between Drusus and what he wanted, yet he had done just that. Like the esteemed Julius Caesar, he had crossed the Rubicon. There was no turning back. Tiberius could not undo what he had done, nor did he want to.

Riding into the open air marketplace, the centurion and the maid were met with cold stares, most of which were squarely aimed at the soldier. Undaunted by their overt hostility, Tiberius guided his horse through the throng of humanity and slow moving carts laden with a variety of fresh produce, exotic spices, savory meats and imported wares. He had not ventured very far into the market fray when he caught sight of a small boy on the verge of hurling a rock in his direction. Finding himself hemmed in on all sides by man and beast, he was unable to maneuver his horse out of the youth's throwing range and having no path of escape, he warned the maid to hold on tight and braced for what was coming. Then out of nowhere, the boy's mother appeared and seized her son's arm, casting a frightened look at the centurion for she saw her child had not escaped his notice. Heaving a sigh of relief, Tiberius rode on by, eyeing the would be culprit fiercely. Shaken, the mother quickly ushered her foolish child away from the soldier, verbally scolding her offspring as they faded into the sea of people. Maintaining his guard, the centurion continued onward, coming upon a vendor selling a visually appealing assortment of fruits and vegetables. Stopping in front of the well stocked booth, he commanded from atop his steed, "You there...bring some figs...and choose well."

The gray haired vendor begrudgingly did as he was told. He had lived more years than he cared to remember under the oppressive rule of the Romans and he knew better than to disregard a soldier's order. Selecting two heaping handfuls of his most appetizing figs, he quickly wrapped the tasty fruit in clean paper, tied it with twine and brought it to the unwelcome customer.

"Give it to the woman," the centurion directed.

Handing the packaged figs to the maid, the vendor stared at her intently, noting her sad, tear stained face and bloodied apparel. Feeling certain the Roman soldier had done her some unspeakable harm as they were notorious for mistreating the weaker members of society, the vendor concealed his righteous indignation behind an expressionless visage. He did not see how a few measly figs could ease the young woman's misery, but he kept his opinion to himself, knowing if he voiced it, he would be asking for trouble and if there was one thing he did not need, it was trouble. Sympathetic as he was to the maid's plight, he spoke not a word to her for fear of the centurion.

"Name thy price," said Tiberius stiffly, marking the vendor's interest in Tamar.

Stepping back from the soldier's fine specimen of horseflesh, the vendor looked up at the centurion, squinting as the sun met his eyes. "I ask nothing," he muttered half heartedly.

Discerning the man's animosity, Tiberius' dark orbs grew narrow and flinty. The vendor could not hide his hatred from the battle hardened soldier with a few disingenuous words. Thinking no more highly of the vendor than the vendor did of him, Tiberius withdrew one sesterius from his leather money pouch, tossed the small coin at the man's dirty, sandaled feet and rode off.

Stooping to pick up the coin, the vendor cursed the centurion under his breath, despising all things Roman, except their money.

Awhile later, the soldier and his passenger entered an affluent neighborhood situated at the top of Palatine Hill, where the Emperor's palace also stood, overlooking the homes below. Tamar had never ventured into the exclusive district, nor did she have the birthright to attain entry. Hers was a modest existence, bordering dangerously on the brink of poverty, unlike Tiberius, who had been born into the wealth and power of a patrician lineage. His was a family of aristocratic distinction, of noble heritage and political privilege.

Bringing his horse to a halt in front of a grand estate which was flanked on both sides by tall, graceful trees and lush greenery, Tamar realized the centurion had reached his intended destination. Gazing at the impressive house that stood before her, she found it lovelier than anything she had ever seen or imagined. Her people lived in no such splendor. Their homes did not boast of towering, majestic marble columns or fragrant gardens filled with statuesque fountains. The prospect of entering the fine residence would have excited her if not for her sorrow, coupled with a strong measure of fear for Tamar knew not what fate awaited her behind the stately, carved doors of the centurion's home.

Upon Tiberius' arrival, a male servant of Greek descent came scurrying forward to render his services. He did not speak for he could not. His tongue had been tied since birth, so he greeted his master with a pleasant countenance and a reverential nod of his head. Taking hold of the reins, the capable servant affectionately patted the horse's broad nose as Tiberius turned in the saddle and assisted the maid from his steed.

Safely on the ground, Tamar regarded the Roman soldier as he dismounted, finding him more tolerable than the rest of his barbaric ilk.

Slapping his horse on the hind quarters, Tiberius dismissed it and his stable servant, who led away the magnificent stallion with notable proficiency. Turning around, he surveyed the bereaved maid, who stood humbly in his presence, bearing in her hands the parcel of fruit he had given her. Noting it had not been opened, he inquired, "Woman, why did thou not eat of the figs?"

"I could not…" Tamar answered meekly, staring down at the packaged figs she held. "Grief hath stolen my hunger."

"Thy hunger shall return," said Tiberius, gently placing his hand under her chin and lifting her face upward.

Raising her sorrowful dark eyes, Tamar met the centurion's steady gaze.

"Woman, thy tears shall pass…but the memories shall remain with thee always. What hath befallen thee this day shall either destroy thee or strengthen thee. The choice is thine. Choose wisely," he advised and having spoken, he withdrew his hand.

Pondering the soldier's counsel, Tamar's gaze fell from his, the gravity of his words weighing on her soul.

Unbeknown to Tamar, Tiberius knew whereof he spoke for he too had borne grief. The sudden death of his beloved Dinah, only days before their wedding was to have taken place had utterly shattered his faith in the gods. It had been two years since Dinah's untimely demise and still, Tiberius refused to worship the gods, supposing they had conspired against him. Neither had he sought female companionship.

"Domina, thy son hath returned," announced the door attendant to Flavia, who had been eagerly anticipating Tiberius' home-coming from the local garrison. "He hath brought with him a woman," added the servant, shutting the door softly so as not to rouse his master's attention.

Shooing the attendant away from his post, Flavia discreetly cracked open the portal again and peered outside. To her astonishment, Tiberius was standing in front of the house speaking to a woman, whose back was to the door, obscuring her face from view. Curious about the female her son had brought with him, Flavia tried to get a better look at her, but she could not for the mysterious woman had not yet turned about. Could this be the one she had asked the goddess, Juno to send?

Religious, Flavia made regular pilgrimages to the public temples to appease the sovereign powers of the universe. Fearful the gods would punish Tiberius for his neglect of worship, she offered up prayers and sacrifices on his behalf, paying special homage to Jupiter, the supreme god, who guided men and protected their military endeavors. She also rendered offerings to Mars, the god of war and to her personal favorite, Juno, the goddess of women. Believing a woman's love would restore her son's faith in the deities, Flavia had asked Juno to send Tiberius a suitable wife of patrician birth. Hoping her petition had finally been answered; she quietly closed the door, murmuring a reverence to Janus and Vesta, the gods presiding over the door and the hearth.

Moments later, the attendant heard his master knock at the door and opened it pretending he knew not that it was the lord of the house. Appearing pleasantly surprised, the servant bowed humbly and said, "Welcome home, Domine."

"It is good to be home," said Tiberius, stepping foot into the atrium, the main reception room of wealthy Roman households. Removing his helmet, he handed it to the servant, who received it dutifully, stealing a quick look at the young woman who stood behind his master.

Unable to maintain her customary reserve, Flavia rushed toward her son. It had been too long between furloughs to suit her maternal heart.

At twenty-nine years of age, Tiberius had served in more campaigns than Rome required of him and he had done so with honor. Although he had made a quite a name for himself in the military and presently served in the prestigious Praetorian Guard, his mother desired he would take up politics like his father before him, but to her dismay, Tiberius had shown no interest in affairs of state. Still, Flavia clung to the hope and never more so than upon his return home.

"Tiberius Marcius, my son...I hath sorely missed thee," she declared, wrapping her arms about him affectionately.

"It is good to lay eyes upon thee, Mater," Tiberius responded cordially as he embraced his mother, finding her demonstrative greeting highly unusual. Glancing over her shoulder, he spied Priscilla entering the atrium and he wondered if she would receive him with the same degree of warmth.

Priscilla was younger than her brother, fifteen to be exact, but she was no less physically striking. A mirror image of her mother, Priscilla had long, silky brown hair which she wore arranged in a braided bun at the nape of her graceful neck, pleasing facial features, a flawless olive complexion, thick dark lashes and large brown eyes. Her willowy body was finely clothed and adorned with costly jewelry. Priscilla had inherited her comely physical attributes from her mother, but her testy disposition was her own.

"To what honor do we owe the return of the great and mighty warrior...Tiberius Marcius Maximus...who hast killed thousands in the name of Rome," Priscilla quipped, her tone rife with impudence as she bowed before him in a mock gesture of adulation.

Hearing Priscilla's impertinent salutation, Tiberius' handsome aspect hardened. He was tired from travel and he was in no mood for an altercation, least of all, with his own sister.

Withdrawing from her son's embrace, Flavia turned toward her daughter and reproved her, saying, "Priscilla, thy sarcasm is most unbecoming. Remember to whom thou doth speak. Thy brother is deserving of thy utmost respect."

"May the gods forgive me," said Priscilla smirking, her tone unchanged. "Truly, I hath erred...forgive me...oh, most noble one..."

"Please...Priscilla," her mother entreated. "Mind thy tongue."

"Sister, I am weary of confrontation. I hath no desire to turn my home into a battlefield," voiced Tiberius, regarding Priscilla sternly.

"Thou art a mighty warrior...thou ought to relish a battle...wherever thou doth find one," goaded Priscilla.

"Woman, I relish it not," replied Tiberius, struggling to control his temper.

During her children's banter, Flavia studied the maid standing quietly behind Tiberius, taking her into account. Judging by the homespun fabric of the young woman's clothing, the ghastly stains thereon and her meek demeanor, the Roman matron quickly surmised the maid was not of noble birth. Clearly, the young woman was not the answer to her prayers. Still, Flavia wondered about her. The maid was certainly lovely despite her wretched attire. Had her uncommon beauty caught Tiberius' eye?

Fixated on the small, decorative pool in the center of the atrium, Tamar gazed intently as streams of sunlight shone through an opening in the ceiling and danced sprightly upon the crystal, clear water below. Lost in the brilliant illumination, she was oblivious to Flavia's inspection of her person, the bickering siblings and the door attendant, who had been staring at her unabashedly.

"Son, why hast thou brought this woman with thee," questioned Flavia, silencing her brood.

Jarred back to reality by the subsequent hush that followed the Roman matron's inquiry, Tamar lowered her dark eyes to the colorful mosaic floor beneath her small sandaled feet, timidly enduring the scrutiny of the patrician family.

"What evil hast befallen her," asked Priscilla, noticing Tamar's blood stained dress, showing from beneath her cloak.

"I hath acquired her from Drusus by pledge," answered Tiberius, deliberately withholding the details of Tamar's misfortune.

"The son of Caesar," his mother queried, furrowing her brow. "What hath he to do with this young woman?"

"She was in his possession, Mater."

"Caesar's son made thee a pledge...and thou hast used it to procure a female slave," remarked Priscilla, looking Tamar up and down with disdain. "Surely, thou could hath had much more!"

"Priscilla, I deliver this maid into thy hands," said Tiberius, bringing Tamar before his sister. "I pray she serves thee well."

"I hath no need of another maidservant."

"Daughter, accept thy brother's gift and let there be peace between thee," urged Flavia, detesting the fact her children were at odds with one another.

"This wretched maid can hardly be seen as a gift...much less a peace offering! I do not want her," voiced Priscilla, unwilling to be appeased for she was determined to make Tiberius pay for what he had done. "She shall not serve me!"

"She shall indeed serve thee..." asserted Tiberius, losing patience. "...or thou shalt serve her. It matters not a whit to me."

"May Jupiter strike thee dead, Tiberius Marcius...the day I serve the likes of her!"

"Priscilla!" her mother gasped in horror, quickly murmuring a prayer to undo her daughter's curse.

His countenance darkening like an impending summer storm, Tiberius thundered, "Mater, leave us and take the maid with thee!"

"Come child," Flavia beckoned Tamar, who was only too willing to withdraw from yet another conflict.

Having provoked her brother's fury, Priscilla fled to the safety of her chamber, slamming the door behind her, but that did nothing to deter Tiberius, who went after her with a vengeance. Flinging open the door to her cubicle, he stepped inside of her sanctuary. "Leave us!" he demanded, dismissing Priscilla's bevy of maids, all of whom left the room promptly, leaving the master alone with their mistress for they wanted no portion of his wrath. His anger kindled, Tiberius grabbed his sister by the arms.

"Thou art hurting me! Unhand me this minute!" shrieked Priscilla, helpless against her brother's formidable physical strength.

"Woman, I shall not unhand thee until thou dost state thy cause against me."

"Dost thou take me for a fool, Tiberius Marcius? Dost thou think I know not that it was thee who sent Claudius away?"

"Priscilla, I did what was best for thee," Tiberius defended himself, astounded his sister knew what he had done.

"I shall never forgive thee for sending Claudius to that miserable outpost in Judea! Never!"

"Woman, it is my right to do as I will concerning thee. Need I remind thee of the power I possess? I am the paterfamilias. I alone hath jurisdiction over thy life...and thy death," he stated ominously, exerting painful pressure on Priscilla's pampered flesh. "It is thy duty to obey me."

Priscilla did not need reminding of Tiberius' power as the paterfamilias. The law of the Roman state was very clear. The paterfamilias had absolute authority over the occupants of his household. His will and his word was law. He could by his own hand, put to death his servants as well as members of his immediate family if they disobeyed him or transgressed the code of decency and he could do so without fear of reprisal from any outside source. His was an autocratic rule sanctioned by Rome and those under his authority were obligated to obey or suffer the consequences.

"Thou art to marry the man chosen for thee, Priscilla. This is proper. This is the patrician way of marriage…the way of our ancestors. Thou wilt abide by it or thou shall meet with an unfortunate fate."

"I shall not abide by a practice which ignores love," announced Priscilla, knowing she was on dangerous ground, but having come too far in the confrontation to back down, she stayed the course. "I shall not allow thee to dictate whom I shall marry! I am old enough to make my own decisions!"

"Thy age hath no bearing on the matter," retorted her brother sharply. "The decision was made for thee by thy father. It was his will that thou should marry Lucius Servilius and I intend to see that his will is done."

"Pater is dead! His will no longer matters! I shall marry Claudius and no other," declared Priscilla with all the passion her youthful heart could muster.

"I forbid it," stormed Tiberius, appalled by Priscilla's defiance. "Claudius is not a suitable husband!"

"Claudius loves me!" Priscilla insisted, suddenly bursting into tears. "He loves me…truly, he doth!"

"Woman, Claudius is neither capable of love nor fidelity! Trust me when I tell thee, he is most unworthy of thee! His intentions are not honorable!"

"Thou art a liar, Tiberius Marcius," cried Priscilla bitterly, her emotions getting the better of her.

"Priscilla, I swear by the gods, I hath spoken truthfully."

"I believe thee not…for thou doth swear by gods thou doth not worship! Thou art not only godless, but thou art a liar!"

Realizing it was futile to go on arguing with his sister, Tiberius released her. He could not force Priscilla to forgive him, neither could he make her understand what he had done, he had done for her sake. He had protected her from a man of questionable reputation, who had an insatiable appetite for women and power. The rogue soldier had set his sights on Priscilla, desiring not her, but the wealth and prestige of her family name that he might gain political leverage in the Senate. Learning of the soldier's plan through an informant, Tiberius called in some favors owed him and had Claudius assigned to a post as far away from Rome and his sister as was physically possible. Priscilla's welfare was in his hands and he intended to do what was right for her. She was to be married into a family as aristocratic and powerfully endowed as her own. She was to be given in marriage to Lucius Servilius upon her sixteenth birthday. This, Tiberius had promised their father on his deathbed and nothing could prevent him from keeping his word. He would not break the binding oath he had sworn. He would honor his father's dying wish and see to it that Priscilla married Lucius Servilius, whether or not it suited her childish fancy.

"Priscilla, thou wilt marry Lucius Servilius," stated Tiberius firmly, his aspect rigid. "I will hear no more of Claudius. Never mention him again."

"Love means nothing to thee, Tiberius! Thou hast dwelt too long among the dead…and thine heart hath grown cold! Thou dost no longer live…save in thine own eyes," sobbed Priscilla, shooting a verbal arrow deep into her brother.

Pained by her assessment of him, Tiberius left Priscilla's room, but he could not escape her stinging words for they carried with them an element of truth. His heart had indeed grown cold as she had said. It had grown cold with Dinah's demise. He knew he was living in the dark shadow of the past. He was living among the dead. He had tried to comfort his grieving heart with military campaigns, but no matter how many victories he achieved or how widespread his fame, nothing could satisfy him or dispel his sorrow. Living by the sword had skewed his perception of life. He no longer desired the love of a woman for he had pledged his heart, not to frail flesh and blood, but to the mighty army of Rome. Her glory would never die.

III

Determined to escape the centurion's residence, Tamar refused to succumb to her weary body, despite her need for rest. Surveying the dimly lit cubicle she occupied, her tired eyes took in the small, sparsely furnished room which was illuminated by an oil lamp as there were no windows. Impeccably clean, the furnishings consisted of a bed, suitable for one person, covered in pale yellow linens, having a matching bolster. Next to the bed was a table on which sat the oil lamp, a basin of water for washing and a neatly folded white hand towel. In one corner of the room was an ornately carved wood bench and in the opposite corner stood a tall slender column, having upon it a marble statute of the goddess Dinah, the protector of women. Painted in soft muted tones were depictions of half clothed gods and goddesses frolicking in the heavens and though the color palate was pleasing to the eye, Tamar did her level best not to look at the walls too closely, finding the artwork utterly offensive to her Jewish faith. Having no appreciation for her pagan accommodations, she longed for her own familiar bed chamber in Subura.

Anxious for the centurion and his household to retire for the evening, Tamar passed the night hours pacing the ivory colored marble floor in order to stay awake, contemplating her impending escape with every step. Waiting till the dead of the night when all were asleep, Tamar slowly cracked open her door, careful not to make a sound. Peering out into the atrium, she spied the door attendant sleeping at his post. Seeing no one else, she ventured from her room and tiptoed toward the rear of the house, praying the servant would not awaken. Quietly, she stole past the looming, decorative columns and the numerous sleep cubicles that lined both sides of the atrium, the large, private domain of the paterfamilias and the dining room. Leaving the atrium, she entered the spacious garden courtyard, located at the back of the house. Navigating by the soft light of a crescent moon, Tamar slipped past the servant's rooms, the kitchen, the library and the stable, disturbing only the centurion's stallion, which whinnied as she went by. Encountering the villains of nature, Tamar's delicate skin suffered cuts and scratches as she groped amidst thick shrubs and foliage, trying to find a way out of the landscaped courtyard. Frantically, she searched the garden for an exit, until finally; she came upon a freight gate, covered with vines. Mustering her strength, she pushed the heavy gate open and fled down the dark alley, putting distance between her and the residence. Moving swiftly through the narrow corridors of prosperous Rome, she ran homeward under the cover of night, spurred onward by sheer determination.

Running as fast as her exhausted legs would carry her, she could not outrun the awful feeling that she was responsible for Josiah's death. If only she had known what evil Drusus was capable of…if only she had not stumbled…if only the soldiers had not caught her…if only…if only…Josiah were still alive, she lamented, blinking back tears of remorse. How could she ever forgive herself? Josiah had sacrificed his life to save her. His blood was on her hands. How could she face her family again? Perhaps, it would be better for everyone if she never returned. Coming to a fork in the road, Tamar paused to catch her breath, considering whether she should turn to the right and follow the dusty road home or continue down the paved road which led to places and people unknown. Torn in her spirit, she cried out to God for direction. She had barely finished uttering her prayer, when suddenly; the evening silence was nightmarishly shattered by the cacophony of carousing soldiers. Terrified, she darted behind a free standing wall of some long abandoned building and hid herself. Through its time worn cracks she peered, her heart beating rapidly. Shaking with fear, Tamar watched the soldiers, wondering if they had seen her.

Unaware they were being observed, five intoxicated Roman soldiers staggered by, laughing and cursing at one another, while they took turns drinking from a jug they passed amongst themselves. A cadet, who could not hold his wine as well as the others, fell to the ground and remained there until he was assisted to his feet by two seasoned soldiers, who ribbed the young man with a barrage of crude insults.

Tamar had never heard such a litany of vulgarity before, except from the lips of…

Then to her horror, a recognizable voice distinguished itself from among the crowd, more chilling to her ears than the other four combined. It was a voice she would never forget as long as she lived. She desperately wanted to burst forth from the safety of her hiding place and attack the Prefect, who had ordered Josiah's execution, but she found herself immobilized by fear. Outnumbered and no match for him or his soldiers, she looked on as he reveled in drunkenness, hating him for what he had done. How dare he laugh! How dare he taste of sweet wine! How dare he even breathe! The

Roman pig had no right to live for he had committed murder and according to the law of her people, he deserved to be stoned to death.

Stooping down, Tamar skimmed the ground with purpose. Finding a rock, she grasped it tightly within her trembling hand, which ached with the desire to execute judgment upon Josiah's murderer.

"Vengeance is not thine," a knowing voice whispered in the darkness.

Startled out of her wits, Tamar jumped to her feet and spun around, her back against the weathered wall, her heart racing with fear as she beheld the apparition. Half wondering if she was hallucinating, she stared in disbelief as a tall figure appeared out of the murky mist. Taken aback, Tamar encountered the most unlikely foe, an elderly man, whose physical attributes were like nothing she had ever seen.

White of hair and beard, his was a face alight with the wisdom of the years and his bright, knowing eyes shone with compassion. His pure white luminous robe was fashioned with threads of silver and gold that flickered despite the dim light of the heavens. So uncommon was his handsomeness that Tamar found him strangely beautiful.

"Do not be afraid, child," his melodic voice soothed her frazzled nerves. "Thy enemy hath not seen thee."

"Who art thou?" she tried to ask, but before she could even speak the words, he answered.

"I am the one who shall lead thee safely to thy uncle's house. Come," and having spoken, he turned and started down the dusty road.

Utterly bewildered, Tamar hesitated. Was it wise for her to go with a man she did not know? Yet, oddly, he seemed to know her. But how? Who was he? And how did he know her destination?

"Come," the elderly man beckoned again, looking back at the timid maid.

Gazing at the benevolent stranger, a sense of peace washed over Tamar and she went trailing after him with childlike trust, letting go of the rock in her hand. Then in what seemed but a blink of an eye, she found herself standing at the doorstep of her uncle's home, tapping lightly upon the time ravaged door. Feeling as if she had awakened from a pleasant dream, she glanced over her shoulder to bid the mysterious stranger farewell, but to her amazement, he had vanished without a trace. Before she could even reflect on his disappearance, the door opened and she was abruptly yanked inside of the dreary, ill lit dwelling.

Unhanding his niece, Laham eyed her coldly.

Tamar shivered as her eyes met her uncle's. Hurt and confused by his indifference, she stood weak kneed and speechless before him.

"Why hast thou returned," Laham snapped nastily. "Dost thou wish us death?"

"Tamar!" her aunt exclaimed in disbelief, hastening toward the maid with outstretched arms. "My dear sweet Tamar…it is thee! Praise the God of Abraham! I feared thou wert dead!"

"I wish she were dead! Her beauty is a curse," uttered Laham bitterly. "Josiah is dead…dead because of her and her wretched beauty! I say, let the Emperor's son hath his way with her…lest we all suffer the fate of Josiah!"

Brutalized by Laham's heartless comments, Tamar broke down and began to weep uncontrollably.

"Laham, she is thy brother's child," Ruth scolded, sheltering the distraught girl within her protective arms. "Hast thou no pity?"

"Pity! Wife, do not speak to me of pity! I took her in when she was but five years of age! I cared for her like she was my own daughter and twelve years later…she hath betrayed me! Pity! I hath no pity for her!"

"I hath not…betrayed thee…Uncle," sobbed Tamar. "I hath not…"

"Thou hast indeed betrayed me!" countered Laham angrily, shaking his stubby fist at her. "Thou hast turned the head of that Roman swine and brought death upon my house!"

Biting her tongue, Ruth cast a hard reprimanding look at her husband and ushered her niece from his sulfurous presence before he could inflict any more verbal harm. Ruth's heart was heavy with sorrow, but she did not blame Tamar for her son's death as Laham did. Escorting her niece to her room, Ruth accounted for her husband's harsh words, saying, "Thy uncle is beside himself with grief, Tamar. Forgive him; he doth not know what he is saying. He speaks from a broken heart."

"He speaks the truth! Josiah is dead…dead because of me…" Tamar wailed, overcome with emotion.

"My child, thou art not to blame for Josiah's death."

"…but I am! I might hath saved Josiah if only I…"

"Stop this foolish talk, Tamar," admonished Ruth gently. "I will hear no more of it. Thou could not hath saved Josiah, except thou had sinned in the sight of Almighty God. Art thou to be faulted for loving God and obeying His commandments? I think not…neither do I fault thee…nor would Josiah."

Grieving the loss of her son, Ruth did not understand why evil had befallen him or why the righteous suffered at the hands of ungodly, but she did understand Tamar's misplaced guilt served no good purpose.

"Tomorrow, thy uncle shall find thee a safe haven," Ruth promised solemnly, helping her niece slip out of a garment befitting a woman of means and into a night dress of the less privileged. Tucking Tamar into bed, she drew the covers snugly about the young woman and kissed her lightly upon the forehead, breathing a silent prayer for her safety. Extinguishing the flickering candle upon the table, Ruth departed, leaving her niece alone in her bed chamber.

Overcome by physical and emotional exhaustion, Tamar fell into a deep slumber and was not awakened by the embittered argument taking place in the next room between Laham and Ruth.

IV

When Tiberius awoke the next morning, he instinctively knew that something was amiss in his household. Remembering his confrontation with Priscilla the day before, he quickly rose from his couch and dressed, not waiting for Anatole, his personal body servant to assist him as was his daily routine, whether at home or in the barracks. Putting on a spotless white toga and brown leather sandals, Tiberius left his bed chamber and headed straight to the sitting room located at the back of the house, facing the courtyard. Priscilla often spent her mornings there with her maidservants, all of whom enjoyed passing the time with their mistress as they were permitted to do needlework and various other activities with her. Checking the sitting room, Tiberius found his sister conversing cheerfully with two of her maids as they endeavored to create an appealing floral arrangement comprised of fragrant blossoms they had gathered from the garden.

Catching sight of Tiberius standing at the door, the maids respectfully bowed to the master of the house and their mistress acknowledged him with a timid smile. Trying to decipher her brother's staid expression, Priscilla thought he seemed relieved to see her, but this, she very much doubted, given all she had said the day prior. Holding his gaze, she waited with bated breath for Tiberius to verbalize the reason for his visit, conjuring up all manner of troubling suppositions, but nothing could have rattled Priscilla quite as much as his silent departure.

Finding his sister where she ought to have been, Tiberius returned to the main house, still plagued with the feeling that something was not right. Trusting his instincts, he went to Tamar's cubicle for after his sister, she was the next most likely to have done something foolish. Not bothering to knock, he entered the maid's room and found it empty of its occupant. Noticing the couch had not been laid upon; he rightly concluded she had escaped during the night. Irked because he had underestimated the maid, Tiberius stormed from the cubicle.

Certain Tamar had returned to Subura, Tiberius knew he would need help in finding her for the area was far too dangerous to venture into alone. Preparing to go after the runaway maid, he dispatched a servant to fetch

Quintus Atilius, a trusted friend and fellow centurion with whom he had fought many military campaigns. He could always count on his assistance. Returning to his private chamber, Tiberius summoned Anatole, who was adept in outfitting him in his military attire for he intended to enter Subura, clothed with the authority of Rome.

As Tiberius was an officer in the Roman army, his uniform was more impressive than the average soldiers. This was especially evident in the form fitted leather cuirass, designed to protect the shoulders, chest, abdomen and back. Adhered to the cuirass were shaped, metal breast plates that were fashioned so as to give the officer the appearance of great muscular development which further enhanced Tiberius' naturally fit physique. Sleeves made of leather straps extended from his broad shoulders and fell midway down his muscular upper arms. About his trim waist, he wore a kilt of leather straps that descended to his knees. A belt known as the baldric was slung over his left shoulder and under his right arm, having a sheath attached which housed Tiberius' exquisite gold hilted sword. His feet were shod in ankle boots similar to sandals, studded with hollow head nails. A cloak of red hung off his shoulders and a bronze helmet with imposing metal flaps on each side protected his face, head and neck. In the event of a parade, which took place after successful campaigns, Tiberius would carry a hard vine wood staff as a symbol of his rank and display for the people of Rome the magnificent decorations awarded him for acts of valor, along with the spoils he had taken from the enemy. However, these symbols of grandeur would be of no use in his search for Tamar, so he left them in his closet with his mess kit and other combat gear. Arrayed in his officer's uniform, Tiberius exited his chamber room and strolled out to meet Quintus Atilius, who stood ready and waiting in the atrium.

Quintus Atilius was not a particularly handsome man, neither was he unappealing to the eye. He was of medium height and build. His hair and eyes were brown, his skin olive in tone. His facial features were largely average with the exception of his long straight nose which dominated his aspect. A man of integrity, Quintus Atilius took seriously his commission to uphold and enforce the laws of Rome. Opposed to lining his pockets at the expense of another man, he was not tempted by bribes or intimidated by the threats and tactics of his enemies. Tiberius could not have chosen a better friend for few men were as upright and trustworthy as Quintus Atilius.

"It is good of thee to avail thyself on such short notice," Tiberius greeted Quintus Atilius, who was also dressed from head to toe in uniform.

"I gladly do so, Tiberius Marcius," replied Quintus Atilius. "Tell me, what need hath thee of me?"

"Come, time is of the essence. I shall explain everything as we travel," said Tiberius, leading the way out of his house.

"Friend, need I remind thee…this is our first official day on furlough," grinned Quintus Atilius, following on the heels of Tiberius. "I pray this matter hast something to do with wine or women…preferably both."

"It concerns a woman."

"Friend, thou hast my full attention," chuckled Quintus Atilius, eager for a diversion from his usual military duties.

Both men were seasoned soldiers, having achieved their rank by promotion and had promising military careers ahead of them. As centurions of distinction, they had the honor of serving in the Praetorian Guard, whose responsibility it was to protect the Emperor and his family, but that was where the similarities ended between Quintus Atilius and Tiberius Marcius.

Quintus Atilius was a propertied man. However, the property he owned did not compare in value with that of Tiberius for he was not of patrician birth neither had he any ancestors of whom he could boast. Of plebian origin, Quintus Atilius had enlisted in the army and worked his way up through the ranks, the acceptable method of military advancement for his social standing. Whereas, Tiberius hailed from a long line of patricians and could have gone the designated route of the privileged, entering the military with rank above that of centurion, but he had not done so, choosing instead to prove his worth and merit as a soldier on his own terms. Determined his worth would not be found solely in his birthright, Tiberius concealed his privileged background by enlisting in a city where he was not known. His patrician heritage remained undisclosed till his promotion to centurion, at which point it became necessary to apply to the Emperor for a commission. The news of the young officer's lofty social status spread quickly throughout the camp, earning him the respect of the rank and file soldiers and the ire of his patrician born superiors, who were none too pleased to inform Caesar of Tiberius' peculiar deception. Intrigued by the story, Caesar summoned Tiberius Marcius back to Rome at once, desiring to judge for himself what manner of man he was. An accomplished military man in his own right, Caesar was impressed with the soldier's fine military record and the accounts of his bravado, but he did not know the half of it, until his own son, Drusus recognized Tiberius and recounted how he had saved his life on the battlefield. A stern judge of character, Caesar verbally reprimanded Tiberius and threatened to relieve him of his duty because he had deceived his superior officers. Although Caesar had no intention of denying the soldier his hard earned rank, he thought it best to put some fear into the young upstart. Ultimately, however, he granted Tiberius Marcius a commission, but he did not assign him a campaign as was customary. Instead, he appointed the soldier to the esteemed Praetorian Guard. Despite Tiberius' unorthodox methods, he had found favor with Caesar, who respected above all, a soldier that had proved himself militarily invaluable and yet did not think more highly of himself than others.

Quintus Atilius admired Tiberius for much the same reasons. In spite of their class variance, Tiberius had never treated him with disdain or indifference and because he had not, they had forged a strong bond of friendship, built on sincerity and equality. There was nothing they would not do for one another. Sticking together through thick and thin, they were united in purpose. And so it was that Tiberius explained his personal dilemma to Quintus Atilius as they rode their horses down the cobbled streets of Rome toward the rutted, muddy roads of impoverished Subura.

Subura was densely populated, the citizens diverse in language and in custom. Yet, for all their cultural differences, the residents were bound together by the common thread of poverty. Rundown shops, taverns and apartment houses dotted the landscape. Many structures had been abandoned altogether, their crumbling walls battered by the passing years and defaced by obscene graffiti. Appearing to outsiders to thrive on belligerence, the people of Subura were very aggressive, so much so, that fierce altercations and vulgar speech were interwoven into the fabric of their everyday lives.

As the centurions made their way through the crowded, bustling streets of Subura, they encountered the bellicose human population, of whom, the greater share were afoot while others rode in trundling carts pulled by oxen. Bleating sheep could be heard along with squawking birds and barking dogs. The air was heavy with the stench of the public latrine. Accustomed to their odious surroundings, the residents went about their daily business, seemingly oblivious to Subura's less than appealing attributes. Small shops and open air stalls offered buyers a wide assortment of merchandise to delight and entice the eye. There were fresh fruits and vegetables, spices from exotic lands, perfumes, brightly colored cloth, sparkling jewels, pottery and every other imaginable treasure worth attaining. In addition, there were taverns that served up wine, women and treachery to free men and slaves alike.

It was the treachery that most concerned Tiberius. He knew all too well thieves, assassins and every ilk of reprobate could be found in Subura. Countless times Rome had come out against the malefactors, squelching revolts and crucifying those found guilty of insurrection and treason. But Rome's swift and brutal punishment did little to dissuade the troublemakers from their criminal acts and Subura remained a thorn in the side of the authorities. Surveying the wretched environment from atop his moving steed, Tiberius could not fathom how Tamar had survived in such squalor. Truly, she was a beautiful flower in the midst of the mire, he thought as his dark eyes took in all that was Subura.

Arriving at a residential section known to be heavily settled by the Jewish people, the centurions began their search for Tamar among the many apartment buildings known as insulae. Traveling from one insula to the next, they knocked on every door, physically intimidating the inhabitants in order to secure information on the maid's whereabouts.

Loathing the Romans and all that they stood for, the children of Abraham answered the soldier's questions, fearing imprisonment or death, although neither centurion verbally threatened such punishment.

After nearly two hours of insufferable heat and diligent door to door questioning, the centurions found themselves at a small, detached dwelling, said to be the residence of Tamar's kinsmen. Prepared for a physical confrontation, Tiberius approached the humble abode and pounded his fist on the weather-beaten door. Standing with his friend, Quintus Atilius withdrew a hand knife from his belt, ready to defend himself and Tiberius should it become necessary.

Ruth answered the door and to her utter horror, she was met by two soldiers, who wasted no time in pushing their way past her. Left at the threshold, she looked on helplessly as the centurions conducted a quick search of her modest home. Not finding what they were after, the taller of the two soldiers grabbed Laham by his coarse tunic, pulling him up from the crude wood bench on which he sat.

"Tell me, old man, where is the maid Tamar," demanded Tiberius, his aspect menacing as he stared into the patriarch's aged face.

"I know not of any such maid," Laham lied feebly.

"Old man, I ask thee again and thou best answer truthfully! Where is the maid, Tamar?"

Coming to herself, Ruth ran to her husband's aid, but was skillfully detained by Quintus Atilius, who blocked her path; determined Tiberius would suffer no interference from her.

"Leave him alone! We know nothing of the maid!" she shrieked, fearing for her husband's life.

Peering into the fierce countenance of the Roman centurion, Laham saw an opportunity and he intended to make good use of it, even if it meant dealing with the enemy.

"Hath pity for I am old and poor," said Laham shrewdly. "The maid whom ye seek provides for me in my infirmity."

"What is that to me," barked Tiberius impatiently.

"I am destitute without her," Laham continued, undaunted. "If thou were to offer a price…a price worthy of her…I could be persuaded…"

"Husband, do not sell thy brother's child into bondage! I beg thee…do not do this evil deed," cried Ruth, mortified by Laham's disloyalty.

"Of a truth, my wife is very fond of the maid," Laham remarked coolly, seizing upon Ruth's emotion to further his proposal. "I too am fond of her, but I am a practical man. I must think of myself and my wife lest we perish. Consider my meager circumstances, most noble servant of Rome and give me a price befitting the maid."

"Old man, if it is a price thou doth want, I shall render it," replied the centurion, eyeing with hostility the contemptible specimen of humanity he held in his grasp. Even though Tiberius knew Tamar was his for the taking, he saw an advantage in financially acquiring her from her kinsman. Viewing Laham with disdain, he demanded, "Where is the maid?"

Laham lifted his dim brown eyes upward to the small loft that had miraculously gone unnoticed.

Tiberius followed Laham's gaze and seeing the loft, he released the old man with a callous shove, causing him to stumble backwards.

"The ladder is hidden behind the drapery," volunteered Laham, steadying himself.

"Husband, thou art no better than these pagans!" screamed Ruth, blinking back bitter tears. "I shall never forgive thee for what thou hast done to Tamar!"

Turning a deaf ear to his wife, Laham paid no mind to her words for it was of no importance to him what she thought.

Leaving Quintus Atilius to the task of guarding the old man and his wife, Tiberius located the ladder and leaned it against the small opening in the ceiling. Climbing up to the loft, he cautiously surveyed the room from his place on the ladder. Spying Tamar's bare feet showing out from beneath a drawn curtain that hung in a corner of the upper chamber, he scanned the premises once again, making certain he was not walking into a trap. Seeing no one but the maid, he entered the room. Standing outside of the drapery, he summoned the maid with authority. "Woman, come forth," and when Tamar did not obey his command, he spoke again, but more sternly. "Woman, come forth!"

Frightened, Tamar's pulse quickened. Trapped and knowing there was no hope of escape, she uttered a desperate prayer for deliverance. Who but God could save her from the dreaded Romans?

Losing patience, Tiberius ripped the curtain aside and snatched Tamar, who did everything she could to resist his efforts to remove her from the closet, but his overpowering strength was more than she could physically withstand. Plucked from the safety of her hiding place, she screamed and thrashed about wildly, trying to escape him.

"Woman, cease thy struggling! I fear I may harm thee," warned Tiberius, mindful of his might as he fought to subdue the frantic maid. "I take no pleasure in such things!"

"Let go of me…you brute!"

"Woman, thou cannot overcome a centurion! Cease thy struggling!"

"Thou art hurting me," she cried breathlessly, fighting him.

"I do not want to hurt thee, woman! Be still and I will unhand thee!"

Anxious to be released from the soldier's vise, Tamar stopped struggling and being a man of his word, Tiberius released her.

Free of the centurion, Tamar stepped back from him. She desperately wanted to turn and run, but run where? Where could she go that he could not find her? Who would dare to rescue her from this fearsome centurion? No one would dare, save Josiah and he was dead. Dead because he had tried to rescue her from the Romans…dead! Suddenly, a horrifying picture of Laham and Ruth flashed before her consciousness. Had they also perished trying to protect her? Were they at this very moment lying in a pool of blood, mortally wounded? Had the centurion ordered their deaths on account of her?

"Answer me…I pray thee…what hath befallen the inhabitants of this dwelling? Do they yet live," Tamar inquired shakily as she looked upon the soldier, her dark eyes filled with apprehension.

"No harm hath come to them," assured the centurion, his eyes keen on her.

Relieved, Tamar drew a small breath and lifted an inaudible prayer of thanks to her God.

"Woman, I hath answered thy question and now thou must answer mine. Why hast thou fled my house?"

Believing she owed him no explanation, Tamar averted his inquiring eyes and fell silent.

Infuriated by her silence, Tiberius grabbed Tamar by the arms with a force that conveyed his anger and ignited hers. Pulling her near his armored body, he questioned her again.

"Why didst thou run away? Answer me when I speak to thee, woman," he snapped harshly.

Meeting his piercing gaze, Tamar responded indignantly, "I am free-born! I belong to no man!"

"Woman, behold the man to whom thou doth belong! Thou art my servant and thou wilt render unto me thy service and thy respect!"

"I will render thee nothing!"

"Caesar himself surrendered thee into my hands! Thou art my property! Woman, this cannot hath escaped thy understanding!"

"I shall not abide by Caesar's decree; neither shall I serve thee or thy sister!"

"Thou wilt serve whomever I say," asserted Tiberius, forcibly escorting Tamar across the small upper room to the loft opening.

"Unhand me, you arrogant, self serving Roman p…" said Tamar angrily, stopping short of the common slur.

Taking exception to her words, Tiberius shot Tamar a sharp look of disapproval and she returned his look with one of defiance, adding to his displeasure. Knowing what she had left unsaid, Tiberius wondered why she had not finished saying it. He had no doubt, she considered all Romans to be pigs. Why then, had she declined to address him as such? Dismissing the foolish contemplation from his mind, Tiberius spoke again, his tone unnervingly somber. "Woman, wilt thou follow me down the ladder or must I carry thee over my shoulder?"

"I will follow thee," she yielded, not daring to provoke him further.

"See to it, thy word is true," he advised and took to the ladder.

Tamar had barely descended to the bottom rung of the ladder when she was roughly accosted by Tiberius. Seizing her, he dragged the maid before Laham and Ruth, who stood under the watchful guard of Quintus Atilius.

Laying eyes on Tamar, Quintus Atilius was awestruck by her beauty. Little wonder Tiberius had been so determined to find her. She was no ordinary maidservant. She was a magnificent work of art, created to be loved and treasured. Had he been a lesser man, he would have sought some means to have her for himself, but as he was committed to serving the interests of Tiberius above his own, he stayed focused on the mission and maintained his dutiful stance.

Placed in front of Laham, Tamar beheld him, but she was not prepared for what she saw. Confused by her uncle's callous expression, she turned to look at Tiberius, trying to make sense of it.

"Woman, he hath betrayed thee," Tiberius answered her unspoken question.

"Betrayed," she repeated in utter disbelief.

"Forgive him, Tamar…forgive him…" Ruth cried out, unable to bear Tamar's inconsolable expression.

"Silence, wife," rebuked Laham gruffly. "I want no forgiveness! What I hath done, I hath done!"

What had he done? Surely, he had not betrayed her into the hands of the Romans! Turning back to Laham, her eyes discerned what her heart did not want to accept. There in his impenitent face, she saw the horrible truth and being unable to shoulder the rejection of her kinsman, Tamar hung her head, shutting out the vision of her betrayer.

"Is this man thy uncle?" Tiberius queried, regarding the maid.

Wounded to the core of her soul, Tamar struggled to find her voice.

"Answer me, woman!"

"He is…" she faltered, not lifting her tear filled eyes.

"Then it is better for thee to dwell with strangers," remarked Tiberius, shifting his attention from her to Laham.

"I beg thee, hath mercy! Do not take her from us," pleaded Ruth tearfully, her hands clasped together in supplication. "Hath mercy…I entreat thee! She is all I hath left!"

"Wait outside, woman," ordered Tiberius, not bothering to look at her.

Attending to Tiberius' directive, Quintus Atilius hastily escorted the old woman from her home. Ruth did not realize Tiberius was sparing her more heartache nor would she have believed him capable of such consideration. Pitying the old woman, he had sent her from the house that she might not witness the painful transaction between him and her husband. Although he had dispensed mercy to Ruth, Tiberius could not do the same for Tamar. She had to be made to understand she was his property.

"Old man, I offer thee thirty pieces of silver for the maid," declared Tiberius, withdrawing his leather money pouch.

"Come! Come," Laham threw up his hands in exasperation. "Is she not beautiful and worth far more than thirty pieces of silver? She is worth twice as much," Laham bartered, not caring that his niece had begun to cry softly.

"Old man, I hath offered thee a fair price. Thirty pieces of silver is the price of a common slave."

"True, but it is customary to pay more for beauty such as hers! Not even the Greeks hath beheld such a vision of pure loveliness! A price befitting her…that is what we agreed upon! Is it not?"

"So be it," conceded Tiberius, casting his money pouch at Laham's sandaled feet.

Stooping down, Laham eagerly retrieved the leather pouch and opened it. Grasping a silver coin in his thick fingers, he placed it between his teeth, gingerly biting it to test its authenticity. Satisfied the coin was indeed silver, Laham spilled the contents of the pouch into his hand and greedily began counting his treasure unaware that Quintus Atilius had rejoined them.

Responding to a silent cue from Tiberius, Quintus Atilius yanked Tamar out of the path of impending peril. Her startled cry came too late to warn Laham.

Feeling the centurion's cold, sharp sword resting precariously at his throat, Laham stared helplessly at the long, shiny blade, swallowing what might be his last breath.

"Get up," barked Tiberius, keeping his sword to Laham's neck.

"What is this?" asked Laham, rising to his feet, oddly aware of the money tumbling from his grasp onto the dirt floor. Even with the threat of death looming over him, he felt strangely compelled to gather up the fallen coins.

"This is a warning, old man! If thou doth value thy miserable life, then heed my words and heed them well," threatened Tiberius, his black eyes narrowing. "If the maid returns here and thou give her shelter with the intent of hiding her…it shall cost thee thy life. Make no mistake…thy life shall be forfeited for hers."

"I swear thou wilt know if she returns," vowed Laham, visibly shaken.

"See that I do," quipped Tiberius, pressing his sharp blade against Laham's neck for emphasis.

"I give thee my word," Laham winced with pain. "Please...grant an old man mercy!"

"Why should I grant the likes of thee mercy," sneered Tiberius, half tempted to slit his throat and be done with him.

"Soldier, I beseech thee...do not harm him," Tamar pleaded, afraid for her uncle. "I will go with thee...but do not harm my kinsman! I entreat thee...do not hurt him!"

"Old man, how doth it feel to hear the maid beg for thy worthless life...even after thou hast handed her over to thine enemy?"

"Hear me, noble servant of Rome! Hear me! I trust her not! She will return and bring thy judgment upon me because I hath sold her unto thee! How shalt thou discern this matter?"

"I see thy dilemma," Tiberius said, finding the idea of Tamar seeking revenge on the crafty old man rather absurd. "If thou doth fear the maid's return, then leave Rome," he advised dryly, withdrawing his sword from Laham's neck and sliding it back into its sheath. Claiming what was rightfully his, Tiberius took custody of Tamar and left Laham standing on the price of her.

Clutching his spared neck, Laham watched as the centurions exited the house with his niece, feeling no remorse for what he had done. "Good riddance, Tamar! May thou toil all thy days under the ruthless Roman dogs," he cursed her under his breath. He hated Tamar as he had never hated anyone before. Not even his hatred for the Romans and their tax collectors could match the intense hatred he felt for his niece. As far as he was concerned, Tamar was guilty of Josiah's death just as if she had done the murderous deed herself. He had taken an eye for an eye and a tooth for a tooth and it had not been without profit. With visions of prosperity filling his gray head, Laham bent down and greedily retrieved his new found wealth.

Outside of the humble dwelling, Tiberius was met by Ruth, who upon seeing the centurion; fell at his feet, weeping.

"Hath mercy and grant my sorrowing heart a brief farewell! I beg thee...be merciful to an old woman!"

Quintus Atilius moved toward Ruth, but Tiberius stopped him, signaling to let her be and said, "Woman, rise and bid thy niece farewell."

Picking herself up from the dusty ground, Ruth embraced Tamar and through heart-rending tears, cried, "My dear child, thou hast been like a daughter unto me…and I hath loved thee as such. Be strong, my child. The Lord God shall give thee the strength to endure what thou must. Remember…He is able to deliver thee from this evil."

"Why hath my uncle cast me out," Tamar asked tearfully, suffering the pain of rejection.

Ruth struggled to find a reply that might somehow explain the unexplainable. Why had her husband done this terrible evil? Why had he betrayed his own flesh and blood? How could she have lived with him for so many years and not known what evil he was capable of? Emerging from her own personal agony, Ruth pulled back from the embrace and looked upon her niece with compassion, saying, "I know not why he hast done this, Tamar, but this I do know…God shall provide someone to care for thee."

"Those were…Josiah's last words…" said Tamar numbly, her voice trailing off.

"What were Josiah's last words," Ruth inquired, lovingly pushing back the loose tendrils from Tamar's face that had escaped her long braid.

"God shall provide…someone…to care for thee…" Tamar repeated slowly, her eyes strangely drawn to Tiberius, who stood intently watching her. No! It was not possible, she reasoned within herself. God would not send a Roman centurion, a man of pagan beliefs to care for a daughter of Abraham! Yet as her eyes met his, the startling revelation became reality.

"No!" she screamed from the innermost depth of her being, unable to accept the intolerable curse. "No! I cannot bear it!"

Beholding her anguish, Tiberius intervened and separated the maid from her aunt, prying the women apart with the aid of Quintus Atilius, who restrained Ruth. Paying no heed to their tearful pleadings, Tiberius led the distraught maid to his waiting stallion. Mounting, he leaned down and extended his hand to Tamar, but she would not take it, though he demanded she do so. Beside herself, she refused to obey Tiberius and ran toward Ruth. Going after her, Quintus Atilius brought her back to Tiberius and forced the crying maid into compliance. Pushing her against the horse's withers, he laced his fingers together, shoved them under her bare foot and hoisted her upward. Tiberius, who had slid back in his saddle, grabbed hold of Tamar and seated her in front of him, insuring she could not escape. Bringing his strong arms around her, he gathered his reins. Quintus Atilius then swiftly mounted his own horse and off the centurions rode, having plucked the fairest flower of Subura.

V

The journey from poverty ridden Subura to the affluent dwellings of aristocratic Rome was an arduous one. It was especially difficult for Tamar who suffered the trek in silence, devastated by the betrayal of her uncle. As for Tiberius, his mood was somber which came as no surprise to Quintus Atilius. He was accustomed to the ways of his serious minded friend and held his peace until the time of his departure.

"Tiberius Marcius, thou doth owe me a flagon of wine," quipped Quintus Atilius, sitting tall in the saddle, grinning ear to ear.

"That is the very least I owe thee, my friend," responded Tiberius, grateful for the assistance rendered.

"If she runs off again…let me know," said Quintus Atilius, eyeing Tamar appreciatively.

"I assure thee, she shall not be afforded the opportunity," Tiberius stated resolutely.

"No…I suppose not," laughed Quintus Atilius, laying his whip to his horse's hind quarters and galloping off.

Arriving at his residence, Tiberius was met by his stable servant, who had kept an eye out for his return. Noting his master's grim countenance, the servant quickly assisted Tamar from the horse, aware of her escape as word of it had spread through the household. Knowing Tamar had caused the master a great deal of trouble, the faithful servant gave her a disapproving look as he set her upon the ground with intentional roughness. He for one judged her attempt at escape most unwise. It was the kind of behavior that resulted in the harshest of punishments and although he had never personally seen the master punish any slave to the fullest extent of the law, it was inadvisable to presume he would not. If the maid had any sense, she would plead for mercy and accept her lowly position. After all, if one was fated to be a slave, better to be one in the house of Tiberius Marcius Maximus for his was a house of nobility.

Dismounting his steed, Tiberius seized Tamar roughly by the arm and escorted her to the house. Unable to keep pace with the centurion's long strides, the maid lost her footing and would have fallen if not for the soldier's firm hold on her. Halting momentarily as she regained her balance,

Tiberius considered the young woman in his possession. He could not help but notice how utterly defenseless she was. There was something frustrating about her frailty, something that caught him off guard. He was a soldier. He had been trained to take full advantage of weakness in others, not to accommodate it. Now he was in charge of a delicate creature that required a great measure of patience and gentleness, neither of which, he came by easily.

With the maid in tow, Tiberius entered the tablinum, his private domain, where he conducted business and met with clients. No one was permitted inside unless invited or summoned. The room was bright and spacious, tastefully furnished, containing a substantial looking desk situated near a window that looked out into the garden courtyard. An imposing chair sat behind the desk and another chair, slightly less grand in appearance, known as the client's chair was in front of the desk. Set apart a little distance was a couch upholstered in a deep blue fabric with several matching bolsters. Next to the couch was a small table, upon which sat an oval tray and wine decanter of polished silver. Clustered in an adjacent corner were three blue ceramic urns of varied height. In a corner behind the desk, stood a tall pedestal resembling a column, bearing a stone likeness of Alexander the Great, his lethal sword drawn, standing triumphantly over a fallen enemy. An ornate light fixture hung on each of the four painted walls, which boasted of battle depictions and mighty gods caught up in a pale blue swirl of sky and white clouds. Located in the very back of the room was the sleeping cubicle and linked to it was a smaller cubicle used for wardrobe and storage.

Seating Tamar in the client's chair, Tiberius strolled around to the other side of his expansive desk, removed his helmet and placed it next to a neatly stacked pile of sealed scrolls. Summoning his steward with a clap of his hands, the efficient servant did his master's bidding and brought forth a large, silver tray bearing a flagon of wine, a flagon of water and two silver goblets.

Dismissing his steward, Tiberius filled a goblet to the brim and guzzled its contents. His thirst quenched, he then poured a little wine into the other goblet for Tamar, watering it down heavily as women of virtue did not drink their wine undiluted. Certain the maid was thirsting, he offered the goblet to her, but she refused the draught. Surprised by her silent refusal, which he rightly discerned had more to do with her dislike of him than her moral upbringing; he again offered her the goblet.

"Drink it," he commanded, watching her.

Obeying, Tamar accepted the goblet and cautiously tasted the watery concoction. Finding the Roman and his wine offensive, she passed the cup back to the centurion, noting his displeasure.

Frowning for she had but sipped of the wine, Tiberius leaned across his desk, took the goblet away from her and set it upon the tray. Sitting down in his comfortable chair, he fixed his dark eyes on Tamar and began to speak, his tone and aspect stern.

"Woman, I will not suffer thy foolishness again. I hath secured thee by pledge and by silver. I hath taken thee from the house of Caesar and from the house of thine kinsman. Thou doth belong unto me. I own thee according to Roman law and according to the law of thine own people. Thou art in my hand. I am thy master and thou art now a servant in my house."

Brought low by the severity of his words, Tamar bowed her head in quiet acknowledgment.

"I shall not tolerate anything less than thy full obedience. Thou wilt render unto me the respect to which I am entitled. I am the lord of this house and as such…I could flog thee for trying to escape…sell thee to barbarians or kill thee with my bare hands. None of which are too harsh a punishment for thy transgression and all are within the bounds of Roman law," stated the centurion, making plain the scope of his authority. "However, for thy sake, I shall assume thou wert ignorant of the law and I shall make an allowance for thy ignorance. I shall temper thy punishment…just this once."

"…but I am not a slave…I am freeborn," protested Tamar, fighting back tears.

"The past is of no consequence now," said Tiberius curtly.

"I beg thee…reconsider this matter and permit me to return to my kinsmen," she pleaded, timidly meeting the centurion's unwavering gaze.

"Woman, the matter hath been settled. Caesar hath sealed thy fate. Thou shalt meet with certain death should he lay eyes upon thee again. What is more, thy kinsman hath cast thee out. Thou hast no home to return unto."

"My kinsman feared thou might harm him. He would allow my return…if thou would but speak the word."

"Woman…" thundered Tiberius, "thou art trying my patience! Thy kinsman cared more for silver than he cared for thee! He feared only that I would take thee without compensating him!"

"Please…I beg thee to reconsider…" she implored, her voice trembling with emotion. "I want to return to my home…and to my people."

"Woman, thou shalt never return to Subura. Though why in the name of Jupiter, thou would even want to return to that cesspool is beyond my understanding," remarked Tiberius, opening his desk drawer and pulling out a razor-sharp knife. Rising from his chair, looking every inch the Roman warrior he was, he came around the desk with purpose.

Seeing the shiny blade in the centurion's hand, Tamar's body stiffened in fear.

Taking the frightened girl by the arm, Tiberius forced her to her feet and demanded, "Give me thy belt."

"Why?" asked Tamar, confused and startled by his peculiar request.

Offering no explanation, Tiberius grabbed the woven belt about the maid's slender waist and severed it with his knife. Reaching around her shoulder, he took hold of her long, thick braid and brought it forward.

"Please...not my hair!" she cried, her dress hanging limply about her small frame. "I beg thee, do not cut my hair!"

"Woman, I hath no intention of harming a hair on thy fair head...only to keep thee from doing so," he said, cutting the band that bound her dark brown tresses.

Shaken, Tamar began to cry. Unaffected by her tears, Tiberius called for his steward, who obeying his summons, immediately reappeared for he had been listening just outside the door as was his habit.

"Steward, the maid is to be confined to her cubicle," voiced Tiberius sternly. "See to it, a sturdy bolt is fitted to her door at once. She is to remain locked in her room till I say otherwise.

Is that understood?"

"Perfectly understood, Domine," replied the steward, showing no emotion.

"Before her confinement commences, a bath is to be prepared for her. No trace of Subura filth is to remain on her person. Burn her old clothes," ordered Tiberius, tossing her belt to his steward, who caught it. "She is to receive clean raiment having no belts or ribbons with which she may do herself harm. Remove from her room any objects that could prove useful, should she attempt to do herself violence and make certain her food trays contain no utensils. She is not to be afforded an opportunity to hurt herself or others."

"I shall do all thou hast said," assured the steward, stepping forward to escort Tamar from his master's sight.

"And set a guard outside the door while she is bathed, lest she take a notion and try to escape again," added Tiberius, shooting a hard look at Tamar. "She is not to be trusted."

"Yes, my lord."

Ignoring the steward that stood ready to whisk her away, Tamar tearfully addressed the centurion. "Must thou bolt my door?"

"Woman, consider thyself fortunate I hath not punished thee more severely," he replied and having spoken, Tiberius looked from the maid to his steward. "Inform my sister, I wish to see her at once."

Attending to his master's will, the steward laid hands on Tamar and ushered her from the room to the servant's quarters at the back of the house, where a bath could be prepared.

Imparting the master's instructions word for word to several robust women and one man, who would guard the maid, the steward left Tamar in their capable hands and sought out Priscilla.

Having duly punished Tamar, Tiberius decided he might as well address Priscilla's errant behavior too, since it seemed to please the gods to surround him with so much dissension. He would attend to the task of straightening out Priscilla's un-Roman like attitude toward her impending marriage and with that settled, he would then be in control of his household and those that lived in it. Truly, he had been absent too long for his authority as paterfamilias was being tried on all fronts. It was time for him to squash the rebellion that threatened his domain and it mattered not whether it came from servant or family member. Both would know his wrath, both would come to respect his word as law or be crushed under it.

Seating himself at his desk once again, Tiberius waited for Priscilla, who arrived looking rather unsettled, which did not escape the notice of her brother. "Be seated," Tiberius said, motioning to the client's chair.

Trying to maintain a semblance of calm, Priscilla gracefully took the place her brother had indicated, bracing herself for what, she did not know. She did, however, suspect his summons had something to do with her most recent outburst. An outburst, she instinctively knew she would come to regret.

"Priscilla, I hath called thee here hoping thou hast come to thy senses concerning thy future marriage," he began, his gaze fastened on his sister. "Lucius Servilius is the man father chose for thee. He esteemed him a patrician worthy of thee as do I. I am well aware that father's choice doth not please thee. Nevertheless, his will shall be done. Thou wilt marry Lucius Servilius."

"I cannot," declared Priscilla, her calm facade shattered. "I cannot marry Lucius Servilius! I do not love him!"

"That will come with time, Priscilla."

"Tiberius Marcius, how can thou be so heartless? Do not make me marry a man I do not love," Priscilla cried, her large, brown eyes clouding with tears.

"Is it heartless, sister, to want what is best for thee?"

"I will not marry him…I will not!" she said defiantly.

"Thou wilt marry Lucius Servilius. Woman, it is thy duty to obey me."

"I cannot! I will not marry Lucius Servilius," she rose to her feet, hot tears streaming down her face. "I will not!"

"Priscilla, it grieves me thou hast refused to obey me willingly. Thou hast left me with no alternative, but to force thee to comply with my wishes," stated Tiberius, genuinely unhappy that he had to take stiff measures against his sister.

Disciplining Priscilla was unpleasant, but as the paterfamilias, it was expected of him. She was his responsibility until the day she entered her husband's house and he did not take his responsibility lightly. He would not rest until she was safely married to Lucius Servilius and out of the reach of the despicable Claudius, whose name had not surfaced, much to his relief. Yet, he knew that Claudius had captured his sister's heart, though how he had managed to do so, Tiberius was uncertain. He had instructed his cousin Cassius to keep a tight rein on Priscilla's comings and goings in his absence and evidently, Cassius had failed to do so. Somehow, Claudius had succeeded in reaching Priscilla and souring her affection for Lucius Servilius, a man far more worthy of her attention and whose patrician background equaled her own. Bound by duty to safeguard the family's honor and position, Tiberius was determined to act in the best interest of all concerned, most especially his lovesick sister.

Rising from his chair, Tiberius beckoned his steward, who was on the other side of the door, eavesdropping. Answering his master's call, the steward entered the tablinum, bowed humbly and waited for his orders.

"Priscilla hath displeased me and I regrettably must punish her," Tiberius said stoically.

"From this day forward, she is not permitted to leave the premises for any reason. No one is to be admitted into this house to visit her, neither is she to send or receive any correspondence. If her friends call upon her, tell them she hath taken ill. And inform her doting maidservants that if they assist her in disobeying my will, they shall incur a fate far worse than hers. Do I make myself clear?"

"Perfectly clear, Domine," said the steward, concealing his sorrow at having to enforce punishment on Priscilla for he was very fond of her. Even so, he knew Tiberius would not have disciplined her if it had not been necessary. The master was not unkind, neither was he cruel, but he did demand respect and obedience from the members of his household.

"Imprison me in my own home if thou wilt, but be warned…Claudius shall find a way to me," Priscilla announced, pretending to be unruffled by her punishment.

Hearing his sister's response, Tiberius glanced at his steward, who quickly shook his head in the negative. Claudius would not find his way inside of the master's house, nor would he ever set eyes on Priscilla as long as he was steward. Fiercely loyal to Tiberius, he would see to that.

Pleased with his steward's silent assurance, Tiberius dismissed Priscilla with an abrupt wave of his hand and she left his presence, holding her head up high just as if she had won the confrontation, though she knew she had not.

VI

Confined to a small cubicle, Tamar's only visitor was Talia, an aged slave woman with a strong maternal instinct, who tended to Tamar as she would to a child. Meticulous in the performance of her duty, Talia looked after the maid's needs, including her hygiene, despite the young woman's assertion that she was capable of caring for herself. However, Tamar's protests fell on deaf ears and having no choice in the matter, she relinquished her personal care to the slave woman at the expense of her modesty.

Monitoring Tamar's grief-stricken state, Talia reported daily to Tiberius Marcius as he had instructed her to do. Seven days had come and gone and Talia's report had remained unchanged for Tamar had shown no sign of emerging from her melancholy state of mind. Quiet and introspective, the maid kept to herself and would not speak unless spoken to. She wept often, so much so, that each time Talia looked in on her; she found the young woman's eyes brimming with tears. Neither did she have an appetite which greatly concerned Talia, who tried to entice the maid to eat, but her efforts were unsuccessful. Mindful of Tamar's fragile emotional constitution and fearing her health would soon suffer as a result, Talia interceded on her behalf, urging Tiberius to grant the maid some measure of liberty lest she become ill. Unmoved by Talia's dire summation, Tiberius let his decision stand and Tamar remained locked in her cubicle for another seven days.

Having no diversion, except Talia's visits which she bore as patiently as she could given the circumstances, Tamar spent her time in prayer and fasting. Taught that suffering was a direct result of sin, Tamar looked inward for the answer as to why misfortune had befallen her. Was she being punished by God? Had she unknowingly violated one of His Holy Commandments? Was she suffering because of some unconfessed trespass? Believing she had offended God, Tamar carefully examined her conscience and humbly repented with tears and fasting.

Unable to account for the origin of her suffering, but nonetheless contrite of heart, Tamar remembered the trials of the great patriarch Job, who like her, did not know why he suffered. He had endured the loss of his good name, his position, his flocks, his children, his possessions and his health. His wife had offered him little in the way of comfort and had gone so far as to suggest he curse God and die. His friends, who had come with the intent of offering solace, added to his misery by accusing him of sin, though he was righteous before God.

Tamar understood the anguish of being falsely accused. Blamed for Josiah's death, her uncle had passed judgment upon her, just as Job's friends had upon him. She too, had experienced the loss of what she held most dear. Gone was her beloved Josiah, her precious freedom, her meager possessions, her ties to family and home. Nothing in the small cubicle belonged to her, not the bed on which she slept, not the lamp which illuminated the darkness, not even the clothing on her body was her own. Alone and destitute, all she had left was her God, the same God in whom Job and so many others before her had put their trust.

Though Job knew not why he suffered, he had remained faithful in the midst of great affliction. Could she, a daughter of Abraham, do any less? Could she turn her back on God just because suffering had entered her life? No, such a deed would be unthinkable. She, like Job had accepted blessings from God and now had to accept her portion of trouble, bearing it in faith. Regardless of whether God allowed blessing or suffering in her life, she would honor Him and keep His commandments. This was the way of the patriarchs. She would follow in their path, the path of the righteous. She would trust God and wait for deliverance for it would surely come to her as it had to Job.

As for Priscilla, she had no use for the God of the Jews. Her allegiance belonged to the gods of Rome, numerous as they were. Reigning over every aspect of Roman life, one was never at a loss for a deity to call upon in time of trouble. There was Jupiter, chief of all gods, Juno, his consort, Mars, god of war, Mercury, god of commerce and luck, Vesta, goddess of hearth and fire, Diana, goddess of childbirth and on and on went the vast assembly of deities. The citizens of Rome believed in a world filled with gods and could not conceive of one god governing the affairs of all men as the Jews believed. Not even Jupiter, the greatest of all Roman gods who presided over the state, its laws, the weather and more could manage the entire universe single-handedly. It took a whole host of gods to rule the fate and fortunes of mortal men. Ones destiny was in the hands of the gods. This was the Roman creed, the creed in which Priscilla put her faith.

For two weeks, Priscilla had called down curses from her pagan gods, beseeching them to chastise her brother for restricting her freedom and thwarting true love. Invoking Venus, the revered goddess of love, Priscilla vowed to visit her temple as soon as she was physically able and offer a sweet sacrifice of honey cakes. She believed her promised sacrifice would please Venus and compel the goddess to answer her prayers, which she uttered daily, careful not to make a mistake in their recital, lest they be rendered worthless. If an error was made, the entire petition had to be repeated in order to find favor with the gods, who desired above all, perfection. This requirement did not deter Priscilla as she maintained a standard of perfection in all she did and prayer was no exception. Reciting her prayers flawlessly, she appealed daily to the powerful goddess for divine assistance.

With a new dawn breaking and curses still fresh on her lips, Priscilla sat at her dressing table, clad in her night gown as her maidservants dutifully busied themselves tending to her grooming. A maid was combing her long, brown hair and another was manicuring her nails and still another waited patiently to apply some cosmetics to the young patrician's lovely aspect. Aware of their mistress' sour mood, the astute maids performed their tasks in near silence so as not to provoke her ire. Priscilla usually took pleasure in being pampered by her maidservants and often joined in their lively chatter, but everything had changed. Since her chastisement, she had paid no mind to her servants or their idle talk. She could only think of herself and her marriage dilemma.

Soon, she would be summoned by Tiberius as she had been for the past fourteen mornings. Without fail, two male servants would come for her and escort her to the tablinum, whether or not she consented to go willingly. Only once did Priscilla resist her escorts, forcing them to haul her to the tablinum kicking and screaming, but her antics availed her nothing. Having suffered the loss of her dignity, she was left with no alternative but to accompany them of her own accord and she went quietly from that day forward. Entering the domain of the paterfamilias, Priscilla would find Tiberius standing behind his desk, his formidable stature expertly draped in a toga, his face hard and expressionless. He would then ask her one question and one only, his voice stern, his manner aloof. "Sister, art thou prepared to marry the man thy father hath chosen for thee?" Always, the same question came from his lips. Always, the same answer came from hers. "I shall marry none, but Claudius." To which, Tiberius would declare, "Thou shalt marry Lucius Servilius or thou shalt not marry," and having the final word, he would dismiss her from his presence. The menservants, who had not left her side, would then usher her from the room, only to escort her back again at the beginning of the next day and the whole unpleasant scenario would be repeated.

At odds with her brother, Priscilla was engaged in a fierce battle of wills. A battle she stubbornly fought knowing she could not win, unless the gods chose to alter her fate. Held prisoner within her home, stripped of her liberty and the company of her friends, Priscilla felt isolated from the outside world. If the gods did not intervene, she would be forced to spend the remainder of her days locked away or worse yet, married to a man she did not love. She had hoped Tiberius would suspend her sentence, but he had not, nor would he even consider her plea for clemency until she consented to marry Lucius Servilius. Still, she refused to give into her brother's demand. Severe as the penalty was in her mind, it had failed to dampen her love for Claudius. If anything, her affection for him had increased in its intensity. Blinded by love, Priscilla could not see Claudius for the scoundrel he was. If she could have, she never would have loved him, thus sparing herself a great deal of hardship.

Upon completion of Priscilla's beauty routine, her dressing attendant helped her slip out of her night gown and into a lavender silk stola, an intricately arranged floor length dress that draped one arm and had a full, pleated blouse which hung over girdling worn tightly at the hips. Having fitted the dress to near perfection on Priscilla's willowy body, the attendant presented a pair of comfortable, white leather slippers, knowing her mistress would have no need of heavy footwear, since she was not permitted to venture out of the house.

"Bring my amethyst necklace…and do be quick about it," Priscilla ordered, admiring her countenance in the nearly flawless mirror held before her by the dressing attendant's young daughter.

"Yes, Dominilla," the attendant replied, leaving her child and running off to fetch the requested jewelry.

Gazing at herself with no thought of the little girl, whose arms were tiring from holding the mirror, Priscilla caught sight of Tamar in the shiny refection and frowned. Given the gravity of the maid's offense, she ought to have been killed, flogged or sold away at the very least. Instead, she had been confined to her room and waited on as if she were of noble birth. And now it appeared her internment had come to an end. Irritated, Priscilla wondered how the maid had managed to elicit mercy from her brother when she, his sister, a patrician, could not.

"Why art thou here? I did not summon thee," snapped Priscilla, turning about in her chair to face Tamar, her displeasure evident.

"Thy brother hath sent me," answered Tamar timidly, lowering her eyes.

"Dominilla, thy brother desires she serve thee," interjected Priscilla's most efficient slave, Talia, whose advanced years and knowledge of the family had made her not only invaluable, but esteemed in the eyes of those she served. "He hath instructed me to teach her the ways of a Roman household."

"Let her learn elsewhere! I hath no need of her! Inform my brother, he can keep the maid for himself," said Priscilla sharply, hoping the old servant would repeat her reply to Tiberius.

"Is it wise, Dominilla, to further provoke thy brother?" the servant inquired gently, adept at handling Priscilla's difficult disposition.

"Old woman, dost thou dare to question me?" Priscilla retorted indignantly, her large brown eyes flashing with anger.

"I beg thy pardon, Dominilla."

"As well thou should," Priscilla scolded as the dressing attendant fastened the necklace about her neck.

Finding herself a point of contention between Talia and her mistress, Tamar grew uneasy.

"Dominilla, I fear what may befall thee if thou doth persist in trying thy brother's patience. He is the paterfamilias and as such…his word must be obeyed. Why fight against what cannot be changed?"

The death of Priscilla's father had changed everything. The balance of power had shifted from him to her brother and she resented the transference. For her the paterfamilias would always be her father. No other would ever occupy his exalted place in her life, yet she was not so naïve as to think she could do whatever she pleased. Tiberius was now the paterfamilias and whether she liked it or not, he had control over her. Priscilla realized challenging his authority had done nothing to strengthen her position; neither had it won her any latitude. As it was, her liberty had been restricted because she had defied her brother. Dare she oppose him again?

"Train the maid and train her well for I will not be patient with her," said Priscilla, conceding to the old woman's wisdom.

"Dominilla, I shall do as thou hath instructed," said Talia, pleased Priscilla had acted sensibly. Glancing at Tamar, Talia gently nudged her. "Maid, give reply to thy mistress."

Caught off guard, Tamar hesitated. She did not want to acknowledge Priscilla as her mistress for if she did, it would mean that she was a slave, a fact, she still had not accepted. Nor did she want to disappoint the slave woman who had been so kind to her during her incarceration and who now stood anxiously waiting for her to speak. Fearing the consequences of insubordination should she refuse to comply, Tamar swallowed her pride.

"Dominilla…" voiced Tamar meekly, addressing Priscilla by her customary title as she had been taught to do. "I shall endeavor to please thee."

"Nothing about thee pleases me or ever shall," declared Priscilla coldly and then departed from her cubicle, not caring she had frightened Tamar to tears.

Comforting Tamar, Talia took her hand and patted it reassuringly, saying, "Little bird, do not fear thy mistress. She is not unkind."

"I cannot help but fear her as I fear all Romans," cried Tamar. "They are a cruel lot."

"That is not true of all Romans, little bird. Thy mistress is merely unhappy for she hath suffered her brother's wrath and having no recourse…save to obey him…she vents her anger where she can. Fear not. Her anger shall pass and she shall remember it no more. Now come, I hath much to teach thee."

But Priscilla's anger did not pass as Talia had said, but rather increased with each passing day.

VII

Assigned the task of washing Priscilla's long silky hair, Tamar performed her duty as she had been taught, thankful for the simplicity of her work. She had rendered the service several times without incident. However one morning, Priscilla was particularly difficult to please and Tamar struggled to stay on the good side of the young patrician. Mindful of Priscilla's disposition, Tamar carefully ran a comb through her mistress' hair, but when she happened upon a tangle, Priscilla screamed at the top of her lungs and her cry of distress was heard throughout the cubicle. Instantly, frantic maids came rushing to her aid from every direction, ever protective of their mistress. Stricken with fear, Tamar dropped the ivory comb and stepped back as Priscilla sprang from her dressing table.

"Thou hast hurt me intentionally!" shrieked Priscilla, turning on Tamar with a vengeance. "I know thou hast!"

"Not so, Dominilla," replied Tamar, trembling.

"Thou art a wretched slave! I knew it when I first laid eyes upon thee!" exclaimed Priscilla nastily, closing the distance between her and Tamar. "Thou ought to be crucified!"

"Dominilla, I know I am not the handmaid of thy choosing…but I hath done nothing…deserving of…crucifixion!"

"Thou art certainly deserving of crucifixion!" Priscilla said angrily, striking Tamar across the face with all the strength she could muster. "If I say thou art…thou art!"

"Dominilla…hath mercy," pleaded Tamar tearfully, straightening herself up from the fierce blow, her stinging cheek bearing the rosy handprint of her mistress. "I meant thee no harm!"

"Depart from me!" Priscilla commanded, fortified by the presence of her doting maidservants, who though they dared not show it, pitied Tamar far more than their high handed mistress. "I loathe the sight of thee!"

Fleeing from her mistress, Tamar ran from the room into the atrium, moving swiftly past the large marble columns gracing both sides of the bright corridor, the decorative pool and the vibrantly colored murals painted on the walls. Frightened and bewildered by the pagan world in which she found herself, she was assaulted by the strangeness of her environment. Afraid to look upon the painted images of Roman gods, Tamar averted her eyes from the pagan depictions that adorned nearly every inch of the atrium walls and raced past the room of the paterfamilias and the steward's room, both of which were empty of their occupants. With the terrifying idols behind her and no one on her heels, she darted from the main house, seeking asylum in the spacious garden.

Running to the garden fountain which bore the stone likeness of Neptune, the Roman god of the sea, Tamar took refuge behind the bushes encompassing the fount, unaware that another pagan lurked nearby. Sinking to her knees, she wept bitterly, believing she was doomed to die by crucifixion.

To be crucified was the most painful and agonizing death one could suffer. Citizens of Rome could not be put to death in this fashion, no matter how heinous the offense as it was prohibited. Crucifixion was reserved for criminals having no citizenship, rebels against the state, felonious slaves and the most barbarous of offenders. Although Tamar had glimpsed the dark side of man's inhumanity to man, she had not witnessed a crucifixion. She had been spared the hideous, barbaric spectacle of a man being flogged to the point of near death and marched through the streets to the place of crucifixion. Nor had she seen the Roman soldiers drive long, iron nails through the wrists and feet of the condemned. But she had seen the gruesome end result of Roman violence, the crosses. Too upset to think clearly, it had not occurred to Tamar that she had never seen a woman crucified as it was seldom done.

Tiberius had been enjoying the serene beauty of a new morning when Tamar came running into the garden. Catching sight of her hasty entry, Tiberius rose from the unpolished marble bench where he had been sitting, sensing the maid was fleeing from something or someone. Naturally, he assumed that he was that someone. It was a reasonable assumption given the fact she was his prisoner and one that suited his cunning military mind as he was familiar with prisoners and their attempts at escape. However, this prisoner was a woman and by reason of her gender, he had underestimated her, a mistake he would never have made with a male prisoner.

Ordinarily, women did as they were told; lacking the strength to fight against their formidable male counterpart, but this woman had not accepted her inferior status in the male dominated world. She had dared to beat her weak fists against Sejanus' armored chest and call him a murderer, a dangerous accusation, though Tiberius knew it to be true. But even more remarkable than her attack on Sejanus was her refusal of Drusus' attentions and her subsequent escape from him. After failing to outrun his soldiers, she had refused to pay the royal Roman obeisance, thereby jeopardizing her life. At the time, Tiberius had admired her courage and spirit. Had it ended there, he would not have faulted her, but it had not. She had continued to defy male authority, his authority and he did not relish the notion of being outmaneuvered by a woman. She had escaped him once, but he had thought it unlikely she would try a second time having been warned of the stiff consequences. Now, he was not so sure.

Tiberius had gone to a great deal of trouble and expense to acquire Tamar and he was not about to let her escape again. She was his property and he was legally and morally responsible for her. It was his duty to look after her welfare. There was no telling what horrible fate could befall one so innocent and lovely should she try to return to that pigsty she called home. Concerned for her safety and detesting the thought of scouring Subura again, Tiberius went after Tamar.

Strolling across the garden with purpose, Tiberius came upon the fount where she had disappeared from his sight. Hearing the trickling waterfall, his sharp ears detected yet another sound intermingled with the cascading waters. Upon listening closer, he heard the maid sobbing and though it troubled him, he was relieved to discover she was still safely on the premises. Walking the perimeter of the shrubbery surrounding the fountain of Neptune, Tiberius found Tamar kneeling, her face buried in her hands, weeping uncontrollably. Moved with compassion, Tiberius entered her sanctuary.

"Woman, why weepest thou?" he inquired, gazing down on the distraught maid, whom he found beautiful even in the midst of her distress.

Startled, Tamar lifted her face from her hands. Beholding Tiberius standing tall before her, having the sun at his back and his fit frame draped in an ivory colored toga, she fell at his well shod feet, quivering with fear and appealed for clemency. "Domine, I entreat thee, hath mercy upon thy humble servant."

"What troubleth thee, woman?" he asked, stooping down and assisting her to her feet, recalling she was in the same emotional state the first time he laid eyes on her.

"My mistress…I can find no favor in her eyes," cried Tamar, her head bowed, her long, unsecured tresses hiding her tear streaked face from view.

"What hast this to do with thy tears?" queried Tiberius, aware that no one was finding favor with Priscilla as of late. "Tell me, what troubleth thee?"

"My…mistress…she…"

"What about thy mistress?" questioned Tiberius, bracing himself for Priscilla's latest antics.

"She said I should be…crucified!" sobbed Tamar. "Domine, I hath done nothing deserving of death! Save me from thy sister's wrath!"

Beholding Tamar's anguish, he now understood the reason for it. Learning his sister had threatened the maid with such a cruel punishment did not sit well with him. As a centurion, he had been called upon to administer this punishment more times than he cared to remember and knowing the full extent of the suffering it inflicted upon the human body and spirit, he wished it on no one, least of all, the fair maid.

"Look at me, woman," said Tiberius, gently lifting Tamar's head.

"Domine, I beseech thee, save me from thy sister's wrath!" Tamar pleaded, obediently raising her dark eyes to his, tears streaming down her cheeks. "Grant thy servant…mercy!"

Noticing the right side of Tamar's face, Tiberius turned her head slightly to have a better look. "Hast thy mistress laid a hand against thee?" he asked, his expression hardening.

"Yes, my lord…" Tamar answered weakly, lowering her teary eyes.

"For what cause?"

"I was combing her hair…she thinks I intentionally hurt her! Domine, I did not…I did not mean to hurt her! Please believe me!"

"Woman, dry thy tears. Thy minor infraction doth not warrant crucifixion. No harm shall befall thee," assured Tiberius, lightly brushing his hand against Tamar's crimson cheek.

Drawing a ragged breath, Tamar recoiled from his touch, turning her face away from him.

Noticing her discomfort, Tiberius withdrew his hand, inwardly suffering his own discomfort which had nothing to do with Tamar shrinking from his touch for that he understood, but he did not understand his own forward gesture. What had moved him to caress her cheek? Had he done so merely out of pity or had he a weakness for her? Not since Dinah's untimely death had his heart been vulnerable and the possibility that it could be so again unsettled him in the worst way. Shaking off the troubling thought, Tiberius said, "Woman, go thy way. No harm shall come to thee."

Immensely grateful to the Roman for sparing her life, Tamar bowed down humbly and kissed the hem of his toga, finding his woven garment far less intimidating than his military attire.

"Domine, thou art merciful."

Priscilla shall not think so, Tiberius said to himself, determined to inflict upon his sister a most severe scolding.

Walking off, Tiberius left Tamar and headed to the sitting room, where he found Priscilla looking lovely in spite of her ugly behavior. Entering, he dismissed her favorite slave companion with an abrupt gesture of his hand. Reading her brother's grim countenance, Priscilla knew she was about to reap his wrath. Abandoning her loom, she attempted to escape him and tried to exit the door with her maidservant.

"Remain here with me, Priscilla. I hath somewhat to say to thee," said Tiberius sternly, catching his sister by the arm before she could leave. "It hath come to my attention thou hath mistreated thy maidservant, Tamar."

"I do not see why that concerns thee. Thou gave her unto me," said Priscilla rigidly, pulling her arm from his grasp.

"Answer me truthfully, Priscilla. Did thou strike thy servant?"

"And if I did?" she retorted defiantly.

"Woman…did Pater ever lift his hand against thee?" asked Tiberius, his piercing black eyes resting ominously upon his sister.

"No…thou knowest he did not," Priscilla replied haughtily, turning away from her brother, who grabbed her arm and pulled her toward him with such force that she could do nothing to counter it.

"Woman, do not walk away from me when I am speaking to thee! Thou shalt render me the proper respect," he reprimanded harshly, his expression one of severe displeasure.

Priscilla tried to maintain her composure as she stared into Tiberius' countenance, but something inside of her would not be calmed for his eyes flickered and burned with anger, threatening violence at the least sign of provocation. This was a side of him she had never seen and it scared her. Powerless to escape his hold upon her arm which seemed to grow ever stronger, pressing her flesh almost to the point of pain, she braced herself for the storm brewing within him. Like a vessel that had ventured into stormy seas, she waited for the mighty waves to crash over her, knowing instinctively there would be little left to salvage.

"Woman, hath I ever lifted my hand against thee?" he continued, sensing his sister was uneasy. "No, I hath not," he answered for her, his voice unnervingly somber. "I hath not because Pater bade me to follow his example. He believed it possible to gain the respect and obedience of a woman with a firm, but gentle hand. If this be true, why then, do I find thee so disrespectful and so utterly defiant?"

Unable to formulate a response worthy of verbalizing, Priscilla answered with silence.

"Sister, thou hast been dealt with kindly. Why hast thou lifted thy hand against thy humble maidservant?"

"She failed to perform her duty to my satisfaction," replied Priscilla, trying to appear unruffled.

"She failed to perform her duty to thy satisfaction," repeated Tiberius sarcastically, a smirk overtaking his grim expression. "Thou hast failed to perform thy duty as a Roman woman to my satisfaction. Thou hast not rendered unto me thy respect or obedience. Perhaps, I should smite thee."

"Thou art trying to frighten me," Priscilla asserted feebly, her countenance paling.

"I hath never approved of striking women for their disobedience as is the accepted practice, but thou hast caused me to reconsider my position and that of Pater's," he continued darkly, noting with some satisfaction that he had completely unnerved his sister. "It is my right as the paterfamilias to deal with thee as I see fit…such is the law! Priscilla, thou hast tried my patience long enough! Any more of thy foolishness and I will be forced to take stiff measures against thee! Dost thou understand?"

"I…I understand, Tiberius Marcius," said Priscilla, suddenly very afraid of her brother. "I shall not give thee cause against me."

"See that thou dost not! And see that thou dost not smite thy maidservant again or threaten her with crucifixion lest thee suffer as thou hast never suffered," warned Tiberius, reminding Priscilla of his weighty power and having done so, he released her and exited the room, leaving his sister more frightened of him than she had ever been in all of her life.

Not since their father's death had Priscilla regarded any man with respect, nor had she feared any man, including her brother. Now, quite unexpectedly, she saw her sibling for the man he was, a man of military might, wealthy beyond what others imagined and powerful in more ways than she had ever bothered to ponder. No longer was he merely her brother. He was the paterfamilias. The tremendous power that once belonged to their father was now his and he was prepared to use it to the fullest extent of the law. Faced with the sobering realization, Priscilla knew she had been permanently defeated for she would never again be able to stand before her brother, unafraid.

Tiberius was not a man who tolerated disobedience, especially from his soldiers. When he issued a command, he expected it to be followed to the letter. Military men lived and died by the orders issued them and there was no place for a soldier who would not obey orders. But his sister was not one of his soldiers; she was a woman, a frail liability that he must care for until she entered into her husband's house. Taking that unalterable fact into consideration, he had been lenient with her in a way he had never been with any soldier under his command and what had his brotherly indulgence accomplished? Nothing…in his estimation. Priscilla had only grown more impertinent and unmanageable. Roman men did not tolerate such behavior from women any more than commanders tolerated insubordination from their soldiers.

Still, Tiberius did not intend to let his anger get the best of him nor did he intend to strike his sister if he did not have to, though he found it to be to his advantage to let her believe he would. With any luck, the mere threat of physical punishment would bring about the reverence he desired from Priscilla and force her to behave like a proper Roman woman. If it did not, he would have to make good on his threat and do what his father before him had never done. He would have to strike Priscilla for her own good. It was not what he wanted to do, but he could not put what he wanted before family honor, nor would he allow Priscilla to do so. She had to learn to conduct herself in a manner befitting her nobility. If she was ever to be a credit to her family, her ungovernable temperament would have to be dealt with. As paterfamilias, it was his duty to take whatever measures were necessary to preserve the honor and standing of his family, no matter how distasteful the task, including administering physical punishment upon his beloved sister.

VIII

Weary of handling the foolishness of his sister and her new maidservant, Tiberius looked forward to discussing with his clients matters of weightier proportions. A patron of means, Tiberius had many clients, men born free or of freed status who had pledged themselves to him. The oath was morally binding and was not given without due consideration. A client committed himself to his patron's interests and carried out his directives. In return for his loyalty, he would receive financial gifts or some other manner of assistance from his patron, assuring continued fidelity. Like most Roman businessmen, Tiberius received his clients with as much regularity as he could manage between military campaigns. Through their eyes and ears, he kept abreast of political and financial matters. Possessing an ability to discern the course that would yield wealth, Tiberius often made business decisions on the strength of his client's information. His financial ventures required a great deal of his time, but he found it to be an endeavor worthy of his attention and more rewarding than monitoring the frivolous doings of women.

He had wasted too much time dealing with women as of late; in particular, Priscilla and he faulted no one, but himself. Had he squashed her rebellious spirit from the beginning, he would not have had to endure the battle of wills that had been waged over virtually everything, including her future marriage. For years he had been patient with her, overlooking her temper tantrums which had begun shortly after their father's death. With his demise, Priscilla's temperament changed from sweet and submissive to sour and defiant. In spite of the disturbing transformation, Tiberius could not bring himself to discipline his sister. He, like the rest of the household pitied Priscilla. She had taken her father's death especially hard. Lamenting with her, family members and slaves alike tolerated Priscilla's unbearable behavior, believing she would come out of it in time, but four years had passed and she had yet to recover her gentle personality. During most of these trying years, Tiberius had been away on campaigns, fighting the enemies of Rome. He had neither the opportunity nor the inclination to address his sister's conduct, but he could no longer ignore his sister's behavior. He had to correct what his years of neglect had wrought in her lest her difficult personality fail to please Lucius Servilius and ruin the lucrative business relationship Tiberius had forged with him.

Aware his clients would soon be gathering in the atrium, Tiberius sent the steward to collect Priscilla and bring her to him. The routine of questioning his sister each morning before seeing his clients had become tedious and inconvenient. Nevertheless, he was determined to continue the daily inquiry until she consented to marry Lucius Servilius.

Seated at his desk, Tiberius broke the seal of a scroll left for him by his cousin, Cassius and read it as he waited for Priscilla. Expecting to see his sister, he was caught off guard when his mother entered the tablinum, unannounced. On her heels was the steward, whose countenance was one of apology as he stood awkwardly behind the matron of the house. Noting the steward's frustration, Tiberius laid the scroll aside and spoke to him, his tone un-punishing.

"Steward, inform my clients I will see them shortly, but before I do, I will see Priscilla. I want her brought to me upon my mother's departure."

"Yes, Domine," said the steward taking his leave, relieved he had not incurred the master's displeasure.

Shifting his attention to his mother, Tiberius addressed her; curious as to why she had barged into his office.

"To what do I owe this visit, Mater?" he asked, motioning for her to take a seat which she did, settling herself in the client's chair.

"Forgive the intrusion, Tiberius Marcius. I must speak with thee before thou dost speak with thy sister."

"Hath Priscilla sent thee?"

"No…but I hath come on her behalf," Flavia answered, keeping the truth from her son. Priscilla had asked her to speak to Tiberius, a request which Flavia agreed to, but only in part. She had her own reasons for wanting to speak to Tiberius and they were not in full accordance with her daughter's wishes.

"Dost thou disapprove of my handling of her?" Tiberius questioned, interested in his mother's opinion, but having no intention of altering his chosen course.

"It is not my place to make such a judgment," Flavia replied evenly, having long ago accepted the fact the paterfamilias had a right to do as he pleased with the members of his family. "Thou hast done as thou hast seen fit. Thy sister's wayward conduct must be dealt with."

"Indeed, it must. Priscilla hath been in need of a firm hand since father's death. Unfortunately, I failed to see to it. It was a grave error on my part...and one which I fully intend to rectify."

"Fault not thyself, Tiberius Marcius," said his mother warmly, catching a fleeting glimpse of her deceased husband in her son's handsome face.

At times, Flavia found it difficult to believe her husband was dead and her son was no longer a child. Where had the years gone? Tiberius Marcius was now a man in his own right, a man worthy of respect. He had embraced his responsibility to family and country, assuming the role of paterfamilias, protecting the family wealth and reputation, serving Rome militarily with honor and courage. He had fulfilled his duty as a Roman with all the vigor of his father before him.

However, Tiberius had chosen to assert his physical strength through prolonged military service rather than assert political strength in the Senate like his father, a fact which greatly worried Flavia. Sooner or later, she feared her son's physical strength would fail him and he would be lost to her, perhaps dying on some foreign battlefield. Proud though she was of his military career, she prayed he would put aside his sword and follow in his father's footsteps. Then and only then could she rest, knowing he was not caught up in some life threatening conflict. Seated before her son, her dreams for him yet unfulfilled, she was thankful he was now stationed in Rome and relatively safe from harm.

But was Priscilla safe from him? Flavia's most pressing concern had always been for Tiberius' safety, but now she feared for her daughter who was dangerously close to reaping Tiberius' physical wrath. She knew she had to address this most sensitive of subjects, but the words seemed to fail her and she could not help but wonder if too many years of military service had made a brute of her son.

Silence stood between the patricians.

Tiberius knew something was bothering his mother, but she seemed reluctant to reveal it to him. Pushing the conversation forward, he patiently inquired, "What troubles thee?"

"My son, though I hath sought thee out...I hesitate to voice my concern for fear I may overstep myself..." stated Flavia, seeking permission to speak freely.

"Fear not...speak thy mind, Mater," said Tiberius, granting his mother license to speak without fear of reprisal.

"Tiberius Marcius, thou art the head of this house and when thou dost speak, thy word is to be obeyed. Therefore, I do not question thy word...or thy decisions…only the manner in which thou hast chosen to enforce them," she paused timidly.

"Continue…I shall hear thee out," said Tiberius, his face displaying a calm, indulgent expression.

Selecting her words carefully, Flavia put them to her son as gently as she could. "I stand in agreement with thee that Priscilla should marry Lucius Servilius. I know this marriage doth not please her, but it was the will of her father. And I want to see his will done. Yet, I am deeply troubled. Priscilla hath informed me thou hast threatened to do her violence. Dost thou think it prudent to lift thy hand against her? Is there not another way?"

"None that she understands," replied Tiberius flatly.

"Then, my son, I entreat thee…temper thy anger. Thy father would hath wanted it so."

"I assure thee…I hath no intention of harming Priscilla, but I find it useful to let her think what she will. If it takes threatening her with violence to restore her reverence for the position of paterfamilias and bring her under my authority…then so be it! She must learn to respect and obey the will of the paterfamilias. For her sake, I caution thee to maintain the integrity of my threat. She must go on believing I meant what I said. I do not want to lift my hand against her, but if need be, I shall exercise my right to do what must be done."

"Thou art wise, my son. I see that I need not fear. I shall heed thy advice," promised Flavia, rising to her feet, satisfied her son did not intend to use physical force against his sister if he could possibly avoid doing so.

A snap of Tiberius' fingers brought his steward running. "Bring Priscilla in," he commanded as his mother made her way out of his office, her luxurious silk robes flowing behind her, leaving in their wake a soft floral scent.

Passing her mother in the hallway, Priscilla eagerly sought her face and was discreetly met with a negative nod of her mother's head, the prearranged signal indicating she had been unable to persuade Tiberius in her daughter's favor. Disheartened, Priscilla entered the tablinum escorted by two male slaves and standing helplessly between them, she was the picture of humility, despite her privileged birth and rich attire.

Seated behind his desk, Tiberius regarded his sister, wasting no look on her finery, but rather focusing on her comely face. Beholding fear in her eyes, his heart sank. It did not please him she was in mortal fear of him. But what choice had he? She had been nearly impossible to subdue and only the threat of physical punishment seemed to speak volumes to her rebellious spirit. It bothered him he had been forced to treat her so harshly. Still, he was determined Priscilla would not see in him any trace of remorse and he hid his feelings behind an impassive countenance.

"Sister, art thou prepared to marry the man thy father hath chosen for thee?" inquired Tiberius, asking the same question he had asked of her for nearly three weeks.

Instead of giving him the same worn out answer, Priscilla made a request. "Tiberius Marcius, I would that we might speak privately."

"Woman, thou hast been warned about trying my patience," he said sternly, having no intent of granting her anything until she complied with his wishes. "Answer my question. Wilt thou marry Lucius Servilius?"

Priscilla cast her eyes downward and blinked back bitter tears.

"Wilt thou marry Lucius Servilius?" Tiberius repeated, his patience wearing thin.

"I will…" she yielded, her voice quivering with pent up emotion, her lovesick heart throbbing with defeat.

"Alas, Priscilla, thou hast chosen wisely," said Tiberius, concealing his pleasure. Knowing his sister as he did, he did not want her to see him gloating as it would only rub salt in her wounds and what was the sense in that. He had conquered her will and that was satisfaction enough. Rising to his feet, he dismissed Priscilla's slave escorts, granting her the privacy she had requested. "Sit, Priscilla. Thou hast permission to speak."

Priscilla took a seat in the client's chair, trying to compose herself, but it was no use. She could not quiet her pounding heart or still her trembling flesh. She feared her brother and she was certain he knew it.

Advancing to the front of his desk, Tiberius stood near Priscilla's chair, his tall stature towering over her. He knew his close proximity would intimidate his sister and he meant for it to do just that. Out of fear, Priscilla had yielded to his will and out of fear she would obey him. Striking an authoritative stance, he folded his arms in front of him, fastened his eyes on her and awaited her words.

Feeling the intensity of his gaze and the power of his presence, Priscilla took a deep breath and lifted her eyes upward to his, but she found no warmth in her brother's eyes for they were cool and distant, offering her nothing in the way of compassion. Realizing that none would be forthcoming, Priscilla endured his gaze. "Tiberius Marcius, I submit to thy will. I cannot withstand thee any longer. Thou art the paterfamilias and I am at thy mercy," she admitted, nervously twisting her slender hands in her lap. "I shall do thy will and marry Lucius Servilius, though I bear no love in my heart for him. But I ask thee and I do so earnestly…how shall I dwell with a man I do not love?" she questioned, tears slipping from her eyes, betraying her anguished heart.

"Priscilla, I advise thee to treat Lucius Servilius with the utmost reverence," admonished Tiberius. "Thou must never give him any indication that he is not the husband thou desired lest he come to hate thee and treat thee shamefully. Heed my words and it shall be well with thee."

"How shall I bear his touch when I do not love him?"

Tiberius paused for a moment, a ready answer he did not have. It was a question that would have been better answered by a woman, but since Priscilla had posed it to him, Tiberius did his best to supply an answer. "In time, sister, thou shalt come to love Lucius Servilius, welcoming his affection, but until that day, thou shalt bear his touch out of duty to thy husband…and to thy family."

"Duty…always duty," Priscilla mumbled to herself, weary of being reminded of her obligation as a Roman woman. "Can one ever escape duty?"

"No Roman escapes duty. Priscilla, as long as there is life in thy body, thou must fulfill what is expected of thee. Thou must honor and obey thy husband, rendering him thy respect…such is thy duty."

Priscilla could not imagine giving herself to a man she did not love, but she was not the first nor would she be the last woman forced into a marriage alliance deemed suitable by the paterfamilias. Having little say in their fate, women did as they were told, marrying the men chosen for them and Priscilla, like the rest of her gender had to comply. She had hoped to convince her brother to let her choose her own husband, to let her exercise some control over her life, but it was not to be. With her fate already decided, she had to accept what she could not change. She had to accept what no woman could change…the balance of power.

"Art thou prepared to do thy whole duty as a Roman woman?"

"I shall please my husband to the best of my ability," she replied tonelessly, giving the answer she knew Tiberius wanted to hear and the only answer she could give as a woman bound by duty.

Though her response lacked enthusiasm, Tiberius found it acceptable. "Very wise, indeed," he remarked coolly. "And quite timely…thy future husband hath accepted my invitation to dine with us tomorrow evening.

I expect to see thee at dinner, splendidly dressed, radiant with beauty and more importantly…good natured. I will tolerate no less than perfection in thy appearance and in thy attitude."

"Thou shall find me a most pleasant addition to thy table," Priscilla said, her countenance expressionless.

"See that I do," warned Tiberius, a menacing look flashing across his face.

"Tiberius Marcius…if thou hast no further need of me…I would very much like to return to my sitting room," Priscilla ventured meekly, her nerves frazzled.

"Thou art dismissed," Tiberius said stiffly.

Priscilla rose from her chair and left the room, anxious to be alone for she had to reconcile herself to a fate she thought worse than death. Expected to dutifully embrace her marriage to Lucius Servilius, she wondered if she had the fortitude to achieve her brother's lofty expectation.

And Tiberius wondered the same.

IX

Tiberius Marcius escorted his two male guests to the triclinium, the dining room of a Roman house for wine and conversation before dinner, while the women entertained themselves in the sitting room until summoned.

Glowing with soft candlelight, the triclinium was furnished with three stately couches arranged in a horseshoe configuration. Each couch was elongated and had an ornately carved arm at one end and a bolster. Situated inside of the horseshoe, in front of each couch was a long, narrow table which stood slightly lower than the couch. Off to one side of the dining room stood a small assembly of servants, prepared to render their services.

Seating himself at the left end of the middle couch, Tiberius offered Lucius Servilius the place to his right which was the place of honor and to his cousin, Cassius, the couch to his left which he alone would occupy. The couch opposite Cassius would remain vacant as no other male guest had been invited, neither would it be occupied by a female as women of virtue did not recline in the presence of dining men. Seated, Tiberius and his guests were attended by a male servant who removed the men's sandals and washed their feet. Upon completion of this social ritual, the men reclined on their couches, adjusting the bolsters under their left elbows for support and comfort. When the master and his guests were comfortably situated, the wine steward stepped forward, accompanied by the cup bearer, who bore a silver tray containing three large silver goblets. Setting a goblet before each man, the cup bearer then gave way to the steward, who carefully dispensed a crimson wine of fine vintage into each vessel. After performing their duty, the wine steward and the cup bearer retreated to their corner of the room to wait until their services would again be required.

Raising his goblet, Tiberius toasted his guests, wishing them continued health and prosperity, to which they all drank, though none among them lacked for anything. The three men possessed robust constitutions and the financial wherewithal to out buy and sell the wealthiest of their competitors. Shrewd in business, they had told no one of their financial partnership, concealing their collective power till such a day it behooved them to do otherwise. Operating individually, they acted in unison to protect their financial standing and increase their mutual wealth.

To further insure their prosperity and loyalty one to another, Lucius Servilius offered his sister, Turia, not yet of marriageable age to Cassius, who accepted as he was quite fond of Turia and she of him. As for Lucius Servilius, he intended to take Priscilla for his wife in spite of his suspicion that she did not find him to her liking, a matter which grieved him as he found her very desirable. Tiberius was to have married Lucius Servilius' cousin, Dinah, had she not passed away two years earlier. Although Tiberius had no marriage on the horizon, he was nonetheless, the vital link in their alliance. It was he who had masterminded their partnership and it was largely his business aptitude that had made them wealthy beyond imagination. Their respective family fortunes had increased so tremendously, each man was now wealthy in his own right, having no need of his father's wealth. Lucius Servilius and Cassius carried out Tiberius Marcius' financial directives and they did so with utmost confidence, completely trusting him with their lives and their fortunes.

Lucius Servilius was the same age as Tiberius, twenty-nine, though he was not as militarily accomplished, but by no means was he without soldiering qualities. He had not aggressively pursued opportunities to display his military prowess in the war arena for he realized he was not a natural born soldier like Tiberius. And he knew his future was full of promise whether or not he marched off to battle as his father was politically well connected. Tall and of medium build, Lucius Servilius was a likable man whose bone structure was distinctly masculine, every feature sharply defined upon his rugged face. His eyes were brown as was his hair and his nose long, his lips thin. Of privileged birth, he carried himself with great poise, ever mindful of his esteemed ancestry and political future.

Three years younger than his business partners, Cassius was an ambitious man who possessed good looks and intelligence, but it was his physical attractiveness that caught the attention of all who saw him. Tall and graced with an imposing physique, he was dark of hair and eye. His head was crowned with tight black curls, his fine features, regal in appearance. His handsomeness was so arresting those who saw him wondered if he was a god incarnate, a unique physical attribute which he shared with his cousin, Tiberius; and one which they both found annoying as they were not given to vanity or self worship. Like Tiberius, Cassius was well educated for no male of their linage had ever been deprived of tutors or books. Possessing a sharp mind and a gift for rhetoric, Cassius hoped to ascend the political ladder and fulfill his lofty aspirations. With politics perpetually on his mind, Cassius opened the conversation with his favorite topic.

"Tiberius Marcius, most noble cousin," he began soberly, as politics to him was a matter of great importance. "It is said thou would make a fine tribune of the soldiers. Thy military achievements make thee a worthy candidate. Fortune hath smiled upon thee for thou hast both the favor of men and the favor of the divine Tiberius Caesar! Thou wilt not go unnoticed. When the Assembly of People gather to elect this year's tribunes, the people shall remember thy outstanding military record and thy name shall certainly be put forth. Wilt thou seek election?"

"I hath given it no thought, Cassius," replied Tiberius, raising his wine goblet to his lips and drinking deeply.

Unable to stomach the possibility his cousin might actually throw away an important political opportunity, Cassius continued, his tone reprimanding. "Tiberius Marcius, it is time for thee to give politics some serious consideration. Thou art wasting thyself serving in a military position that is beneath thee and if thou dost continue this foolishness, thou wilt soon find thyself without any hope of a political career. Do not squander another day working thy way up through the ranks. This is not the way of a patrician. Every soldier, irrespective of rank, knows thou art a true military man. Thou hast earned the admiration of thy men, thy officers, the Roman people…the Senate…and the divine Caesar! What more dost thou need? Thou art a patrician, Tiberius Marcius, not a plebian! Thou wert born into privilege and power! It would greatly benefit thyself and Rome if thou wouldest remember thy birthright and take thy rightful place!"

"With all due respect, Tiberius Marcius…Cassius hath a point. Thou need not go on proving thyself militarily. Thou hast achieved recognition," stated Lucius Servilius, supporting the position of Cassius. "Why not use it to further a political career?"

"Remember thy birthright," reminded Cassius, visibly frustrated.

"I am well aware of my birthright," said Tiberius dryly. "Nevertheless, I shall consider thy counsel."

"Consider it well," admonished Cassius. "Dangerous men such as Sejanus are advancing politically. Noble men of Rome can ill afford to be politically idle. We must stop Sejanus from obtaining more power. We must not allow this wily Etruscan to rule in the affairs of Rome and overshadow us. We are the true Romans and Rome belongs to us!"

"Truly, Sejanus is a danger to Rome," said Lucius Servilius, picking up where Cassius left off. "And he is no admirer of thee, Tiberius Marcius. As long as he is Prefect of the Praetorian Guard, thou wilt never advance past the rank of centurion. He shall rob thee both of thy career and thy life if thou art not careful! I do not trust him and neither should thee."

"I am well aware of his dislike for me," assured Tiberius, unruffled by the verbal aggressiveness of his two guests.

"That is not the worst of it, Tiberius Marcius," Lucius Servilius continued. "He is not only a threat to thee, but to Caesar's house. It is rumored…Sejanus believes himself destined to rule Rome. He hath his eye on the throne. It is fortunate for Rome, Caesar's heir lives…may the gods preserve him."

"Surely, Sejanus dost not think he can ascend to the throne!" voiced Tiberius in disbelief. "That is utter insanity!"

"Do not underestimate thy enemy, Tiberius Marcius," warned Cassius, studying his cousin's face intently. "He hath not underestimated thee."

"It might sound like utter insanity to thee, but I assure thee, Sejanus hath set his sights upon the throne!" retorted Lucius Servilius, prepared to make his argument. "He commands nine thousand troops…and all are quartered within the city limits. That alone is cause for concern. There are many who regard Sejanus with suspicion and put nothing past him! He exercises his power as Prefect with unparalleled arrogance…selling offices to the highest bidder…bending regulations to suit his purposes. He doth make a mockery of his post. He hath committed countless murders and not a one can be traced back to him for he covers his murderous tracks well. Any man who crosses him winds up mysteriously dead. He is a treacherous viper, who bears watching. Make no mistake; Sejanus will murder anyone who gets in his way…including Drusus. Even as we speak, he hath gained the coveted position of Caesar's friend and advisor. Statues of Sejanus are being erected in the city and Caesar publicly praises him. Drusus seems oddly unaware of Sejanus' dangerous ambition…or of his sordid affair with his wife, Livilla. The Prefect intends to take everything that rightfully belongs to Drusus. He already hath acquired Caesar's ear and Livilla's affection. All he lacks is the throne itself."

"Drusus is aware of Sejanus' warped loyalty," submitted Tiberius. "I hath witnessed a change in him where it doth concern Sejanus. Drusus doth not trust him even in matters of minor importance. He hath of late turned a watchful eye upon the Prefect. I suspect he resents Sejanus' growing influence over his father."

"That may be, but Sejanus is clever and will do what is necessary to maintain the favor of Caesar and his house," stated Lucius Servilius, having tasted of his wine. "He hath even taken to procuring females for Drusus' entertainment…no doubt, to hide his affair from Drusus. There was one particular maid said to be quite beautiful, a Jewess, I believe, who caught Drusus' eye…not too difficult a feat…if one is a woman," remarked Lucius Servilius with a grin. "Drusus sent Sejanus after her, but the maid refused the royal invitation, so Sejanus took her by force from her family, along with another member, a male which he imprisoned with the intent of insuring the maid's cooperation."

"A fascinating story…but what relevance hath it?" asked Cassius, having no interest in what he thought was gossip.

Lucius Servilius turned to Tiberius, looked him in the eye and said, "It hath a great deal of relevance if thou art the man who hast taken the object of Drusus' desire and thwarted the efforts of Sejanus."

Digesting Lucius Servilius' remark, Cassius looked to Tiberius, suddenly very interested.

Tiberius knew his guests expected a response from him, but he felt no obligation to render one and so did not, much to their disappointment. Instead, he nonchalantly picked up his goblet and finished off his wine.

"Bring forth this maid that we might see why thou hast risked thy future and the favor of Caesar's house," requested Cassius.

"Summon her," voiced Lucius Servilius.

"She is a woman like any other. I see no reason to put her on display," said Tiberius evenly, motioning to his wine steward, who immediately came forward and refilled the men's goblets.

"Tiberius Marcius, thou hast not even so much as noticed a woman since Dinah…and thou saith she is like any other," declared Cassius, wanting very much to see the female who had captured his cousin's attention. "If thou hast dared to take her from Drusus, risking his royal wrath…as well as Sejanus' wrath…truly, she must be worth having. Bring forth the maid that we might judge her worthiness."

"It is time the women join us for dinner," stated Tiberius, ignoring Cassius' request. Looking to a servant, he directed, "Inform the women, we await their arrival."

"How unfortunate we are, Cassius. Our esteemed host refuses to allow us even a glimpse of the maid," remarked Lucius Servilius, smiling broadly. "What a pity. I should liked to hath seen this vision of loveliness."

"Take heart, my friend. One appointed day, fortune shall smile upon us and we shall see this maid whose beauty is such that it cast a spell over otherwise sane men," said Cassius, winking at Lucius Servilius.

Having had their fun at Tiberius' expense, the two men made no more mention of the maid.

Upon the women's entrance, the servants set up chairs for them on the opposite side of the table, facing the men. Priscilla was seated across from Lucius Servilius; Turia was seated across from Cassius and Flavia across from her son.

Instructed by Tiberius on how she was to dress and behave, Priscilla conducted herself accordingly, mindful her brother would be watching her every move. Upon taking her seat, she smiled demurely at her intended which pleased Lucius Servilius immensely.

Turia smiled at her intended too, but not because her brother expected it of her. She smiled because she could not help herself for so in love was she with Cassius, who received her smile as he would a gift, with pleasure.

The instant Flavia laid eyes on her son; she knew something of importance had transpired between the men prior to her arrival. Tiberius appeared to her to be disturbed, whereas the other two men were enjoying themselves. The guests did not seem to notice anything unusual about their host's demeanor, but Flavia did not expect them to. No one knew her son as well as she nor could they see like she could behind the mask of his rigidly held countenance. She was the only one who knew that something was bothering him and she wondered what that something was.

The presence of women at the table lightened the conversation considerably as the men did not discuss subjects that might upset or bore their female companions. They spoke no more of politics, but instead, participated in what they felt to be frivolous conversation. There was talk of the circus and its wonders, upcoming chariot races, fierce gladiators and juicy tidbits of scandalous gossip. While conversing, they dined on roasted hens, freshly baked bread, a salad of assorted lettuces seasoned with a flavorful oil and vinegar dressing, a medley of steamed cauliflower and broccoli florets, large green olives imported from Spain, a variety of cheese and at meal's end, an enticing selection of sweet fruits and honey filled pastries.

All in all, dinner was a pleasant affair consisting of savory dishes and lively conversation.

During the meal, Tiberius said very little. His mind was preoccupied with the words of his guests. Cassius and Lucius Servilius had made a point of warning him about Sejanus and to ignore their counsel would be foolish. Hearing the Prefect had the favor of Caesar troubled Tiberius. Equally troubling was Sejanus' affair with Drusus' wife. Tiberius had always known his enemy to be ambitious, but never had he suspected Sejanus of reaching for the throne. Did Drusus suspect the Prefect's real motive or was he simply jealous of Sejanus' elevated status in the eyes of Caesar? And what of Caesar, was he completely blind to Sejanus' thirst for power? How long would Sejanus' ambitions go unnoticed? How many lives would be destroyed before he received his due? Armed with Caesar's favor and a position of power, the Prefect's victims were defenseless against him. So it was with Tamar, caught in the midst of political intrigue, an unwilling participant in the Prefect's cleverly devised plan of destruction. She had been offered to Drusus like a mouse to a hungry cat. How many other women had the Prefect procured for Drusus to gain his favor and dull his royal senses? How many good Roman men had perished at Sejanus' hands? Someone had to put a stop to his treachery. Dare he be the one? To do so would be suicide, but he could not stand by and do nothing. Too much was at stake. He had to find a way to warn Drusus.

Coming out of his contemplative state, Tiberius suddenly realized he had not watched Priscilla as closely as he had intended. Turning a keen eye in her direction, he observed her. As usual, she looked beautiful and even more so when she smiled at her intended, which he noticed she did quite often. It pleased him to see she was treating Lucius Servilius with what appeared to be genuine interest. Had he not known otherwise he would have sworn she liked Lucius Servilius for her performance was flawless.

Feeling her brother's gaze upon her, Priscilla met his eyes, hoping to find something in his expression that would convey his approval, but she found nothing in his somber countenance as he did not feel it necessary to reward her for behaving as she ought. As his stoic expression seared her heart, Priscilla found herself struggling to maintain her composure. Lowering her eyes, she hid her disappointment beneath her long dark lashes. Why did it matter to her whether or not she pleased him? Why was she seeking his approval? Having no answer to her questions, Priscilla regarded the man across the table from her, considering his person. Her fate could have been worse; her brother could have forced her to marry an older, unattractive man. At least Lucius Servilius was young, pleasing to look upon, well born, intelligent and wealthy. In addition, he seemed to genuinely care about her which was more than she could say about her brother.

Sensing in her a need, Lucius Servilius reached across the table and gently squeezed Priscilla's hand. He did not know the reason behind her melancholy eyes, but he was certain if she gave him half a chance, he could banish it forever.

Touched by his tenderness, Priscilla smiled at him, wondering how she could have dismissed his affections so easily. And Lucius Servilius returned her smile, encouraged by her warm response.

X

Dawn was breaking as Tiberius awoke from a sound sleep, his internal clock proving reliable. Sweeping aside the fine mosquito netting which hung about his bed of bronze, Tiberius looked across the dimly lit room, his eyes drawn to the sword which hung at the entrance of his dressing cubicle, complete with scabbard and baldric. It was time once again to take up his weapon, to meet the life and death challenges that lay ahead. He had readied it for this day, honing and polishing his sword until it shined brightly with fierce anticipation. The warrior within him yearned to feel the weight of the blade in his hand and hear the sound of it clashing against enemy weaponry. He had fought and won many battles with his trusted sword, bloodying it more times than he could remember. He had never tasted the bitterness of defeat. It was as if Mars, the revered god of war had himself consecrated it, granting victory after victory to its bearer. And in truth, it was no ordinary weapon. It was beautifully crafted, its blade of the purest steel, its handle of gold crowned by an eagle's head of exquisite detail. Bearing the standard of Rome upon its golden hilt, the striking sword had been presented to Tiberius by his father upon his entrance into manhood. It was a gift unlike any other and Tiberius treasured it above all he owned. To him, the magnificent sword represented more than just a weapon of defense. It symbolized the bond of father and son, the rite of passage into manhood, the brevity of life and the certainty of death.

Finding his sleeping cubicle uncomfortably warm, Tiberius left his bed and strolled into the front room, past his desk to the window at the far end of his study. Mindful of his naked state, he opened the shutters just enough to let in some fresh air from the garden and still maintain his privacy. Bringing relief to the tepid surroundings, a heady fragrance and a gentle breeze filled the room, awakening his senses and cooling his nude body. Somewhere off in the distance, he heard a bird chirping and it seemed to him, the feathered creature was as eager as he to begin the new day. Peering through the parted shutters, Tiberius saw the early morning sky still held the full moon of the night before. It would not be much longer till the sun chased away the radiant orb, replacing its resplendent glow with blazing illumination. Rome was unbearably hot during the summer and he preferred to rise at dawn and accomplish what he could before the stifling heat set in.

Leaving the window, Tiberius returned to his sleeping cubicle and clothed himself in a short linen tunic before attending to his personal hygiene. Roman morality dictated that slaves could not be called upon to assist their masters in extremely personal activities which suited Tiberius just fine. In the practice of caring for himself, Tiberius walked over to the table beside his couch on which sat a jug of water and an empty bowl. Pouring some water into the bowl, he washed his face and smoothed back his wavy hair. Taking the fresh towel provided by a slave the night before, he dried off the excess water remaining on his skin. Deeming himself presentable, Tiberius summoned his personal body servant Anatole with a loud clap of his hands and his servant whose ears were inclined to his master's call appeared without delay.

As the routine was the same each morning Anatole knew his master was ready for his daily shave. So he brought with him a sharp blade, an aloe balm and a steady hand with which to perform the task. After carefully shaving his master's face, leaving no cuts behind to mar his fine appearance, the servant ran a comb of ivory through Tiberius Marcius' thick black hair. Noticing some unruly strands of hair behind Tiberius' ears, Anatole snipped them with a pair of scissors. Satisfied with his work, the servant handed his master a mirror which Tiberius glanced into and then quickly laid aside for he was not one to gaze long at himself. His grooming completed, Tiberius entered his dressing cubicle, his servant following on his heels. There, he donned his military attire with the help of Anatole, who after outfitting his master in army regulation began collecting the centurion's gear.

The competent servant placed a bronze food box, a mess tin, a kettle, some rope, a pickaxe, a chain, a saw and a hook inside of his master's tool bag. He then laid the packed bag next to a tightly woven wicker basket used to move earth. His master would have need of these implements if he and his soldiers went on campaign for not only were they required to defend Rome and her interests, but they were sometimes called upon to build roads and bridges along the countryside.

"Take my gear to the atrium," ordered Tiberius, feeling physically and mentally prepared to return to military duty. "And see that my horse is readied."

"Yes, Domine," said his body servant, who was eager to accompany Tiberius on another military expedition. Anatole was proud to serve a soldier of distinction, to travel with him wherever duty called. He never wearied of pitching camp under the wide open sky, exploring new lands and fighting barbarians. The latter of which did not fall to him as often as he would have liked for he was merely a servant, untrained in the ways of war and considered to be of little use in combat. Even so, Anatole thrived in the military. At his master's side, he had seen much of the world, most of which had been conquered by the mighty army of Rome. Although he was not Roman by birth, he took pleasure in their conquests and adhered to their customs, rejecting the culture of his own Greek ancestry, much to the chagrin of his mother, Talia. Born in his master's house, Anatole was a young man of short, stocky proportions who despite his small stature, lowly status and ethnic background fancied himself a Roman soldier, living and breathing the military with the same zeal as the patrician he served.

Entering the triclinium in full armor, except for his helmet, Tiberius did not recline at the table as he had the night before. His uniform made doing so rather awkward due to his sword and the fitted leather cuirass which covered his chest and back from neck to waist. Making use of an upright chair, he sat down to a breakfast of boiled eggs, freshly baked bread, honeyed fruits and water. Not knowing when he would return again to enjoy the palatable meals prepared by his cook, Tiberius took time to savor his meal. Though camp was only a few miles from the Palatine where he lived, he would not avail himself of the comforts of home, electing instead to do without them as his soldiers did. Others of his caliber and class often indulged themselves with frequent visits to their residences while in the service of Rome, but Tiberius felt it best to resist the temptation. Maintaining the respect of those he commanded was more important to him than his personal comfort.

Tiberius had just finished his breakfast when Priscilla and Flavia entered the dining room and looking upon them, he found their beauty and gracefulness pleasing to behold. They were arrayed in long robes of shimmering silk that covered their shapely forms in a most attractive, yet modest fashion. Brilliant jewels adorned their necks, arms and fingers. Their delicate facial lineaments were framed by their brown tresses which were stylishly parted in the center, waved and puffed out, circling the head and bound with ribbon. Taking them in with an appreciative eye, Tiberius considered his mother and sister, who were remarkably similar in appearance, despite the difference in age. The passage of time had in no way detracted from his mother's good looks. Both women were equally beautiful, a credit to his noble house. Tiberius knew it would be some time before he would again see such unadulterated loveliness. His mother and sister were untainted by the ugliness of poverty and war, but soon he would encounter women who were not so fortunate, whose beauty had long since vanished, if ever it had existed.

The women he would come across while serving in the military would be those who offered themselves for a price or those unfortunate creatures captured and distributed among the officers and soldiers as part of the spoils of battle. In either case, Tiberius did not take advantage of the women for he did not care to consort with prostitutes or ravish defenseless maids, barbarian or not. He chose to forego the fleshly pleasure of a woman and did so amid ridicule from his fellow officers, who seemed to think him less than a man because he would not join them in their wanton reverie. For Tiberius, to be a man was to bear responsibility, to live by discipline and impart discipline when necessary. Manhood was honor, integrity and self-control. It was not overcoming the lesser sex for one's own pleasure. Such coarse behavior was unworthy of a man for a woman could not properly defend herself against so strong an adversary. Women had not the strength or wit to do so, rendering the conquest of little merit in his estimation. Adhering to his father's instruction that violence against women was contemptible and beneath a man, Tiberius bore the ridicule of his peers and while they lay drunk with wine and women, he saved his strength for combat.

Seeing her son in military dress, Flavia's heart sank within her. She had hoped he would remain home for awhile longer, but as always, there was some pressing military conflict that demanded his attention. What was it this time? Had a pompous king in a far away country refused to pay tribute to Rome? Had he and his kingdom dared to throw off the mantle of Rome's awesome power? Or was Rome itself seeking out some unconquered territory to devour, ever hungry for new riches, new peoples to rule and to enslave. Whatever the reason for his departure, it was cause for concern. Flavia dreaded the thought of her son marching off to battle and even more so, the thought he might never return. Invoking the goddess Fortuna, she prayed Tiberius would remain safely within the city gates and guard Caesar as he had been appointed to do. Flavia knew serving in the Praetorian Guard was not without danger, but she did not think it nearly as dangerous as being on a foreign battlefield with barbarians.

In spite of their strained relations, Priscilla was no more pleased to see Tiberius in uniform than her mother was. Like Flavia, she worried she would never see him again, that some violent fate would befall him while he was away. And that worry, coupled with the possibility she might never enjoy a moment in his good graces, moved her to breathe a prayer to the household gods for his safe return.

"Must thou leave so soon?" Flavia inquired, taking a seat at the table beside her daughter.

"I must," Tiberius replied, rising to his feet, cognizant of the sadness in his mother's voice. "Cassius shall care for thee and Priscilla in my absence. He shall see to thy need as he hath in times past."

"My son, it is not our need that concerns me," said Flavia earnestly, looking up at the centurion who stood before her dressed in the splendor of Rome.

"Be not troubled, Mater. I shall return to thee as soon as I am able," Tiberius assured, meeting his mother's loving gaze.

"Where goest thou?" Priscilla questioned anxiously, oblivious to the servants who busied themselves with setting breakfast before her and her mother. "When shall thou return?"

Fixing his black eyes upon his sister, Tiberius searched Priscilla's face trying to discern whether her inquiry was free of motive. Not convinced it was, he put forth a stern warning. "Priscilla, I know not where I shall go or when I shall return, but I caution thee against disobeying me. If thou dost see my absence as an opportunity to challenge my authority, think again. I hath informed Cassius of my wishes concerning thee and instructed him to use whatever measures are necessary to achieve thy cooperation. Dost thou understand?"

"I understand, Tiberius Marcius," answered Priscilla meekly, her eyes falling from his, unable to bear his piercing gaze.

"Tiberius Marcius, thy sister intends to do thy will and marry Lucius Servilius," stated Flavia, coming to the defense of her daughter. "Do I not speak the truth, Priscilla?" queried Flavia, turning to look at the young woman who bore her likeness.

Deriving courage from her mother's verbal intervention, Priscilla regarded her brother, who stood staring at her, his face rigid and without expression. Addressing him, she spoke in a tone cool, but tranquil. "I shall do thy will whether or not thou art present, Tiberius Marcius."

"Then I shall be pleased with thee, Priscilla," remarked Tiberius and having spoken, he exited the room, not realizing he had given his sister what she needed most from him, a kind word.

XI

Tiberius led the way as he and Anatole steered their horses down the cobbled streets of Rome toward Viminal Gate, where the Praetorian Guard were stationed. The elite branch of soldiers, whose duty it was to protect the Emperor were concentrated within a single barracks just a few miles from the capital. Their close proximity to the palace seemed harmless to most citizens, even prudent, but those who knew the astute Prefect of the Praetorian Guard thought differently. Among them was Tiberius, who was convinced Sejanus had an underlying motive in quartering troops within the city.

Traveling toward his destination, Tiberius recalled the conversation he had with Cassius and Lucius Servilius the night before. Valuing their counsel, he turned their words over carefully in his mind, giving special consideration to those concerning Sejanus. Cassius had stressed the danger of allowing Sejanus to continue on his path of power and Lucius Servilius had presented valid reasons to heed his warning. Both men were remarkably adept at separating the truth from hearsay. If they were of the opinion the Prefect was seeking the throne, then he probably was. Tiberius had long suspected Sejanus of employing underhanded methods to achieve his political objectives, but he had not surmised the ultimate objective was the royal seat of power. No wonder Sejanus had positioned soldiers so near the palace. If he was to successfully further his quest for power, it was absolutely crucial he ingratiate himself with the emperor and his heir. And what better way was there than to be strategically placed, highly visible and readily available.

Undeniably, Sejanus was a dangerous man. He posed a threat to Caesar's house and to the stability of Rome. The empire could not endure under the leadership and rule of a treacherous, self-serving cutthroat like Sejanus. Someone had to put an end to the Prefect's abominable aspirations. The most expedient way, short of murder, was to achieve a position of power equal to or higher than his. Perhaps, Cassius and Lucius Servilius were right in urging I stand for tribune in the next election, thought Tiberius, seriously considering their suggestion.

Not a word passed between master and servant during the short journey and none was forthcoming for Anatole knew his master preferred to ride in silence, contemplating whatever men of his status contemplated. But this day was unlike previous days for Anatole marked a difference in his master's demeanor which concerned him. Tiberius Marcius was so occupied with his own cogitations that he appeared to be oblivious to his surroundings. Though Anatole was used to seeing his master deep in thought for he was a serious minded man, he could not recall ever having seen him in such a pensive state outside of his private domain. It was not like the centurion to ride through the streets of Rome paying no heed to the hazards that might be lurking along the way. Whatever was weighing on the master's mind had to be of great importance for him to throw caution to the wind.

Anatole knew for certain it was not Priscilla's upcoming marriage to Lucius Servilius that troubled Tiberius Marcius for he had broken his sister's will and forcibly bent it to his own. This he had heard from Priscilla's maids who daily imparted gossip to those willing to listen. And listen he did to them and the kitchen slaves, the latter of which had reported Priscilla had vowed to obey her brother's wishes. So Priscilla was not the problem. What then? What was weighing so heavily upon him? Anatole had rarely been privy to his master's thoughts for Tiberius Marcius kept his feelings and matters of an intimate nature locked within him. What Anatole knew of his master's personal life, he had learned from those slaves who took it upon themselves to eavesdrop, but even they had precious little information to offer. This time it was quite apparent they had overlooked something the master had said as being of no significance. If they were going to eavesdrop on the master's private conversations, the least they could do was recognize what had value and what did not, thought Anatole, frustrated by their inability to discern what was worthy of reporting.

Reaching camp, Tiberius and Anatole abandoned their headwork and turned their attention to their respective duties. Dismounting his steed, Tiberius handed the reins to Anatole, who dutifully led the horses away to the military stable to care for them. Standing ram rod straight, his soldierly mien coming to him naturally, Tiberius Marcius entered the headquarters to report to Sejanus, his commander.

As Tiberius respectfully presented himself to his commanding officer, the Prefect scrutinized him with a keen eye, hoping to find something amiss in the centurion's appearance that warranted disciplinary action. But as usual, Tiberius Marcius was the epitome of military perfection from helmet to boot and he could find nothing for which to upbraid him. Irked, Sejanus curtly dismissed the two officers who had been briefing him on the state of security inside the palace. Obeying his directive, they gathered up their palace diagrams and departed, silently acknowledging the most respected centurion in their cohort. Left alone with Tiberius, Sejanus' eye lingered a moment on the centurion's magnificent sword, coveting it.

Tiberius had grown accustomed to the critical examination of his person and endured it patiently, concealing his contempt for his commander behind a rigidly held countenance.

Sejanus had not seen Tiberius Marcius since the day he had snatched the pretty Jewess from his grasp, robbing him of his pleasure and the credit of her return. Adding insult to injury, he, the Prefect of the Praetorian Guard had been forced to take orders from the centurion, an officer of lower rank. The very remembrance of that humiliating incident could bring Sejanus to the brink of rage, a rage which he now held in check as he faced his archenemy. Though he knew Tiberius Marcius had acted on orders from Drusus and not of his own account, the knowledge did nothing to assuage the Prefect's injured pride. He was determined to avenge himself at the centurion's expense for not only had Tiberius Marcius been insubordinate to his commanding officer, he had foiled a well crafted plan.

Sejanus would not tolerate being upstaged by any man. Rightfully, he should have been the one to deliver the maid to Drusus, to present her to him and receive his due. Instead, he received a tongue-lashing from Drusus, who blamed him for the loss of the maid to Tiberius Marcius. Blame which he inwardly refused to accept, though outwardly, he pretended to cower to Drusus' ravings so as not to further agitate him. How in name of Jupiter was he to know Tiberius would ask for the maid and Caesar himself would grant him his request. If Drusus had not sent Tiberius to find the maid and bring her back, the centurion would never have had the opportunity to ask for her. Had the royal donkey left well enough alone, he would be happily entertaining himself with his latest plaything, instead of mourning its loss.

Although his plan to deliver the maid to Drusus had been thwarted, Sejanus had gained useful insight into Caesar's son. He now knew that despite his efforts to satisfy Drusus' voracious appetite for pleasure, the royal ingrate distrusted him. Why else would he have issued Tiberius Marcius the same orders? Galled as he was by the revelation, Sejanus was no less confident in his ability to master Drusus and gain his trust. All that was required to subjugate the lecherous heir was to implement an insidious plan of destruction. He would destroy Caesar's son with lust. He would present Drusus with maiden after maiden, each fairer than the one before, each able to arouse in him a burning desire. Basking in fleshly pleasure, the noble rake would eventually become enslaved to his passions, living from one conquest to the next and fit for nothing. The day of Drusus' destruction was nearing. The gods had ordained it. Soon Drusus' throne and his lovely wife, Livilla would be his for the taking. But first, he must deal with Tiberius Marcius. The haughty centurion would come to rue the day he interfered in the affairs of his commander.

"I hath been anticipating thy return, centurion," Sejanus said gruffly, his dark menacing orbs fastened on his formidable foe. "I hath an assignment for thee…one for which thou art well suited."

"I shall endeavor to be worthy of it, Prefect."

Sejanus smiled malevolently and continued, "Thou art to meet with an informer…a man called Barnabas. Thou wilt find him at the temple of Venus Libitina late tomorrow afternoon. He hath chosen this particular temple as he must register a death in his family, a most unfortunate occurrence, but ever so timely. I applaud his cleverness. His selection of a meeting place is as novel as it is functional."

"How shall I know this man?"

"No need to concern thyself with his appearance. He hath knowledge of thee and shall seek thee out. Await his arrival among the cypress grove at five o'clock tomorrow and he shall find thee. He hath in his possession a list of assassins who are plotting the demise of several highly esteemed senators. A quid pro quo hath been arranged. The informer shall be given this bag of gold," stated the Prefect, drawing from his person a small pouch and handing it to the centurion, "In return, he shall give thee the list. Once thou hast the list in thy possession, deliver it to me directly…without delay. Understood, centurion?"

"Understood, Prefect."

"Centurion, be it also understood that no one is to accompany thee on this assignment or know thy destination," added the Prefect. "Thy departure from camp must be inconspicuous. Roman lives depend on it. Hath I made myself clear?"

"Yes, Prefect."

"Thou art dismissed, centurion."

Tiberius left feeling as though he had just been handed a death sentence. He suspected he was being lured into a trap, but there was not much he could do about it. He had no proof. He had only his instincts. It was his duty to obey his commanding officer and duty dictated. He would not run the risk of compromising his military career. He would do as he was commanded and should his instincts prove true, he would have to fight to escape Venus Libitina, the goddess who presided over the extinction of the life force. He did not want to be ushered into her realm any sooner than was necessary.

Dismissing the grim notion, Tiberius spent the remainder of the day and the better part of the next conducting inspections, posting guards about the camp and overseeing an inventory of arms and equipment. Enlisting the assistance of two clerks, he made certain all stock was accounted for and in working order. It also fell to him to verbally discipline his soldiers and when necessary order corporal punishment. But most of his day was devoted to the daily training of the rank and file, a task which Tiberius found personally gratifying.

He had just finished demonstrating how to properly wield a sword to a group of young cadets when it came time for him to set out for the temple of Venus Libitina. Tiberius was no more at ease with his assignment than he had been the day before. Nevertheless, he was determined to see it through, proceeding with the utmost caution. Turning the cadets over to the supervision of another officer for the completion of their training exercises, Tiberius made his departure, rousing the notice of no one or so he thought.

Occupying the position of authority in the house of Tiberius Marcius, Cassius dutifully saw to the business of his cousin, meeting with his clients and imparting to them the customary favors. He recorded the transactions that took place so when Tiberius returned, he would have knowledge of what had been promised to each client and why.

On the second morning of Tiberius' absence, Lucius Servilius joined Cassius in the tablinum, offering his assistance with the clients which had gathered in the atrium to await their summons.

"Before we begin seeing clients, I am compelled to ask thee one question," said Lucius Servilius, standing across from Cassius, who had already comfortably settled himself in the chair behind Tiberius' desk.

"What is the question?" Cassius inquired, regarding Lucius Servilius with interest.

"What manner of woman stands outside this domain?"

"I am not aware of any such woman," replied Cassius.

"She seems to be waiting for someone, but she troubled none of us. Perhaps, she is waiting for Tiberius Marcius. Dost thou suppose he hath a female client that he failed to mention," said Lucius Servilius, breaking into a mischievous grin.

"Lucius Servilius, that is unheard of! Frankly, I doubt Tiberius Marcius would sanction such a ludicrous idea! The very thought of women as clients…ugh! Let us not speak of it! I cannot bear the thought," said Cassius, finding the idea wholly objectionable.

"Art thou not interested in who this woman is? Dost thou not wish to know why she stands outside of Tiberius Marcius' residence? I for one…am most intrigued."

"I see we shall accomplish nothing till I satisfy thy curiosity," Cassius remarked testily, summoning the steward for questioning, who dutifully appeared before the two patricians.

"Tell me, steward, hast thou noticed a woman standing outside of this residence?" asked Cassius, leaning forward in his chair, his gaze fixed upon the servant, his folded hands resting on the desk.

"Yes, Domine, the door attendant brought her to my attention," the steward answered, ill at ease with Cassius as he was short tempered with servants.

"Well…speak up!" Cassius snapped impatiently. "What dost thou know of her?"

"I know this is the second day she hath appeared on the premises. More than this I know not," said the steward, bracing himself for a reprimand, certain one was coming.

"Steward, I shall judge what thou knowest," Cassius said coolly, intending to ply the steward with more questions.

"Yes, Domine."

"Hath she spoken to any man?"

"No, Domine. She hath kept to herself, speaking to no one," answered the steward, growing increasingly nervous.

"Hath she badgered the clients?"

"No, Domine."

"Hath she made a spectacle of herself or acted in some ill manner?"

"No, Domine."

"Steward, why hast thou not informed me of her presence on the property?"

"Domine, I did not want to trouble thee on account of her. The woman is low born. I presumed her to be of little importance."

"Nevertheless, I ought to be informed of who is on the premises. I am responsible for the affairs of Tiberius Marcius while he is gone. I rule this house in thy master's absence. I determine what I shall do and whom I shall see…not thee or any other," lectured Cassius sternly. "Steward, I counsel thee to respect my authority and remember thy place."

"I beg thy pardon. I hath erred in my judgment, Domine," said the steward meekly.

"In the future, steward, I shall be informed of such matters. Is that understood?"

"Yes, Domine."

"Steward, I shall see this woman…after the clients hath been dispersed."

"Shall I escort her into the atrium, Domine?"

"No, let her remain outside. I shall see her in due time."

"Yes, Domine."

"That is all, steward."

"Yes, Domine," said the steward, who departed, relieved he had not met with a harsher admonishment.

"Cassius, my friend, it is apparent thou art in no hurry to unravel the mystery of this woman," stated Lucius Servilius, feeling disappointed. Then a thought struck him and he brightened. "Tell me, hast thou seen the maid Tiberius Marcius took from Drusus?"

"Lucius Servilius, we hath already wasted enough time on the subject of one woman. Must we squander more time on another? We hath clients waiting…men of substance…men who rule the civilized world. What need hath we to discuss women? What rule they of importance? I advise thee to marry Priscilla as soon as possible and discuss the miserable subject with her," he said scornfully. "I for one do not care to spend any more time discussing females."

"Make sport of me if it pleases thee, Cassius, but thou wert just as interested in seeing the maid as was I. Dost thou deny it?"

"I deny it not!" retorted Cassius irritated. "Art thou satisfied?"

"Satisfied? How so? Thou hast not yet answered my question. Hast thou seen her?"

"I hath not nor hath I made any attempt to do so. When I encounter her, it shall be soon enough. There! I hath answered thy question! Now…art thou satisfied?"

"I am," replied Lucius Servilius, grinning ear to ear as he enjoyed their verbal sparing even if Cassius did not.

As there were many clients to see, Cassius and Lucius Servilius spent the next several hours hearing what each man had to say. Some brought useful information, others had performed a service, still others presented themselves as new clients and all expected something in return from their wealthy patrons. When the last client left, the two men calculated the cost of the information and services received, weighing them against the day's profit which was invariably in their favor. They had not only profited financially, but they had received a number of interesting reports concerning their political adversaries that would undoubtedly be advantageous in the days to come.

Having recorded a wealth of information, Cassius rolled up a scroll and placed his personal seal upon it, employing his gold ring and a bit of hot wax to insure none other than Tiberius would read what had been written within. Laying the scroll aside, he turned his attention to Lucius Servilius who was sitting on the couch across the room, reflecting on what he had heard. Cassius knew the same disturbing revelation that occupied his own mind, occupied that of his colleague.

The morning had ended with a strange old man, unknown to Cassius and Lucius Servilius, presenting himself as one of Tiberius' clients. Not knowing whether or not the peculiar looking man was truly a client, they chose to hear him, finding him a rather fascinating character to behold.

Dressed in coarse raiment and leaning upon a staff, the stranger was clearly a shepherd for the smell of sheep clung to him. Past his physical prime, his frame was frail and withered, his hair and beard were the color of the wool he harvested and deep lines etched his time weathered face. Though his years were many and his strength appeared to be failing him, the vitality of youth still shone in his brilliant blue eyes, emitting an energy which illuminated his aged countenance. Despite his earthy appearance, it was apparent he was a man of learning for he spoke flawless Latin which amazed Cassius and Lucius Servilius for they were certain he was no

Roman. When he began to utter knowledge about them, known but to them alone, they realized he was no ordinary shepherd. Unnerved by his uncanny ability to see into their lives, both public and private, they maintained their guard and listened, acknowledging nothing the old man said as being the truth. As he went on spouting his mystical knowledge with all the zeal of bona fide seer, a feeling of awe overtook them. Unaffected by the patrician's silence, the shepherd's blue eyes danced as he uttered revelations shown him by the divine ones. As hoped for and expected, the future held prosperity, happiness and political accolades for both Cassius and Lucius Servilius, but when the seer began to speak of Tiberius Marcius, his wrinkled face darkened and his words grew foreboding.

"I hath come to warn the one called Tiberius Marcius Maximus…it is for his sake that I hath traveled the long journey here. The gods hath chosen him for their purpose. I speak of things to come. Tiberius Marcius is in grave danger. His enemy plots his death even now and will not rest till the murderous deed is done."

"What can be done to prevent this evil from happening," asked Cassius, rising from his chair, alarmed and sickened by the prediction.

"Tell us, sage," insisted Lucius Servilius, equally disturbed.

"Alas, nothing can be done. It is written in the stars. It is the will of the gods. Tiberius Marcius will taste of death this very day."

"Death!" stormed Cassius, flying around the desk and grabbing the seer out of the client's chair, forcing the frail man to his feet. "Old man, why hast thou informed us of Tiberius' impending death…if we can do nothing to prevent it? What manner of warning is this? It cannot be heeded!"

"Take hold of thyself, Cassius. He is but the bearer of bad tidings. He is not the murderer," reasoned Lucius Servilius as calmly as was physically possible given the grim enormity of the seer's revelation.

"Answer me, old man! Why hast thou informed us?" Cassius demanded; his anger unabated.

"I perceive that thou lovest him greatly," replied the seer, unruffled by the fury that held him captive. "Tiberius Marcius hath not only the favor of men…he hath the favor of the gods. It is because he is so favored that he shall taste of death…so that he may drink of the god's nectar…"

"Thou art making no sense, old man! Speak plainly!"

"Love…love is the god's nectar," declared Lucius Servilius, deciphering the mystic's meaning.

"Tiberius Marcius shall taste of death…but he shall not die. He shall walk among the dead, but in due time, he shall return to the land of the living by the divine hand of the goddess Venus."

Cassius released the old man feeling somewhat comforted, but not altogether sure he believed or understood the seer's strange babblings.

Free of Cassius, the old man smoothed out his crumpled garment, took up his shepherd's staff and started for the door, but was momentarily detained by Lucius Servilius who offered him a denarius, a day's wages for a laborer. The seer refused the silver coin and went on his way, surprising Lucius Servilius and Cassius. It was not often they saw their money declined.

Greatly troubled by what the mystic had said concerning Tiberius Marcius, both men found their spirits dampened for they did not take his prediction lightly. And his refusal of their money only heightened their anxiety.

Brooding over the seer's visit, Cassius left the desk and walked over to the table beside the couch where Lucius Servilius was sitting, pondering the mystic's warning. Taking the flagon of wine from the table, Cassius poured wine into two goblets and handed one to Lucius Servilius and together they drank deeply.

"We must try to warn Tiberius Marcius," said Lucius Servilius after finishing his wine. "We must send word to him somehow."

"I fear it would not reach him in time. If the seer is to be believed, fate hath already taken its course. The gods hath willed it so. All we mortals can do is wait and pray," said Cassius solemnly, putting his empty goblet down on the table. "In the meantime, we shall attend to the woman that stands outside."

"Her presence is a harbinger of things to come," Lucius Servilius said gloomily, rising to his feet and setting his goblet down beside Cassius'.

"In light of the seer…it appears so," agreed Cassius, his heart heavy as he and Lucius Servilius exited the tablinum.

The heat of the day had taken its toll on the woman's stamina. She was resting in the shade, beneath the canopy of a tall cypress tree at the edge of the property when Cassius and Lucius Servilius first laid eyes upon her. Observing her sitting under the tree that symbolized death, Cassius swallowed hard and vowed, "I swear to thee Lucius Servilius if Tiberius Marcius dies…I shall put to death his steward for allowing this ill omen to escape my notice. He should be flogged…the incompetent fool!"

Seeing two Romans approaching, their eyes fastened upon her, their white togas expertly draped upon their fit bodies, their manner and bearing undoubtedly that of the well born, Ruth rose to her feet hastily, her heart pounding. Drawing a deep breath, she stood her ground as the patricians drew near.

"Woman, what business hath thee here?" demanded Cassius, staring intently at the foreign woman before him.

"I desire to speak with the master of the house," she answered nervously, enduring the Roman's penetrating gaze.

"I am he."

"Noble Roman, thou dost bear him some resemblance, but thou art not he. I seek the man called Tiberius Marcius."

"Why dost thou seek him?" inquired Cassius, eyeing the woman warily, wondering if she was another fortune teller.

Intimidated by the Romans, particularly the one who addressed her, Ruth found it difficult to withstand their brazen scrutiny. It was all she could do to maintain some semblance of calm and continue speaking. "I prefer to state my business in his presence," she asserted, timidly meeting the dark eyes of her interrogator.

"Woman, Tiberius Marcius is not in residence. I am charged with overseeing his affairs. Thou would do well to state thy business lest I lose patience with thee," warned Cassius, anxious to be rid of her.

"When shall he return?"

"Not for some time," growled the Roman.

Fighting back tears of disappointment, Ruth lowered her gaze and wiped her beaded brow. "Forgive me…I am weary and do thirst. Grant me a drink of water, noble Roman."

Taking his cue from Cassius, Lucius Servilius walked back to the house and asked the door attendant to fetch a cup of water and bring it out to the woman. Overhearing the request, the steward promptly sent the first available servant he saw to do the patrician's bidding, irritating the door attendant who longed for a chance to leave his post.

Returning to the cypress tree, Lucius Servilius heard the old woman stating her business and he suspected his friend had pressured her into doing so.

"I hath come to redeem my kinswoman, Tamar, who was unjustly sold into slavery by my husband. I beg thee to release her," Ruth pleaded, her voice trembling with emotion.

"Woman, ought not thy husband be the one to put forth this request? Is it not his right?"

"He cannot, noble Roman, for he is gravely ill and lies upon his deathbed. He hath sent me forth to undo his grievous deed that he may look upon her once more and die in peace. He wishes to return the centurion's money," said Ruth, producing a money pouch which she offered to the Roman. "It is not the full price of her, but I am prepared to sell myself into bonds that she might hath freedom. I ask only that I be allowed to bury my husband," she said, tears welling up in her eyes.

"Woman, the maid is the property of Tiberius Marcius. I can do nothing to change this fact," stated Cassius, declining the pouch offered him which he recognized as having belonged to his cousin. "Go back to thy husband and tell him…what is done is done."

"Please, noble Roman," Ruth entreated, her eyes desperate. "Take the money! I beg of thee…permit me to redeem my kinswoman!"

Unmoved by the woman's petition, Cassius voiced sharply, "Leave and do not return. Forget the maid. She shall never return unto thee. Her fate hath been decided."

"I cannot forget her," declared Ruth in despair. "She is like unto my own child! Hath mercy on an old woman!"

"Depart from here, woman," Cassius ordered, but his command was not obeyed for Ruth's attention shifted suddenly to another. Her distressed countenance brightened so dramatically that Cassius knew at once her kinswoman was approaching.

Seeing her beloved aunt from afar, Tamar quickened her step. "Ruth," she cried out with joy, tears clouding her eyes as she hurried forward, losing water from the cup she carried.

Turning about, Cassius and Lucius Servilius beheld the maid and neither one was quite prepared for what they saw. They had heard she was beautiful…but that was an understatement. Truly, she was a woman of inordinate beauty…possessing exquisite skin, delicate features, long dark wavy tresses, compelling dark eyes and a most comely form. She was the personification of Venus…a living, breathing goddess. It was easy to see why Drusus had desired her and why Tiberius Marcius had risked his future to have her. What man or god would not desire one so beautiful?

Not one to waste time admiring a woman, especially one of low birth, Cassius was the first to shake off the lovely vision. Moving swiftly, he caught the fair maid by her arm before she could reach her kinswoman.

Dropping the cup, Tamar struggled against Cassius, fighting to extradite herself from his firm grasp, but to no avail.

Ruth rushed forward trying to make her way to Tamar, but Lucius Servilius blocked her path and held her back.

Amidst the crying and pleading of both women, Cassius addressed Ruth sternly, "Woman, depart from here and do not show thy face again for if thou dost…thy kinswoman shall suffer the consequences!" And to Lucius Servilius, he said, "Escort her off the property!"

Constrained by the Roman's unyielding strength, Tamar was powerless to alter the course he forced her to take. He was in full command of her physical being and she could do nothing to counter him.

"Please…hath mercy! Hath mercy, noble Roman," Ruth cried after Cassius as he forcibly escorted Tamar back to the house.

"Down the street with thee," thundered Lucius Servilius, ushering Ruth from the property against her will.

Detesting public displays of emotion, Cassius rebuked Tamar harshly as they entered the atrium. "Woman, cease thy crying! Emotional outbursts are not tolerated in a Roman house!"

"Thou hast ripped my heart asunder," Tamar wept bitterly, casting a backward glance at Ruth who was being led away by her Roman escort.

"I am capable of ripping more than thy heart asunder," he remarked darkly, his grip upon her arm tightening to the point of pain. "I counsel thee to remember that."

Alarmed, Tamar bore the pain he inflicted upon her in silence, afraid to cry out lest he make good his threat.

Speaking to the steward, Cassius directed, "Take this hysterical woman to her cubicle and bolt the door. I do not want to lay eyes on her for the remainder of the day…and withhold her meals," he added as an afterthought, intending to teach her a lesson she would not soon forget.

"Yes, Domine," said the steward, gingerly taking hold of the distraught maiden.

"Woman, thy tears avail thee naught in a Roman household. Remember this when thou art hungry," admonished Cassius, his hardened aspect portraying a look of superiority.

"Why art thou so cruel hearted?" she lashed out, tears streaming down her flushed cheeks. "I weep for want of my kinswoman and for this cause…I suffer thy wrath! What manner of man art thou? I pity thee! Thou art less than a …dog!"

Fearing for Tamar, the steward tried to usher her from Cassius' presence before she could say any more.

"Halt, steward! I would hear her!"

Obeying the command, the steward stopped in his tracks.

"Woman, dost thou dare to speak to a Roman in such a manner? Answer me, Jewess," demanded Cassius, his handsome face dark with rage.

Regarding the Roman standing before her, Tamar instantly regretted her emotional eruption. Looking as fierce as a lion, it seemed to her he was ready to pounce upon her and tear her apart, limb by limb. Did he not say he was capable of such violence? Why had she not heeded his warning? Why had she resisted the gentle tug of the steward who had tried to silence her?

"Hast thou gone dumb, woman?"

Frightened, Tamar bowed her head, praying a show of submission would pacify his anger.

"Ah…the mortal Venus hath come to her senses…and not a moment too soon," declared Cassius, mollified by her sudden change in conduct. "It is wise of thee to hold thy tongue, woman, for thou art in no position to speak thy mind!" Addressing the servant beside her, Cassius barked an order, "Steward, do as I hath commanded thee…lock her away!"

"Mortal Venus…" repeated Lucius Servilius to himself, watching the maid being led from the atrium.

Cassius swung around and saw his colleague standing in the doorway. "What say thou?" he demanded impatiently.

"Laugh if thou must…but I am persuaded the maid is Venus…Venus incarnate."

"Lucius Servilius, thou hast gone mad! I called her so merely in jest!"

"In jest, Cassius? It is a truth! Did not the seer foretell Tiberius Marcius would return to the land of the living by the power of Venus? Art thou blind to the maid's beauty and deaf to the words of the seer? Can thou not see the maid for who she is? I tell thee, she is Venus…the one who shall restore Tiberius Marcius to life!"

"Ye gods! Thou art speaking of women again! And what is worse…thou art speaking of this Jewish bondswoman as if she were truly a Roman goddess!" exclaimed Cassius, throwing his hands up in exasperation. "Go home, Lucius Servilius! I can bear no more!"

And having spoken, Cassius went into the tablinum and shut the door behind him. He had had enough of Lucius Servilius, enough of women, enough of the gods and their fiendish tricks!

XII

The steward stood watch at the front entrance, performing the vigilant duty of the door attendant, who now slept soundly as did the rest of the household. He was the only person awake; the only servant not permitted a restful repose. Physically tired and weary of his post, he leaned against the door, his arms crossed in front of him, pondering his fall from favor. For the life of him, he could not understand why Cassius had ordered him to keep vigil at the door as it was not his appointed duty. He resented being assigned to a task beneath him, especially one that kept him stationery. He was no ordinary slave; he was the steward of the house, the most respected and indispensable of all his master's servants. Never had his master or any member of his noble family treated him or his position with such utter disregard, but the same could not be said of Cassius. He was a stern, unduly exacting sort of patrician, given to impatience with those under his authority. Knowing this, the steward had thought better of questioning his judgment and just obeyed his command, mutely accepting what he could not change. Still, he wondered why Cassius had inflicted upon him the unenviable station of door attendant. Was it due to his failure to bring the low born woman to the patrician's attention? Was she the cause of his fall from favor, his misfortune? Had she brought upon him the displeasure of Cassius, the contemptible post he manned and the deprivation of sleep he now suffered?

Surrounded by an eerie silence, the steward contemplated his dismal situation, his stream of consciousness wandering through the recesses of his mind, his bleary eyes roaming the shadowy realm he occupied. As the night wore on, he drifted deeper and deeper into himself, his eyelids grew heavier, his thoughts escaped him and he fell asleep at his post.

In such state he remained until a dull thump struck the door behind him and startled him awake. Snapping to attention, he listened, his heart and mind racing. Had he been dreaming or had he heard something? What phantom haunted him? Was its presence real or a figment of his imagination? Leaning his ear against the door, he listened for the unwelcome specter, his hands resting on the secured bolt. Again, he heard the thump, but this time, he detected urgency. Suddenly, he realized that something or someone was kicking the door.

"Who goes there?" demanded the steward, unnerved by the late night visitor.

"It is I, Quintus Atilius. I bear thy master."

Recognizing the voice that spoke, the steward threw the bolt and opened the door with great haste. There before him stood Quintus Atilius and in his muscular arms lay the limp, bloodied body of Tiberius Marcius.

"Ye gods! What terrible fate hath befallen him?" exclaimed the steward in horror, beholding the unconscious body of his master.

"No time to explain…Tiberius Marcius is in dire need of medical attention," replied Quintus Atilius, stepping into the dimly lit atrium. "Wake Cassius!"

The steward fled the atrium and a moment later returned with a lamp in hand. "Come," he said, hurriedly leading the way into the tablinum.

Quintus Atilius followed the steward and upon entering the room, encountered Cassius, who with somber countenance gravely surveyed the wounded body of his cousin. "Lay him upon his couch," he directed, accompanying the steward and Quintus Atilius into Tiberius' bed chamber.

The steward placed the lamp on the night table and then quickly swept the bed curtains aside, clearing the way for Quintus Atilius.

"He was bleeding to death amongst the cypress grove of Venus Libitina," said Quintus Atilius, gingerly laying Tiberius down upon his bed. "It was Anatole, who found him. He had followed Tiberius from camp and watched for his return, but when he never showed, Anatole grew concerned and ventured into the grove to seek him. It was there, he happened upon him…in this terrible state. Before losing consciousness, Tiberius told him he had been ambushed by three men…Sejanus had set him up."

"Curse that ruthless, bloodthirsty cur!" declared Cassius vehemently, clenching his teeth. "He shall pay for this!"

"He shall indeed!" said Quintus Atilius darkly, turning an eye on Cassius. "I did not think it wise to transport Tiberius Marcius back to camp. I feared Sejanus would finish the work of the assassins and suffocate him whilst he lay unconscious…so I brought him here and I sent Anatole after a physician. I instructed him to escort the physician to thy door and then return to camp…lest he arouse suspicion."

"Thou hast done well and I am greatly indebted to thee, Quintus

Atilius," said Cassius, drawing near the bed. "Steward, bring some fresh water and plenty of bandages. Be quick about it!"

"Yes, Domine!"

Bending over Tiberius, Cassius began the process of removing the bloodied uniform, assisted in the tedious undertaking by Quintus Atilius. Working as gingerly as he could so as not to cause any further injury, he unbuckled the baldric, noting his cousin's fine sword was missing from its sheath. Flinging the belt to the floor, he then applied himself to the difficult task of removing Tiberius' fitted leather cuirass which was caved in on the left side, just under the ribs. The deep puncture was oozing bright red blood and Cassius was anxious to stop the flow of blood, but he could not do so until he had divested Tiberius of his outer armor. Realizing the ordeal would have been too painful for his cousin to endure, Cassius was thankful Tiberius was unconscious.

"What hast become of his weapon?" asked Cassius, stripping away the protective armor that had failed to ward off injury, its removal, revealing a blood soaked tunic beneath.

"I searched for it, but it was not to be found," answered Quintus Atilius, flinching slightly at the sight of the crimson tunic. "I suspect the assassins took the blade to prove they had done the deed…find it and we find them."

The steward returned with a large basin of water and an armful of bandages. Placing them on the table beside the bed, he asked, "Domine, shall I fetch someone to care for his wounds?"

The question caught Cassius' attention and he turned toward the steward, recalling the words of the seer. "…by the divine hand of Venus," he mumbled to himself.

Hearing him, Quintus Atilius regarded Cassius with curiosity.

"Wake the maid, Tamar! Bring her here at once!" commanded Cassius, deciding to act upon Lucius Servilius' assertion that the maid was Venus incarnate. Cassius did not believe she was anything more than a bondswoman, but he could not afford to dismiss the possibility she might be more, not when Tiberius' life hung in the balance.

"Domine…" ventured the steward nervously. "I doubt she is capable of…"

"Do as I hath commanded," came the curt reply.

"Yes, Domine," said the steward, hurrying off to Tamar's cubicle.

Arriving at her door, the steward tapped lightly, threw the bolt and stepped inside, his shadow falling across her couch.

Startled, Tamar sat upright in her bed, frightened by the ethereal figure standing in her cubicle.

The steward drew near and saw the maid was wide eyed with terror and looked as if she were about to scream. "Fear not, maid," said he. "I mean thee no harm. Cassius hath need of thee and hast sent me to fetch thee."

"What need hath he at such a late hour?" she inquired warily, unsettled by the steward's presence.

"That is not for me to say. Rise and make haste, maid, lest thou try his patience."

"I fear he hath sent for me that he may do me some unspeakable evil! I dare not go with thee!"

"I assure thee, maid, he shall do thee no evil. He hath need of thee. Make haste! His temper is short and I fear for myself and thee if thou doth not obey his summons! Make haste," urged the steward.

Convinced of his sincerity, Tamar yielded, saying, "I would see to my appearance before I go to him. Leave me that I may rise from my couch."

"Again, I say unto thee, make haste!" said the steward, exiting her cubicle.

Heeding his words, Tamar rose from her couch quickly. Mindful of her modesty and uncertain of Cassius' intentions, she covered her night dress with a cloak which draped her body from head to foot. Feeling uneasy, she left the security of her room for what reason, she knew not. Her mind filled with frightening scenarios, Tamar's anxiety intensified as the steward hastily led her through the ill lit atrium and into the shadowy tablinum.

Coming to a halt outside of Tiberius' sleeping cubicle, the steward turned to Tamar and said, "Enter, he awaits thee."

"Must I enter alone?" she asked, fear gripping her.

The steward nodded affirmatively.

"Thou said no evil would befall me, but now I fear thou hast deceived me, seeing thou hath brought me to the master's bed chamber."

"Fear not, maid. I hath not deceived thee. Enter! Thou art needed!"

"Why am I needed? Tell me," she pleaded, clutching her cloak close to her body.

Offering her no explanation, the steward nudged Tamar forward into the sleeping quarters.

Upon entering the room, her initial fear was laid to rest, but another instantly rose in its place as she gazed upon her wounded master, lying lifelessly upon his bed, his body and clothes heavily stained with blood. Standing over him on one side of his couch was a centurion, whom she recognized and on the other side was Cassius, whom she dreaded. Daunted by the sanguine scene before her, she stood frozen in the doorway, her delicate constitution unable to withstand what her eyes beheld.

"Come hither, woman. Help us disrobe him," ordered Cassius sternly, sparing her no look as he was busy cutting away Tiberius' bloodied tunic from his body.

Feeling light headed, Tamar stammered, "I…I…cannot!"

At her words, Cassius looked up from his work and cast a menacing eye in her direction. Quintus Atilius also regarded the maid, but his face held none of Cassius' hostility.

"Come hither, woman!" demanded Cassius, his ire whetted by her noncompliance.

Paralyzed by fear, Tamar remained where she stood, unable to move.

Enraged by what he took to be a willful act of defiance, Cassius flew at Tamar, his dark eyes flashing violently as he seized her with one hand and wielding the other, struck her across her pallid face. And having administered one swift blow, he abruptly released her.

Tamar let out a cry and fell back against the wall in sheer terror, her cloak falling from her shoulders to the floor, her heart pounding, her burning cheek throbbing and her body shaking.

"Woman, thou wilt do as thou art commanded!" stormed Cassius, his fierce eyes keen upon the frightened maid. "I shall not tolerate thy impertinence! Thy master lies near death on account of thee! Better it had been for him had he left thee to Caesar's son! Woman, thou hast brought calamity upon thy master and upon his house! I will not watch him die for the likes of thee! Thou art unworthy of his noble Roman blood!" declared Cassius bitterly; thrusting his blood stained hand in her face, hate emanating from his dark orbs. "Unworthy…I say!"

Having regained consciousness, Tiberius heard what had been said by Cassius; but he did not realize Tamar had been struck prior to the verbal reprimand. Troubled by the harshly worded rebuke, Tiberius rose to his servant's defense. He did not want Tamar to feel responsible for his ill fate. No one was responsible, no one except Sejanus and his hired assassins.

His body racked with pain, Tiberius groaned, "Cassius…she…is not…to blame…"

Upon hearing his cousin, Cassius returned to Tiberius' bedside, but not before he shot Tamar a threatening look.

Recoiling from him in fear, Tamar touched her face where Cassius had struck her, but the sting of his brutal words hurt more than the physical pain he had inflicted. Was she truly responsible for her master's wounds as Cassius had said? Had the centurion suffered violence on her account? Was she the reason he lay battered and bloodied? Was there no escaping the wrath of Drusus? How could she have been so foolish? Josiah had perished because of her and now the centurion was facing the same fate. Overwhelmed by a deep sense of guilt, Tamar knew she had to do something.

Crying out to God in desperation, she prayed for the strength to rise above her physical weakness for she had no stomach for blood and torn flesh. Drawing a deep breath, she approached the couch, the color draining from her face as she beheld Tiberius, who lay stripped to his waist, his left side deeply lacerated and caked with blood, his left arm pierced and bloody. Seeing the anguish in his eyes, she was moved with compassion.

"Permit me to clean his wounds," requested Tamar, timidly addressing Cassius, who turning to her, sternly nodded and stepped aside. Taking up vigil at the foot of Tiberius' couch, he and Quintus Atilius observed the maid as she went to work. Nothing escaped their watchful eyes.

Selecting a suitable cloth from among those provided by the steward, Tamar immersed it in the basin and after wringing it free of excess water, she gently pressed the cool cloth against Tiberius' wounded side.

Finding the cleansing of his wound agonizing, Tiberius moaned and grabbed Tamar by the wrist.

"Domine, unhand me that I may care for thee," Tamar entreated, gravely concerned for him. "Thy wounds must be cleaned to prevent infection."

"Doth thou…take…pleasure…in my suffering?" he questioned gruffly, his black eyes filled with pain.

"I hath not a heart of stone, my lord," replied Tamar softly, fighting back tears.

"Woman…do not…care for me…out of…guilt. I…desire…another…" he gasped, his strength failing him.

"Domine, do not send me away," pleaded Tamar, meeting the suffering eyes of her master. "If I am the cause of this evil, it is only right that I tend to thee. I beg thee…do not send me away. Permit me to do what needs to be done."

Too weak to argue, Tiberius released his hold on her wrist and turned his face to the wall to hide the anguish that would surely manifest itself upon his countenance with every excruciating touch of his pierced flesh.

Resuming the cleansing of her master's wounds, Tamar rinsed the bloody cloth in the basin and ever so gingerly, she again pressed the cloth against his side. Knowing his pain was unbearable, she attended him with tenderness and heartfelt prayer.

Marveling at her change of heart, Cassius and Quintus Atilius glanced at one another, equally astounded.

"I understand her not," said Cassius to the centurion at his side. "She refused to obey me when I called upon her services, but yet, she implored Tiberius Marcius to let her render them."

His gaze fixed on the maiden of mercy, Quintus Atilius replied, "Cassius, thou wert too hasty in chastening her. Her refusal to heed thy command stemmed not from disobedience, but from a fragile constitution. Did thou not notice her pale aspect? Did thou not notice she could neither speak nor move at thy command? The sight of blood weakened her. I suspect the maid was on the brink of a fainting spell."

"Gods preserve thee! Thou art enamored with her, Quintus Atilius! So much so…thou dost think nothing of rebuking me on her account!"

"If thou did not wish to hear my thoughts, Cassius, thou should not hath engaged me in conversation," retorted Quintus Atilius, stiffly.

The tense moment was diffused when the steward entered the room and announced the arrival of the physician, who stepped forward, prepared to offer his medical expertise despite the late hour. He was a man of many years, his kindly face, though not particularly handsome was pleasant to look upon. Silver haired, gray eyed, tall and lean, he was the best physician in Rome and he took great pride in his reputation. Unlike some of his esteemed profession, he cared immensely for the fate of those he treated. No one was more important to him than a person in need of medical attention. This was evident in his manner for he wasted no time on formalities, but went immediately to his patient. He did not need to squander precious time asking questions. He had already been briefed on the patient's condition by the servant who had escorted him to the house.

Moving away from the bed, Tamar gave place to the learned man of medicine.

Nearing the couch where the patient lay, the physician glanced at the discarded military uniform lying on the floor. Noting the garments were heavily saturated with blood, he surmised the blood loss was severe. Leaning over Tiberius, he felt his neck for a pulse, finding it quite weak. He then examined the deep hole in his patient's side and the long gash on the underside of his arm. The side injury was by far the more serious of the two wounds as the underlying tissue had been lacerated.

"Art thou in pain?" he asked knowingly, raising his soft gray eyes to his patient's face.

His patient nodded; the anguish plain on his ashen countenance.

"I am going to give thee something to ease thy pain," he said and then turned to Tamar, "Bring some strong wine, woman."

Rushing from the bed chamber into the adjoining room, Tamar quickly located the decanter of wine and filled a goblet with the requested draught. Returning with the cup, she presented it to the physician, who poured into the wine, a syrupy substance derived from poppies.

"Raise his head," directed the physician, stirring the concoction with a sterile utensil.

Tamar did his bidding and gently cradled her master's head within her small hands.

Addressing his patient, the physician said, "Drink this, soldier," and he put the goblet to Tiberius' lips, encouraging him to swallow the medicated wine. When it came to alleviating pain, poppy syrup was an effective drug. If ever he had seen a patient in need of the medicine, it was this man. He knew the soldier was suffering terribly and strongly suspected he was repressing cries of agony. He could not help but admire him for his heroic effort. Here is a true Roman, brave till the bitter end, thought the physician, withdrawing the empty goblet and setting it down on the table beside the couch. With the potent drug administered, the physician turned his attention to sterilizing and bandaging the wounds. Enlisting the help of Tamar, he lectured her on the importance of changing the bandages frequently, a task he felt her capable of, having duly noted her thorough cleansing of the patient's wounds and attentiveness to his care. Finishing, the physician handed Tamar a vial of the syrupy medicine, giving her implicit instructions on how it was to be dispensed. And having done all he could, leaving the rest in the hands of the gods, he walked over to where the two men stood, both grave in appearance.

Addressing them in a low dignified tone, he said, "I hath eased his pain…more than this I cannot do. He is beyond the skill of a physician. He hath lost much blood; his life force is weakened to the point of death. It is highly unlikely he shall live to see the sun rise," said the physician, grimly shaking his head of silver.

"Can nothing be done to save him," inquired Cassius, a sense of disbelief washing over his countenance.

"Nothing…in my power," replied the physician. "All that can be done for him is to see that he is properly cared for while he lives. The maid shall fulfill this of her own accord."

Looking past the physician, his mind desperately seeking a glimmer of hope, Cassius' eyes fell upon Tamar. Why did everyone continually make mention of the maid as if she were somehow important in the scheme of life? Was she? Had he misjudged her? Was it possible she possessed divine power? Was she Venus incarnate? Could she do what the physician could not? Could she save Tiberius and restore his vitality? Oh, how he longed to believe she was more than a mere bondswoman of Jewish decent, but as he beheld her small frame clothed in servant's attire, her braided hair hanging down her back, her lovely face as pale as her master's, he found she looked more like a mortal than a goddess. A goddess would not fear man, Roman or otherwise, nor would a goddess tolerate being smote by a mortal man. A goddess would have lashed out against her inferior, striking him dead where he stood, but this goddess endured the blow, she cried out, she was weak kneed, she was frail in body and mind. No, she was no goddess…she was but a mere woman…man's inferior, thought Cassius sadly, hope vanishing from his mind.

Having nothing more to say for what good were words in times like these, the physician left the room, accompanied by the steward, who had been standing in the doorway quietly weeping for the master he loved.

Suppressing her own grief, Tamar picked up the water basin intending to dispose of its bloody contents, but as she turned to leave, Tiberius reached out his bandaged arm and detained her. "Woman…what said the physician? I adjure thee by the gods…to tell me."

"I know not, Domine. I was not privy to his diagnosis," she replied meekly, lowering her eyes lest he see the truth in them. She knew very well what the physician had said for she had read it plainly on the faces of Cassius and the centurion, but she had not the heart to say.

"Tell me, woman…am I dying?"

Before Tamar could formulate an answer, Cassius and Quintus Atilius came to his bedside.

"Woman, empty the basin," Cassius ordered, sparing her the unenviable task of divulging the bad tidings.

"Wilt no one answer me?" asked Tiberius, swallowing hard as he looked from face to face.

"Tiberius Marcius, the physician saith thou art beyond his skill," stated Cassius evenly, concealing his emotion behind an implacable mask.

"Alas...the truth," said Tiberius solemnly, accepting his grim fate.

"I vow to thee, Tiberius Marcius, I will not rest till I avenge thee," said Quintus Atilius, his face hard as stone, his sober words filled with weight and promise. "I shall find the men who did this to thee and they shall pay with their lives...and so shall Sejanus. When I am through with him, the cursed dog shall beg me to let him die!"

"Quintus Atilius...no man ever had a more loyal friend than thee," voiced Tiberius easily, the drug having already lessened his physical torment. "I hath trusted thee in life and I shall trust thee in death to keep thy oath."

"Farewell, my friend," said Quintus Atilius, taking leave before emotion could break through his hardened aspect.

Alone with Cassius, Tiberius fastened his eyes upon his cousin's finely featured Roman face. "Cassius, into thy capable hands do I place my family and fortune. I ask thee to care for my mother and sister as thy own. Be patient with them, especially Priscilla, who shall surely try thee. Rule her with an even hand and see she doth wed Lucius Servilius. It was the will of my father that she be so joined. I swore to him I would see his will done. Now, I must entrust thee with this vow."

"Priscilla shall marry Lucius Servilius and no other. I give thee my word, Tiberius Marcius. Thy father's will shall come to pass."

Tamar returned to the bed chamber bearing in her hands a basin of fresh water.

Seeing her, Tiberius said, "Woman, wake my mother and sister and bid they wait till they are summoned."

"Yes, Domine," replied Tamar, setting the basin down and departing from the room, an ill feeling lingering in the pit of her stomach.

"Cassius," continued Tiberius, his eyes returning to his cousin's somber face. "I hath more to say to thee...hard things. Wilt thou hear them?"

"I wilt hear all thou hast to say."

"Cassius, thou art a noble Roman. Fortuna shall surely shine her face upon thee, but thy temper shall be thy undoing if thou art not careful. I caution thee to mind thy temper lest it earn thee the hatred of those around thee, slave and free. I ask thee to remember my words and treat my servants kindly...in particular, the maid Tamar. She is as fragile as a flower...she shall not thrive if thou art harsh with her. Be patient and do not mistreat her."

"Why art thou so concerned for his maid? She deserves to be dealt with harshly," Cassius sneered, unable to conceal his contempt for Tamar. "Is she not the reason thou art wounded unto death?"

"She is not the sole reason...and thou knowest this as well as thou knowest thy name. Do not lay guilt at her feet, Cassius. It is not right to burden her so. Lay the guilt where it belongs...at the feet of Sejanus."

A brief silence transpired between the two men. Cassius pondered what Tiberius had said, while Tiberius fought against the unseen forces waiting to usher him into the nether world.

Holding them at bay a little longer, Tiberius spoke again, his voice considerably weaker than before. "I might hath loved her had my days permitted."

"Loved who?" inquired Cassius, suddenly confused.

"Tamar..."

Cassius could not believe his ears. Convinced Tiberius spoke the maid's name out of drug induced delirium; Cassius let it pass without comment.

"Bid her sit with me till I die," uttered Tiberius, clutching the arm of Cassius.

"If it pleases thee..." replied Cassius, perturbed.

"Mater...Priscilla...my time grows short."

Cassius went to the door and commanded the steward to show the two women inside and seeing Tamar, he beckoned her as well. He could not bring himself to deny Tiberius his dying request. If Tiberius Marcius wanted the maid to sit with him, then sit with him she would.

The three women entered the cubicle. Flavia and her daughter rushed to Tiberius' bedside. Tamar stood in the doorway looking on, the steward beside her.

"My son," said Flavia, stroking his forehead tenderly, her heart wrenching inside of her, her face rigid and tearless as she looked down upon him. She would not cry or make a spectacle of herself though every fiber in her body wanted to give way to emotion. She wanted to scream, to cry, to curse the gods, but she restrained her emotions and conducted herself properly as she had always done. It was the Roman way. It was the only way.

"Mater, I must leave thee," said her son, his voice almost a whisper, his strength dwindling. "Cassius...shall care for thee...and Priscilla."

"Oh, Tiberius Marcius! Do not leave us!" cried Priscilla, tears streaming down her cheeks.

"I hath no choice, Priscilla. Fortuna hath abandoned me," he smiled weakly. "I should hath…listened to thee, Mater. I should never…hath ignored the gods…I hath incurred…their…wrath…" and having spoken, he closed his eyes and fell into a deep sleep.

"My son is dead," Flavia announced stoically, her voice sounding strangely distant. "I hath no husband and I hath no son. The gods hath seen fit to rob me of both."

Priscilla laid her face in her hands and began to wail, her unbridled sobs reverberating throughout the house, waking the rest of the inhabitants.

Laying hold of Priscilla, Cassius shook her violently. "Priscilla, collect thyself! This is no way for a Roman woman to behave!" he scolded and then callously handed her over to the steward. "See her to her chamber," he snapped, in no mood for theatrics.

The steward, whose eyes were red with sorrow, took the weeping girl and walked her back to her cubicle, supporting the weight of her against him. Flavia fell in behind them, her beautiful face devoid of emotion.

Tamar remained standing in the doorway, observing Cassius, who outwardly appeared to be as emotionally unaffected by Tiberius' death as Flavia. Wondering if the Roman was even capable of mourning, Tamar wiped the tears from her eyes as she watched him place a chair beside Tiberius' couch. Then, turning in her direction, he approached her.

"Sit with him till I return," he said simply, handling Tamar with unusual gentleness as he took her by the arm and led her to the couch where Tiberius lay still and lifeless. Placing her in the chair, he left the room.

Alone with Tiberius, Tamar sat by his couch, gazing intently at him. Tears drew into her eyes, his death gripping her heart. It distressed her to behold his youthful body, once so strong and full of vitality. He should not have died. He should have married, sired children and lived a long satisfying life, but his days had been cut short by violence. Her master had met with the same horrible end as Josiah, she thought guiltily. Both men had rescued her from Drusus and both had paid the ultimate price.

Standing outside of the bed chamber, Cassius watched Tamar, anxiously waiting for her to exercise her mystical power over death, hoping against his better judgment she was indeed Venus, a notion revived in his mind by Tiberius. Tiberius Marcius had said he might have loved her had his days permitted. Perhaps, the power of Venus had brought forth the strange declaration, thought Cassius, unwilling to let go of the possibility that the maid might be Venus, though everything inside of him said differently. Still, his Roman sensibilities refused to abandon hope. The gods were after all the gods. They did as they pleased. They toyed with the lives of men, watching them as one would an actor upon a stage. Perhaps, it pleased the gods to use a lowly servant girl in their melodrama.

Believing she was responsible for the centurion's death, Tamar slipped off of the chair and onto her knees beside Tiberius' couch. Taking his still warm hand in hers, she cried softly, "Forgive me, Domine. I am to blame for this evil. I hath brought death upon thee…please forgive me for what I hath done! Had I known what was to befall Josiah…and now thee…I would never hath fled Drusus! Forgive me, Domine! Forgive me!"

Cassius grew uneasy as her tearful words assaulted his ears. Was Tiberius truly dead? Had the seer been mistaken? Where was Venus…if not before him? It was her power that was supposed to restore him to life! Where was she? Where in the name of the gods was she? Curse the gods and their games! "Curse them," he stormed inwardly, tears escaping him.

Tiberius heard Tamar's sorrowful confession. He felt her soft touch and her tears upon his skin, but he could not lift his eyelids to gaze upon her or open his mouth to speak words of absolution. His body no longer obeyed his commands. He was a prisoner in a strange dream like world. He was not dead and he was not fully alive. Struggling desperately to master his body which now lay helpless upon his couch, he tried to reach out to Tamar, but his limbs would not move. Determined to overcome the mysterious force that rendered him immobile, he fought against it, until finally, after much concentrated effort; he moved the fingers of his left hand. Would this slight stirring be enough? Would she see he yet existed?

Stunned by what her tearful eyes witnessed, Tamar gently squeezed her master's hand. "Domine, thou livest!" she exclaimed, her heart swelling with hope, her eyes searching his still, expressionless face.

Cassius wiped the tears from his eyes, fearing they had clouded his vision. Had he seen what he thought he had seen? He rushed forward for a closer look.

"He lives!" announced Tamar exuberantly. "He lives!"

Cassius stared at her in amazement and wonder. Her tears had stirred life in Tiberius Marcius! Never again would he curse the gods! Never again would he rail against the powers that be! And never again would he lay a hand on Venus!

XIII

Cassius gazed at Tiberius Marcius, who lay still and seemingly lifeless upon his couch, his countenance ashen, his breathing barely detectable. In spite of the life threatening wound he bore in his side, he had survived the night. The gods had seen fit to spare his life, for what divine purpose Cassius knew not, but he felt certain the gods had destined his cousin for greatness and the thought pleased him immensely. But even with a god ordained destiny waiting in the wings, Cassius realized Tiberius' road to recovery would not be easily traveled. For not once during the long night had he awakened from his deep slumber, neither had he manifested any other sign of emerging from the black abyss that held him captive. It seemed only his maidservant possessed the power to reach into the darkness that imprisoned him.

Pondering the maid's mystical ability, Cassius turned his eye on Tamar, who stood beside him wringing out a cloth in a basin of water, which she then used to wipe Tiberius' brow. Observing her, Cassius could see nothing extraordinary about the maid aside from her physical beauty. He could not understand why the gods of Rome had bestowed divine power on a bondswoman. Could they not find a noble Roman to restore Tiberius Marcius to life? Why had they chosen a woman of low birth to serve their purpose? Though Cassius dared not doubt the maid's power, lest in doubting, Tiberius die, it nevertheless troubled him that she looked so weary, so humanly frail. He simply could not fathom a Roman deity with frailties. Despite Rome's national faith having been infected by the Greeks, who attributed to the gods weaknesses and passions, he rejected the idea gods were plagued by mortal weakness. Yet this Jewish bondswoman turned goddess was surely as weak a vessel as he had ever laid eyes upon.

Feeling his gaze, Tamar turned toward the Roman, half expecting him to speak, but he said not a word as he looked upon her lovely, pale face. She appeared fatigued and Cassius suspected she was as hungry as she was weary. He knew she had not eaten since he had commanded her meals be withheld nor had she any rest since being summoned to care for Tiberius. Though her toil worn state was obvious, Cassius elected not to address her physical needs, but to put her to the test. If she was of divine origin, she would address her own needs, if indeed, it was even necessary. If she were not a deity, but mortal, then she would be unable to meet her needs without his knowledge. Either way, her true identity would come to light. He was tired of second guessing himself as to who she really was and he looked forward to the moment of truth. Leaving Tiberius' bedside, Cassius departed from the chamber and returned to the study to wait the arrival of Lucius Servilius.

At daybreak, he had sent the steward to the house of Lucius Servilius, forbidding the servant to breathe a word about Tiberius Marcius to patrician or slave, under the threat of crucifixion. His threat was most effective on the steward, who understood all too well what a torturous form of death he would suffer if he dared disobey. Cassius was not about to risk others discovering Tiberius was still alive before he had an opportunity to confer privately with Lucius Servilius. Together, they would devise a course of action, but until then, Tiberius Marcius was dead for all practical purposes. Cassius had not even informed Flavia or Priscilla, much less the rest of the household servants that Tiberius lived. Only he, the steward and the maid knew and he had taken measures to insure their silence.

Staring out the window, his arms crossed in front of him, Cassius was deep in contemplation when the steward entered the tablinum and announced Lucius Servilius, who entered the room, visibly agitated.

"Why in the name of Jupiter hast thou sent for me at such an hour as this? What could be so pressing that a man must leave his house without having tasted a morsel of his morning meal?"

Turning slowly from the window, his countenance more somber than usual, Cassius said without preamble, "Tiberius Marcius was ambushed last night by three hired assassins and left for dead."

Taken aback, Lucius Servilius faltered momentarily, "I…I…knew not the urgency of thy summons! The steward said nothing of Tiberius Marcius!"

"I forbade the steward to speak of him," said Cassius dryly, unfolding his arms and straightening out the drape of his toga.

"Ye gods," exclaimed Lucius Servilius, calling to mind the seer's prediction. "The old shepherd knew whereof he spoke! How did this come to pass?"

"The seer warned of an enemy…the enemy is Sejanus. In typical fashion, the Prefect made unethical use of his authority and sent Tiberius Marcius to the temple of Venus Libitina on the pretense of an assignment.

It seems the treacherous cur fully expected the underworld deity to aid him in robbing Tiberius of his life. He did not count on the goddess Fortuna hindering his efforts for Anatole followed Tiberius from camp without his knowledge. He kept watch from afar and when Tiberius did not return to his horse, Anatole became alarmed and rode forward to seek him. He found Tiberius Marcius bleeding to death amongst the cypress grove. Tiberius conveyed to Anatole what befell him and sent him after Quintus Atilius, who brought him here in the dead of night."

"Doth Tiberius Marcius yet live?"

"He hovers somewhere between life and death, appearing more dead than alive," replied Cassius gravely. "He sustained a deep laceration on his left side and a lesser laceration on the underside of his left arm."

"Wilt thou permit me to see him?"

"Come," beckoned Cassius, leading the way into the bed chamber.

Upon their entrance, Tamar rose from her chair and stood by Tiberius' bedside as the two patricians approached.

"Woman, remove the bandage from thy master's side," barked Cassius, not bothering to look at Tamar for his attention was fixed on Tiberius Marcius. "And see thou dost not cause him pain."

"Yes, Domine," replied Tamar, moving to obey the command though her weary body resisted the effort.

"Tiberius Marcius hath suffered greatly because of this wound," stated Cassius, standing over Tamar as she carefully undid the bandage.

Exposing the wound, Tamar stepped aside. The men drew closer to examine the injury, which was raw and crimson and hideous to behold.

"I hath never seen a more grievous wound inflicted upon a man and he live," commented Lucius Servilius, shaking his head. "I can scarce believe Tiberius Marcius hath survived. If I did not know differently, I would think he had battled barbarians in the war arena."

"Had the encounter taken place in the war arena, he would hath had a fighting chance, but Sejanus and his hired assassins were not interested in a fair battle," stated Cassius, anger churning in his gut. "If Tiberius had not been outnumbered, I doubt he would hath been seriously wounded. He is far too skilled with his sword to be easily cut down and Sejanus knew it! He accounted for Tiberius Marcius' skillful use of his blade when he sent three men to assassinate one! Despicable cowards!"

"Sejanus must be made to suffer for his part in this!" growled Lucius Servilius, his temper rising. "Tiberius Marcius must be avenged!"

"Rest assured, Quintus Atilius shall see to that!"

"Hath he vowed revenge?"

"He hath and I trust he shall keep his vow. It is to our advantage to see he doth not fail. We must plan accordingly. The odds against Sejanus need be no more equitable than those given Tiberius Marcius," uttered Cassius savagely.

"I agree with thee. Let us plot the cowardly Prefect's demise. Destroying him will be a pleasure!" voiced Lucius Servilius, savoring the thought of revenge.

Turning to Tamar, who had heard an ear full, Cassius directed, "Woman, bind thy master's wound," and having spoken, he and Lucius Servilius left the room with vengeance burning in their hearts.

"The maid hath tended to him well, Cassius," remarked Lucius Servilius as they entered the study. "His bandages were fresh, his wound clean and he appears as if he were in a comfortable sleep. Her concern for his well being is apparent. I believe she would care for Tiberius Marcius whether or not thou commanded it of her."

"Thou would hath seen differently last night. She was not so willing."

"Odd. I felt certain I observed in her a genuine concern for Tiberius Marcius. Art thou saying, I am mistaken?"

"Thou art not mistaken. The maid did care for him, but whether it was due to the chastisement she received or mystical forces, I cannot tell. I hath witnessed a strange thing concerning her and it hath left me quite baffled," admitted Cassius, returning to the desk and seating himself. Settled in a chair, he invited Lucius Servilius to do the same.

Lucius Servilius took a seat in the client's chair across the desk from Cassius, intent on finding out what had addled the razor sharp mind of his colleague. "Tell me, Cassius, what strange thing hast thou witnessed?"

"How am I to explain the unexplainable?"

"Try, Cassius. I am prepared to hear thee."

"It began when I commanded the maid to assist Quintus Atilius and myself in divesting Tiberius Marcius of his bloodied uniform, but she would not comply. Her defiance so infuriated me that I rose up against her. I had scarcely finished reprimanding her when Tiberius regained consciousness and in his debilitated state, he spoke in her defense."

"What then, Cassius?"

"Moments later, the maid sought my permission to care for Tiberius Marcius and care for him she did. Even when Tiberius tried to dismiss her, supposing her services were rendered out of guilt, she refused to leave him, insisting she must cleanse his wounds. Her sudden change of heart greatly puzzled me."

"Clearly, there is a bond between Tiberius Marcius and this maid," said Lucius Servilius, finding the narrative very interesting.

Though Cassius strongly suspected there was a bond between them, possibly one of love for Tiberius had stated as much, he thought better of divulging Tiberius' deathbed confession to Lucius Servilius. After all, it was made while under the medicinal influence of poppy syrup and the duress of impending death. One could hardly hold a man accountable for words spoken under such circumstances. Choosing not to confirm Lucius Servilius' astute observation, Cassius let the comment pass and continued speaking.

"While the maid attended to Tiberius, Quintus Atilius and I anxiously awaited the arrival of the physician. When he arrived, he examined Tiberius Marcius and finding his wounds cared for, he employed the maid whose handiwork pleased him. Medicine was administered to relieve Tiberius' excruciating pain, but little else could be done for him. The physician then informed me in the presence of Quintus Atilius that Tiberius would not live to see the sun rise…and he added…the maid would tend to him of her own accord. True were the words of the physician on both accounts for the maid did indeed care for Tiberius Marcius…till his death!"

"He died?" exclaimed Lucius Servilius, thoroughly confounded.

"Bear with me, Lucius Servilius. I know it is difficult to believe, but Tiberius Marcius did in fact die. He died in the presence of Flavia, Priscilla, the steward, the maid and I. Upon his death, I sent all from the chamber save the maid, whom I bade, sit by his side. Lastly, I left the room, but did watch the maid, careful to remain unseen. Curiously, the maid began to weep over Tiberius Marcius and through her tears, she spoke to him. Then a most remarkable thing occurred…he moved his fingers…and I seeing rushed forward into the chamber. There, I beheld the maid holding Tiberius' hand and heard her tearfully proclaim him alive. And so he is."

"Truly, the maid is Venus incarnate!" declared Lucius Servilius, his face brightening. "The seer foretold his death and return to life by the divine hand of Venus! And it hath quite literally come to pass! The goddess hath bestowed her divine favor upon Tiberius Marcius! Of a truth, he is destined for greatness!"

"His destiny is clear to me as well," said Cassius, sighing heavily.

"Why then art thou cast down?" inquired Lucius Servilius, unable to digest Cassius passionless response. "Venus hath visited this noble house and restored Tiberius Marcius to life! Is not this cause for rejoicing?"

"I find it impossible to rejoice whilst I am troubled."

"What troubles thee, my friend?"

"Tell me, Lucius Servilius, what am I to do with this supposed goddess? Shall I erect a new temple in her honor and offer pleasing sacrifices? Shall I climb the highest pinnacle in Rome and loudly proclaim a goddess walks among us? What am I to do with this…this Venus? I am greatly troubled on account of her. She appears to be mortal in all ways and I frankly struggle to view her otherwise despite her manifested power over life and death. I am torn as to whether I should regard her as a servant of this house or as a deity of Rome."

"Call her forth that we may question her," suggested Lucius Servilius thoughtfully. "Perhaps a word from her shall convince thee of her divinity and ease thy mind."

Following his colleague's advice, Cassius left his chair and called Tamar from Tiberius' couch. "Come hither, woman."

Detecting impatience in the Roman's voice, Tamar promptly obeyed his command so as not to provoke him to anger. She did not wish to bring his mighty wrath down upon herself again. Unsettled by his summons, she entered the tablinum. There, she found the two men seated; their eyes keen upon her.

"Draw nearer," instructed Cassius. "I would examine thee."

Nervous, Tamar reluctantly approached his chair, maintaining what she deemed a safe distance from him.

Sensing she was afraid of him, Cassius asked, "Woman, dost thou fear me?"

"Thou knowest I fear thee, Domine," she answered, timidly meeting Cassius' piercing gaze.

"Woman, why dost thou fear him?" inquired Lucius Servilius, amused by the maid's straightforwardness.

"Not daring to answer the question posed to her, Tamar lowered her eyes, escaping Cassius' glare which had rendered her dumb with fear.

"What reason hast thou? Hath he mistreated thee?"

"Woman, answer the questions put to thee," prompted Cassius, unconcerned that Lucius Servilius would learn of the physical punishment he had levied against her.

"Domine, must I speak of that which I rightfully suffered at thy hand?" asked Tamar meekly, humbling herself before Cassius. "Hath I not already been made to know my place?"

"Woman, thy words please me. Therefore, I shall answer for thee and spare thee the discomfort of doing so," replied Cassius, his tone cavalier. Turning to Lucius Servilius, he said, "The maid fears me for I hath raised my hand against her, which as thou can plainly see hath benefited her immensely."

Thinking it unwise to smite Venus, Lucius Servilius shot a reproving look at Cassius, who ignored the silent reproach of his colleague.

Rising from his seat of power, Cassius walked around the maid, scrutinizing her person. His intense inspection discomfited Tamar, who despised the brazen way in which he regarded her, but could do nothing to hinder his view and so endured it.

"Woman, who art thou?" he demanded, slowly circling her.

"I am called Tamar, Domine."

"Art thou born of the Jews? Tell the truth!"

"I am."

"Dost thou possess divine power?"

"I possess no power, Domine."

"Knowest thou magic incantations or spells?"

"No, Domine…my people forbid such practices," answered Tamar, disturbed by his line of questioning.

"Dost thou worship the gods of Rome or the God of the Jews?" he asked, coming to a halt, face to face with her.

Tamar's heart accelerated as his dark orbs searched her face for an answer. Fear took hold of her and she began to tremble.

"Dost thou worship the gods of Rome or the God of the Jews?" Cassius repeated, managing a level of patience rarely found in him.

Believing he intended to punish her for not embracing the gods of Rome, Tamar fell at his feet and pleaded, "Hath mercy, Domine! I hath served thee with all of my strength! Let not thy wrath fall upon thy humble servant!"

Cassius turned to Lucius Servilius, a satisfied smile resting upon his lips. "What more evidence is needed than this," he asked, pointing triumphantly to the maid at his feet. "A goddess would not prostrate herself before a mere mortal and beg for mercy! We must seek Venus elsewhere for she doth not exist in this lowly maid! Sadly, she is as much flesh and blood as we!"

"My friend, thou art too quick in judging her," asserted Lucius Servilius, abandoning his chair. "Hast thou already forgotten what good fortune she hath bestowed upon Tiberius Marcius?"

"I am now inclined to believe that it merely appeared as if it were of her doing."

Assisting Tamar to her feet, Lucius Servilius reassured the frightened maid. "Woman, why dost thou beg for mercy? We intend thee no harm. We only seek answers from thee."

Lifting Tamar's face upward, Cassius stared into her dark eyes and demanded, "Answer, that we may know thee."

"Art thou the goddess called Venus?" questioned Lucius Servilius, taking in her lovely features. "Tell us, that we may worship thee?"

"Hath I not suffered enough at the hands of thy people? Must thou also make of thy lowly servant…a fool," cried Tamar, addressing Cassius, her voice quivering with emotion. "Thou knowest I…I …am no…goddess," she stammered, pushing back tears of frustration. "I am Tamar…the bondservant of Tiberius Marcius, whom he secured from Drusus, son of Caesar…now made fool for thy pleasure! Thou knowest I merit no worship, noble men…neither do I desire it!"

"The maid hath answered well. Let us put this nonsense aside," stated Cassius, thoroughly relieved to find the maid no more a deity than he. "It is not right that we should make sport of Tiberius' servant," he added, pleased she seemed none the wiser for their questioning.

Confounded by the maid's declaration, Lucius Servilius left her to Cassius, who sent Tamar back into Tiberius' bed chamber with a promise of food and rest to come.

"Lucius Servilius, I am indebted to thee for thou hast relieved me of one burden," said Cassius, strolling over to the couch where his associate had seated himself. "Yet, one remains that is far more pressing."

"Doth thou speak of Sejanus?"

"I do."

"Let us plot his downfall and be rid of the cursed dog!"

"It pleases me the fire of revenge still burns within thy belly," remarked Cassius. "I feared thou might hath lost thy appetite for it."

"Why should I?" snapped Lucius Servilius, defensively. "Hast Sejanus fallen upon his sword and saved us the trouble of killing him?"

"Thou art clearly disappointed to learn the maid is not Venus."

"Friend, thou art too full of thyself. Dost thou think I know not what thou art implying? Dost thou truly think the maid hath negatively affected my resolve to avenge Tiberius Marcius?"

"Come, Lucius Servilius, admit it! Learning the maid is mortal hath left thee disillusioned to say the least!"

"Cassius, just because the maid doth not recognize the favor of the gods rests upon her, doth not lead me to conclude she doth not have some degree of divine power," retorted Lucius Servilius, his face red with anger. "She did by thy own admission; bring Tiberius Marcius back from the land of the dead. She was spoken of by the seer and whether thou doth acknowledge her as the Venus he foresaw, she hast done as he foretold. If I were thee, Cassius, I would mind how I treat her, if not for thine own good, then for the good of Tiberius Marcius. His very life may depend upon it," warned Lucius Servilius, eyeing Cassius sternly.

"I shall keep in mind thy words, Lucius Servilius," Cassius said evenly, regretting he had offended his colleague. "Come, let us put aside our differences concerning the maid and be about the business of avenging Tiberius Marcius."

After plotting what they hoped would be the swift and sure destruction of their mutual enemy, Lucius Servilius left the tablinum and went to Priscilla's sitting room, while Cassius went in search of Flavia. They had decided to reveal that Tiberius Marcius was alive for they saw an advantage in letting it be known. The women of the house, the servants and the clients would all be informed with the latter being of the foremost importance. The clients were crucial if the news was to reach Sejanus. Without their unwitting participation in the plan, it would be next to impossible to draw Tiberius' assailants out into the open and that was their objective.

Lucius Servilius entered Priscilla's sitting room, finding it strangely quiet. There was none of the usual chattering and activity that ordinarily filled the bright and airy space adjacent the garden. The mood was solemn and Lucius Servilius felt the pain of the room's patrician occupant as sure as if it were his own. Though he had not yet taken Priscilla to wife, his heart was bound to hers and when she suffered, he suffered.

Priscilla did not realize Lucius Servilius was in the room for she was seated with her back to him. A maidservant noticed the visitor and informed her distraught mistress of his presence. Turning in her chair, Priscilla regarded her future husband and he her. The depth of her grief was apparent as tears were visible upon her face. She had cried through the night and into the morning. So profound was her sense of loss, mingled with guilt, that none could comfort her or stem the tide of her tears. Assisted by two maids, Priscilla appeared almost feeble as she slowly rose from her chair to greet Lucius Servilius.

Closing the space between them, Lucius Servilius drew near to her and took her slender hands in his, hopeful the visit would take a turn for the better once she learned her brother lived. Having Priscilla in his possession, he dismissed the maidservants. He wanted to be alone with her, to bask in her presence, to feel the warmth of her gaze upon him. He longed to speak words of love to her, to hear the same from her lips, but he restrained himself from expressing his innermost feelings. He would not bare his heart until he knew for certain he had won her favor. He, a Roman of noble ancestry would not make a fool of himself over any woman, even one as magnificent as Pricilla. It was not the best of situations in which he found himself, but he was bound and determined to preserve his dignity. He was betrothed to a woman who seemed to have little interest in him, while he on the other hand had interest in little else but her, an interest which for the most part, he concealed. Still, he was hopeful. With any luck, fortune would smile upon him and he would receive from Priscilla's well guarded treasury some small token of affection.

"It is kind of thee to visit me in my grief, Lucius Servilius," she said softly, her semblance mournful.

"Priscilla, I hath somewhat to say to thee concerning thy brother," he said, kissing her forehead fondly.

"Nothing thou canst say shall ease my sorrow, Lucius Servilius…for I hath murdered my brother!"

"My dear Priscilla, thou art speaking as one who hath taken leave of thy senses. Thou art overcome with grief. Be comforted…thou wielded not the sword that pierced him."

"Thou art mistaken…I wielded the sword of prayer. Prayer is more lethal than the sharpened blade. I cursed Tiberius Marcius unto death and the gods granted my evil prayer," she cried miserably.

"Woman, why didst thou curse thy brother?" questioned Lucius Servilius, stunned by her confession.

"I cursed him because he forbade me to love…ugh…" she blundered, stopping mid sentence. Remembering Tiberius had warned her against telling Lucius Servilius of her love for Claudius, she bit her tongue and swallowed hard, knowing she had said too much.

"Go on…" urged Lucius Servilius, wondering if she would dare admit what he already knew. Neither Tiberius nor Cassius had breathed a word of her infatuation with Claudius, but Lucius Servilius had sources of his own and he was aware of her feelings for the man. He had hoped she would come to her senses where Claudius was concerned and see him for what he was…a worthless, womanizing soldier with dangerous political aspirations who was far beneath her station in life. He had intended to wait out Priscilla's infatuation and marry her when it ceased to be, but now his wisdom seemed as foolishness. Realizing she still held to her witless infatuation, Lucius Servilius felt rejected and angry. And his countenance hardened.

"Lucius Servilius, the reason matters not," she cried, tears brimming in her sorrowful eyes. "My brother is dead because I called down the wrath of the gods upon him! I must live with the evil I hath done!"

"Woman, thy evil prayers were not answered. Thy brother lives and it is well for thee that he doth," he said harshly, dropping Priscilla's hands in disgust.

"Thou art mad, Lucius Servilius! I saw with my own eyes his death, I and others also!"

"The favor of the gods is upon Tiberius Marcius and he lives in spite of thy curses."

"I must go to him," she exclaimed, starting for the door, but Lucius Servilius seized her by the arm, his fingers tightening about her flesh with purpose.

"Priscilla, thy brother lies in a deep slumber. It is not known when he shall awake. Thy presence shall be unknown to him."

"I must go to him! I must care for him," insisted Priscilla, surprised to find herself constrained by the man she thought too gentle to treat her roughly.

"He is well cared for. There is no need for thee. Thy brother would be better served if thou wouldest repent of thy ill will towards him and honor him as thou ought. He is a man worthy of thy respect and it is thy duty as a Roman woman to render him his due. Thy trespass against Tiberius Marcius hath caused me to question thy understanding of the paterfamilias' power. It is a fearful thing to fall into his hands for none can save thee. Thou would do well to seek his forgiveness and plead for mercy. Be assured the gods are not pleased with thee for cursing the paterfamilias, nor for that matter, am I," he scolded, abruptly releasing her. "Woman, I hath never looked upon thee with as much disfavor as I do now!"

Filled with shame, Priscilla turned her back to Lucius Servilius, bitter tears spilling from her large brown eyes. She knew she had earned his condemnation for she had not conducted herself as befitted a patrician woman. She was a disgrace to her noble lineage. She had defied and cursed the paterfamilias and her utter disregard for him had nearly resulted in his untimely death. It came as no surprise Lucius Servilius now looked upon her with disfavor. How could any Roman man admire such a woman as she had become?

Having said all that needed to be said, Lucius Servilius exited the room, leaving Priscilla to ponder the error of her ways, while he pondered the wisdom of taking her to wife.

XIV

The hour was late as Sejanus made his way through the dark narrow alleys of Subura accompanied by his Greek hire, Xenos the gladiator, whose duty it was to protect the Prefect from the plebeian rabble that roamed the streets. It was not safe to travel alone in Subura, especially after nightfall. Opportunists were everywhere, peering out of shadowy corners, leaning in doorways, slinking along every path that one might lay a foot upon. However, Sejanus was not intimidated by the coarse, violent men he encountered for one look at Xenos and they forgot any ideas they might have had of attacking him.

Xenos was far too formidable an opponent to be easily overcome. Mammoth in size, tall and muscular, Xenos had never lost a fight to another gladiator, much less to anyone else, an accomplishment he was extremely proud of. Having retired undefeated from performing his trade for audiences, Xenos hired himself out as a bodyguard, but unlike others, he had only one employer. He was Sejanus' man through and through. Paid handsomely for his services, his loyalty was unwavering.

Guarding the Prefect with the utmost vigilance, Xenos was prepared to defend his employer. With muscles taut and eyes alert, he searched every corner and every alley they traveled for potential trouble, but none was encountered this night. Reaching their destination, a crossroad tavern, Sejanus entered ahead of Xenos, who delayed his entrance as instructed.

Spying the three assassins he had hired to murder Tiberius Marcius, sitting at a table in the back of the tavern, Sejanus went over and joined them. Drunk on cheap wine and eager to get their money from the Prefect, they greeted him heartily. As the tavern was crowded and noisy, the Prefect had no fear of being recognized or heard, so their exuberant greeting caused him no discomfort.

One of the assassins shouted at the bartender, "A flagon of wine for our esteemed guest! Be quick about it!"

The bartender, adept at hearing over the noise and taking orders from drunken patrons, heeded the request with amazing alacrity.

Lifting the wine goblet to his lips, Sejanus swallowed a mouthful of the sour draught as his throat was dry and he was thirsty. He was accustomed to finer wine, but one could not expect such fare in a Subura tavern. Making due with what was served; he drank another mouthful and set the goblet down on an obscenity carved into the tabletop.

"Hast thou done the deed?" asked Sejanus gruffly, his dark menacing eyes traveling from one man to the next.

"We have," answered the self-appointed leader of the trio.

"Is that so?" the Prefect inquired of the other two.

"Yes," they replied in unison, backing their leader.

"Where is the proof I requested?"

"Here," said the leader, reaching beneath the table and bringing up from the dusty floor, a sword wrapped in linen, which he placed on the table in front of the Prefect.

Sejanus drew back the cloth, uncovering Tiberius' sword, its sharp, polished blade stained with dried blood.

"It is his," volunteered the second assassin, referring to the blood.

"We have done what thou asked. Now give us our due," said the third assassin impatiently as he was eager to find himself a woman for the night.

"The blood proves only that he was pierced," said Sejanus, unimpressed, tossing the linen covering back over the sword. "I asked more of ye than that."

"We left him for dead in the grove of Venus Libitina," growled the leader, worried he and his men were not going to be paid. "That is what thou asked!"

"But was he dead?" demanded Sejanus, his fierce orbs narrowing.

"Someone came upon us as I was about to slit his throat and make certain of it," explained the leader, aware the Prefect was not pleased. "But I assure thee…the wound he sustained likely proved fatal. He was bleeding heavily when we left him."

The leader's explanation was met with stony silence. Word had reached Sejanus that Tiberius was still very much alive and knowing this, he marveled the assassins had dared to come forward, expecting payment for their failed attempt at murder. Rather than point out their gross incompetence and run the risk of drawing unwanted attention, Sejanus held his tongue. He had more complicated measures in mind, requiring of him far less energy than it would take to rebuke the three idiots before him.

"Wert thou seen?" he asked sharply, regretting he had not sent Xenos to kill Tiberius Marcius.

"No," said the leader confidently.

"Didst thou see who came upon thee?"

"We saw no one for it was dark."

Xenos watched as the Prefect withdrew three small bags of silver, sliding one across the table to each assassin, who greedily snatched their precious pouch and shoved it deep within the fold of their garment. The gladiator paid close attention to where each man stashed his booty.

"It was a pleasure doing business with thee," expressed the leader, happy to have his money in hand. "Do call on us again."

Sejanus stood to his feet, took up the wrapped sword and smiling sinisterly said, "I intend to." Then, he turned and disappeared into the drunken crowd of patrons. Passing the gladiator on his way out of the tavern, he snarled, "Kill the incompetent idiots!"

Xenos acknowledged the command with a nod, his predatory eyes darting to his intended victims. By dawn, the three would be dead, their throats cut from ear to ear, their silver his with a promise of more to come. Doing the Prefect's dirty work had made a rich man of the gladiator, who had no qualms about committing murder as he valued no life but his own. Killing was mere sport to him. The more difficult the challenge, the better he liked it. In Subura, where the streets were filled with cutthroats and thieves, murder was but child's play. Who would notice one more assassin this side of Rome, thought Xenos, downing the remainder of his wine, his eyes fixed on the doomed threesome. He had carried out far more difficult assassinations for his employer than this. To get in and out of Rome's affluent neighborhoods and murder a citizen of importance without being caught was tricky business indeed, but to kill a few common criminals in Subura was no trouble at all. No one would miss the likes of them. No one would launch an investigation into their deaths. Rome would consider herself well rid of the vermin. And so too, would the Prefect.

Early the following morning, Sejanus sent for Quintus Atilius, who appeared before the Prefect, concealing his loathing for his superior behind a phlegmatic expression and military deference.

A stickler for military decorum, the Prefect eyed the officer intently. Finding the centurion's appearance and stance to his satisfaction, Sejanus proceeded to address him.

"Centurion, Tiberius Marcius was ambushed two days ago while on special assignment. Fortunately, he survived the attack," stated Sejanus, managing to sound incredibly sincere. "He now lies at home, severely wounded. It is my hope he shall recover his former strength and return to his post. I can ill afford to loose a centurion."

It had been reported to the Prefect that Quintus Atilius had been seen returning to camp shortly before daybreak on the morning following the attack on Tiberius. Having been informed of this, Sejanus suspected the officer had played a part in aiding Tiberius and had thwarted the efforts of the assassins.

"Prefect, I knew not of his grave misfortune! I had supposed he had taken leave," lied Quintus Atilius, feigning surprise, an effortless feat as he was truly astonished to learn Tiberius was still alive. "Dost thou know who attacked him?"

"Centurion, I made it my business to know," retorted Sejanus, a diabolical sneer coming over his dour aspect. "Rome was searched, the perpetrators found and executed! I will not tolerate my soldiers being assaulted! Their deaths shall serve as a grim example to those who think otherwise!"

"Why art thou informing me of these things? What would thou hath me do, Prefect?"

"Quintus Atilius, I tell thee these things because I know thou art a friend of Tiberius Marcius. Is that not so?"

"I am, Prefect," answered the centurion, discerning his superior had a two fold reason for asking.

"Hast thou fought many campaigns together?"

"More than I can remember, Prefect."

"Then, I hath chosen the right man to deliver this message to him," announced Sejanus, looking rather pleased with himself as he handed a sealed scroll to the centurion. "In addition, I would hath thee escort his servant back to him and return his weapon," stated the Prefect, picking up Tiberius' sword from off his desk and turning it over to the officer. "Quintus Atilius, I could not entrust such valuable property to just any soldier. I had to find a man who could be trusted and who better than a friend of Tiberius Marcius."

Quintus Atilius accepted the sword from Sejanus, noting the dried blood upon its blade, the sight of which made his own blood boil, but he did not allow his emotion to be seen. Resisting the urge to drive the exquisite sword into his superior and kill the smooth talking dog, he slowly exhaled his anger. This was neither the time nor the place for revenge.

It was apparent to the centurion that Sejanus thought himself above suspicion, but Quintus Atilius was not in the least bit deceived by the Prefect's flowery sentiment. He had no doubt Sejanus was behind the attempt on Tiberius' life, neither did he doubt he would try again. Question was, how much did Sejanus know of his involvement? Did he know it was he who had borne Tiberius Marcius to his home that near fatal night? Had one of the Prefect's spies seen his comings and goings from camp? Only time would tell. It was best to assume the worst, especially where Sejanus was concerned. Dismissed from the Prefect's presence, Quintus Atilius left to do his bidding, having surmised there was a price on his head.

When the centurion was safely out of hearing distance, Sejanus cursed and railed against him, "Quintus Atilius, thou art chief among fools! Thy friendship with Tiberius Marcius shall cost thee thy life! Prepare thyself fool for death awaits both thee and thy high born friend!"

XV

Held captive by the impenetrable slumber, now in its third day, Tiberius still had not awakened and it seemed as if he never would. Only the rise and fall of his chest as he drew breath gave evidence of life and cause for hope.

Ordered to look after Tiberius, Tamar made every effort to see he rested comfortably. Though her work was physically harder, she welcomed it as it released her from Priscilla's beck and call. Unlike her mistress, whose demands were of a frivolous nature, her master had serious need of her. Putting all of her energy into caring for Tiberius, Tamar watched him closely, doing everything she could to alleviate any discomfort he might suffer. Never did she allow a sweat to break across his brow or a bedsore to manifest itself upon his anatomy. Twice daily, assisted by a male slave, Tamar moved Tiberius' limp body, changing the position in which he laid. She kept his bed linens and body clean, his bandages changed, his face shaved and his hair combed. She cooled his skin with a damp cloth and fanned him when the afternoon temperatures rose to unbearable heights. In the dead of night when no one was present, she invoked the God of Abraham, praying audibly for Tiberius, petitioning her God to show him mercy and heal his wounded body. Although she was weary physically and emotionally, she put her master's needs above her own and rendered every service selflessly.

Having noticed Tiberius' lips were dry, Tamar was applying ointment to them when Flavia entered the chamber and approached the couch where her son lay. Seeing the mistress of the house, Tamar respectfully acknowledged her and withdrew slightly from the bed.

Flavia gazed upon her son, her motherly instinct to cradle him in her arms properly suppressed. In spite of her effort to restrain herself, an expression of maternal love did manage to escape her. Breathing her son's name, she leaned down and affectionately stroked his clean shaven face, finding it cool to the touch. "Tiberius Marcius, my firstborn…return to me. Flee the darkness of the underworld and return to those who love thee, my son."

Detecting emotion in Flavia's voice, Tamar could not help but pity her. What mother could withstand the sight of her child lying perilously between life and death? There was no difference between the Romans and the Jews when it came to loving their children, thought Tamar, observing her mistress with compassion.

Raising her large brown eyes to Tamar, Flavia inquired, "Hast he yet stirred from this sleep?"

"No, Domina."

Upon hearing the maidservant's response, Flavia's eyes fell on her son once again. She could not understand why the gods permitted him to linger between the two worlds. What purpose did his life serve in such a powerless state? Why did they not release him from their divine grasp? As a Roman, Flavia believed the gods intervened in the lives of men in an orderly and natural fashion, but was it natural that her son should lie in a state of limbo? She wondered.

Stepping away from Tiberius' couch, Flavia looked upon his caretaker, addressing her with benevolence. "Tamar, thou hast done a great service for thou hast cared for my son in a manner which benefits him and pleases me. In no other hands could he be better served."

"Domina, I hath done no more than my duty," replied Tamar modestly.

"Thou hast indeed done more than thy duty," said Flavia softly. "Thinkest a mother's eye cannot see? Thou hast cared for my son with tenderness and reverence. I am most grateful to thee."

Touched by Flavia's gratitude, Tamar scarcely knew how to respond. Not since the day she had stepped foot into the Roman household had she been spoken to kindly by those she served.

"Send word to me should he awaken," instructed Flavia, preparing to leave the chamber. "I care not the time of day or night."

"I shall, Domina," assured Tamar, her heart warmed by her mistress' benevolent words.

Passing from the bed chamber into the study, Flavia noticed Cassius sitting at her son's desk. He appeared deep in thought as he moved his reed pen across the parchment spread before him. Having no desire to disturb him or draw his attention, Flavia quietly made her way through the study. She had nearly reached the exit when she heard Cassius speak.

"Why dost thou steal past me, my dear Flavia?" he asked, returning his pen to the ink well.

Slowly, Flavia turned about and faced him, finding his dark discerning eyes fixed upon her. Collecting herself, she replied levelly, "What reason dost thou suppose, Cassius?"

"If I knew...I should not ask," he grinned, admiring his aunt's composure.

"I did not wish to disturb thee, Cassius, but it appears I hath done so."

"Thou dost not like me much, Flavia," he remarked deliberately, endeavoring to fluster the Roman matron.

"Nonsense, I like thee well enough. Thou art my brother's son."

"Nicely stated, my dear aunt, but that is hardly an answer."

"Cassius, what doth thou hope to gain by pressing me?" she inquired stiffly.

"Why the truth, of course!" exclaimed Cassius, reveling in the verbal exchange as it was providing him with a much needed diversion.

Flavia had never really liked Cassius, in spite of his being her nephew, but the idea of admitting it to him or anyone else was unthinkable. She found him arrogant, self righteous and high handed just like her brother. Even so, it was hard to fault the son for being like his father. So rather than focus on her nephew's negative traits, she preferred to focus on the one redeeming quality of which she was certain. Cassius willingly fulfilled his patrician duty. He accepted responsibility for her and Priscilla during Tiberius' long military absences. As far as Flavia was concerned that was reason enough to spare his feelings.

"If it is truth thou seekest, then I am obliged to say, I hold thee in high esteem," she lied, having no trace of emotion on her face or in her tone.

"Come now, Flavia! Out with it! I know thou dost not..." he began and then suddenly fell silent, his gaze shifting from his aunt to the steward, who had entered the tablinum. "What is it, steward?"

"Forgive the interruption, Domine...Domina," said he, respectfully acknowledging each patrician. "Quintus Atilius hath arrived and desires to speak with thee, Domine. He says the Prefect hath sent him."

"Then by all means, show him in."

"Yes, Domine," answered the steward, bowing deeply as he backed out of the tablinum.

"What a pity, dear Flavia, that I must curtail our conversation. It was just beginning to become interesting," remarked Cassius, rising from his chair.

"So it was," responded Flavia, thankful for the steward's timing. Relieved, she fled the tablinum, realizing she had narrowly escaped her nephew's inquisition. He had fully intended to press her for the truth, though why, she did not know.

Quintus Atilius entered the tablinum on the heels of Flavia's exit, followed by Anatole, who bore Tiberius' sword in hand.

"Greetings, Cassius. I bear a message from the Prefect," said the centurion, withdrawing a scroll from his leather cuirass and handing it to Cassius, who broke the seal and read it.

"The Prefect informs me that Tiberius Marcius' assailants are dead… there were three…and his sword was recovered in their possession. He goes on to state that he wishes Tiberius a swift recovery," sneered Cassius, rolling the scroll up and tossing it on the desk. "It seems the Prefect takes us for fools, Quintus Atilius."

"I concur, Cassius. He spoke to me as if he were truly concerned for the well being of Tiberius Marcius. Yet, I know differently."

"Is the sword that of Tiberius?" questioned Cassius, eyeing the servant in whose hands the weapon laid, concealed in linen.

"It is," answered Quintus Atilius.

Cassius stepped out from behind the desk and the servant came forward, relinquishing the sword to Cassius, who stripped away the covering exposing the bloodied weapon.

Silence fell over the room, each man's eyes fastened on the soiled weapon, each harboring his own dark thoughts of revenge.

"Take it and clean it," directed Cassius, giving the sword back to Anatole. "And when thou hast done so, return the weapon to its rightful place among Tiberius' military gear. When he awakens, he will surely take up his sword again. I want it standing ready. Understood?"

"Understood, Domine," replied the servant.

"After thou hast done this…thou may take two days for thyself, doing whatever pleaseth thee. When Tiberius Marcius awakes, he shall decide how better to reward thee for thy faithfulness. In the meantime, I grant thee liberty for two days. Thou art dismissed."

"I thank thee, Domine," said Anatole, who was sorely in need of rest. He had not slept soundly since the attack on his master, fearing the Prefect would murder him while he slumbered.

"Some wine, Quintus Atilius?" offered Cassius, upon the servant's departure.

"One cup to quench my thirst and then I must return to camp. I am certain the Prefect awaits me."

Pouring the crimson fluid into a fine silver goblet, Cassius handed it to the centurion. "Art thou in danger from the Prefect?"

"I suspect I am," answered the centurion, raising the goblet to his lips and drinking deeply.

"Then thou best sleep with one eye open and thy back against the wall," warned Cassius. "If Sejanus discovers it was thee who bore Tiberius to safety, he will no doubt exact revenge."

"I warned Tiberius' servant of the same and judging by the looks of him, he heeded my warning. As for me, I am prepared for just such an attack. I only fear it will not be Sejanus who comes after me, but one of his minions. I would much rather kill the Prefect. It would be more satisfying," confessed Quintus Atilius, finishing his draught.

"More wine, soldier?"

"No. I hath had my fill and must be on my way, but before I depart, I would like to know the condition of Tiberius Marcius. The Prefect shall expect a report from me and I myself desire to know. I was certain Tiberius was as good as dead when last I saw him and I knew no different until the Prefect informed me otherwise. Tell me, how did he come by that information?"

"Clients, Quintus Atilius! Clients! I and Lucius Servilius intentionally spread the word through our clients in order to draw out the assailants. As planned, the news reached the Prefect, who promptly put an end to the assailant's worthless lives, thereby saving us the trouble. That only leaves us with Sejanus to deal with and deal with him we shall...all in good time. Thou may inform that venomous snake that Tiberius Marcius lies in a deep sleep and it is not known whether he shall awaken. But to thee, I say...take heart. Thy friend shall recover. It was foretold by a seer that an attempt on Tiberius' life would be made, but he would not die. Since the gods hath seen fit to preserve his life thus far, I am now inclined to believe the seer knew whereof he spoke."

"This is welcomed news which shall not reach the Prefect's ears!" declared the centurion, genuinely pleased. "I bid thee good day, Cassius."

"May the gods go with thee, Quintus Atilius. I trust thou shall keep thy sword at thy ready."

"Rest assured, I shall," said the soldier, patting the hilt of his weapon. And turning about, he exited the room.

XVI

Awaking, his vision blurred, Tiberius Marcius fastened his eyes on the hazy figure that hovered near. Unaware she was being observed; Tamar removed the bandage from Tiberius' side and gingerly attended his wound with a damp cloth. She had just finished her task when her patient reached out and laid his hand upon her arm. Taken by surprise, her eyes flew to the face of her master.

"Domine, thou hath awakened!"

"I thirst," he said weakly to the now clear image.

"I shall fetch thee a draught," said Tamar, casting aside her cloth and darting from the bed chamber into the study.

Hastening to the table where the wine sat, she took possession of the flagon and one goblet. Having what she sought, she turned about to leave, but stopped dead in her tracks when she saw Cassius sitting behind the desk, staring at her, his brow lifted in consternation.

Abandoning his seat of power, Cassius came across the room, grabbed the flagon and goblet away from Tamar and set them down on the table. "Woman, if thou thirst…water only may thou hath," he said sharply.

"Not I…but my lord doth thirst," Tamar responded, unnerved by the patrician.

"Thy lord! Why didst thou not say so, woman?" barked Cassius impatiently, snatching the flagon and goblet off the table and rushing into the bed chamber.

Entering the room ahead of Tamar, Cassius approached Tiberius' couch. Finding his cousin awake and alert, he quickly poured some wine into the goblet and leaning down; he raised Tiberius' head and placed the cup to his lips.

"Drink thy fill, Tiberius Marcius," said he, conscious of his cousin's weak physical condition. "The wine is sweet and potent. It shall renew thy strength."

Tamar stood on the other side of the couch, watching, relief flooding her as Tiberius drained the goblet of its contents. Her master would not die. God had answered her prayer and spared his life. Jehovah had shown mercy to a Roman who knew Him not.

"Assist me, Cassius. I desire to leave my couch," said Tiberius, anxious to know the measure of his strength.

"Dost thou think it wise? Thy wounds are not yet healed. Rest thyself a day or two more and then rise from thy couch," advised Cassius, worried Tiberius would further injure his side.

Tiberius' countenance darkened. "Cassius, question not my judgment! Assist me this instant!"

"Domine, I beseech thee to heed the words of thy kinsman," said Tamar, voicing concern. "Thy wound is severe and doth require time to heal. Thy flesh hath only just begun to mend itself. Thou art still in danger of losing more blood!"

Perturbed by the maid's outspokenness, Cassius could not decide whether or not he approved of it. That would depend entirely on Tiberius.

Determined to leave his bed, Tiberius tried another approach, this time, striking at his cousin's ego. "Cassius, doth a woman now speak for thee?"

His ego sufficiently stung, a heat of temper rose within Cassius and he threw Tamar a menacing look, which was not lost on her or Tiberius. "No woman speaks for me, Tiberius Marcius, least of all this Jewish bondswoman," he retorted, his tone rife with contempt.

"I thought not," replied Tiberius, achieving his purpose. "Now, lend me thy assistance, Cassius."

Powerless to stop Tiberius from leaving his couch or Cassius from aiding him, Tamar could do nothing but stand and watch the two Romans do what ought not be done. Why, she asked herself, had she even bothered to speak? Her words had only served to draw the displeasure of both men, neither of whom found her opinion of any merit. Hurt by Tiberius' remark and Cassius' subsequent response, Tamar felt utterly worthless and insignificant.

Enlisting his cousin's assistance, Tiberius sat upright on the edge of his couch, groaning as he rose up from his prone position. Drawing a ragged breath, he put his uninjured arm across Cassius' broad shoulders and pulled himself to his feet relying heavily on his cousin's strength. Supporting the weight of Tiberius' unsteady frame, Cassius slowly guided him out of the bed chamber and into the study.

"To the window," directed Tiberius, desiring some fresh air.

Blinking back tears of exhaustion as well as frustration, Tamar turned her attention to the couch, stripping and changing it of its linens. While she labored, disquieting thoughts assailed her weary mind. The Roman culture did not hold women in high esteem and her own culture was little better in comparison. Yet, she refused to believe as a woman, she was somehow less valuable than a man. Inwardly, she rejected the low status accorded women, though outwardly, she yielded to the male dominated hierarchy. She submitted herself to their authority. She obeyed their commands. She endured their harshness. Why then, had she taken her master's words to heart? She should have understood her place, his right to disregard her, but try as she did, she could not expel Tiberius' barbed comment from her mind or the notion that she was deserving of better treatment. Brushing aside her tears, she gathered the soiled linens in her arms and left the bed chamber.

Passing the two men in the study, Tamar averted her gaze from them, lest they should catch a glimpse of her tear streaked face, but her attempt at hiding her countenance was in vain. Tiberius was acutely aware of her distress.

"Shall I order the cook to prepare food for thee?" asked Cassius, upholding Tiberius, who was in obvious pain, but made no complaint.

"Do not trouble thyself," answered Tiberius, gazing out the open window into the colonnaded garden. "The maid will see to it…as she hath seen to all my needs. I hath awakened to find myself bathed and clean shaven and lying upon my couch as comfortably as if I suffered not. The maid hath cared for me well, Cassius. I hath no reason to doubt she will provide…the necessary…sus…tenance," he faltered, suddenly overcome by a sharp stab of pain.

"I think thou shouldest return to thy couch, Tiberius Marcius," urged Cassius, sustaining him as he doubled over.

"It appears I must, Cassius," Tiberius said, laying his hand against his side. "I am bleeding."

Tamar returned to the bed chamber to find Cassius tending to Tiberius' wound. Seeing blood trickling from her master's side and his anguished expression, she rushed to the couch where he sat, seized a cloth and inserted herself between the two men. Relieved the maid had returned, Cassius retreated, though he would have liked nothing better than to shove her aside, so intense was his dislike of her, but reason prevailed. The maid knew how to care for Tiberius and Cassius felt it was best left in her hands until the physician could be summoned. Standing off to the side, he watched as Tamar placed the cloth on Tiberius' wound and applied pressure to the injury. When she had stemmed the flow of blood, she covered the wound with a fresh bandage. Then, laying her hand against his chest, Tamar silently directed Tiberius to lie back on his couch, which he did with her and Cassius' assistance.

"Tiberius Marcius, the physician should be summoned at once," stated Cassius soberly. "Thou art in need of his services."

"No, Cassius. The maid hath done well by me," replied Tiberius, speaking more for his servant's benefit than his cousin's.

"She is no physician," argued Cassius. "I strongly advise thee to reconsider."

"Cassius, what more could the physician do that the maid hath not already done? I need only to rest…now leave me."

Frowning, Cassius departed.

Alone with Tamar, Tiberius looked at her and said, "Sit thee beside me, woman. I hath somewhat to say to thee."

Obeying, Tamar sat down on the edge of his couch, clasping her small hands in her lap.

"Woman, I hath offended thee, hath I not?" he asked, studying her with interest.

Astonished at his perceptiveness, she lowered her gaze, his discerning eyes causing her discomfort.

"So, I hath offended thee," he answered for her, understanding her silence. "I thought as much. Woman, I took no pleasure in it. What I said, I said merely to enlist Cassius' assistance…to achieve my end."

Struck by his sincerity, Tamar lifted her gaze and beheld her master's face. Had she misjudged him? Had her emotions clouded her perception of him? Had her ears deceived her? Was he, a man of noble birth apologizing to her, a woman of low birth?

"Wilt thou admit I offended thee?" he questioned, his eyes intently searching hers.

"Domine, I ought not to hath taken offense. I am thy humble bondservant. It is thy right to speak unto me as thou wilt," she answered prudently, knowing her master's apology in no way implied equality between them.

"Well said, my faithful servant," voiced Tiberius and then suddenly groaned as an agonizing pain shot down his left side.

"Domine, thou need not suffer so! The physician hath supplied medication to ease thy discomfort! Dost thou desire it?" she asked anxiously, rising from the couch, her gaze fixed on Tiberius.

"Wine…give me wine," he moaned, his aspect contorted with pain.

Hastily emptying the remainder of the flagon's contents into the goblet,

Tamar leaned over Tiberius, gently lifted his head up and put the cup to his lips.

Consuming the last of the wine, Tiberius fell back on his pillow, his pain only slightly abated. "Woman, I shall require more wine."

As if on cue, his mother entered the chamber, followed by Talia, who carried a large tray of enticing food and drink. Informed by Tamar that Tiberius had awakened, Flavia had ordered the kitchen to prepare a fine meal, a meal which she personally intended to see that her son ate. If he was to fully recover, he needed to regain his strength and Flavia was determined to see that he did.

Hearing her son's request, she said, "Tiberius Marcius, I hath brought thee plenty of wine and food. Thou shall hath thy fill of both."

Clearing a space for Talia to place the tray, Tamar removed the bandage cloths and the basin of crimson water from the bedside table.

"Tamar, go and refresh thyself and return after a time of rest," directed Flavia, granting the maidservant a much deserved break from her duty. "I and Talia shall tend to Tiberius Marcius in thy absence."

"I shall do as thou hast said, Domina," replied Tamar, departing with the basin in hand.

Encountering Cassius in the study, Tamar was abruptly ushered to the corner of the room furthest from the bed chamber door. There, Cassius detained her, refusing her passage from the tablinum. Finding herself at his mercy, her arms weary with the load she bore, Tamar braced herself for his wrath.

"Woman, what manner of spell hast thou cast over Tiberius Marcius?" he growled, his dark orbs as piercing as sharp daggers.

"I hath cast no spell, Domine," said she, wide eyed with fear.

"I say thou hath…when he refuses the esteemed services of a physician and prefers instead…the likes of thee!" contended Cassius, his voice eerily low, mindful of the occupants in the adjoining room.

"I assure thee, Domine, I too desire that my lord should be seen by a physician! I do not wish him to rely solely on my humble ability!"

"If that be true…then convince him to summon the physician! Do so before the day is out! I warn thee…if he should die, I shall put thee to death… a slow excruciating death from which there shall be no escape!" threatened Cassius, backing her against the wall, his eyes flashing dangerously.

Frightened out of her wits, Tamar dropped the basin, shattering it, the fragments and bloody water splattering Cassius, herself and the floor.

Infuriated, his toga spotted with blood, Cassius seized Tamar by the arm, painfully squeezing her flesh in his strong hand. "Clean it up, woman," he snarled through clenched teeth, violently throwing her to the ground. "I do not want to find one drop of blood or one piece of the broken bowl left anywhere in this room!" Turning on his heels, Cassius stormed out of the study, leaving in his wake, a terrified servant.

Thinking she had heard something in the next room, Flavia glanced at the door and listened, but only the voices of those in the bed chamber met her ears. Dismissing the thought, she focused her attention back on her son.

"Mater, I desire more wine."

Obliging her son's request, Flavia filled his cup to the brim with fresh wine and served it to her offspring, an affectionate smile resting on her lips.

After cleaning the tablinum floor and changing her garment, Tamar returned to Tiberius' chamber, looking noticeably less rejuvenated than when she left. Upon Tamar's entrance, Flavia rose from her chair, leaving the bedside of her son, who was sleeping soundly and approached the servant.

"Art thou ill? Thou dost look pale," remarked Flavia, noting the maid-servant's pallor. "What hath befallen thee?"

"Domina, I dare not say," answered Tamar shakily.

"And why not?" inquired Flavia gently, feeling concern for the servant who had cared so diligently for her precious son.

"Please, Domina...spare me thy questions," pleaded Tamar, losing control of her emotions and bursting into tears.

"Tamar, I command thee to tell me what hath upset thee."

"Cassius..." she cried softly, burying her lovely face in her hands. "He hath laid upon me an impossible burden."

"Maid, heed my words," said Flavia, lowering her voice and casting a backward glance over her shoulder, making certain Tiberius still slept. "Whatever he hast commanded thee to do...thou must not disobey. Thou must do exactly what he requires of thee. He is not a man of patience. He tolerates nothing short of absolute obedience, especially from servants. Do not make the mistake of thinking thou canst reason with him. A woman is no man's equal, least of all...one of inferior birth. Tell me, what doth he require of thee?"

Pulling herself together, Tamar lifted her face and answered, "He requires I convince thy son to summon the physician...threatening that should he die...I too shall die! I do not want to die, Domina!"

"Then thou must do as he says," stated Flavia solemnly.

"But Domina, what if I cannot? Thy son hath refused the physician, declaring I hath done for him what the physician would hath! How shall I convince him otherwise when Cassius cannot?"

The Roman matron laid her slender hand against her throat and thought for a moment, a plan quickly formulating in her mind. Having a solution to the maid's dilemma, she took Tamar aside, saying, "Leave my son to me. Return to thy chamber and there remain, feigning illness…which should not be too difficult seeing thou art so pale and shaken. I shall inform Cassius thou hast fallen ill and request the physician be summoned. He shall not refuse my request for he desires the physician's presence in this house. Fear not, the physician shall attend to my son…either by my will or Cassius'. Now, go and do as I hath told thee."

"Domina, thou art merciful," exclaimed Tamar, kissing her mistress' hand in gratitude.

"Return to thy chamber," Flavia instructed. "And do whatever is necessary to maintain thy pale aspect."

Departing, Tamar made her way back to her cubicle to await the physician and Flavia sought out Cassius.

Tiberius awoke to find his mother sitting in a chair beside his bed, her beautiful face, serene.

"Son, what might I do for thee?" she inquired, rising and taking his hand in hers. "Tell me and it shall be done."

"Mater, hast thou been long at my side?"

"I hath been here nearly three hours, my son."

"Where is the maid, Tamar?" he asked, not seeing her. "Hath she not returned?"

"She hath taken ill. I sent her to her chamber to rest. I fear she hath exhausted herself seeing to thy care. For her sake, I besought Cassius to send for the physician and he granted my request. We do presently await word from the physician concerning her. I fear he shall confine the maid to her bed, thus leaving thee unattended."

"See to it that she receives the proper care and rest," stated Tiberius, regretting he was the cause of Tamar's illness. "Burden her no more, but send in her stead, Talia."

"Tiberius Marcius, Talia is an old woman. She doth not hath the stamina required to care for thee, neither doth she hath the knowledge," said his mother reasonably.

"Talia hath cared for me since the day I was born. She hath seen me thru childhood and into manhood. How canst thou say, she hast not the knowledge? She is capable of caring for me as well if not better than any servant under my roof, save perhaps, Tamar."

"But she is of advanced age…"

"Her age hast no bearing on her service," said her son stubbornly.

"Tiberius Marcius, I shall not thwart thy will. If thou desireth Talia to care for thee, then so be it. But as thy mother, I ask that the physician be permitted to examine thee."

"I see no reason to trouble the physician further. I need only to rest and my strength shall return."

"Son, wilt thou not grant thy mother this one petition? I desire to be assured of thy health by one who is skilled in such matters."

"Very well, Mater, if it pleases thee…I shall see the physician," he yielded wearily, closing his eyes.

Pleased with herself, Flavia left the room and summoned the steward, instructing him to escort the physician to Tiberius' chamber. Her objective nearly accomplished, she returned to Tiberius' bedside and resumed her vigil, secure in the knowledge that her son would receive the best of care from both the physician and the maidservant, whose life he had unknowingly saved.

XVII

Early the next morning, Flavius set out to visit his sister, Flavia and her family. He had heard the account of his nephew's brush with death from his wife upon his return to Rome, she having heard it from their son, Cassius. And Flavius was to hear it again and again. It seemed all of Rome was talking about his nephew. Even the hallowed halls of the Senate were a buzz. Strangers, clients and fellow senators alike informed him of Tiberius' misfortune. Each man offered his opinion as to what had happened and by day's end, Flavius could not discern fact from fiction, so numerous were the accounts.

Home from battle but two days, Flavius barely had time to digest the news of his nephew, much less, recover from military service. Having hankered after a spell of army life, he had volunteered for a campaign which had lasted eight grueling months. His senatorial status had entitled him to serve as a legate to the general, a most prestigious post as he was answerable only to the general himself. Though an elder statesman, Flavius was not content to merely make speeches on the Senate floor. He loved soldiering and frequently embarked on campaigns of his own choosing. Serving in Rome's formidable army was as much a part of his life as was the Senate. As campaigns went, this one had not only been successful, but lucrative. Decimating the enemy, the army had taken spoils of gold, silver and precious stones. They had enslaved every man, woman and child left alive of the barbarian tribes that had dared to threaten fledgling Roman provinces. Their loss of wealth and liberty was Rome's gain. Rome's treasury was handsomely increased, her provinces saved from destruction and her defenders generously rewarded for their victory.

Battle weary, Flavius returned to Rome. The years were taking their toll on his body, though he would not admit it to himself or anyone else. He had anticipated making a smooth, quiet transition back into civilian life, but it was not to be. Instead, he found himself faced with another enemy. Feeling it his moral obligation to find out who was responsible for the attempt on his nephew's life and destroy the yet unknown adversary, he vowed to Mars, the god of war and bloodshed that he would see justice done.

His Palatine home just a short distance from his sister's, Flavius strolled down the familiar cobbled street, contemplating all he had heard concerning his nephew. Reaching his destination, he knocked on the door, his callused hand sounding his unexpected arrival.

The great door was opened by the servant in attendance, who bowed respectfully and welcomed the esteemed visitor inside.

"Inform Flavia that her brother wishes to see her," said Flavius, his imposing physique draped in Senate garb.

The slave left to do his bidding, leaving Flavius standing in the sunny atrium, his eyes settling upon a magnificent rendering of Alexander the Great painted on the atrium wall. Whenever he visited, the senator took time to admire the painting which depicted a young, brave soldier sitting upon a majestic black steed, his sword raised triumphantly in battle, his enemies slain at his feet. There was something about this particular rendition of Alexander the Great, King of Macedonia that struck Flavius, but he could never quite put his finger on it. Was it the young warrior's fiery eyes, so dark and determined? Was it his victorious pose or was it the man himself? Whatever the appeal, the painting continued to captivate Flavius, time and time again.

Flavia entered the atrium and seeing her brother, smiled warmly and said, "Flavius wilt thou never cease to admire Alexander the Great?"

Hearing her, Flavius turned from the painting and beheld his sister, still as lovely as he could ever remember. "My dear Flavia, Venus hath favored thee with lasting beauty," said he, approaching her and kissing her affectionately upon her forehead.

"Flattery from the lips of my brother," said his sister, still smiling.

"I...Flavius, flatter thee? Thou knowest better. I say only what I mean, my dear sister. Now tell me, Flavia, what is this I hear of thy son?" he inquired, looking down into his sister's face, his visage somber.

"Of details, I know little," answered Flavia, her smile fading as she met her brother's gaze. "I only know what my eyes hath seen. My son journeyed into the realm of the dead and remained there the space of three days before returning to the living. He is weak and suffers much pain. His left side was severely injured and I greatly fear; he may never fully recover."

"Flavia, if Tiberius Marcius can muster the strength to return from the land of the dead, he can surely overcome physical adversity. I trust the gods shall strengthen and restore him," said Flavius, taking his sister's hand and patting it reassuringly. "Where is thy son? I wish to speak with him."

"He is in the garden with Cassius."

"Hath my son served thee well, Flavia?"

"He hast."

"I could not hath asked the gods for a better son than he."

"Truly, he is like his father," remarked Flavia, looking thoughtful.

"So he is…" agreed Flavius, swelling with pride. He loved his son more than anyone or anything. His birth was the only joy that had come out of his loveless marriage. There had been no more children born, partly because his wife had shown little interest in their son and partly because Flavius had shown little interest in his wife. He simply could not bring himself to love a woman who could not love her child.

"How is thy wife?" Flavia inquired politely. "I hath not seen Calpurnia in months. Is she well?"

His expression souring, Flavius replied flatly, "Calpurnia is well and sends her regards."

Regretting she had asked about Calpurnia, Flavia dropped the subject, having noted the change in her brother's countenance and tone. "Flavius, thou need not tarry here with me. Go to the garden. Thy son and thy nephew shall welcome the sight of thee."

"Why are not all women like thee, Flavia?" he sighed wistfully, before taking his leave.

Sensing that something was amiss between Calpurnia and her brother, Flavia turned and watched him disappear down the long atrium hall. She had not suspected his marriage to Calpurnia was anything but happy for he had never given any indication he was not pleased with his wife. Over the years there had been rumors to the contrary, but Flavia had not taken them seriously. She had heard it said in whispered tones that her brother had an eye for women. Was it true, after all? Had he turned to other women for pleasure? Had he a mistress or two? As a Roman woman, Flavia accepted the fact that a great many men indulged in pleasure outside of marriage, particularly when on campaign, yet it distressed her to think her brother was among the ranks of men that did so. It was not the women that bothered her, but knowing her brother was unhappily married. That, she found hard to take. Pitying him, Flavia left the atrium for her sitting room, her heart a little heavier.

Flavius entered the garden and found Cassius and Tiberius, sitting on a white marble bench, heatedly discussing some point of dissension. He went unnoticed as he approached the two young Romans.

"My son…my nephew…why art thou at each other's throats? Thou ought not bicker among thyselves," admonished Flavius, taking them by surprise. "We must unite to fight our common enemy!"

Genuinely pleased to see his father, Cassius rose from the bench and embraced him. "Pater, it is good to look upon thee again," greeted Cassius, electing to ignore the scolding. "I trust thou hast greatly profited from thy latest campaign."

"Son, it is most presumptuous of thee to think I can be side stepped," said Flavius, withdrawing from the embrace and eyeing his son sternly. "I meant what I said to thee and Tiberius Marcius. And to that end, I shall repeat myself. It is unwise to waste thy energy fighting one another when thou hast a common enemy."

"Pater, I meant thee no disrespect," Cassius said apologetically.

Tiberius made an effort to rise, but Flavius reached out and laid his hand upon his nephew's shoulder. "Do not trouble thyself, Tiberius Marcius. Save thy strength for thou shalt need it to overcome thy adversary."

"Then, thou hast heard?" inquired Tiberius of his uncle, regarding him with respect.

"I hath indeed heard as the account hast spread throughout the whole of Rome. Trouble is; I can barely discern the truth from fabrication. Tell me, what really happened?"

"Uncle, there is not much to tell. I was given an assignment by Sejanus…the details of which matter not as it was no assignment, but a trap. The Prefect set me up. I was ambushed by three men. I would likely be dead if it had not been for my servant Anatole, who unbeknown to me followed me to the ill fated destination. When I did not not reappear in due time, he grew concerned and searched me out, finding me nearly unconscious and bleeding profusely from my wounds."

"Didst thou recognize the men that attacked thee?"

"No, I knew them not. Neither were they seen by anyone, but me. My servant saw nothing."

"Dost thou think the three assailants were the same men found dead in Subura?"

"I am fairly certain they were for Sejanus is not the sort of man who tolerates failure, nor doth he leave behind a trail. I am convinced he had them murdered to silence them."

"I and Quintus Atilius are of the same opinion," interjected Cassius. "Sejanus made a point of informing us the assailants had been found and executed. He would not hath informed us if he had not already silenced his hired assassins."

"Then we hath only Sejanus to deal with," Flavius stated soberly. "Doing so will be difficult as he is the Prefect of the Praetorian Guard. We must be careful not to incur the wrath of Caesar for any action we take against the Prefect might adversely affect the security of Rome. I warn ye, should this occur, Caesar will not look kindly upon us," said Flavius, glancing at his son.

"Pater, Quintus Atilius hath sworn revenge as hath I and Lucius Servilius! Surely, thou art not suggesting we are powerless to act against Sejanus, merely because of his position as Prefect," said Cassius, stunned.

"We are not powerless, my son, but we shall be under intense scrutiny. Caesar seems for the moment to favor Sejanus and we cannot afford to risk the Emperor's wrath by acting rashly. We would be wise to bide our time and wait for an opportunity to present itself...preferably one not of our own making."

"But that could take years!" exclaimed Cassius impatiently, his face reddening. "Sejanus deserves to die now!"

"Cassius, I more than any man hath reason to want Sejanus dead, but we must bide our time, lest we be the ones who end up dead," warned Tiberius.

"Tiberius Marcius, thou hast yet to say why thou art counted as an enemy of Sejanus. What was the cause of this enmity?" asked Flavius.

"A woman," blurted out Cassius, not giving Tiberius a chance to answer. "A woman of Subura, no less."

"Is this so, Tiberius Marcius?" questioned Flavius, astounded by the revelation. "A woman is the cause of all this trouble!"

"Not entirely," Tiberius answered tersely, shooting Cassius a reproving look.

"I see," said Flavius, smiling, clearly amused. "I take it this woman is worth the pain and suffering thou hast endured."

Comprehending his uncle's insinuation, Tiberius replied testily, "It is not as thou thinkest. She serves Priscilla."

"Tiberius Marcius, I find thy answers rather evasive! Enough of this! I want to know who this woman is and exactly how she fits into the circumstances in which thou hast found thyself!"

"She is a common woman of Subura on whom I took pity," retorted Tiberius, reluctant to elaborate.

"Tiberius Marcius...thou art beginning to weary me!"

Realizing his uncle's patience was wearing thin and knowing Cassius would undoubtedly give his version if he did not speak for himself, Tiberius decided to tell his uncle what he wanted to know. "It all started when Drusus, son of Caesar, laid eyes upon a young woman of Subura…"

"Continue…I am listening."

"Desiring the maid, Drusus sent Sejanus to retrieve her. She was forcibly brought to the palace and her brother was imprisoned to insure her cooperation. Somehow, the brother managed to escape and rescue her and together they fled the palace guards. Sejanus was again sent after the woman and ordered to execute the brother when he caught up with them, which he did. But Drusus apparently did not trust Sejanus to return the woman to him unharmed and I was assigned the task of seeing to her safe return. I arrived on the scene after the woman's brother had been executed. Following Drusus' orders, I took custody of the woman and escorted her back to the palace, thus appearing to my commander to be usurping his authority. For this reason, I am numbered among the enemies of the Prefect."

"Most fascinating…" remarked his uncle, his brow furrowed. "But thou still hast not said how this woman became thy property."

"I secured her by pledge from Drusus."

"Ye gods! This grows ever more complicated," declared Flavius, visibly troubled. "Tiberius Marcius, I would venture to say thou hast made an enemy of Caesar's son as well. I take it he did not give this woman to thee willingly."

"He did not. Caesar himself gave the woman unto me."

"Tiberius Marcius, I must put one more question to thee and I require thee to answer truthfully. Hast thou taken this woman unto thyself and known her pleasures?"

"I hath not," replied Tiberius dryly, no flicker of emotion on his face.

"Then, I do advise thee to return the woman immediately. Since thou hast not enjoyed her pleasures and she remains untouched by thee, her return would no doubt be welcomed. Deliver her to Drusus by the hand of Sejanus and thou shall end the enmity between thee and Caesar's son. As for Sejanus, he shall likely be caught off guard by thy action and though he shall continue to pose a threat to thee, he shall no longer hath a legitimate motive for murder. Though practically speaking, I do not think he needs one from what one hears of him. Even so, it is worth a try. With any luck, Sejanus will be pacified and will not seek further revenge against thee."

While his father spoke, Cassius scanned his cousin's rigid aspect for clues as to what he was thinking. Tiberius Marcius was a difficult man to read, but that did not hinder Cassius from trying. He hoped Tiberius would take his father's advice and relinquish the maid to Drusus, though he rather doubted it. Cassius was convinced things would not improve for his cousin as long as the maid remained in his possession. From the moment she had entered Tiberius' life, it seemed as if fortune had abandoned him. Cassius could think of no better solution than ridding his cousin of the accursed maid. To that end, he was determined to work. "I concur with my father, Tiberius Marcius," said he, when Flavius had finished speaking. "Return the maid to Drusus. She is not worth thy life."

Tiberius rose from the bench of his own accord, though weak, he managed to stand, aided by a hard wood cane. "I shall not return her to Drusus or Sejanus," he announced stubbornly, his facial expression darkening. "I will deal with them as I must…with or without thy support."

"Be reasonable, Tiberius Marcius," urged Flavius, perplexed by his nephew's obtuseness. "Rome is full of women…find thyself another. What is one woman in the light of so many?"

"It is because of this woman…that I live. For three days and three nights, she cared for me, rendering every service necessary to my well being and comfort as I laid lifeless upon my couch. I should hath died, but I did not and I am persuaded it was due to the constant care she bestowed upon me. Can I reward her faithfulness by delivering her to men who mean her harm? Do I not owe her my life?"

"Nonsense," snapped Cassius. "Thou owest thy life to Quintus Atlius and thy servant, Anatole! This woman did no more than was her duty as thy servant!"

"I do not wish to discuss the point further, Cassius," stated Tiberius in a tone which brooked no argument. "I hath made up my mind concerning the maid and I shall not be moved." Turning to Flavius, Tiberius said, "I thank thee for thy advice and now if thou wilt excuse me, I feel the need for rest."

"By all means rest thyself, Tiberius Marcius, but think on what I hath said. It is for thy own good that I speak," said his uncle, patting him on the back with affection.

Departing, Tiberius made his way through the garden, his steps slow and deliberate, every movement causing him immeasurable pain which he silently endured. A male servant saw his slow gaited progress and ran forward to assist him.

Waiting until Tiberius was out of hearing distance, Flavius turned to his son and said, "Cassius, I take it thou hath seen this woman."

"I hath," answered Cassius, sitting down on the cool marble bench.

"What dost thou think of her?" inquired his father, joining his son on the bench.

"I find nothing redeeming in her aside from beauty. She is low born."

"When a woman is attractive, her status matters not."

"Pater, surely thou art not in favor of such unions?"

"For the mere sake of pleasure…yes. However, I do not favor patricians marrying below their station in life. It dilutes the noble bloodline, endangering the very foundation of Rome. Tell me, Cassius, doth Tiberius Marcius hath feelings for this woman?"

"I would say he hath grown attached to her," said Cassius, remembering his cousin's deathbed confession.

"I suspected as much as I hath never seen him quite so adamant. I must assume his intentions are honorable toward her, though I would that his intentions were solely that of pleasure. I fear it was a mistake allowing him to mourn Dinah for as long as he hast. I fault myself for this grievous oversight. I must find Tiberius Marcius a Roman woman of suitable birth and means before he takes a notion to legally join his noble body to that of his lowly maidservant. May the gods help us!"

"Pater, marriage is but half the solution. As long as the maidservant remains within the walls of this house, she shall present a problem."

"Of that, I am well aware, son. It may be we shall hath to deliver the maid to Drusus ourselves."

Unable to conceal his pleasure at the thought, Cassius smiled ear to ear. Nothing his father could have said could have pleased him more.

XVIII

The day had passed into night, the hour was late and the Prefect had been called to appear before Caesar. He was escorted through the dark streets by two tight lipped palace guards, who volunteered no information on the reason for the summons, which greatly irritated Sejanus. He did not like not knowing what lie ahead of him; neither did he appreciate the abrupt manner with which the guards delivered the message nor did he take well to being hurried to his destination. He was after all the Prefect of the Praetorian Guard, not some low ranked soldier to be ordered and herded about from pillar to post. What in the name of the gods could be so important that he must leave the comfort of his warm bed in the middle of the night, wondered Sejanus as he entered the palace gates, flanked by a guard on either side.

Inside the royal court, softly lit by lamps that lined the long walls, Caesar sat waiting in the divine seat of power, his heir seated next to him, their fit bodies cooled with large fans held by servants who were adept at moving the air about in a most comfortable fashion. The grand court was guarded by two loyal soldiers who stood inside the room, one on each side of the door and two equally loyal soldiers manned the outside of the door, all with eyes alert and weapons at the ready.

In one of his dark moods, which seemed to be occurring with more frequency, Caesar was grim faced and silent as he sat erect upon the throne. Drusus did not dare to question his father as to why he had insisted on his presence at such an hour. He knew he would soon know. Content that he occupied a place beside his father and he was to be privy to something of importance, Drusus cast a wandering eye on a pretty servant girl who was fanning him. Caesar noted his son's interest in the servant and was about to address it when the royal doors swung open wide and Sejanus was ushered inside, accompanied by the two palace guards that had been sent after him.

"We hath been awaiting thee, Prefect" said the Emperor, his tone somber, his countenance dark and foreboding.

Sejanus came forward before Caesar and his heir as was the custom and struck his breast in deference and said, "Hail Caesar," rendering the proper respect due to Rome's Emperor. "Sire, what need hath thee of me?"

Before answering the question, Caesar dismissed the guards which had escorted Sejanus, as well as the young maid who had caught his son's fancy. He wanted Drusus' full attention to be on the matter at hand, not on some foolish female and her secret pleasures.

Drusus pretended not to notice the servant girl had been dismissed, but the silent rebuke of his father was hard to ignore. Caesar had a watchful eye and it was apparent it was on him. Drusus straightened up in his chair, assuming his royal role with dignity, determined not to give his father another reason to correct him.

"Prefect, I want to know what thou knowest about the attempt on Tiberius Marcius Maximus' life," queried Caesar, regarding Sejanus closely.

"I know only that he was ambushed by three men of Subura, all of whom, I searched out and when I found the perpetrators, I had them executed," replied the Prefect evenly, hiding his displeasure with the late night interrogation.

"Dead men do not tell tales, do they, Prefect?" goaded Caesar, leaning forward in his chair, his brown eyes cold and discerning.

Drusus looked from Sejanus to Caesar. What was the meaning of his father's remark? What was he saying? Had the Prefect something to do with Tiberius Marcius' misfortune? Oh, how he loathed Sejanus. He half hoped it was true, not that he wished Tiberius Marcius any ill will, but if his misfortune could topple Sejanus from his lofty position, then so be it. If it was true, then perhaps his father would finally recognize the Prefect for what he truly was; a low down, lying, scheming, murderous snake.

Sejanus swallowed hard and collected his thoughts before answering. He had not expected Caesar or anyone else for that matter to be overly interested in the details of Tiberius Marcius' brush with death. Clearly, he had underestimated Caesar's interest in the centurion. "Tiberius' attackers confessed to having done the deed," stated Sejanus cautiously, choosing to ignore Caesar's insinuation.

"Prefect, nasty rumors are circulating round about Rome...that thou art the one behind the attack on Tiberius Marcius! I do not like hearing such rumors!"

Drusus' eyes widened and a sly smile threatened to break forth on his thin lips, but he bit his lip to prevent its emergence. It would not do to look pleased. Oh, but this was too exciting, much more satisfying than frolicking with the pretty servant girl! Watching Sejanus' feet being held to the fire was proving to be immensely pleasurable.

"Caesar, thou knowest I am not well liked. An enemy hath devised this lie to destroy me…to ruin my reputation…to damage my dignitas. Why would I try and kill one of my own centurions? What sense doth that make?" said Sejanus craftily, pleading his case. "Centurions are invaluable assets and Tiberius Marcius is as fine a centurion as I hath ever commanded."

"Prefect, Tiberius Marcius Maximus is more than a centurion. He is a patrician! His esteemed ancestors made Rome great! He is deserving of the utmost respect and honor! And what is more…he hast earned it!" thundered Caesar, unimpressed with Sejanus' lame argument. "I know not whether thou art guilty of plotting against him, but if I should find out that thou art, I shall not deal with thee kindly. I shall show thee no mercy. I shall turn my back on thee. I shall forget thou art my friend and advisor! I shall do to thee what is rumored thou hast done to others!" vowed Caesar, his eyes narrowing ominously.

The Prefect had never seen this side of Caesar before. There was something darkly complex in his intellect, a force to be reckoned with, not as easily persuaded as Sejanus had thought. He did not know Caesar as well as he had supposed and that gave him pause. "I swear to thee, Sire, I had naught to do with Tiberius Marcius' ill fate," lied Sejanus coolly, doing his best to sound sincere.

"I warn thee, Prefect, do not lay a hand upon him, his house or his servants, his family, his friends or anything that is his! Whatever he loses, whether it be by thy hand or another's, I shall require twice of thee…up to and including thy very life!" threatened Caesar angrily, his voice reverberating through the royal court.

Humbling himself, the Prefect concealed his outrage behind an empty expression and said, "I shall assign him a guard. No harm shall come to him, Caesar. I give thee my word."

"Thou shalt assign to him, his trusted friend, Quintus Atilius to be his guard and no other!" ordered the Emperor, bent on making certain Tiberius Marcius would be protected by one who revered him.

"I shall do as thou hast said," complied Sejanus, knowing he had been outfoxed.

"Thou art dismissed," said Caesar curtly and with an imperial wave of his hand, he shooed the Prefect from his royal presence.

Sejanus fled the court, fuming.

The late night exchange between his father and Sejanus had been entertaining and quite revealing in Drusus' estimation. The loss of sleep had been well worth the sacrifice. Witnessing the tongue lashing of the Prefect had been extremely gratifying to behold. Caesar had set the haughty Prefect on his ear and in an indirect way; he had done so on account of his heir. Realizing this, Drusus contemplated the marvelous revelation and its full implication. If Caesar had insured the safety of Tiberius Marcius because he had saved the life of his royal heir, then it stood to reason, the father still honored the son, despite the son's inability to measure up to his father's strict standards. Drusus knew he was not what Caesar wanted him to be, but now he understood that blood was indeed thicker than water. Up until tonight, he had not been so sure as Sejanus seemed to have more favor with his father than he. Now, he knew Caesar's loyalty was to him, not the Prefect. Regarding his father with renewed reverence, Drusus basked in the knowledge that Caesar did care for him, that he did matter to his father and because he did, the Prefect had been rebuked and Tiberius Marcius had been granted the favor and protection of Caesar.

XIX

"Rouse thyself, Domine!" exclaimed the steward, his face beaming, unable to contain his excitement as he swept back the curtain from Tiberius' couch with a grand gesture. "This day shall be a great day, a day of remembrance! Drusus, son of Caesar hath sent thee word of his coming! Arise and make ready!"

"Steward, it is not yet dawn," snapped Tiberius irritably, waking from a restless night's repose. "Why should Drusus trouble himself at this untimely hour?"

"He hath chosen to visit thee, Domine! What doth the hour matter?" asserted the steward, adjusting the bed curtains as he spoke. "Caesar's son does as he pleases...when he pleases! It is his right! Arise and make ready! A great day is at hand!"

Tiberius' countenance darkened and his eyes flashed with anger for he did not tolerate disrespect from anyone, least of all, his servants. "Mind thy tongue, steward," rebuked Tiberius sharply. "Though I lay afflicted upon my couch, do not presume I am powerless...lest I do show thee differently!"

"Domine, hath mercy," entreated the steward, swallowing hard, realizing he had overstepped himself. "Hath mercy on thy foolish servant and his foolish tongue."

"If I am to arise and make ready as thou hast said...then I shall need some assistance. Will I not? Where are they who assist me?"

Having no worthy reply, the contrite servant lowered his eyes to the floor, feeling the sting of his master's reprimand.

Tiberius stared at his servant for several moments, allowing the admonishment to fully infiltrate the steward's consciousness.

Regretting the careless manner in which he had addressed his master, the servant waited with bated breath for Tiberius to speak again, which he did, much to the relief of the steward.

"Send Anatole to my chamber that he may help me from my couch... and Tamar," commanded Tiberius, eyeing the steward. "I hath need of her. Instruct the servants to prepare for the honor of Drusus' presence. Spare nothing in my hand. Render unto Caesar's son the very best of my house...take no account of the cost. Inform my mother and sister that they may properly present themselves. Send for Cassius and Lucius Servilius! I desire they be present when Drusus arrives! Go now…make haste! There is much to be done!"

"It shall be done, Domine," replied the humbled steward, quickly departing with his orders, feeling fortunate his master had not dealt with him more severely.

Within moments of the steward's exit, Anatole appeared and helped the centurion rise from his couch and perform the necessary tasks of making oneself presentable, but when it came to caring for Tiberius' wounds, he left that task undone at the directive of his master. After completing his appointed duties, the body servant stepped outside of the cubicle and called in Tamar, who had been patiently waiting in the study to be summoned.

Carrying clean strips of cloth over one arm and a bowl of fresh water in her small delicate hands, Tamar entered the cubicle, prepared to minister to her master. She was content to serve the centurion and to do all she could to insure his full recovery. To that end, she willingly performed her duty whenever it was required of her and this day was no different.

Beholding the vision of graceful beauty, Tiberius viewed Tamar with a keen eye as he had not seen her in three days. "Come and dress my wounds, faithful servant," said he, noting the color had returned to her cheeks and she appeared well. It was clear the rest had done her good for whatever had ailed her, now ailed her no more.

Upon hearing her master speak, a faint smile emerged on Tamar's lips, but she did not meet her master's gaze, mindful of her lowly status. Placing the bowl of water on the bedside table, she set about organizing the cloths according to their length and purpose. Keeping the lengthier ones close at hand, she turned to the centurion, who was standing near the table and began to gingerly remove his soiled bandages.

Tiberius had never seen Tamar smile before. Though her smile was ever so fleeting, he was quite certain he had seen it. Why had she smiled? Was she more at ease with him? Was it her good pleasure to care for him? Observing the lovely servant girl, he considered her as she tended to his wounds, cleaning and applying fresh bandages with gentleness and quiet duty. Her reverent devotion to his physical care pleased him and he looked upon her with favor.

While Tamar attended Tiberius, Anatole busied himself in the wardrobe closet, searching for the perfect raiment in which to arraign his master. Making his selection, he exited the closet bearing in his arms a finely woven fabric of white, bordered with threads of gold. "Domine, I trust I hath chosen well. I find this garment suitable for the esteemed occasion of Drusus' visit. Dost thou agree?" inquired Anatole, extending his arms, the expensive fabric draped over them in anticipation of his master's approval.

Realizing Drusus was coming to the master's house, a low involuntary cry of distress escaped Tamar, which was heard by Tiberius as she was near to him, still dressing his wounds.

"I commend thy choice, Anatole," stated the centurion, praising his manservant, while at the same time cognizant of his troubled maidservant. "When I am bandaged, I shall dress."

"Very well, Domine. I will return with thy best sandals," replied Anatole, visibly pleased his master approved of his wardrobe selection.

Overwhelmed by the fearsome prospect of encountering Drusus again, Tamar began to tremble uncontrollably causing her capable hands to falter as she tried to bandage the centurion's wounded arm.

Halting her progress, Tiberius placed his steady hand lightly over Tamar's and looking down on the comely maid said, "Woman, be not afraid."

"Domine...surely, Drusus hath come for me! How can I not fear? He did not grant me to thee willingly and because he did not...thou hast suffered grievously on my account! My heart breaks for I know the trouble I hath caused thee," she said earnestly, her large, dark eyes meekly meeting his. "Drusus shall not rest until..."

"Be not afraid," said Tiberius again.

"Domine, if thou art willing...I beseech thee...let thy servant remain with thee."

"Be not afraid," he repeated, his gaze steady upon her.

"Domine, how can thou say unto me, "Be not afraid." I greatly fear Drusus and with good cause. I hath suffered much at his hands. Hath pity on thy servant and permit me to remain in my cubicle while he doth visit thy noble house," Tamar pleaded, not wanting to see or be seen by Drusus.

"Woman, I will not permit thee to hide thyself from Drusus. Thou must face thy fear. It is the only way thou shall gain a strong measure of courage."

"Domine, thou art a soldier...not I! Thou art brave and courageous...I am neither...I cannot face Drusus! I cannot!" she cried, her voice quivering with emotion as tears filled her eyes. "I cannot face him again!"

"Thou can...I hath faith in thee," stated Tiberius and having spoken, he withdrew his hand.

Understanding he had said all he was going to say, Tamar fell silent, brushed aside her tears and returned to bandaging his arm. She knew she could not change his mind and she did not dare try. With stifled emotion and trembling hands, she finished wrapping the centurion's arm. With that accomplished, Tamar gathered up the soiled bandages that had been discarded upon the floor. With arms full, she left Tiberius' presence, pondering his words.

Arrayed in a well draped toga, leather sandals and leaning on a cane, Tiberius emerged from the tablinum to find a flurry of servants rushing to and fro. Every servant he owned was busy preparing for the visit of Rome's royal son. It was as he expected it to be. As he stood watching, suddenly, without warning, a sharp excruciating pain struck him with such intensity that he fell back against the wall, losing his balance and his grip upon his cane, which tumbled to the floor. Several servants saw Tiberius falter and they immediately rushed to him. Talia was the first to come to his side, saying, "Domine, what would thou hath me do for thee!"

"I hath need of medicine," groaned Tiberius as a second wave of pain swept over him. "Wine…wine!"

Two male servants came swiftly to Tiberius' aid and walked him back to his bed chamber, seating him upon his couch.

Doing her master's bidding, Talia poured a cup of red wine and quickly brought it to Tiberius, who drank it and then another, after which, he sent her to find Tamar.

Tamar was laundering the bandages she had removed from Tiberius' body when Talia found her. Looking up from her work, her hands immersed in a tub of water, Tamar knew instantly by Talia's countenance that something was amiss.

"Come quick, child! The master is not well! He asks for thee!"

Concerned for her master's welfare, Tamar wasted no time. Pulling her hands out of the water tub, Tamar followed Talia, drying her wet hands on her dress as the two women hastily made their way to their master's cubicle.

Entering the room, Tamar was reminded of the night the centurion had nearly died and fearing he might yet do so, she uttered a fervent prayer to her God. She could see Tiberius was in extreme pain. His eyes had lost their brightness, his breathing was labored and the color had drained from his face. Wondering what had brought on the dreadful change, Tamar hurried to the bedside table where the medicine was kept. Laying hold of the medication, she went to her master, took the cup from his hand and gave it to

Talia, instructing her to fill it with more wine. Talia quickly refilled the goblet and handed it back to Tamar, who then carefully added the prescribed dose of poppy syrup into the crimson liquid. After stirring the contents, Tamar offered the medicated draught to Tiberius, watching as he drank it without hesitation or comment.

Tamar knew the centurion did not want to depend on medicine to battle pain; that he preferred instead to find relief in wine alone. She understood his reluctance to rely on strong medication, but she did not believe sweet wine could take the place of potent medicine. It concerned her he had taken to drinking wine in order to combat pain, but she kept her opinion to herself out of deference to her master.

Not since the night of his ambush had Tiberius succumbed to taking the medicine. He hated to use it, but now, he had no choice, the suffering was too great and time was running out. Drusus would soon arrive. He did not want the Emperor's son to see him weak and racked with pain. It was a matter of pride for he was a Roman soldier, strong and able to endure all manner of hardship. There was nothing weak or cowardly about a Roman warrior and to preserve his image, his dignitas; Tiberius swallowed the entire contents of the goblet, hoping it would quickly alleviate his pain so he could save face before Drusus.

Bearing in his hand the discarded cane he found outside the tablinum, the steward entered the bed chamber, wearing a worried expression, having heard from several servants the master had been overcome by pain. "Domine, art thou well enough to receive the Emperor's son? Shall I send word to him that thou art unable to receive him this day?"

His head bowed, Tiberius nodded in the negative, the pain unbearable, his countenance ashen and his brow heavily beaded with perspiration.

"Domine…I regret I must trouble thee at this time…seeing thou art suffering greatly. Forgive me. I bring strange news," stated the steward awkwardly, leaning the cane up against the chamber wall. "Quintus Atilius stands outside thy house. He hath been ordered by the Prefect to stand watch over thee."

Considering the information rather odd, Tiberius lifted his head and looked at the steward, who continued speaking.

"He states he is to guard thee day and night. He is not to leave thee. He hath requested to speak with thee privately. What shall I say unto him?"

"Tell him…we shall speak…later."

"Very well, Domine."

"Watch and...inform me...of Drusus' approaching," said Tiberius, finding it difficult to speak through the pain. "Depart all ye...that I may rest...till then."

At his word, the steward ushered all the servants from the room, but when Tamar tried to leave, Tiberius took hold of her arm and constrained her, saying, "Stay...with me."

"If it pleases thee, my lord," said Tamar softly, her heart wrenching inside of her for she could not bear to see him so afflicted. Looking upon his aspect, the torment sitting silent in his eyes, she was moved with compassion. Picking up a soft cloth from the bedside table, she reverently wiped her master's brow and having done so, she knelt down beside his couch, took his strong hand in hers and administered comfort and heartfelt prayers through his anguish.

Experiencing another wave of agony, Tiberius moaned, tightened his grasp on Tamar's small hand and exhaled deeply, battling the throes of pain.

Entering the tablinum unannounced, Cassius and Lucius Servilius made their way back to Tiberius' bed chamber having already been informed of his condition. Cassius was the first to enter the chamber and see Tamar kneeling beside Tiberius' couch, his sharp eye noting her hand intertwined with his cousin's. "Ye gods, what must I do to be rid of her," he mumbled to himself, despising the caretaker and her tenderness. Lucius Servilius did not view the scene before him with the same disdain. Unlike Cassius, he saw nothing disturbing about Tiberius finding solace in the maid's presence.

"Tiberius Marcius, art thou able to withstand the pain?" asked Cassius, regarding Tiberius with genuine concern. "Hath the physician been summoned?"

"Tiberius Marcius, I think thou should lie down upon thy couch," suggested Lucius Servilius, finding it uncomfortable to watch his friend suffer.

"No time...I await Drusus," grunted Tiberius, throwing his head back and closing his eyes as he endured yet another strike of misery.

Seizing the moment, Cassius reached down and took hold of Tamar's arm, discreetly applying painful pressure as he forcibly raised her to her feet. His cousin was in too much agony to notice the deed and his friend's attention was staid on Tiberius. "Leave," he commanded under his breath, his dark eyes narrowing with purpose, wanting her out of his sight and out of Tiberius' life.

Held in a painful vise, Tamar looked to Tiberius, but he was unaware of anything save his own misery. Feeling her own measure of discomfort at the hand of Cassius, Tamar fled the room upon her release, escaping the ill tempered patrician. She knew he loathed the very sight of her; that he blamed her for his cousin's misfortune, the latter of which she understood as she faulted herself too. In spite of Cassius' obvious dislike of her, Tamar submitted to his authority. She no longer tried to reason with him or defend herself as she had in times past. She simply served him to the best of her ability, enduring in silence his commands, but to her dismay, Cassius persisted in treating her harshly.

Left alone with Tiberius, the two patricians stood silent, watching helplessly as he battled his flesh.

"Domine…Domine! Drusus and his entourage are drawing near," announced the steward to the room's occupants and then departed, spreading the word throughout the whole house.

Collecting himself, Tiberius drew a ragged breath and glanced from Cassius to Lucius Servilius saying, "Assist me to my feet. I shall hath to depend …on ye to uphold me…in the presence…of Drusus. I am…unable to stand…without assistance."

"Tiberius Marcius, we are honored to assist thee," stated Lucius Servilius with sincere affection for his friend, admiring his fortitude.

"Whatever thou doth require of us, we shall do," added Cassius, ever loyal to his cousin.

The two men helped Tiberius to his feet and escorted him into the atrium, where Flavia, Priscilla and all the servants of the house stood waiting to greet Drusus, the divine heir of Caesar, Rome's future.

Entering the sunlit atrium, Tiberius Marcius surveyed all those assembled. He beheld his mother and sister with an appreciative eye for they were beautifully adorned and pleasant to look upon. His servants were clean and presentable, behaving properly. His steward was standing proudly in front of all the servants with the exception of the door servant, who was anxiously awaiting the arrival of Drusus. All appeared in order, but one servant had escaped notice. Where was Tamar? Tiberius looked again, this time more carefully, scanning the faces of his servants and then he saw her, hidden in the center of the back row, standing beside Anatole. Pleased she had not cowered to fear; Tiberius took his place as head of the house, standing in front of everyone with Cassius on his right and Lucius Servilius on his left, each man supporting him.

Having arrived at his destination, Drusus exited his sedan chair with great pomp and circumstance, surrounded on all sides by palace guards, whose sharp eyes surveyed the premises and then swiftly encompassed it. Flanked by two body guards, Caesar's son studied the domain of Tiberius Marcius with interest, finding it attractive and worthy of a patrician. Standing guard at the door, he saw a centurion and he knew it had to be none other than Quintus Atilius. Drusus smiled to himself recalling the humiliation of the Prefect the night before. Evidently, Sejanus had wasted no time in obeying Caesar, thought Drusus, laughing inwardly.

Approached by Caesar's heir, Quintus Atilius paid him homage, concealing his surprise behind a hardened professional visage.

"Art thou Quintus Atilius?" asked Drusus, regarding the centurion in front of him.

"I am he, Sire," answered the centurion, wondering how Drusus knew his name.

"Centurion, guard Tiberius Marcius with thy life for Caesar hath need of him."

"Yes, Sire."

Drusus patted Quintus Atilius on the shoulder and then looked to a palace guard, expecting him to knock on the door of the residence, which the guard did. The door swung open and four royal guards entered the house, taking up position on both sides of the entrance. Following his guards, Drusus entered the atrium finding it full of subjects who upon seeing him, bowed down in obeisance. Pleased with the grand reception, he took a moment to bask in it. Ah, it was good to be the son of Caesar, he thought as he looked out over the humbled assembly gathered before him.

"Welcome, most noble, Drusus," greeted Tiberius, managing to sound like himself in spite of persistent physical torment. "I am honored at thy visit."

"As well thou should be, Tiberius Marcius," answered Caesar's heir, full of self importance.

"Noble Drusus, I ask thy pardon. I am physically unable…to render thee the respect which thou art due," admitted Tiberius, hating to state his weakness before one so powerful.

"Tiberius Marcius, do not trouble thyself. I know thou dost honor me in all ways," replied Drusus, closely scrutinizing the centurion. Realizing Tiberius was being upheld by the two men at his side, he marveled the once strong and capable soldier was now weak and incapable of standing on his own two feet. "Tiberius Marcius, thou dost not look well. It appears thy enemy nearly had his way with thee," remarked Drusus, sobering at the sight of his faithful subject, who had barely survived the lethal determination of the Prefect.

"I am pleased to say the gods had other plans for me."

"I too am pleased," said Caesar's son, shifting his attention to the patricians at Tiberius' side, who were about to bow down when Drusus spoke again, raising his jeweled hand. "Good citizens, do not trouble thyselves on my account. Serve Tiberius Marcius and I shall be well pleased with thee."

Though they had been excused from rendering the customary deference, Lucius Servilius and Cassius respectfully lowered their heads before Drusus. It was apparent to both men that Tiberius Marcius had favor with Caesar's house and they were not about to do anything that might reflect negatively on one so greatly favored.

"Tiberius Marcius, thou hath a house filled with beauty," declared Drusus, catching sight of Flavia and Priscilla, the sunlight illuminating their jewels and their fine facial features. "Who is this lovely vision before me?" inquired Drusus, his royal eye settling upon Priscilla, who feeling his gaze, gracefully bowed before him again.

Lucius Servilius felt a twinge of jealousy as he witnessed Drusus' careful inspection of his betrothed.

"She is my sister, Priscilla," answered Tiberius Marcius, receiving the compliment. "She is betrothed to Lucius Servilius, the patrician on my left."

Drusus tore his eye from the beautiful girl and acknowledged her future husband, saying, "Fortune hath smiled upon thee, Lucius Servilius. She shall make thee a fine wife."

"Sire, I consider myself a most fortunate man," replied Lucius Servilius stiffly.

Relieved to hear his kind words, Priscilla stole a look at Lucius Servilius, but his attention was not on her, but on Caesar's son.

"Thy house is filled with beautiful women, Tiberius Marcius. I fail to see why thou did rob me of the little Jewess," remarked Drusus, his expression souring as he surveyed the occupants of the room. "Thou hast no need of her for thou hath plenty of lovely women and servants to do thy bidding."

"I could say the same of thee, Drusus," replied Tiberius Marcius lightly.

"Thou doth never cease to amaze me, my friend," said Drusus testily, turning to look at Tiberius. "Thou dost always manage a ready reply. Though I appreciate thy quick wit, I shall not be put off. Tiberius Marcius, I demand to see the maid whom thou did take from me."

Tamar's heart had been pounding in her chest from the moment Drusus entered Tiberius' house. It had required all of her strength and determination to remain in the same room with her formidable enemy. She wanted desperately to run and hide, but she stood where she was. Her master had faith in her, but it was all she could do to have faith in herself. Hearing Caesar's son refer to her, Tamar became lightheaded and was nearly on the verge of fainting, so great was her fear when she heard a voice close to her. Momentarily distracted, she heeded the voice.

"Remember the master's words," whispered Anatole, encouraging the weak kneed girl. He knew she was afraid of the Emperor's son. He had overheard the master's conversation with Tamar and though it was none of his affair, he pitied her. Unsure if she had heard him the first time, he again whispered, "Remember the master's words."

Prompted by Anatole, Tamar recalled Tiberius' words to her. "Be not afraid." Despite the advice, she was afraid...very afraid. She knew her master could not save her from Drusus, not without God's intervention. Only Almighty God could save her from Caesar's son. The centurion could do nothing to help her. No one but God alone could save her from her enemy. Taking hold of the revelation in a way she never had before, Tamar made a conscious decision to trust in God and not in man. For too long, she had looked to man to save her, now she would look solely to God. Praying for deliverance and the courage to endure what she must, she surrendered her fear to God and prepared to face Drusus.

"Where is the Jewess?"

"She stands in the last row," answered Tiberius.

"Tiberius Marcius, call forth thy servant," ordered Drusus, intent on looking upon Tamar.

"Tamar, come forth and present thyself," summoned Tiberius.

In obedience, Tamar stepped forward and made her way through the household servants, who parted, allowing her to pass among them. Servants and patricians alike watched in silence as the lowly servant girl approached the royal heir to the throne.

Cassius whispered to Tiberius Marcius, "Return her to Drusus. He yet desires her."

Tiberius made no response; his attention was steadfastly fixed on Tamar.

Reaching Drusus, Tamar bowed down humbly before him, dutifully submitting herself, determined not to provoke him to anger as she had done before. This time she yielded to his authority that she might not bring shame or violence upon herself or her master.

Drusus marveled at the change in Tamar's demeanor since last he saw her. Lifting her face, he beheld the servant girl, finding her exquisite in every way imaginable. As he feasted his hungry eyes upon her, a most peculiar sense of loss washed over him. He wanted her terribly, but knowing his friend had suffered mightily on account of her, he could not in good conscience begrudge him the beautiful young woman. She belonged to Tiberius Marcius. He had earned his right to her, thought Drusus as he turned away from the object of his desire, miraculously choosing friendship over lust.

Tamar was stunned. Drusus no longer desired her! God had delivered her from her enemy! God had not forgotten her, nor turned His face from her. A scripture from the book of Job flooded her mind, "Thou shalt be secure, because there is hope...and thou shalt take thy rest in safety." With a heart full of gratitude, Tamar offered a silent prayer of praise and thanksgiving to God for she was safe from her enemy. Free from the fear which had held her captive for so long, Tamar looked to her master whose eye was upon her and he nodded ever so slightly and she seeing; received his approval.

"Come, Drusus, let us enter the triclinium. A grand feast hath been prepared for thee," said Tiberius easily, the pain having subsided somewhat. And to his servants, Tiberius directed, "Return to thy duties."

Anatole went to Tamar, who was still on her knees, offered his hand and assisted her to her feet. "Well done, maid," said he. "Thou hast conquered thy fear."

Talia drew near and looked upon her son, marking his interest in Tamar.

"God hath delivered me," declared Tamar, tears of joy shimmering in her gentle eyes.

"Which god hath delivered thee?" asked Talia. "There are many gods, child."

"There is but one God!" proclaimed Tamar with such conviction that it startled Anatole and Talia, who being Greek believed in a myriad of gods.

And having spoken, Tamar left their company and disappeared into the dispersing crowd of servants, offering up praise to her God, the God of Abraham, Isaac and Jacob.

Seated in the dining room, the Emperor's son and the patricians were waited upon hand and foot with special attention given to Caesar's heir. The men were served warm breakfast pastries, an assortment of melons and cheese, eggs, meat and sweet wine. Pleased his guests were hungrily partaking of the food set before them, Tiberius began the conversation.

"Tell me, Drusus, why hast thou so honored me with thy visit?"

"Friend, I bear good news from the lips of Caesar concerning thy enemy," smiled Drusus, his ring clad hand choosing a sweet pastry from the finely crafted silver tray in front of him.

"What enemy hath I?" quipped Tiberius, grinning.

"The one I made for thee, my friend. My ardent pursuit of the pretty little Jewess hast much to do with thy present suffering, Tiberius Marcius," said Drusus, raising the pastry to his mouth and taking a bite. "I never imagined my want of her would nearly cost thee thy life."

"Give him Tamar," whispered Cassius into Tiberius' ear.

Sipping from his cup, Tiberius ignored his cousin and regarded the Emperor's son with reverential interest, waiting on his words.

Lucius Servilius saw Cassius lean over and whisper into Tiberius' ear and he knew instinctively what he had said. It bothered him that Cassius continued to press Tiberius on the subject of the servant girl. When the opportunity presented itself, he intended to speak with Cassius concerning the matter, but now was not the time or the place.

"Answer me this, Tiberius Marcius. Hast thou broken her will? She doth not seem as spirited as I remember," remarked Drusus, studying the centurion.

"I did not find it necessary," answered Tiberius.

"Truly, thou hast a way with her, Tiberius Marcius...but, I digress. As intriguing as she is, she is not the reason for my visit. I hath come to thy house to personally relay Caesar's words. It is my hope the good news shall add health to thy bones and peace to thy sleep."

"Drusus, my friend, I thank thee for thy concern. I feared the maid had come between us...severing our bond of friendship. It pleases me to know our friendship remains strong and intact."

"Thou feared...what fear hast thou? Thou took her from my hand as though I were but a child. Fear did not hinder thee, nor did our friendship for that matter," laughed Drusus, no longer angry over the loss of the maid. "Thou hast always been fearless, my friend…perhaps…a little too fearless."

Tiberius smiled.

Cassius swallowed hard.

Lucius Servilius breathed a quiet sigh.

Drusus continued speaking, "Late last night, Caesar summoned Sejanus to the palace. I was there to witness my father's rebuke of the Prefect, which I must admit…I thoroughly enjoyed. The rumors concerning Sejanus and thy attack reached Caesar's ears. He did not like hearing such rumors and told the Prefect so, warning him that should he discover the rumors to be true, he will do to him what hath been rumored, he hath done to others. What is more, Caesar stated that should any harm come to thee or thy house, twice thy loss shall be required of him…up to and including his very life! I for one heartily approve of Caesar's decree! I should like to be rid of Sejanus…mind thee…but not at thy expense!"

"I understand," said Tiberius, appreciating the sentiment.

"My friend, thou hast the divine protection of Caesar's house. The wily Prefect will not be permitted to do thee further harm. If he harms thee…he harms himself."

"This is welcomed news, Drusus," declared Tiberius, feeling a measure of relief, but knowing Sejanus as he did, he knew the Prefect would not give up entirely.

"This is good news," agreed Lucius Servilius, realizing Sejanus would still require watching.

"Can that vicious dog be trusted to obey Caesar?" inquired Cassius, not altogether convinced Tiberius would ever truly be safe from Sejanus.

"It is difficult to know for certain," replied Drusus, matter of factly. "Sejanus is crafty. I strongly advise thee to keep a close watch on him. Go nowhere without thy guard. He was appointed by Caesar to protect thee. The Prefect is a dangerous man, a man of ambition. Even so, I do not believe he will risk losing Caesar's favor for he thrives on power and ambition. He possesses an insatiable appetite. He is so ambitious that I sometimes think…he desires the throne for himself."

The three patricians were somewhat encouraged by Drusus' visit, but they each were cautiously optimistic where it concerned Sejanus. The

Prefect would no doubt find some way to punish Tiberius Marcius, maybe not in the near future, but down the road, he would be waiting to exact his revenge. The longer he had to wait, the more deadly his strike would be and no one knew that better than Tiberius Marcius.

XX

After Drusus' departure, Lucius Servilius and Cassius helped Tiberius to his bed chamber, encouraging him to rest for the remainder of the day.

"Tiberius Marcius, I strongly advise thee to remain in bed and allow thy body time to heal," said Lucius Servilius, voicing his concern as he and Cassius assisted Tiberius onto his couch. "Thy flesh hath not yet mended itself."

"Thou ought to rest and summon the physician daily that he may monitor thy progress," added Cassius, noting Tiberius looked pale and exhausted.

"I thank thee both for thy concern," uttered Tiberius wearily, lying down upon his couch. "I shall heed thy advice."

"Shall I summon the physician for thee," asked Cassius.

"I shall do so later…if need be…" replied Tiberius, feeling weak.

Perturbed, Cassius frowned, saying, "Tiberius Marcius, surely, thou dost not intend to leave thy medical care in the hands of thy bondswoman Tamar. She is no physician. She hath no knowledge of the body."

Lucius Servilius shook his head in dismay.

Tiberius shot Cassius a disapproving look. He was in no mood to listen to disparaging remarks about his maidservant.

Unruffled by his cousin's silent rebuke, Cassius made his point. "Thou must be seen by the physician. He is schooled in matters of the anatomy… and well able to practice medicine…the maid is not. She is unlearned…and incompetent. It is most unwise of thee to trust in her meager ability."

"That is quite enough, Cassius," breathed Tiberius, keeping his temper in check. "Lucius Servilius, would thou kindly escort my opinioned cousin from my presence. I desire to rest now."

"Consider it done," replied Lucius Servilius with mild amusement.

Highly irritated, Cassius left the room of his own accord with Lucius Servilius following on his heels.

"What in the name of the gods possessed thee to speak ill of the maid," asked Lucius Servilius, catching up to Cassius as he was walking out the front door of the residence.

Seething, Cassius turned on him and said nastily, "What in the name of the gods keeps thy mealy mouth shut when thou ought to speak sensibly? Would thou hath Tiberius Marcius die for lack of proper medical care?"

"Come now, Cassius. Calm thyself. He shall not die. It was foretold by the shepherd that he would live."

"Dost thou suppose I hath confidence in a strange old shepherd and the nonsense he spoke?"

"I think thou knowest it was more than mere nonsense," argued Lucius Servilius, falling in step alongside Cassius as they made their way down the cobbled road. "It is evident the gods hath destined him for greatness…and the maid whom thou dost despise…is part of his destiny."

"What kind of destiny deems one to suffer as Tiberius Marcius suffers? If it were not for that accursed maid, Tiberius would never hath been attacked and left for dead!"

"Thou cannot know whether or not something would or would not hath occurred," stated Lucius Servilius reasonably. "Thou should not fault the maid for Tiberius' misfortune. He doth not…why should thee?"

"Lucius Servilius, thou art a fool! Thou art enchanted with her because she is comely. I for one see no value in her apart from her appearance. I liken her to a snake charmer for all who look upon her fall under her spell…and none more than thee!"

"Cassius, I will not deny the maid is lovely, but there is far more to her than meets the eye. She is bound to Tiberius Marcius for some purpose. Their destinies are intertwined! Thou would do well to remember that! Thou cannot continue to fight against the will of the gods…neither can thou continue to fight against thy cousin. If thou dost…I fear for thee. Each time thou hast spoken against the maid, Tiberius hath rebuked thee. There will come a day if thou dost continue to speak against the maid that Tiberius will banish thee from his presence. I feel it in my bones. I hath witnessed his reaction to thy words and I tell thee, thou dost stand on unsteady ground when thou dost rail against the maid. Cassius, for thy own sake, speak ill of the maid no more."

"Thou dost almost persuade me."

"I would that I could, Cassius, but I know thee. Thou art not easily persuaded."

Cassius knew Lucius Servilius had rightly spoken for the truth of his words resonated deep inside of him. Tiberius was indeed growing impatient with him over the maidservant. Yet, he found it impossible not to speak against her whenever the opportunity presented itself. The very sight of her provoked him to anger and he could not rein in his hostility. He never thought anyone, least of all, a female slave, could drive a wedge between him and Tiberius for they were blood brothers, similarly minded and nobly born. No one had ever come between them. No one had ever been successful in their attempt to do so, no one, except the maid and for that, Cassius hated her all the more.

"We cannot know what the gods intend, Cassius," Lucius Servilius continued, wiping the sweat from his brow as they strolled in the warm afternoon sun. "It is best to leave Tiberius Marcius' fate to them. Do not try to interfere. Let Tiberius do with the maid as he sees fit…as destiny rules. If she hath found favor in his sight and obtained kindness from him, she doth well. She is in his hand and under his authority. She hath been put there by the gods and she must answer to him. It is not for us to judge another man's servant. Let us stand aside, hold our peace and watch as Tiberius' destiny unfolds."

"I fail to see the maid's role in Tiberius' destiny! She is the cause of his misfortune and suffering," argued Cassius stubbornly, stopping in front of his home. "I will not rest until I expel her from Tiberius' life. If I hath to wrap my hands around her pretty little neck in order to be rid of her…I will!"

"Cassius hear me well," warned Lucius Servilius, becoming angry, his countenance reddening. "If thou doth fail to see the maid's role in Tiberius' destiny, it is because thou hast refused to do so! Listen to reason! I plead with thee for thy sake, say no more against the maid…neither do anything to expel her from thy cousin's hand. If thou dost harm her in any way, Tiberius Marcius will turn on thee with a mighty vengeance and the gods will do nothing to save thee from his wrath…nor will I!"

Incensed, Cassius flew into a rage, spewed a mouthful of foul curses, verbally berating his friend and having unmercifully cut him to the bone, he stomped into his house and slammed the door, feeling completely vindicated.

Reeling from the insults he sustained, Lucius Servilius exhaled and bitterly declared, "May the gods show thee the error of thy way, my friend," and having thus spoken, he continued down the cobbled path, greatly persuaded of trouble to come.

XXI

The afternoon had faded into evening and the collective mood of the house was quiet. The royal visitation had exhausted its occupants, patrician and slave alike, but none more than Tiberius Marcius, who had fallen into a deep slumber and had not yet awakened.

Tamar was in her cubicle on her knees in prayer when the Spirit of God spoke within her, urging, "Go to the centurion." Obeying the inner voice, she ceased praying, rose to her feet, took her oil lamp in hand and went directly to Tiberius' quarters. Feeling a sense of urgency with each step she took, she quickly made her way down the narrow hallway and into the atrium.

Arriving at the tablinum, she found no servant in attendance and the door shut. Tamar stared at the closed door, debating whether or not she should enter the patrician's private domain. He had not summoned her and she knew he would not look kindly upon the intrusion. Uncertain as to what she should do, she stood at the door, greatly troubled. Again, the Spirit spoke, this time more strongly, "Go to the centurion." Yielding to the command of the Spirit, Tamar opened the door and entered, finding the room completely dark. Using her lamp to dispel the darkness, she raised it slightly, its soft glow illuminating her path as she made her way through the dismal study toward the bed chamber. Suddenly, she heard the centurion speak, his voice shattering the eerie silence. Startled, Tamar stopped in her tracks and listened, but she could not decipher his words. Continuing on, she reached the bed chamber, her heart racing as she stepped inside the cubicle. Apprehensive, she drew near the couch where Tiberius lay, set her lamp on the table and parted the bed curtains. Beholding her master's flushed countenance, Tamar laid her hand on his forehead and finding him hot with fever; she turned to the water basin on the table beside her, took a small clean cloth and immersed it in the bowl. Wringing out the excess water, she placed the cool compress on Tiberius' forehead and then immersed another cloth which she placed on his chest. Tamar was about to leave and seek assistance when Tiberius began to speak again. She paused to listen.

"Dinah...where art thou," Tiberius cried out deliriously, his eyes closed, his head turning listlessly from side to side. "Dinah…draw nigh…Dinah…"

Alarmed by the intensity of his fever, Tamar ran out of the bed chamber into the atrium, crying aloud for the steward.

The steward, along with four other servants answered her call, among them was Anatole.

"What troubles thee, woman," inquired the steward anxiously, seeing her distress.

"Send for the physician at once! The master hath a grievous fever!"

At her word, the steward immediately dispatched a male servant to fetch the doctor and commanded another to make an offering to the family gods on behalf of Tiberius Marcius at the household shrine in the atrium.

A young servant boy, eager to help, stepped forward and asked, "What may I do?"

"Bring a basin of fresh water and clean linen," instructed Tamar, catching her breath. "Do be quick about it."

The youth darted from the atrium to do her bidding.

"And I…what would thou hath me do?" asked Anatole, his face somber.

"Assist me," replied Tamar, hurrying back inside the tablinum.

Grave in aspect, the steward stood alone in the grand atrium, confronted once again with the sobering possibility of Tiberius' death. Should the unthinkable occur; Cassius would inherit most of Tiberius' property, including his servants. The prospect of belonging to Cassius and serving him for the rest of his days; sent a chill down the steward's spine. Not desiring such a grim fate, he earnestly prayed to the gods to spare his master's life. As it was, Cassius had been given temporary authority over the affairs of Tiberius' house and that in itself was challenging because he was so difficult to please. The steward was not alone in his thinking for all the household servants dreaded the prospect of falling into the hands of the foul tempered patrician. Knowing Flavia would most likely call for Cassius when she learned of her son's condition, the steward considered taking the initiative and sending ahead for him, but he was hesitant to do so. It was against his better judgment. However, he knew the decision was not his to make. It was Flavia's. With this in mind, the steward left the atrium in search of the matron of the house. She would shoulder the decision and her servants had no choice but to bear up under it.

Returning to Tiberius' bedside, Tamar removed the damp cloths she had laid upon him. Finding they had absorbed heat from his feverish body, she immersed them again in the water basin, wrung out the excess liquid and placed them back on Tiberius' head and chest. Taking a third cloth, she dampened it and began to swab the centurion's body, trying to bring down his elevated temperature.

Bearing a cup in one hand, Anatole parted the bed curtains on the opposite side of Tiberius' couch, speaking to Tamar as he did so, "Woman, lay aside thy towel and raise his head that he may drink."

Tamar did as the body servant directed, watching as he held the goblet of water to Tiberius' lips. To her dismay, the centurion scarcely drank a mouthful before turning away from the cup. "Offer him strong wine instead. It will give him strength," suggested Tamar, gazing upon her master's countenance with compassion.

Finding her advice sound, Anatole went to the study and poured a generous amount of red wine into another goblet. Returning to the couch, he waited for Tamar to elevate Tiberius' head again and then he placed the cup to his master's parched lips, expecting Tiberius to drink from it, but he did not.

Refusing the wine, Tiberius moaned, "Dinah…where art thou?"

Wondering for whom the centurion called, Tamar lifted her eyes to Anatole, who answered her unspoken question.

"He loved her…and she him…but their love was ill fated," said Anatole wistfully, remembering the past. "They were to be married…"

Listening to the unfolding story, Tamar dipped a small corner of a clean cloth into the wine goblet held by Anatole and wet the centurion's lips with the crimson liquid, hoping to entice him to drink.

"…but it was not to be," continued Anatole, observing Tamar closely. "Dinah fell sick and died while he was in a far country on a military campaign. No one wrote and informed him of his betrothed's untimely demise. No one wished to be the bearer of bad tidings…most especially…Flavia. She feared the ill tidings would be detrimental to her son while soldiering and she strictly forbade any one to tell him of Dinah's fate till his return from duty. When he learned of her death…his sorrow was very great and he yet grieves…" said Anatole sadly, revealing intimate knowledge of his master. "He hath never loved another."

Tasting the wine on his lips, Tiberius slowly opened his eyes, fixing his fevered gaze on Tamar and spoke to her in a strangely distant voice, "Dinah, surely, it is thee."

"No, Domine, it is I, Tamar…thy maidservant."

Bending near, Anatole offered some wine to Tiberius, who drank a little and after drinking, addressed Tamar again, speaking out of his delirium.

"Lovely Dinah…hast thou returned to lead me into the nether world," he asked, his black eyes fastened upon her as she gently laid his head down upon the pillow.

"Domine, it is I, Tamar…thy maidservant," she repeated, removing the cloth from his forehead and refreshing it in the basin.

As Tamar laid the cool cloth back upon his head, Tiberius reached for her, catching her by the wrist saying, "Dinah, why dost thou say thou art another? I know thee."

Disturbed by Tiberius' belief that she was his dead beloved and had returned from the underworld for him, Tamar pondered the gravity of his illogical assertion. Not knowing how to answer him, she prayed for wisdom and then opened her mouth to speak, her own words taking her by surprise. "Tiberius Marcius, thou hast rightly discerned my identity. I am Dinah…whom thou did love…but thou dost err in thinking I hath come to lead thee into the afterlife," she said tenderly, meeting his feverish eyes, her small wrist still held within his grasp. "I hath not come for this purpose. Thou shalt not die this day. Thou shalt live and not die. I speak life over thee, Tiberius Marcius."

Shocked by Tamar's peculiar declaration, Anatole drew back from the couch, raising his weathered brow in consternation, wondering at her words.

"Is it truly thee…Dinah?"

"It is I."

"I desire to join thee in death."

"No, Tiberius Marcius, thou art to live!"

"Live? How then shall I be with thee?"

"I speak life over thee, Tiberius Marcius…life!"

Unbeknown to Tamar, Cassius, the physician, Flavia and the steward had quietly entered the chamber and all had heard her strange words.

The physician was the first to speak, stepping forward, "Woman, what ails thy lord and master?"

Caught unawares, Tamar looked up from Tiberius upon hearing the physician, turned and found all eyes upon her. Judging by the look on their faces, she realized instantly they had heard her every word. Feeling the weight of their judgment, her face colored and she lowered her gaze, replying humbly to the physician, "He hath a grievous fever. I hath done what little I know to do, but my skill is nothing compared to thy learned skill."

"Of that, I am not convinced," said the physician kindly, coming to the centurion's bedside. "Woman, it appears thou hast some healing knowledge and a good measure of common sense to boot."

Tamar extracted her wrist from Tiberius' hand and stepped back from the couch giving place to the physician, who began examining his patient. Glancing in the direction of the patricians, Tamar encountered the cold, steely glare of Cassius. Unnerved, she cast her eyes downward without regarding Flavia, who was standing at his side, her emotions carefully concealed behind her noble features.

"Woman, come with me," barked Cassius, his tone and visage betraying overt hostility. "I hath somewhat to say to thee!"

Hearing the patrician's stern words, the physician looked up from his patient and regarded the maidservant, reading her body language. Perceiving her anxiety, he turned about and faced Cassius, addressing him on her behalf. "Patrician, I hath need of her as doth her lord. She is well able to assist me in his care."

"Choose another to assist thee, physician," growled Cassius, unaccustomed to his will being thwarted.

Interrupting the tension between the two men, the servant boy entered the room carrying linens, accompanied by a young girl, who bore a basin of fresh water in her small hands, both were stoic in appearance. Together, they went directly to Tamar.

Nervous for she was under the watchful eye of Cassius, Tamar received the items they brought, setting them upon the table and handed the basin of soiled water to the girl for removal, but the distraction was only momentary. The children left as quickly as they had entered and the heated discourse between the men resumed.

"Patrician, thou art wasting precious time. I hath a patient to attend to. I hath need of the maid's assistance," stated the physician, agitated by Cassius' aggressiveness.

"Physician, it is thee who doth waste time, not I. This woman can be of no assistance to thee. She is dull witted and altogether foolish."

"I beg to differ with thee."

The steward and Anatole exchanged looks, both wondering what the outcome of the verbal duel would be.

Tamar was on the verge of tears, frustration welling up inside of her.

"Differ if thou will, but my word stands!" declared Cassius hotly.

"Dinah…draw nigh…" the patient cried out.

Prompted by Tiberius' outcry, Flavia spoke up in a bold, uncharacteristic manner. Unveiling her emotions for all to see, she openly pleaded with her nephew. "Cassius, I beg of thee…consider my son. He is not in his right mind for a great fever hath overcome him. He is in desperate need of medical attention. Grant the physician's request. Permit the maid to assist him…I beg of thee…for my son's sake."

Again, the steward and Anatole looked at one another, equally astonished by Flavia's display of emotion. They had never before seen this side of her. She had always been sedate and measured, maintaining her composure at all times, until now. It was apparent her son's suffering was taking a toll on her Roman sensibilities.

As for Tamar, she feared for Flavia for she knew Cassius despised emotional eruptions of any degree.

True to character, Flavia's public plea immensely irritated Cassius. Fuming inwardly, he reluctantly relented out of concern for Tiberius. "Very well, physician, the maid may assist thee." And having spoken, he exited the bed chamber with Flavia following behind him, offering soft spoken words of gratitude.

Pleased with his victory, the physician returned to the care of his patient, speaking to Tamar as he did so, who received his kind words with modesty as she assisted him in his endeavor.

"Woman, thou art to be praised for thy skilled hand and thy well chosen words. Thy master is fortunate to hath a servant such as thee," said the physician, carefully inspecting Tiberius' injuries for outward signs of infection, but finding none.

Like most doctors, the physician had gained his expertise on the battlefield, mending and caring for wounded and dying soldiers. Rarely had he encountered anyone as knowledgeable as the maid who was not medically trained. Women were midwives, their knowledge limited to childbirth and the care of infants, but the maid possessed an ability surpassing the natural skill of her gender. He remembered how she had cared for the centurion when he was near death and he believed the soldier's survival was due in large part to the fine care she had rendered. Now, once again, the maid had done well by him. The physician respected her so much that he had gladly risen to her defense against the haughty patrician who clearly did not esteem her in the least.

In the midst of the unlit study, Cassius turned on Flavia, who was a few steps behind him, seized her by the arms and rebuked her harshly. "Flavia, cease thy words of gratitude. They do nothing for me. My anger is greatly kindled against thee!"

Held in her nephew's vise, Flavia remained outwardly calm as Cassius' fingers painfully pressed her flesh with cruel purpose.

"Woman, art thou so old and dull of mind that thou hast forgotten how to hold thy feeble tongue? I did not ask thee thy opinion, nor did the physician for that matter, yet…thou spoke! Thou hath no right to speak in the presence of men…unless thou art spoken to! I warn thee, I shall not tolerate another such foolish outburst! If thou doth ever again challenge my authority or interfere with my will, I shall be forced to deal with thee severely! Hath I made myself clear?"

"Quite clear, Cassius," Flavia responded meekly, suppressing her inner turmoil. She knew her nephew was a force to be reckoned with and she did not want to further inflame his anger any more than was absolutely necessary to achieve her objective. She had intentionally provoked his ire, fearing he would punish Tamar for the strange words she had spoken to Tiberius. Flavia had heard her nephew curse Tamar under his breath and knowing him as she did; she knew she had to do something to protect the maid from his terrible wrath. Grateful to the maid for her tireless devotion to Tiberius' care and desiring that nothing should hinder the maid from performing her good work, Flavia willingly stood in Tamar's stead, enduring Cassius' fury.

As for Cassius, his fiery temper blinded him to Flavia's clever manipulation and he was none the wiser, never suspecting his aunt would deliberately put herself between him and the maid whom he despised. Having spewed his venom, he abruptly released Flavia and left the tablinum.

Standing where he left her, her body trembling, her arms aching, Flavia had weathered the storm that was Cassius, successfully deflecting his wrath away from Tamar and onto herself.

"Domina, did he hurt thee?" asked the steward in a hushed tone, having witnessed the episode under the cover of darkness.

Startled, Flavia turned toward the familiar voice.

"Thou wert brave, Domina."

Touched by the steward's concern, tears welled in Flavia's eyes. Thankful for the blanket of darkness surrounding her, she brushed aside her tears, considering them a nuisance and said evenly, "Steward, I should hath heeded thy wise counsel. I should not hath sent for Cassius. I shall not soon forget thy wisdom."

"Nor I…thy bravery, Domina," replied the steward solemnly, coming to her side.

Together, they left the tablinum, each feeling a renewed reverence for the other.

XXII

Priscilla had been brought up to obey the paterfamilias, but she had not always done so. She resented being told what to do and when to do it. When she did obey, her obedience was often in lip service only. Now obedience was no longer optional. Tiberius had made it clear if she did not comply with his mandate, he would force his will upon her through any means necessary. Fearing his threat, Priscilla vowed to marry Lucius Servilius, but her heart was not in it.

Seated at her vanity, her maidservants attending to her daily beautification, Priscilla pondered her impending marriage, ignoring the chatter of her maids as she struggled to reconcile herself to her fate. She did not love Lucius Servilius, but she did think well of him. Still, she did not want to be his wife. She regarded the pre-arranged marriage as just another lucrative business transaction made by her brother, discounting the argument that it was her father who had actually arranged the marriage. She did not believe her father had done so, despite her mother and brother's assertion that he had. She was convinced it was Tiberius who had chosen her future husband and no one could persuade her otherwise. Gazing into the mirror at the young maid who was arranging her hair, Priscilla watched as the servant pinned up her long, brown hair on top of her head with hairpins of silver. Drawing a parallel between herself and the maid, Priscilla felt as if she had no more control over her life than did her servant girl. Though she was born a patrician, what was the good of her aristocratic birthright? It brought her no empowerment. She was not the master of her destiny. Like her maidservant, she was a slave to duty. She would pass from her brother's rule, to her husband's, having no choice in the matter, but to dutifully obey their dictates.

Coming out of her contemplation, Priscilla realized her maids were discussing Tiberius. As she listened to their conversation, her heart sank and her conscience was deeply pricked.

"The steward fears the master may die," said a maid sadly.

Another said, "Yes, even Anatole fears the same. He told me so."

"The physician was summoned last night and so too was Cassius. He remains in the house to keep watch," chimed another maid, warning all within hearing distance of Cassius' presence.

"It is as though the master is cursed with a terrible curse," voiced the young maid who was arranging Priscilla's hair, pinning up the last strand as she spoke.

"Don't be ridiculous! My brother is not cursed!" snapped Priscilla guiltily, remembering the curses she had called down on Tiberius.

Her maids fell silent. "Pray tell, what hath befallen my brother?" asked Priscilla looking from maid to maid. "Why did none of thee inform me? Am I not his sister?"

"Dominilla, we thought thee knew of his terrible fever," spoke the bravest of her maids.

"I knew nothing! How can I know anything when I am told nothing!" said Priscilla testily, rising from her chair. "Finish dressing me, I must go to my brother!"

"Yes, Dominilla," replied her maids, each one scattering to find what was needed to complete the task of adorning their mistress in her finery.

Dressed, Priscilla headed straight to the tablinum. She was about to enter the room when she a heard a male voice behind her speak.

"Priscilla, thou wert not summoned," said Cassius, eyeing her.

Priscilla turned about and faced Cassius. "I desire to see Tiberius Marcius," she declared, maintaining possession of herself as Cassius approached her.

"Thou wert not summoned, Priscilla," repeated Cassius, taking his cousin in with his eyes for he had always found her lovely to behold.

"Nevertheless, I desire to see Tiberius Marcius," she repeated, rising to the verbal challenge.

Amused, Cassius smiled. He appreciated Priscilla's indomitable spirit. In many respects they were similar in temperament. He often pondered what it would be like to take her as his wife, though he tried not to dwell too long on the thought out of respect for Lucius Servilius, to whom she was betrothed. Cassius fully intended to marry Turia, finding her to his liking, but he felt she paled in contrast to his female cousin. He found Priscilla pleasing to his discriminating eye, intriguing in every way imaginable and he could not resist trifling with her whenever the opportunity presented itself.

"My dear Priscilla, thou wert not summoned. I cannot allow thee to enter without permission from Tiberius Marcius," said her cousin, still smiling.

Annoyed with his game, Priscilla responded coolly, "Go then and petition him on my behalf that I may enter his presence."

"Go to thy sitting room. I will send thee word."

"I do not wish to go to my sitting room! I want to see my brother and I want to see him now!"

"Priscilla, thou should learn to control thy temper. It is most unbecoming," remarked Cassius, toying with her.

"I shall do so, Cassius, when thou dost," she fired back, frowning, not as afraid of him as she ought to have been.

The steward entered the atrium, carrying a tray of food and saw the two patricians standing at the tablinum door, conversing. He surmised it was not a pleasant conversation by the expression on his mistress' face. He cleared his throat intentionally as he drew closer to tablinum, to warn them of his approaching. Experience had taught him that there were some things better left unheard.

Cassius turned about as the steward came near having heard his polite warning and as he did, Priscilla seized the moment and rushed forward into the tablinum and was at Tiberius' bedside before Cassius could catch up to her.

Sitting upright on his couch, his fever having broken hours before, Tiberius was surprised to see his sister and wondered at her swift entrance, but he quickly understood it when he saw Cassius enter right behind her, clearly irritated, followed by the steward, who respectfully remained at the door's entrance.

"Forgive me, Tiberius Marcius," began Priscilla, defiantly turning her back to Cassius as she addressed her brother. "I was grieved when I heard thou had a great fever and I desired to see thee. I feared if I sought permission to enter, thou would deny me access for I hath not always found favor in thy sight. I pray thou dost forgive my transgression…and grant me a moment in thy presence."

Tiberius nodded for her to continue.

"I could not trust the word of servants concerning thee. I had to see thee with mine own eyes…to know how it was with thee. It pleases me to find the fever hath left thee and thou doth sit upright upon thy couch. Truly, thy destiny is in the hands of the gods. May the gods preserve thee, Tiberius Marcius. And now, with thy permission, I shall leave, lest I weary thee."

Tiberius nodded again.

Taking her cue, Priscilla turned on her heels and departed the room without acknowledging Cassius, who had been staring at her menacingly.

The steward stepped forward upon her exit and situated the tray on Tiberius' lap that he might eat his morning meal, having found Priscilla's discourse very interesting.

Cassius turned to leave the room and go after Priscilla, desiring to upbraid her for her rash behavior, but Tiberius called after him knowing his intent.

"Cassius, let her depart in peace. She meant no harm."

"Tiberius Marcius, she lacks proper respect for the authority of the paterfamilias. She doth as she pleases, when she pleases, showing no respect for the powers that be. She thinks a few flowery words will erase her transgression. I daresay; Lucius Servilius shall find her a handful when he takes her to wife. I almost pity him."

"He is quite capable of handling her," said Tiberius, biting into a slice of freshly baked bread.

"Ump…I wonder," muttered Cassius to himself.

"Domine, shall I send Tamar unto thee after thy morning meal?" asked the steward, taking note of his master's pale aspect. "She awaits thy summons. It was she who tended thee in thy misery."

"As did the physician…" added Cassius sourly, unwilling Tamar should receive any credit for Tiberius' recovery. "It would be far wiser to summon the physician this morning than Tamar. The maid hath taken leave of her senses. She hath assumed the name of Dinah and now speaks as such. She hath gone mad."

The steward stiffened and glared over his shoulder at Cassius, hating him for stirring up trouble.

"What art thou saying, Cassius?" asked Tiberius, laying down his bread, an uneasy feeling overtaking his weakened body. "I do not understand."

"The maid spoke unto thee whilst thee suffered fever and declared she was Dinah in the flesh."

"Cassius, I know thou dost despise the maid. Therefore, I find it hard to believe thy report."

"Tiberius Marcius, thou dost not hath to believe my report. Ask thy mother…ask Anatole or ask the physician. Better yet, ask thy steward what he heard," suggested Cassius, fixing a stern eye on the servant. "Let thy steward bear witness that what I hath said is true."

The steward swallowed hard, regretting he had mentioned Tamar's name in front of Cassius.

Tiberius looked to his steward and said, "Speak, steward! Be this true?"

Faltering, the steward hesitated in his speech trying to carefully formulate an answer, "Domine…the…maid…Tamar, whilst she cared for thee…spoke unto thee…as Dinah…it is true. I cannot say why she spoke as she did. I know not what transpired before I and the others entered thy chamber. Only she and Anatole know."

"Steward, send Anatole unto me and speak not a word concerning why he hath been called," commanded Tiberius, visibly disturbed. "I would hear from him what he knows of this matter."

Bowing in submission, the steward departed to do the will of his master, resenting Cassius' interference in the affairs of Tiberius' house.

Alone with Cassius, Tiberius confessed his disappointment. "I awoke this day believing Dinah had been at my side and I was comforted. I thought she had returned. I drew strength from her appearance and the words she spoke unto me. But it was not Dinah…it was another…and I find myself troubled by this revelation."

"Be not troubled, Tiberius. Thou had a great fever. It is understandable thou wouldst call for Dinah, but it is certainly not acceptable for thy maidservant to pose as Dinah and speak as such. Fault not thyself, but thy servant. It is she who hath wrought this evil deception," declared Cassius, feeling completely justified in bringing the matter to Tiberius' attention.

Lapsing into silence, Tiberius put aside his tray, his appetite failing him and withdrew into himself.

Cassius noticed his cousin had not finished his morning meal and felt some guilt over the observation, but he ignored his conscience, reflecting instead on the benefits of exposing the maid's misdeed.

Anatole stepped inside the cubicle, having been duly warned by the steward, who had gone against his master's wishes and told the body servant of the matter that he might not be caught off guard. "Domine, thou did send for me?"

"I did," answered Tiberius, his face expressionless as he regarded his faithful man servant in whom he trusted. "What is this I hear of my servant, Tamar?"

"I know not what thou dost mean, Domine? What hast thou heard?"

"Do not attempt to withstand me or forestall the truth," warned Tiberius sternly. "I am in no mood for antics. Did thou hear Tamar speak as though she were Dinah?"

"I did, Domine."

"And thou did nothing…said nothing?"

"I knew not what to do…for thou called her Dinah. I knew not what to think. For all I knew, she was who thou said. I am but a lowly servant and do not understand the ways of the gods. I do not know their intentions. They play their tricks and we mortals can do little about such things. Domine, it was not in my realm of power to do or say anything."

"Utter nonsense," barked Cassius, impatiently.

"Then, it was I who called her Dinah…" said Tiberius, his heart sinking inside of him.

"Yes, Domine. It was thee who did call her Dinah. She tried to tell thee she was thy servant Tamar, but thou insisted she was Dinah. Thy fever was very terrible and thou knew not what thou wert saying. Be not angry with her, Domine," pleaded Anatole. "Thy maidservant hath served thee well; even thy physician said the same of her."

Cassius cringed, remembering the verbal battle he and the physician fought over the maid. "That is merely a matter of opinion," he interjected haughtily.

Anatole maintained his stance in humility, thankful his and Tamar's fate did not rest in Cassius' hands. Even in his master's displeasure, he was measured and merciful, his servants often enduring little more than a stern tongue lashing for their infractions.

Correctly assessing that his body servant had spoken the truth, Tiberius dismissed him without rebuke.

Bowing deeply and backing out of his master's presence, Anatole concealed his relief behind a humble façade, counting himself fortunate.

"Why did thou not chastise thy servants? Not one of the three did thou correct," said Cassius, confounded by Tiberius' handling of the situation. "And thou did not even summon the maid whose fault it was."

"Cassius, how can I chastise my servants? They did nothing worthy of punishment. It was I who called the maid by my beloved's name. Can she be faulted for my deed?"

"Tiberius Marcius, I am beginning to understand why thy household hath no fear of thee," chided Cassius, shaking his head in disgust. "Thou dost not readily chastise thy servants or thy family. Thy sister defies thee. Thy mother speaks out of turn. Thy servants band together to run circles around thee. The maid uses her beauty to beguile thee and thou dost nothing about her or any other. Thy entire house is rife with rebellion!"

"Cassius, is it thy place to judge my house?"

"It is when thou hast given me the authority to do so," answered Cassius smugly, looking superior.

"Perhaps, I should reconsider my decision," countered Tiberius, growing angry. "Thou art quick to judge my house, but not quick to judge thyself."

"I judge thy servants because thou dost not," replied Cassius defensively. "Thou wilt not even hold the maid accountable for the trouble she hath caused thee. Thou dost suffer daily affliction because of her and yet thou dost tolerate her presence…thou dost even seem to favor her."

"Hold thy tongue, Cassius! Do not speak of her again, lest I pass judgment on thee and banish thee from my house," threatened Tiberius, his face hardening.

Realizing he had overplayed his hand, Cassius went silent, bitterly remembering the warning given him by Lucius Servilius; not to speak against the maid. He had ignored the advice of his friend to his own detriment. His brazen attempt to discredit the maid had miserably backfired. Now, his relationship with Tiberius hung precariously in the balance, along with his own future prosperity. With nothing left to do, but concede defeat, Cassius left the tablinum, encountering in the atrium the three servants who had been his undoing.

Reading violence in the eyes of Cassius and knowing his penchant for physical assault, the steward and Anatole courageously positioned themselves in front of Tamar, protecting her from any possible retaliation.

Cassius' eyes flashed dangerously as he beheld their blatant disrespect for him. Outraged, he stormed out the front door and returned to his own house, vowing revenge against the three servants.

XXIII

In spite of his weakened physical condition, Tiberius sat down at his desk, determined to take care of business matters, to recover what had been lost due to the unforeseen circumstances that had beset him. His brush with death had not only had physical consequences, but personal and financial as well. Desiring to return to some semblance of normalcy, Tiberius tackled the scrolls on his desk which his cousin had prepared for him. One by one, he broke Cassius' personal seal and unfurled the parchments, reading and pondering the implications of each recorded message. Of all the scrolls, he found the one concerning the shepherd who had predicted his death and return to life by the power of Venus; the most unsettling.

To start with, he had no client fitting the shepherd's description, nor could he recall any who even remotely resembled such a one. Whoever the strange fortune teller was, he was a man of mystery, however; his words were not altogether mysterious to Tiberius as he had the benefit of hindsight. Deciphering the seer's strange message, he recognized in whom the power of Venus resided, though he did not understand how or why. The unworldly revelation left him with more questions than answers. Setting the scroll apart from the others, he decided to summon Lucius Servilius and hear his perspective on the matter.

Rising from his chair, aided by a cane, Tiberius slowly, but deliberately walked across the room to the table where the flagon of wine sat, relentless physical pain driving him to the source of relief. Pouring a generous serving of wine into a goblet, he drank the contents quickly and refilled his cup. "Steward," he called out, raising the goblet to his lips again, medicating himself.

Appearing in the doorway, the steward answered, finding his master standing at the table, his back facing him, "Yes, Domine."

"Send for Lucius Servilius," ordered Tiberius, not bothering to turn around.

"Is there anything else thou doth wish, Domine," asked the steward, realizing Tiberius was suffering pain, having grown adept at detecting it in his master's voice. "Shall I send Tamar unto thee…with thy medicine?"

"I hath no need of her," Tiberius replied sharply. "Do not ask me again."

"Yes, Domine," said the steward, bowing, perplexed as to why his master had refused the maid and the medicine when he was clearly in need of both. He suspected Cassius had something to do with his sudden change in attitude toward Tamar. Disgusted by the ill will wrought by Cassius' hand, the steward departed the room to execute his master's bidding.

Steadying his cup as he made his way toward the window, Tiberius pondered the shepherd's bizarre prediction. Reaching his destination, he stood and gazed outward at the pleasant garden, his keen eye unexpectedly finding the subject of his contemplation seated on a marble bench with his body servant seated next to her. Perturbed by the seeming intimacy of the scene, Tiberius swallowed the last of his wine, watching the two servants with intense interest.

Anatole took Tamar's hands and declared, "Tamar, I hath grown fond of thee and if thou wilt permit me, I shall petition the master that we may marry."

Startled by his touch as well as his declaration, Tamar withdrew her hands from his and stood to her feet. "Anatole…thou art kind unto me and I do not wish to hurt thee. Let us speak no more of this for I shall never marry."

Anatole rose to his feet and patiently addressed her, "Tamar, it is not good for a woman not to marry. I would be a good husband to thee. I would care for thee in all things. Consider my proposal, Tamar. Do not be hasty with thy decision."

"No, Anatole. I desire no man," she said, her voice trembling with emotion, her knees weak beneath her. "I shall never marry."

"Come, Tamar. Thou art young and beautiful. How can thou say such a thing?"

"Choose another…I shall never marry," she stated with all the conviction she could muster, turning to leave, but Anatole caught hold of her and detained her, drawing her close to himself.

"Tamar, consider me," pleaded Anatole, searching her face for some sign of hope with which to encourage his ardent heart.

"Thou art frightening me! Please…release me," she cried out, turning her face away from his, her mind flashing back to the terrible day the Roman soldiers had seized her and murdered Josiah.

"I intend thee no harm, Tamar," assured Anatole, beholding her fear. "Only consider me…"

"Please…I beseech thee…release me!"

Realizing he had frightened her out of her wits, Anatole let go of Tamar.

Loosed from his hold, Tamar fled the garden.

Rejected, Anatole hung his head and walked away discouraged.

Disturbed by the incident he had witnessed, Tiberius restrained himself. He did not want to make assumptions that could later prove to be untrue. He had not heard their verbal conversation, but he had a strong feeling he knew what had transpired between his servants for he had paid close attention to their body language, especially Tamar's. Seeking to ascertain the truth, Tiberius decided to speak with Anatole and give him an opportunity to explain himself, before passing judgment on his servant.

Returning to his desk, Tiberius summoned his steward with a loud clap of his hands.

The steward appeared quickly, dutifully heeding the second summons. "Domine, thou did call."

"Send Anatole to me at once!"

"Yes, my lord," bowed the steward and left the room, wondering at the impatience in his master's voice.

Tiberius unfurled the scroll having to with the night Anatole had saved his life and re-read the account. If it had not been for Anatole disobeying orders and following him to the temple, Tiberius knew he would have bled to death in the cypress grove of Venus Libitina. Ordinarily, he would punish a soldier or a servant for such gross insubordination, but in light of the seer's prediction, he believed there was no willful intent to disobey on the part of his servant. Anatole's decision to disregard orders was evidently divinely ordained. He had always been one who could be trusted to do what he was told, following orders precisely to the last detail, performing every command with excellence and in this fashion, Anatole had continued.

"My lord, thou did send for me," said Anatole, presenting himself before his master, his aspect uncommonly somber.

"I did, Anatole, but before I address the matter at hand, bring me the flagon," ordered Tiberius, needing more wine to ease his bodily pain.

Anatole did as he was instructed and without being asked, poured more wine into his master's goblet, discerning his physical need.

"Pour thyself some wine also," directed Tiberius, regarding his servant intently.

"Thank you, Domine," answered Anatole, retrieving a goblet from the table. Returning to the desk, he served himself.

"Sit down, Anatole. I hath somewhat to say unto thee."

Anatole sat down. "Say on, my lord," replied Anatole, tasting his wine.

"I hath just finished reading the account of the night thou did save my life. I would no doubt be dead if it had not been for thee. The time hath come for thee to be rewarded for thy faithfulness."

"Domine, I did no more than thou had a right to expect of thy servant," stated Anatole with sincere humility.

"Even so, I desire to reward thee. I am willing to grant thee thy freedom and a handsome sum of money with which to enjoy it. I am prepared to write thy emancipation papers this day."

"Domine, I thank thee for thy generous offer, but I do not desire to leave thy house or thy service. I am content to serve thee all of my days," said Anatole soberly, no trace of emotion showing on his face.

"Thou would turn down liberty in favor of servitude?"

"I am content, Domine, to remain in thy service, to go where thou dost go, to do what thou dost want done, to serve thee in the military…and in thy house…to carry out thy commands…all of my days."

"Anatole, my faithful servant, surely there is something thou dost desire. Tell me, that I may reward thee," urged Tiberius, moved by his servant's loyalty.

"What I desire thou cannot give unto me," Anatole uttered sadly, dropping his head.

Looking upon his servant's melancholy demeanor, Tiberius knew what his servant desired and he was right, he could not give it to him and neither did he want to.

"I desire a wife, but the woman I chose hath rejected my proposal," volunteered Anatole, baring his soul. "She said unto me, she shall never marry. I wonder what terrible thing hath broken the heart of one so lovely that she would deny herself happiness."

Feeling for his servant, Tiberius posed a question which was against his own better judgment to ask, "Would thou hath me force her to marry thee?"

Brightening, Anatole lifted his head, fixing his gaze on Tiberius, the idea holding a glimmer of hope, then suddenly, his countenance fell and he answered, "I would not, Domine. She would only grow to hate me if I insisted upon having my way with her. Over time, my heart would suffer even more than it doth this day. I must accept her decision."

Exhaling with quiet relief, Tiberius' opinion of his servant increased all the more and he said, "Anatole, thou art a man of fine character, a servant most worthy of praise and I am honored to retain thee in my service. Go now and take thy ease. Tomorrow will bring better things unto thee."

Anatole rose up from his chair, bowed humbly and exited the room.

Finishing his wine, Tiberius thought on the words of his servant concerning the heart of Tamar. Though Anatole had never mentioned her by name, Tiberius was positive it was she of whom he spoke. Having knowledge of the terrible thing that had befallen her, Tiberius realized the maid had dealt with her grief the same as he. They had both chosen to deny themselves happiness with another. Shaking off the uncomfortable comparison, he took his pen and scribbled a few words down on the parchment in front of him.

"Domine, Lucius Servilius hath arrived. Shall I send him in?" inquired the steward, entering the study.

"Show him in and bring another flagon of wine," commanded Tiberius, rising to his feet in expectation of his guest.

"Greetings in the name of the gods, Tiberius Marcius," said Lucius Servilius as he entered the tablinum with a cheerful countenance. "It is good to see thee at thy desk. I trust thou hast found things in order."

"Indeed, I hath," replied Tiberius, motioning for his friend to be seated in the client's chair. "I hath spent all morning reading the scrolls written by Cassius. It appears ye had an interesting visitor in my absence and I should like to hear thy perspective on him."

"Ah…thou dost refer to the old shepherd," laughed Lucius Servilius, taking his seat, followed by Tiberius doing the same. "He was quite unique to say the least."

Returning to the tablinum, the steward set before the patricians a shiny, silver tray bearing a fresh flagon of wine and two polished silver goblets. Removing the empty flagon along with the used cups, he replaced them with clean vessels, filling each with wine and then set the flagon on the desk between the two men.

"To thy health, Tiberius Marcius," toasted Lucius Servilius, lifting his goblet.

"And to thine, Lucius Servilius," answered Tiberius, also lifting his goblet.

The steward left the room as the two men drank to their mutual health as was their custom.

"Tell me, was the shepherd a client? Cassius and I were most perplexed with the likes of him. He even refused our money as I recall. Most unusual."

"As far as I can surmise, I hath no such client. The whole encounter is other worldly and makes no sense unless considered from that vantage point. Dost thou agree?"

"I agree with thee, Tiberius Marcius," replied Lucius Servilius, pausing to sip his wine. "The whole day was strange…clearly the handiwork of the gods. They arranged the preordained events and we were unable to alter them. I am frankly surprised they even bothered to serve us notice by way of the seer. His ominous prediction left Cassius and I exceedingly troubled…and desperately clinging to his words concerning the role of Venus in thy recovery. It was a trying day."

"Who is this Venus incarnate the shepherd spoke of?" questioned Tiberius, taking up his cup and drinking, interested in hearing his friend's opinion.

"I believe she is thy fair maid…the one whom thou took from Drusus," answered Lucius Servilius cautiously, watching for a reaction from Tiberius, but seeing none.

"And why dost thou believe this?"

"I can not say exactly, but I know it. Hast thou asked Cassius these questions?"

"I hath not asked Cassius for he cannot keep a civil tongue in his head when it comes to the maid. I seek the truth concerning her. I fear Cassius will not reveal it unto me," stated Tiberius, holding his countenance in check.

Sighing, Lucius Servilius recalled his last encounter with Cassius, but he kept the unpleasantness to himself out of respect for Tiberius.

"Lucius Servilius, how is it possible for a lowly maid to house the power of a goddess? Hath thou an answer to this mystery?"

"No, Tiberius Marcius. I hath no answer worthy of voicing. Suffice it to say, the gods hath destined thee to greatness and the maid is connected to thy destiny. Of this, I am certain. Despise not her lowly position for the gods hath exalted her and sent her unto thee for a purpose. If thou dost despise her, then thou shalt impair thy own future. Thy own greatness is at stake. I know this with certainty, my friend."

"Now, it is thee who doth speak like a seer," remarked Tiberius, wrapping his fingers about the stem of his goblet, giving thought to the words of his friend.

"I am fully persuaded of what I hath said, Tiberius Marcius."

"There is something about her. She hath brought me back from the very brink of death and I myself hath no worthy explanation of her…uncommon power," admitted Tiberius, somewhat reluctantly.

"Did Cassius mention the maid's kinswoman sought her release that same fateful day?"

"He did and I am satisfied with how the matter was handled," said Tiberius, determined Tamar should never again return to the filth and poverty of Subura.

"Are there any other matters of concern, Tiberius Marcius?"

Pouring more wine into his cup, Tiberius responded, "There is…I want to know when thou shalt marry Priscilla. It is time for her to be given into thy hands. She is too much for me in my weakened physical state," joked Tiberius, smiling.

"That, I do not doubt, my friend," laughed Lucius Servilius, sipping his wine. "I should like to speak with her before I give thee an answer."

"By all means, do so," encouraged Tiberius, his mood lightening, his pain finally abating. "Take her to wife today if thou be so inclined. Thy marriage is long overdue. It is time for her to wed."

"Friend, thou art too eager to be rid of thy sister for my comfort. Is there something thou hast not yet revealed unto me concerning her?" asked Lucius Servilius in earnest, aware of Priscilla's love for another, having obtained the knowledge through his own sources. He doubted Tiberius would ever inform him of his sister's misguided affection for Claudius, but he offered him a chance to do so if he dared.

"Go and speak with her," said Tiberius, skirting the question. He was not about to reveal anything that would jeopardize his sister's future and if Priscilla knew what was good for her, she would not either.

XXIV

Seated in the triclinium, Priscilla and her mother had just finished eating their afternoon meal when Lucius Servilius entered, taking them by surprise. Flavia was the first to see Priscilla's intended. Rising from her chair, she said, "Greetings, Lucius Servilius." Following suit, Priscilla rose from her seat and echoed her mother's words, rattled by his unexpected visit.

"Pardon the interruption, Flavia. I would like a private word with thy daughter."

"Certainly, Lucius Servilius," assented Flavia graciously, dismissing the servants in attendance and leaving, hopeful the visit would result in the long awaited marriage of the two young patricians.

Fixing his gaze on his betrothed, Lucius Servilius extended his hand to Priscilla, beckoning her to come to him.

Responding, Priscilla went to Lucius Servilius, placed her slender hand in his and being led, she accompanied him to a couch where they sat down.

"Priscilla, thy brother thinks it is time for us to marry," began Lucius Servilius, his tone and expression both equally grave. "I on the other hand hath reservations concerning thee and I am somewhat hesitant to take thee for my wife."

Priscilla inhaled deeply, the weight of his words burdening her mind with all sorts of troubling scenarios.

"I am aware thou dost not find me to thy liking," he continued, his eyes pinned on her, discerning her growing discomfort. "Under normal circumstances that would not hinder me in the least…but I hath become privy to some very disturbing knowledge concerning thee."

"Lucius Servilius, whatever thou hast heard…hold it not against me," entreated Priscilla, feeling strained physically and emotionally.

"Priscilla, it is not as simple as that. This is a matter of great concern unto me. I must think of my own future happiness and whether thou art truly a suitable wife for me. The goddess Lucina hath brought many things to light and I cannot foolishly ignore what she hath revealed unto me."

Realizing Lucius Servilius had somehow learned of her love for Claudius, Priscilla anxiously tried to convince him otherwise lest she fall from grace. "I will not deny I did not want to marry thee…but I hath come to my senses. I hath seen the error of my judgment and hath corrected my heart's course, setting it solely upon thee. Thou art an honorable man of aristocratic birth. Thy ways are my ways and we are well suited one to another. Hold not my former foolishness against me. If thou doth marry me, thou shall find me a pleasing and obedient wife. I shall do everything within my power to be all thou dost desire in a wife. I pledge myself anew to thee, Lucius Servilius."

"Woman, I want to believe thee, but I cannot. I hath in my possession a letter addressed to thee, delivered this day into the hand of Quintus Atilius, who gave it unto me as I entered thy domain. I deliver it to thee…having read it for myself…" said he, pulling the letter from his toga and handing it to Priscilla, his face unusually stern.

Receiving the letter, Priscilla opened it with trembling hands, reading the words of love written by Claudius. Comprehending the gravity of the moment, she slowly folded the letter, lifted her large brown eyes to Lucius Servilius and asked meekly, "Doth my brother know of this?"

"I said nothing to him concerning this letter."

An uncomfortable silence fell on the two patricians as each battled their own raging emotions, each wondering what the other would do next.

Filled with remorse, tears slipped from Priscilla's eyes as she addressed her betrothed in a small, weak voice, "Lucius Servilius, I hath wronged thee terribly…and I am ashamed of what I hath done. I did not consider thy heart or thy happiness. I thought only of myself and…I fear…I must now face the consequences. Do what doth seem right in thine own eyes."

Taking the letter from Priscilla, Lucius Servilius stood to his feet, the folds of his toga cascading neatly about his frame. Staring down at the scorned object of his affection, he angrily crushed the letter in his fist and threw it to the floor. "I shall consider my options," he declared coldly and having spoken, he left the room, his heart trodden asunder.

 Passing Lucius Servilius in the atrium, the steward noticed the patrician's dour countenance and sensed something was amiss.

Brushing the tears from her eyes, Priscilla rose to her feet, wanting to amend the damage she had done to the dignitas of her betrothed. Running out of the dining room after Lucius Servilius, she caught up to him in the atrium, imploring, "Lucius Servilius, hear me."

Seeing Priscilla, the steward hid himself and listened, his interest peaked.

No Greater Love

The Roman turned about and faced his spurned lover, unmoved by her tear streaked face.

"I hath wronged thee…and I beg for thy forgiveness! I repent of my wrongdoing! The letter means nothing to me! Cast me not away in thy anger, Lucius Servilius!"

"Priscilla, do not make matters worse by making a spectacle of thyself," snapped Lucius Servilius, having no liking for public airing of personal matters. "I told thee…I shall consider my options…and consider them I shall!"

"Consider then…my repentant heart," pleaded Priscilla, reaching for Lucius Servilius.

Hardening his heart, Lucius Servilius withdrew from Priscilla and exited the house without a backward glance.

Giving way to despair, Priscilla fled the atrium, seeking refuge in her cubicle. Shutting the door behind her, she sank to the floor, weeping bitterly.

The steward went to his mistress' room and put his ear to her door, hearing her sobs. Stepping back from her cubicle, he considered what should be done. Having seen the two patricians exit the dining area, he left the door and went into the triclinium, looking about the room for some indication as to what had happened between them. Spotting a crumpled parchment upon the ivory colored marble floor, the steward stooped down, took it in hand, smoothed out the paper and read the tender words of a lover to his beloved. Swallowing hard, the steward stood to his feet and stuffed the incriminating letter into his tunic, knowing what should be done, but not wanting to do it.

"Steward, tell the cook to prepare us an afternoon meal…and bring wine for my thirsty friend," ordered Tiberius, entering the dining room with Quintus Atilius, catching the steward by surprise.

"Yes, my lord," said the steward nervously, turning around to face his master, wondering how much he had seen, if anything.

"Steward, why doth thou appear rattled at my appearing," questioned Tiberius, knowing his servant well enough to recognize when he was upset.

"My lord, I stumbled and fell only moments before thy entrance. I am embarrassed thinking thou hast seen thy servant's folly," lied the steward.

Regarding the steward closely, Tiberius wondered at his strange behavior, saying, "I hath not known thee to be a man easily embarrassed."

"It is indeed most unlike me, Domine," agreed the servant, regaining his composure. "Hath thou any further need of me?"

"No, none at this time," answered Tiberius, his eye still on the servant.

Bowing, the steward departed. Out of his master's sight, he sighed with relief and patted his tunic, making certain he still had the letter on his person.

"Make thyself comfortable, Quintus Atilius," said Tiberius, taking a chair at the table as he was unable to recline upon the couch without enduring pain.

Following his host's lead, the centurion also chose a chair, finding it more accommodating to his military attire.

Several servants came forward, cleared the table of the plates used by Flavia and Priscilla and began busily setting out clean tableware, along with a variety of food and sweet wine before their master and his guest. Completing their tasks, they took up position on the other side of the room, close enough to see and hear their master's call, but not close enough to hear every word of his private conversation.

"Tiberius Marcius, I shall not linger long at thy table. I shall eat quickly and return to my post," said Quintus Atilius, helping himself to some bread and cheese. "I hath noticed a marked increase in passersby and I am discomforted by their frequency. I suspect Sejanus hath set his hand to something malevolent."

"I hath no doubt that he hast, my friend," replied Tiberius, drinking deeply from his wine goblet.

"I do not think the sly dog will ever relent from trying to harm thee," said the soldier, washing his food down with wine. "And I do not believe he is deterred in the slightest by Caesar's threat, nor by my presence at thy door…I regret to say."

"I believe thou art correct in thy assessment. Caesar's intervention only served to increase the Prefect's desire for revenge," said Tiberius grimly. "Caesar meant well, but he doth not know the lengths to which Sejanus will go to achieve his end. To his way of thinking…the end justifies the means."

"Not if I hath anything to do with it," vowed Quintus Atilius, hating the Prefect for what he had done to Tiberius. "I look forward to the day I cut his throat from ear to ear."

"Quintus Atilius, take care it is thee that doth the cutting and not Sejanus," warned Tiberius. "The unrelenting hatred he hath for me is the same hatred he hath for thee. Thou art just as much at risk as I, my friend."

"I am aware of that, Tiberius Marcius. Hath no fear, it is he who shall forfeit his life…not thee…not I!"

The men's conversation quieted as the wine bearer stepped forward and refilled their goblets and began again with the servant's departure from the table.

"I am mindful of the deceptiveness of our enemy and am well acquainted with his trickery," continued the centurion. "So much so…I did not even trust the youth who delivered unto me a letter for thy sister…though he was but a boy. Neither would I leave my post to deliver it into her hands, lest I be found derelict in my duty to protect thee and thy house."

"Give me now this letter," demanded Tiberius impatiently.

"I cannot. I gave it unto Lucius Servilius upon his entrance into thy home. He assured me he would deliver it to thy sister. Was my judgment faulty," asked Quintus Atilius, sensing Tiberius' displeasure. "Is not Lucius Servilius betrothed to thy sister and privy to what concerns her?"

"Thou did as thou thought fit," uttered Tiberius, refraining from critizing the soldier's decision. "My sister is betrothed to Lucius Servilius, but I still prefer to monitor any communications she receives until the day of her marriage."

"It shall not happen again, Tiberius Marcius. I pray I hath not caused thee any undue aggravation," apologized Quintus Atilius, rising from his chair.

"Think no more of it, my friend. Whilst thou dost stand guard, I shall look into the matter for myself."

Taking his leave, the soldier left the room and returned to his post.

Alone in the triclinium, Tiberius recalled his conversation with Lucius Servilius, recollecting nothing out of the ordinary about their dialogue. But as he thought on it, he realized Lucius Servilius had not bid him farewell, neither had his sister come to him with news of her impending marriage. Something had most certainly transpired between them and by all indications, it was not good. Downing the remainder of his wine, Tiberius angrily hurled his empty goblet across the room with violent force, startling his servants who stood wide eyed in disbelief, unaccustomed to displays of temper from the master of the house.

XXV

"Why hath the master not summoned me," Tamar questioned the steward, searching his face for answers. "It hath been two days. Who hath cared for him in my absence? Hath I displeased him? Tell me, why my lord calls for me no more!"

Drawing Tamar aside behind a large marble column, the steward spoke in a hushed voice saying, "Tamar, the master hath not told me why he calls for thee no more. When I ask him if he desires thy service, he denies his need of thee."

"What wrong hath I done?"

"Woman, thou hast done no wrong. I am convinced Cassius hath persuaded the master he hath no need of thee," submitted the steward, feeling sorry for the maid as he could see she was troubled.

"Who then hath cared for him?"

"Anatole doth care for him."

"Oh…" said Tamar, her gaze falling from the steward, remembering her encounter with Anatole in the garden.

"Now, I will ask thee a question…" began the steward, beholding the maid's loveliness. "What hath come between thee and Anatole?"

Lifting her eyes, Tamar met the steward's gaze and looking upon him intently, inquired, "Why doth thou ask?"

"Woman, I hath seen how he hath looked at thee and I hath seen thee flee at the sight of him. Thou hast never before done this. I am perplexed by thy fleeing. Thou need not fear him. He would never do thee harm. Did he not stand in front of thee and shield thee from Cassius' wrath? There is no cause to fear such a man as he."

"I thank thee both for what thou did that day, but I did not ask it of thee. Ye should not jeopardize thyselves on my account. What I must endure at the hand of Cassius…I must endure alone."

"Still, thou hast not yet answered my question," pressed the steward, marveling at her new found courage. "What hath come between thee and Anatole?"

"If thou must know…ask him," replied Tamar, unwilling to reveal what had transpired between them, deeming it too personal.

"Very well," said the steward, accepting her decision. He was about to speak again when he heard his master's call.

"Steward," summoned Tiberius impatiently, walking into the atrium, having left the triclinium.

Heeding his call, the steward stepped out from behind the tall column and answered, "Domine, here am I."

Seeing his steward come from behind the column, Tiberius asked, "Who is there with thee, steward?"

"It is I, Domine," replied Tamar, stepping into the open atrium, the late afternoon sun illuminating her appealing frame.

Laying eyes on her, Tiberius regarded the maid, who being enveloped in light appeared as if she were a vision. For a brief moment, he wondered if she really had been sent by the gods for some divine purpose in his life. Finding it difficult to believe, Tiberius dismissed the idea as nonsense and said, "Woman, return to thy mistress and serve her again as thou once did. I no longer hath need of thee."

Hearing his decree, Tamar's countenance fell as she fought back a myriad of emotions. Bowing humbly, she gave the expected response, "Yes, Domine."

"Steward, I would hath a word with thee," said Tiberius gruffly. "Come with me!"

"Yes, Domine," the steward answered nervously, following his master.

Tamar did not understand why Tiberius suddenly seemed indifferent towards her or why he had sent her back to Priscilla. Feeling the pain of rejection, believing she had somehow displeased him, Tamar left the atrium with a heavy heart, discounting the steward's assurance that she had done no wrong.

"Close the door, steward!" ordered Tiberius, seating himself in his desk chair.

Obeying the command, the steward shut the door and then presented himself to his master, standing in front of the large desk with all the composure he could muster.

Eyeing the servant sternly, Tiberius said, "Steward, I am displeased with thee!"

The steward stiffened, bracing himself for what was coming, suspecting Tiberius had seen more than what he had let on earlier in the triclinium.

"It hath come to my attention that a letter was delivered this day addressed to my sister…a letter from that despicable dog, Claudius!"

His conscience under pressure, the steward's forehead beaded with sweat, his hands grew clammy and his heart began to pound loudly within his chest.

"Thou hast failed to do thy duty! The letter went from the hand of Quintus Atilius into the hand of Lucius Servilius and finally to Priscilla! Steward, I expected thee to be on thy guard for such a communication and keep it out of all hands, save mine!"

"I hath the letter, Domine…" confessed the steward, pulling it from his tunic, too afraid to conceal the matter any longer.

"Thou hast the letter in thy possession…and thou withheld it from me," Tiberius exploded angrily, slamming his fist down upon the desk. Irate, he jumped up from his chair and snatched the letter from his steward, who stood trembling with fear. Unfolding the crumpled love note to his sister, Tiberius read it, growing madder and more disgusted with every written word of the interloper's pen. Finishing, he glared at his servant; his eyes narrow with rage and remarked darkly, "Steward, I ought to put thee to the sword!"

The steward dropped to his knees, begging for mercy, fearing for his life. "Domine, I hid the letter out of concern for thy health…and…for thy sister's well being! I knew the letter would cause terrible trouble! I knew not what to do…I hesitated to bring it to thy attention…for…I feared for thee both! Grant thy servant mercy, my lord! I beseech thee…in the name of the gods!"

"I am he whom thou dost serve, steward! Thou art to do my will!"

"Yes, my lord," agreed the steward meekly, lowering his eyes to the floor, watching the sandaled feet of his master leave the study.

Furious, Tiberius went into his cubicle, entered the closet where his military gear was kept and grabbed a thick leather belt from off a wall hook. Cracking the belt once, he left the cubicle and returned to the study, finding his steward still on his knees.

"Get up, steward," barked Tiberius hotly, his gaze steadfastly fixed on the disobedient servant as he slowly stood to his feet.

Facing Tiberius, the steward swallowed hard, seeing the dreadful belt in his hand. Never before had his master laid a hand on him. Fearing that was about to change, the steward pleaded for clemency. "Please, Domine…I beg of thee…"

"Silence! I will not hear thy pitiful pleas for mercy! Get out of my sight…I will deal with thee later!"

Bowing deeply, the steward choked back his pent up emotion and hastened from the room, too scared to utter another sound.

His anger kindled, Tiberius stormed out of the study, having the belt and letter in hand and headed to Pricilla's cubicle, being seen by several servants, who quickly scattered in every direction, wanting no part of the trouble to come. Reaching his sister's quarters, he kicked open the door and entered, making his way to the far right corner of the room where Priscilla lay upon her couch, her back facing him.

Thinking one of her maidservants had come into the room, Priscilla sniffled, "Leave…thou cannot comfort me."

Like a bolt of lightening flashing dangerously across a darkened sky, Tiberius seized Priscilla by the arm and brutally yanked her from her couch, his powerful vise tightening unmercifully about her delicate extremity. Frightened out of her wits, Priscilla screamed at the top of her lungs, frantically struggling to escape the might and main of her brother.

Hearing their mistress scream, Priscilla's maids came running to her rescue, but upon seeing Tiberius they retreated quickly, knowing there was nothing they could do to save her from her brother's wrath. Fearing for Priscilla, Talia ran down the hall to find Flavia.

"What is the meaning of this foul communication," thundered Tiberius, angrily shoving the letter and belt in his sister's face.

"I swear to thee…Tiberius…I did all I could to persuade Lucius Servilius that the letter meant nothing to me…" cried Priscilla, shaking uncontrollably, fearing the leather belt in her brother's hand. "Please…believe me…"

"The letter meant nothing to thee! What kind of an assurance is that? What is a letter compared to a man? It is the man himself that doth mean something to thee! Thy fondness for Claudius hath vexed us all! Woman, thou hast trifled with the affection of Lucius Servilius…having no regard for him…nor I! Thou hast not respected my authority as paterfamilias or behaved according to my sovereign will! Moreover, thou hast not honored and obeyed the will of thy father! Thou hast done as thou pleased and today thou wilt suffer the consequences of thy actions!"

"Please…Tiberius…hear me…the gods are my witnesses…I assured Lucius Servilius that Claudius meant nothing to me…I pledged myself anew to Lucius Servilius…I truly did…"

"Doth he intend to marry thee," questioned Tiberius, fire blazing in his black orbs.

"He said…he would consider his options…" sobbed Priscilla, knowing her brother would not be satisfied with her betrothed's response.

"So be it! Let him consider his options, while I exercise mine," growled Tiberius, violently throwing Priscilla to the ground, his temper raging out of control. Wielding his belt, Tiberius unleashed his fury, striking Priscilla on her back side, ignoring her screams and tearful pleas as the cruel belt met her soft pampered flesh.

Cowered in fear, Priscilla wailed, her hands clasped together in supplication, pleading, "Please…Tiberius…no more! Thou art hurting me…"

"I fully intend to hurt thee…perhaps even kill thee…" her brother threatened savagely, anger surging through his veins.

"Hath mercy…upon me…Tiberius…Claudius means nothing to me…" screamed Priscilla, in fear of her life. "Please…no more…I am begging thee…"

Bent on teaching Priscilla a lesson she would never forget, Tiberius drew back his belt and was on the verge of lashing her again, when suddenly, Tamar rushed forward, courageously inserting herself between the two siblings, while Flavia and Talia stood at the entrance of the room watching the unfolding drama in horror.

"Domine, I entreat thee…grant thy sister mercy! I beseech thee do her no harm!" implored Tamar, endeavoring to protect her mistress from her master's wrath.

Astounded by Tamar's bold intervention, Tiberius lowered his belt.

Emotionally spent, Priscilla lay on the floor, huddled at her brother's feet, sobbing hysterically.

Tamar stooped down and put her arms about Priscilla to comfort her and looking up at Tiberius said, "Domine, whatever she hath done…grant her mercy!"

"Priscilla, behold the maid whom thou dost despise! She hath saved thee from untold misery," proclaimed Tiberius, violently snapping the belt on the floor beside his sister, who shrieked at the sound of it. "See thou doth remember her kindness unto thee."

"I will…remember…" wept Priscilla, cradling her face in her hands, rocking to and fro like a distraught child.

Reaching down, Tiberius laid hold of Tamar, pulling her from Priscilla, his black eyes fierce as he drew her to himself and severely admonished, "Woman, never stand between my sister and I again! If thou dost…thou wilt suffer twice her punishment! Twice…I say! I wilt not grant thee an ounce of mercy! Next time…I shall not stay my hand!"

"My lord, I will not displease thee again," vowed Tamar calmly, meeting her master's daunting gaze, her knowing eyes softly taking him in.

Finding her sedate response and the softness of her expression quite strange in light of his fury, Tiberius released Tamar, unable to comprehend her.

Glaring malevolently at his sister, Tiberius declared scornfully, "Priscilla, thou best pray Lucius Servilius still wants thee for if he dost not…I shall wed thee to the first man that asks for thee…whether he be old, poor or utterly unappealing…matters not a whit to me! Thou dost deserve whatever evil befalls thee!" Finished with his sister, Tiberius turned on his heels and exited the room, his mother and Talia letting him pass without interference or comment.

Still on the floor crying, Priscilla looked up and saw her mother. "Mater, did thou hear Tiberius? He intends to marry me off to just any sort!" cried Priscilla, trying to elicit her mother's sympathy, but none was forthcoming from the Roman matron, who strongly disapproved of challenging the paterfamilias.

"If he doth…it will serve thee right, Priscilla," rebuked Flavia harshly. "It was most unwise of thee to provoke thy brother! Whatever fate befalls thee, thou hast no one but thyself to blame." Offering no solace, Flavia turned her back on her offspring and departed the room, leaving Talia and Tamar to care for Priscilla.

The two servants came to their mistress' aid, lifted her from the floor and walked her to her couch.

With eyes swollen from weeping, Priscilla looked at Tamar seated beside her on the couch and asked, "Why did thou risk thyself on my behalf? Thou dost know I despise thee…as my brother said…yet, thou stood bravely between us. Why?"

"I did not do so merely for thy sake, Dominilla, but for the sake of thy brother also. I fear the pain hath become too great for him."

"What art thou saying?"

"Thy brother suffers constant pain from his wounds…some days are worse than others. Today is such a day. I beg thee, Dominilla, provoke him no further for all of our sakes," said Tamar, tenderly wiping the tears from her mistress' face and pushing aside strands of her long brown hair that had come undone in the altercation.

Talia kept silent, pondering Tamar's words as she gingerly loosened the back of Priscilla's stola, exposing a long red welt. Rising, she went to the vanity table, selected a healing balm of aloe, returned to her mistress and gently applied the balm, while Tamar held Priscilla's hands, consoling her as she winced with pain and cried fresh tears.

XXVI

By lashing Priscilla and subsequently the steward, Tiberius had made it painfully evident to his entire household that a stricter standard of discipline would be applied to all. He would not tolerate any measure of disobedience from patrician or slave. Every person under his roof would suffer the consequences of their actions, regardless of how insignificant the infraction might be. Nothing less than blind obedience would suffice. The grim change in affairs gave rise to a dreadful silence which pervaded the Roman dwelling as its occupants tried to cope with the sterner expectations put upon them by Tiberius. All served him with fear and trembling with the notable exception of Tamar, who viewed him not as the others did, but through discerning eyes of compassion, which baffled Tiberius.

It had not escaped his notice that Tamar had been strangely unruffled in the face of his fury. Finding the maid's strong command of herself quite remarkable, he once again considered the possibility she might truly be the goddess Venus, come in the flesh as foretold. There was no denying Tamar had played a crucial role in keeping him from death, but was it merely a coincidence that she had done as the seer had predicted Venus would do? Or was his maidservant really a goddess in disguise? Even his trusted confidant, Lucius Servilius was convinced the maid was more than what she appeared to be outwardly. Standing before the household altar to the family gods, unvisited since the demise of Dinah, Tiberius pondered the role of the gods in his life. He had completely ignored them for better than two years, but surprisingly, they had not utterly forsaken him. Still, he could not fathom why his future required a goddess to leave her lofty realm and enter into the circumstances of men, posing as a lowly servant in order that his personal destiny might be fulfilled.

Under the watchful eye of the door attendant, who was careful not to be seen observing his master, Tiberius placed an acceptable offering at the shrine and mumbled some prayers. The servant marveled as his master had not worshiped the household gods for so long that he could scarce remember when he last saw Tiberius visit the altar, much less pay the gods homage at such a late hour. Everyone in the house was sound asleep, save he and his master, who he suspected was intoxicated. It was common knowledge among the servants that Tiberius had begun drinking heavily to combat his physical pain, so heavily in fact, he required several servants to undress him and lay him upon his couch nearly every evening. Amazingly this night, his master had not only left his couch on his own, but was managing to remain steady on his feet without the use of a cane or someone to lean upon. Concerned his master might fall and further injure himself, the attendant discreetly regarded the patrician, standing ready to assist him if need be.

Finished with his prayers, Tiberius left the shrine with purpose, strolled through the moonlit atrium, down the hall and quietly entered into Tamar's cubicle. Finding her sleeping peacefully upon her couch, he studied her for several minutes, beholding the beauty of his maidservant while considering all he knew of her. It was beyond his understanding how a fragile vessel such as she could contain the divinity of a Roman goddess. Perhaps, he simply needed to believe she was Venus for her divine power to be fully manifested. Thinking she could shed light on his ordained destiny, his judgment impaired by wine, Tiberius awakened Tamar out of her dream state, startling her into consciousness.

Waking to Tiberius standing beside her couch, Tamar sat upright, pulled her blanket close to her body and inquired nervously, "Domine, why hast thou come?"

Answering her not a word, he took her firmly by the wrist, led her from her cubicle, down the hall and into the dimly lit atrium. Situating her directly in front of the altar, he then addressed the door servant commanding, "Turn thy eyes away from the maid."

"Yes, my lord," said the door attendant, intrigued by the late night occurrence. Evening after evening, he stood alone at the door having no diversion from the monotony, but this night was altogether different and he could not help enjoying it, even if his eyes were now facing a wall.

Unnerved by her master's peculiar behavior, Tamar did not dare turn from the shrine knowing Tiberius had intentionally placed her in front of it and was himself standing right behind her. Averting her eyes away from the pagan altar which was an affront to her Jewish faith, her anxious mind fixated on her state of dress and she said timidly, "Domine, please permit me to cover myself properly. I hath need of my robe. My modesty doth suffer."

"Did thou not hear my command to the door servant?"

"Yes, Domine…even so…I suffer in this immodest state…clothed only in my night dress…before thee."

"Woman, suffer not. I hath no interest in thy feminine charms," said he nonchalantly, laying his hands upon her soft shoulders. "Tell me, what dost thou see before thee?"

"An altar…to Roman gods…" answered Tamar uneasily, drawing a deep breath, praying her master would not see she had averted her gaze from his idols.

"Thou hast rightly said. Know thee anything about the gods of Rome?"

"No, Domine. I know nothing about thy gods."

"Hast thou ever heard of the goddess Venus?"

"Yes…my lord."

"What know thee of her?"

"I know nothing…my lord," replied Tamar, disturbed by his line of questioning.

"Why trifle with me…" breathed Tiberius into Tamar's ear, his strong hands squeezing her small shoulders. "Thy appearance was foretold."

Smelling wine on his breath as spoke into her ear, Tamar realized Tiberius was inebriated. Collecting her wits about her, she chose her words carefully. "Domine, perhaps my appearance was foretold thee…but this doth seem unlikely as I am only a maidservant."

"Others seem to think thou art more…and I myself wonder at thee."

"My lord, I am what thou dost see."

Turning Tamar around, Tiberius looked upon her countenance intently, his dark piercing gaze penetrating her soul as he spoke frankly. "Woman, in thee I doth see loveliness, gentleness and uncommon virtue. I see in thee the power to heal…thou hast brought me through death and infirmity. I see in thee the mighty strength of a man…the tender heart of a woman. I see in thee courage for thou did stay my hand against my sister…not considering thy own safety…and…in all thy deeds…thou hast vexed me. Woman, I ask thee…who art thou? Reveal thyself."

"Domine, I am but thy Hebrew maidservant," answered Tamar with humility, lowering her gaze to the floor, discomfited by her master's benevolent words.

The conversation was so interesting the door attendant could hardly wait to hear more; barely a word had eluded his attentive ears.

"Surely, thou art more than a Hebrew servant?"

"Among my own people, I am no man's servant, but in thy house, I am a servant and I am subject unto thee," said she, lifting her dark eyes to his, wondering at him.

"If thou art truly subject unto me…then tell me what I desire to know. Art thou of this world or another?"

"I live in this world, same as thee, my lord. Thou dost know from whence I came. Thou found me in Subura…in the house of my kinsman," replied Tamar, suddenly recalling the strange questions asked her by Cassius and Lucius Servilius. It was all beginning to make sense now. Her master's questions were similar to theirs. Clearly, the three patricians believed she was something more than she was and why they did greatly perplexed Tamar.

"From what source dost thou derive thy mystical power?"

"Domine, I hath no mystical power. Such things are an abomination to my people. Whoever thou dost think I am…I am not and whatever power thou dost think I possess…I do not. I am only thy bondswoman. I am nothing more."

Still not fully persuaded of her, but in dire need of wine, Tiberius curtly discharged Tamar saying, "Woman, return to thy chamber."

Relieved the inquisition had ended, Tamar fled the atrium as swiftly as her bare feet would allow, the moonlight taking liberty with her modesty, revealing through her night dress her feminine shape, which caught the attention of Tiberius, who did not take his eye from her until she could no longer be seen.

XXVII

Under the cover of darkness, Xenos escorted Livilla, wife of Drusus through the dangerous streets of Subura to a clandestine meeting with her lover, Sejanus, who was waiting for her inside a pottery shop, having paid the proprietor a handsome sum of money for the use of his property and his sworn silence.

In the darkest corner of the shop, surrounded by the potter's wares, Sejanus occupied a table with a perfect view of the entrance, situated in close proximity to an exit, should a quick departure be necessary. Eyeing the shop keeper's young, appealing daughter as she set before him a flagon of wine and an ornately painted goblet that had been fashioned by her father, the Prefect took note of the girl's well developed figure and her inviting smile. Each time he saw her, he contemplated having her, though he had made no advances toward the girl, nor had he approached her father concerning her. Even so, he continued to be enthralled with the maiden, who was oblivious to his carnal interest in her due to her young age.

Several short knocks at the door put an end to Sejanus' roving eye and wanton thoughts. The shop keeper's daughter answered the door, taking direction from the Prefect, who motioned to her to do so after hearing the prearranged tapping signal he and his hireling had agreed upon. Opening the portal, the girl stood aside and in stepped the large, muscle bound gladiator, Xenos, followed by Livilla, draped from head to foot in a brown cloak, concealed from all who would try to look upon her. She could not risk being seen traipsing about town, especially in Subura, without a proper royal escort and a proper destination, neither of which she had.

Sejanus left the comfort of his chair to greet Drusus' attractive wife. Coming to her, he lowered the hood of her cloak and kissed her affectionately upon her forehead. Taking Livilla by her ring clad hand; he escorted her back to the dark corner and seated her at the table.

"Dost thou thirst, my precious," asked Sejanus of Livilla, observing her regal mannerisms as he took a chair beside her.

"No, Sejanus. I desire nothing except thee, my love," she replied, smiling sweetly, her brown eyes shining with adoration for the Prefect, which immensely pleased him.

Taking her slender jeweled hands in his, Sejanus leaned very close to her and whispered in her ear, "Livilla, my love, it is time we make our move...thy husband must be eliminated if ever we are to be together. We can not go on meeting like this forever."

Livilla pulled back from her lover, startled. "What art thou saying?"

The Prefect withdrew from his belt, a small pouch of white powdery substance and placed it inside of Livilla's soft palm, closing her fingers about the poison. "Take this...and when the opportunity presents itself, empty the full contents into his wine one evening," instructed Sejanus treacherously, plotting the death of Rome's royal heir. "Upon drinking, Drusus shall fall asleep and never awake. Then, after a suitable mourning period, I shall divorce my wife and make request of Caesar for thy hand in marriage."

Livilla could not believe her ears, exhaling; she uttered in a small quivering voice, "I cannot murder my husband..."

"If thou dost not...thou shall remain the pitiful wife of a cruel, weak minded lecher, who hath become nothing more than a slang word to the masses," growled the Prefect malevolently, referring to the fact the Roman people had begun to use Drusus' name as an insult.

"What if I am found out?"

"Thou wilt not be found out if thou dost give due consideration to how the deed should be done. Be clever...employ thy feminine wiles...be creative...thou art an intelligent woman. Do whatever it requires of thee," urged Sejanus, working to ease Livilla's fears so his future could come to fruition. He wanted nothing more than to sit upon the throne and gain a lofty place for himself in history.

With trembling hand, Livilla carefully tucked the lethal pouch into her cloak pocket under the watchful eye of the Prefect, who had Livilla so completely under his influence that she was willing to do whatever he asked of her...including murder.

"Sejanus, I shall do this terrible deed...only because I truly love thee... and I despise Drusus," declared Livilla with feeling, keeping her voice low, her eyes searching the eyes of her lover for reassurance of his devotion.

Astute in handling women, Sejanus responded by taking Livilla's face in his hands and tenderly kissing her. He then whispered in her ear the words he knew she wanted to hear. "My dear Livilla, I eagerly await the day when thou will be fully mine. I will love thee as thou hast never been loved before. There shall not be a love as great as ours. Our love for one another and for Rome will make history. Let us embrace our glorious future...and remember Drusus no more."

Livilla threw her arms about the Prefect's neck, softly admitting, "I needed to hear thee speak of thy love for me…that I might muster the courage to do what must be done."

Smiling sinisterly to himself, his countenance hidden from sight, buried in Livilla's fragrant brown hair, Sejanus knew he was on the verge of achieving his ultimate goal…the throne was nearly his! Ah, life was good!

"I long for the day when we can be seen together in public," said Drusus' wife, picturing herself and Sejanus holding a lavish banquet in the palace hall. "I loathe sneaking about like a commoner."

"Livilla, thou must leave now, before someone discovers thou art missing. We shall not meet again…till the deed is done and a respectable mourning period hath passed. We cannot afford to arouse suspicion," he stated under his breath, removing her arms from about him and gazing upon her intently. "Understood?"

"I understand," came her lovesick reply.

"Escort her home," barked Sejanus, looking to his hired gladiator.

The lovers rose from their chairs and Sejanus placed Livilla under Xenos' care and protection. Walking them to the door, the Prefect asked, "Gladiator, did thou deliver the letter as I commanded thee?"

"I sent a small boy to deliver it," answered Xenos. "Still, the centurion would not leave his post to hand it to Tiberius' sister as hoped…nevertheless, it was delivered. And the results…I am happy to report were better than planned…the letter was transferred directly into the hands of her betrothed."

"Excellent! That stroke of good luck should hath produced a great deal of trouble for Tiberius Marcius," snickered the Prefect gleefully.

"I assure thee it did for I saw the betrothed patrician storm from the house shortly thereafter…his angry countenance proof positive that he had read the letter."

"Excellent work, Xenos! Thou shalt be nicely rewarded! Since I am not at liberty to kill Tiberius Marcius…I shall trouble him at every turn! He will wish he were dead when I get through with him!"

The gladiator grinned broadly, revealing several missing teeth, pleased his employer approved of the job he had done for him.

"Perhaps, we can lure the pretty Jewess from the safety of his house by utilizing her aunt…who lives here in Subura," said the Prefect thinking out loud, formulating another evil scheme. "Locate the maid's kinswoman…for future use…" ordered Sejanus, catching sight of Livilla's perplexed expression out of the corner of his eye. Thinking it unwise she should hear or know too much of his business, the Prefect said no more, though his wicked mind continued to devise his sinister plot.

"Consider her located," answered Xenos confidently.

Kissing Livilla lightly upon her forehead, Sejanus ushered her and the gladiator out the door and on their way, telling them, "Make haste with thyselves."

"I thought thou wert accompanying us," said the gladiator to Sejanus, looking back at his employer, whose tall, fit, uniformed frame filled the doorway.

"I hath some unfinished business to attend to," winked the Prefect, glancing over his shoulder lustfully at the shop keeper's daughter.

XXVIII

Accompanied by his father, Cassius arrived at Tiberius' home an hour before clients were ordinarily seen. Tiberius had not sent for either man and Cassius was not altogether certain his cousin would receive him after their heated argument the week before, so he brought his father along to ease the tension between them.

"Steward, wake Tiberius Marcius," ordered Flavius, standing in the open atrium.

"My lord, Tiberius Marcius is in the triclinium, eating his morning meal," said the steward, visibly humble in the presence of the patricians.

Cassius noticed the change in the steward's demeanor, finding his servile manner, a great deal more to his personal liking. He did not believe a servant should think too highly of himself.

"We shall join him," asserted Flavius, walking past the steward, followed by Cassius, who looked upon the servant harshly, remembering their last encounter.

Bowing, the steward lowered his gaze to the floor and kept it there as the patricians passed him. He did not wish to antagonize either one, especially Cassius, whom he knew had it in for him.

Flavius and his son entered the dining room and found Tiberius seated upon a couch, conversing with his mother, who was sitting across the table from him.

Upon their entrance, Tiberius greeted them pleasantly, saying, "To what do I owe this unexpected visit? Hast thou come to break bread with me?"

"Need I a reason to visit my family?" quipped Flavius, walking over to his sister, who rose to her feet, receiving from her brother an affectionate kiss upon her cheek. Not seeing his niece at the table, he asked, "Flavia, where is thy lovely daughter? Hath she no need of food?"

Thinking it best that Tiberius answer her brother's questions, Flavia looked to her son, waiting on him to speak.

Surmising something was amiss and it had to do with his lovely niece whom he adored, Flavius turned from Flavia to regard his nephew.

"Is she well," inquired Cassius, genuinely concerned for Priscilla.

"She is taking her meals in her room," replied Tiberius dryly, reluctant to discuss his sister as he was still very angry with her. "She hath been punished."

Seating himself, Flavius asked, "Why? What hath she done?"

Waiting on the reply, Cassius also took a place at the table.

Immediately, two servants came forward and set tableware before the men that they might partake of the morning meal, but the guests were not interested in eating, rather in hearing what Tiberius had to say.

"She hath encouraged an ardent suitor of questionable character by the name of Claudius. The scoundrel sent her a love letter…and regretfully the distasteful communication fell into the hands of Lucius Servilius…compromising Priscilla's betrothal. For this cause, I whipped her and banished her from my sight till her fate is decided. I now await the return of Lucius Servilius," explained Tiberius, his countenance stern. "I shall abide by his decision…whatever it may be."

Cassius was utterly surprised to learn Tiberius had beat Priscilla. If he had not heard it from Tiberius' own lips, he would never have believed him capable of whipping his sister. Hearing this and seeing the change in the steward led Cassius to conclude his cousin had given his words serious consideration. The argument between them had not been for naught. Evidently, Tiberius had taken his advice and set his household in order.

"This is most unfortunate," said Flavius, shaking his head and sighing deeply. "I am greatly disappointed in Priscilla. I thought she possessed better judgment. Hast thou given any thought to who she shall wed if Lucius Servilius should decline to marry her?"

"I shall wed her to the first oaf who asks for her!" remarked Tiberius bitterly.

"Tiberius Marcius, be reasonable. She is a patrician. Certainly, thou can find a more suitable husband for her than some common oaf," asserted Flavius, opposed to Priscilla being sentenced to such an awful fate. "I will not permit thee to wed thy sister to a man beneath her social status. Despite her foolish transgression, thou must do right by her."

Scowling, Tiberius looked his uncle in the eye and said stubbornly, "Priscilla's fate lies in my hands, not thine! I shall do with her as I please!"

Seeing an opportunity, Cassius seized it, brazenly announcing,

"If Lucius Servilius wilt not wed Priscilla…then I shall take her as my wife."

A hush fell over the room as each patrician digested Cassius' shocking declaration.

Flavia felt as if she had suffered a physical blow and struggled to catch her breath, her countenance paling.

Tiberius was stunned and it showed upon his aspect.

Red in the face, Flavius broke the silence, angrily rebuking his son. "Cassius, thou cannot be serious! Priscilla is thy cousin! It is not proper! I will not hear of it!"

"Thou hast taken leave of thy senses!" exclaimed Tiberius, reeling at the thought of his cousin and sister joined in marriage.

"What is to become of Turia?" asked Flavius, staring at his son, his face still flushed. "Thou art betrothed to her."

"I shall inform Turia that I hath chosen another," replied Cassius nonchalantly, not in the least bit bothered by the negative reaction of his family.

"Priscilla and thee would not make a good marriage…thou art too much alike in temperament," contended Tiberius, finding it hard to swallow that Cassius desired his sister. "Thou would make one another miserable and what purpose would that serve? Turia would make thee a much better wife."

Flavia agreed with her son, but prudently kept her opinion to herself. Now was not the time for a woman to speak.

Not easily dissuaded, Cassius argued, "Simply because Priscilla and I are alike is no reason for us not to marry. I daresay; it is the very reason we should."

"I absolutely will not permit it," declared Flavius heatedly. "Cassius, I forbid thee to do this thing…I shall disown thee!"

"And what shall be the gain of that? Thou dost punish thyself, not I. I am wealthy whether or not I receive an inheritance from thee," retorted the heir callously. "Pater, I hath no need of thy money or thy approval!"

Stinging from his son's sharp tongue, Flavius stood to his feet, speechless, his face and neck red with indignation.

"Enough!" snapped Tiberius impatiently. "I will hear no more of this nonsense!"

Distressed over the turmoil in her family, Flavia was on the verge of fainting, the conflict having become too much for her. Feeling lightheaded, she leaned forward in her seat and laid her face in her hands.

Seeing his mother, Tiberius abandoned his couch and went to her, gently helping her from her chair. Summoning a male servant in the room, he instructed the servant to assist her to her chamber that she might lie down and rest.

As the Roman matron was escorted from the triclinium, the three patricians watched in silence, each man reflecting on the words he had uttered in her presence. Cassius felt he had said too much, Flavius reckoned he had not said enough and Tiberius regretted having spoken at all.

XXIX

Attending to her mistress' vanity, Tamar was arranging Priscilla's many perfume bottles when one in particular caught her attention. Amber in color and round in shape, the glass vial was crowned with a tall, slender, ornate top of pure gold, having a polished amber stone set therein. Enthralled by its beauty, Tamar picked up the lovely bottle and opened it, smelling the fragrance within. Startled by a servant girl entering the cubicle, Tamar dropped the perfume vial and it fell to the marble floor, shattering to pieces at the foot of the vanity, its sweet aroma filling the room. Horrified by what she had done, tears welled up in Tamar's eyes. Distraught, she bent down to gather up the broken fragments, dreading the wrath of her mistress.

The servant girl saw what happened and immediately raced to tell Priscilla, waking her from an afternoon nap.

Seeing Priscilla's bare feet drawing near the vanity, Tamar looked up at her mistress and cried fearfully, "Forgive me, Dominilla!"

"That perfume was a gift from my father…I was saving it for my wedding night…" moaned Priscilla, discovering her beautiful bottle broken and its treasured fragrance lying on the floor.

"I entreat thee, hath mercy, Dominilla…" pleaded Tamar, her voice quivering, tears streaming down her cheeks. "I should not hath touched the vial. It was so lovely and I…I was drawn to it. I beg thy forgiveness…"

"What dost thou mean…thou wert drawn to it?" snapped Priscilla, looking upon her servant sternly.

"It was so beautiful…I desired a closer look," explained Tamar contritely, gazing down at the amber glass she held in her hand. "I was admiring the perfume vial when it slipped from my grasp. Words cannot express my great sorrow."

"A lash or two across thy back would serve thee well," Priscilla threatened, but as she was yet speaking, her conscience was pricked and her heart softened toward the servant.

"Dominilla…please…hath mercy," begged Tamar. "I entreat thee…hath mercy…"

Recalling the painful sting of Tiberius' belt upon her own flesh, Priscilla reconsidered her rash words. Taking a deep breath, she slowly exhaled and said, "Maid, fear not. No punishment shall befall thee. I shall grant thee mercy for I hath remembered thy great kindness unto me on the day of my brother's wrath."

Receiving clemency from her mistress, Tamar blinked back her tears, scarcely believing her ears.

Addressing the maid who had tattled on Tamar, Priscilla said curtly, "Remove the glass, but do not disturb my perfume top or the fragrance. Leave them where they lie. I shall see to them myself."

Heeding her mistress, the maid found a small basin in which to dispose of the broken glass and began clearing away the shattered fragments, confounded by Priscilla's merciful treatment of Tamar.

Leaving her servants, Priscilla entered her closet and chose a nightdress from among her vast array of clothing. Returning with it, she knelt down beside Tamar and sopped up some of the precious perfume using the chosen garment. After which, she laid the palms of her hands in the remaining fragrance and said to Tamar, "Undo thy hair."

Obeying, Tamar did as she was told, wondering at the strange command.

"Turn thy back unto me," directed Priscilla, her voice benevolent, calming the nerves of her maid.

Again, Tamar complied.

Taking Tamar's long, dark mane in hand, Priscilla gently ran her perfumed hands down the length of her servant's hair, repeating the process several times. Finishing, the patrician further instructed her maid, "Do unto me as I hath done unto thee." Having spoken, Priscilla turned her back to Tamar and removed the band and silver pins from her hair, loosening her brown tresses.

Placing her hands in the spilled perfume, Tamar reverently anointed her mistress' hair, the sweet fragrance creating a bond between the two young women.

"Now…my perfume hath not gone to waste," stated Priscilla, turning to look at Tamar, in whose gentle, dark eyes stood tears. "Maid, be of good cheer. Today thou hast found favor with thy mistress. I shall treat thee with kindness from this day forward," vowed Priscilla, giving the gold perfume top to Tamar. "Take this…it shall be as a remembrance unto thee of my pledge."

Deeply moved, Tamar humbly received the gift. Bowing her head, she kissed Priscilla's hand, saying, "Dominilla...behold thy faithful handmaid."

Expressing good will toward her maid, Priscilla tenderly laid her hand upon the crown of Tamar's head and was about to speak over her when the door to her cubicle opened, disrupting the intimate moment. Glancing upward, Priscilla saw her mother, who regarded her daughter and the maid with intense interest.

Stepping inside, Flavia closed the door behind her and asked, "Priscilla, do I not smell the perfume thy father gave unto thee?"

"Thou dost, Mater," answered the daughter.

"Why is thy hair and that of thy maid's undone?"

"I broke the vial," lied Priscilla, shouldering the blame, unsure of her mother's reaction should the truth be known for the perfume was very costly. "I chose to anoint our hair and my raiment with the fragrance rather than see it entirely wasted."

Flavia discerned there was more to the amiable scene than what she had been told, but sensing good had transpired between the two, she chose not to pry any further. She had weightier matters to address. "Daughter, I must speak with thee...privately," voiced Flavia.

Rising to her feet, Priscilla dismissed her maids.

Retrieving her mistress' night dress from the floor, the servant girl placed it upon the vanity bench and together the two maidservants exited the cubicle, one blessed; the other jealous.

"Mater, what is it? Thou doth not look well," remarked Priscilla, observing her mother's pallid countenance. "Sit upon my couch and rest thyself."

"Only for a moment...I hath not much time. I hath come to warn thee."

"Warn me...of what?"

Reaching the couch, the two women sat down beside one another, Priscilla bracing herself for what her mother was about to say, fearing the worst.

"Early this morning thy uncle and cousin paid a visit to thy brother. I was present at the time of their visitation and was privy to their conversation. A conversation, I found most troubling."

"Why? What was said?"

"Before I answer thee...I must ask thee a hard question. Answer truthfully before the gods, daughter."

"I shall, Mater," replied Priscilla earnestly.

"Hath Cassius ever behaved unseemly towards thee?"

"What dost thou mean…unseemly?"

"Hath he ever made unwanted advances toward thee, Priscilla?"

Priscilla's mouth dropped open, shocked at the inquiry. "No, Mater! Why hast thou asked me this strange question?"

"I ask because…Cassius hath announced he will marry thee if Lucius Servilius wilt not."

Priscilla gasped, mortified at the thought.

"Daughter, didst thou know thy cousin desired thee?"

"No, Mater! I knew not! What did Tiberius say to this?"

"He and thy uncle were adamantly against it!"

"Oh…thank the gods," exclaimed Priscilla, breathing easier, visibly relieved.

"Priscilla, heed my warning. If Lucius Servilius wilt not wed thee, I fear Cassius may take matters into his own hands. Perhaps, the gods hath not yet abandoned thee. Maybe, it was they who arranged for thee to be confined to thy cubicle…to keep thee from his sight. Thy misfortune may be good fortune in disguise. Daughter, thou would do well to pray to the gods that Lucius Servilius wilt marry thee in spite of thy indiscretion. Thy fate doth lie solely in their hands. No mortal flesh can undo the mischief thou hast set in motion."

"Mater, I shall heed thy warning," assured Priscilla, finding Cassius' interest in her very disturbing. "Pray to the gods for me, Mater. I desire a better fate than the one I hath brought upon myself."

"I shall," said her mother wearily, rising from the couch. "I must leave thee now. Say nothing of what I hath told thee."

"My lips are sealed, Mater," promised Priscilla, her heart sinking as she watched her mother exit the room. Left alone, Priscilla fell upon her couch and wept, her future appearing more ominous than ever before.

Tiberius was about to enter his study when he caught the scent of sweet perfume in the air. Turning around, he saw Tamar hastening through the atrium, her unsecured tresses cascading down her back.

"Woman, come hither," beckoned Tiberius, his masculine senses whetted by the sight and smell of his maidservant.

Hearing his command, Tamar turned about and cautiously approached her master, surmising her appearance was the reason for the summons.

Beholding the beauty of his servant, Tiberius stepped aside and motioned for Tamar to enter the study ahead of him, which she did with some hesitancy. Entering after her, he closed the door behind him, eyeing the maid as she stood in the midst of his study. Walking over to where she stood, he drew very near her person, took a handful of her wavy, dark brown hair and lifted it to his face, smelling the lingering fragrance.

Finding his closeness and the intimacy of his touch disconcerting, Tamar drew a ragged breath, which did not escape the hearing of Tiberius.

"Woman, who hath anointed thy head," he questioned, his gaze fastened upon the maidservant, the enticing fragrance filling his nostrils.

"My mistress hath done so, Domine," answered Tamar meekly, not daring to meet his inquiring eyes.

Surprised by her answer, Tiberius laughed. "What? My selfish sister hath used her precious perfume to anoint a servant. I find that difficult to believe."

"It is true, Domine. Thy sister is not selfish as thou dost suppose. She hath treated me with great kindness."

Amused by Tamar's defense of Priscilla, he unhanded her hair and said lightheartedly, "Then, she hath done well. Tell me, woman, why hath she dealt with thee so kindly?"

"My lord, I broke a bottle of her perfume…the one her father gave unto her…" confessed Tamar, her eyes still downcast, ashamed of what she had done. "…and she graciously forgave my trespass…returning the kindness I had shown her on the day of thy terrible wrath."

"Continue, woman," urged Tiberius, finding the story quite interesting as it was unlike Priscilla to forgive anyone, especially a servant. "I would hear this strange tale of my sister's goodness."

"Domine, thy sister was not willing that her perfume should be altogether wasted. For this reason, she anointed my hair and bid me do the same unto her. Then, she spoke these words unto me. "Thou hast found favor with thy mistress. I shall treat thee with kindness from this day forward…" said Tamar, choking back emotion as she repeated Priscilla's vow.

Realizing the maid had been greatly affected by his sister's benevolence, Tiberius asked, "Dost thou believe her?"

"I do, my lord," Tamar responded, lifting her head and extending her hand, revealing the treasure she held. "Why would she give this unto me if she did not intend to honor her pledge?"

Noting the gold trinket in his servant's small hand, Tiberius made no reply to her question. Walking away, he strolled over to the table where the flagon was kept and poured himself a cup of wine with which to medicate himself. Consuming it, he set the empty goblet down on the table, casting his eye upon his lovely servant, who was growing steadily more uncomfortable in his presence.

"Domine, grant me leave," requested Tamar anxiously, feeling the penetrating gaze of her master. "I wish to return to my mistress."

Sensing her discomfort, Tiberius knew she wanted to escape him, but he was in no hurry to dismiss her. He found her a pleasant distraction from his physical affliction and family squabbles, being weary of both. Returning to Tamar, Tiberius closed in upon her, taking her in with his eyes and said, "Tarry awhile, woman."

"Domine, send me from thy presence...for when thou dost drink much wine...I do fear thy intentions," Tamar stated timidly, lowering her gaze once again.

"Woman, what hast thou to fear from me? When hath I done thee harm," questioned Tiberius, put out of countenance by her words. "I hath treated thee well as befits thy station in life. Yet, thou sayest unto me...I fear thy intentions. What manner of speech is this?"

Before Tamar could articulate a reply, there was a tap at the door, providing her with a momentary reprieve.

Responding impatiently, Tiberius glanced at the door and barked gruffly, "Enter."

Flavia opened the door and saw Tamar standing in the room. Struck by her son's close proximity to the maid, it crossed Flavia's mind that Tiberius found the servant desirable.

"Pardon my intrusion," apologized Flavia, reading displeasure upon her son's rigidly held aspect. "It appears I hath come at an inopportune time."

"Thou hast," said Tiberius tersely, not bothering to disguise his irritation.

Retreating, Flavia closed the door, her womanly intuition proving to be sound. It was just as she thought. Her son was interested in the maid. Offering a prayer of gratitude to the gods, Flavia took heart, believing the maidservant had a divine assignment. If the all wise gods had chosen a lowly maid to revive passion in Tiberius instead of a well born Roman woman, then so be it. No mortal was in a position to thwart the will of the gods, but they could assist their divine purpose and Flavia intended to do just that.

XXX

"Steward, are there no clients in the atrium," inquired Tiberius, sitting at his desk, finding the morning unusually quiet.

"None, my lord," replied the servant, his tone and stance meek, ever mindful of the day his master's thick leather belt met his bare flesh. Though he felt his master had been justified in punishing him as severely as he had, the steward had become overly fearful of displeasing Tiberius in word or deed. So much so, he could barely manage to meet his master's gaze.

"If any should arrive, thou wilt find me in the stable," said Tiberius, rising to his feet, aware of the steward's changed demeanor, but choosing to do nothing to ease his apprehension.

"Yes, Domine," said the steward, respectfully bowing before exiting the study.

Leaving the tablinum, Tiberius strolled into the garden courtyard which was surrounded by a paved walkway and covered by a roof supported by tall ornate columns. In the center of the garden was a large fountain bearing the image of a young woman carrying a water pot on one shoulder from which water trickled and danced at her lifeless feet. Encircling the fountain was an elaborate garden of lush greenery, decorative statues, fountain pools and marble benches. On both sides of the courtyard, there were rooms. Bypassing his sister's sitting room, a spare bedroom, the library, the kitchen, the slave quarters, storerooms, toilets and the bathing facilities, Tiberius came to the stables located at the very back of the house.

There he was met by his mute stable servant, who was surprised by the visit. Greeting Tiberius with a reverent nod of his head, the servant showed him to his horse, wondering if he was yet physically able to ride the animal.

Upon seeing his master, the black stallion welcomed him with a whiney, bringing pleasure to Tiberius, who patted his horse affectionately. The soldier had not laid eyes on his magnificent beast since the night of the ambush.

Hearing some commotion in the courtyard, Tiberius peered out of the stable and saw Anatole and Quintus Atilius fast approaching him, their countenances somber. At the entrance of the courtyard, he noticed the steward and several other servants gathered together, engrossed in conversation. Sensing something dreadful had occurred; Tiberius swallowed hard and went out to meet his friend and his servant.

"Domine, Quintus Atilius hath some bad news," proclaimed Anatole, visibly distressed.

Tiberius looked to Quintus Atilius, anxiously waiting his words.

"Tiberius Marcius, I deeply regret to inform thee that thy friend, Drusus, son of Caesar hath died this day of mysterious causes," said Quintus Atilius, feeling the impact of his statement. "Macro sent word of Drusus' demise only moments ago. The entire city is talking about his death…some are even celebrating it."

"Rome hath suffered a great loss…" Tiberius said solemnly, moved by the gravity of the announcement. "Those who do celebrate…are fools!"

"Macro hath ordered my return to camp. He fears there may be trouble in the city."

"I find that rather unlikely, given nine thousand troops are housed within the confines of Rome…courtesy of that crafty vizier, Sejanus," remarked Tiberius sarcastically.

"Tiberius Marcius, I feel compelled to warn thee…Sejanus may decide now is the time to settle his score with thee. Caesar will put aside the affairs of state to mourn his son and when he doth, Sejanus will be given a greater measure of power. May the gods help us all. Drusus' death and my recall provide him with the perfect opportunity to come against thee. Thou would be wise to remain on thy guard. I strongly advise thee to set Anatole at thy entrance to keep watch for I know not if Macro will permit my return."

"Quintus Atilius, I shall heed thy counsel and do as thou hast said. Anatole hath proved himself to be a fine soldier. I am confident in his ability to safeguard my house and my person in thy absence," stated Tiberius, regarding his servant, who appreciated his master's vote of confidence and was eager to rise to the occasion.

"Friend, I leave thee. May the gods watch over thee."

"And also over thee, Quintus Atilius."

Taking his leave, Quintus Atilius departed from the home of Tiberius, following orders to report to his superior at once. In route to the barracks, his mind turned over the fact that Macro, the second in command had summoned him and not the Prefect. Quintus Atilius liked Macro well enough and even respected him, but he could not help wondering if Macro was in cahoots with Sejanus. Pondering the lofty power the Prefect held; which had now increased considerably with the death of Drusus, the centurion suspected Sejanus had orchestrated the untimely demise of Caesar's heir in an attempt to achieve the ultimate position of power. And he was not alone in his thinking, Tiberius suspected the same.

XXXI

Discussing Drusus' death, a handful of clients stood in the atrium talking amongst themselves as they waited to be called by their patron, Tiberius Marcius. Also waiting was Lucius Servilius, Cassius and Flavius, the latter of which noticed his son and Lucius Servilius had nothing to say to one another. The senator was about to look into the matter when the steward called him forth, granting him preferential treatment over the others as he was the highest ranking individual among those gathered.

Taking full advantage of his senatorial status, Flavius insisted his son accompany him. Not daring to thwart the senator's will, the steward mutely escorted the two patricians to the tablinum. Entering, Flavius addressed his nephew, his countenance more somber than usual. Cassius mirrored his father's countenance.

"Tiberius Marcius, I assume thou hast heard the news of Drusus' death," began Flavius, declining his nephew's invitation to be seated.

"I hath, uncle," replied Tiberius Marcius, seated behind his desk which was littered with the scrolls he had been reading all morning.

"Troubling rumors are circulating among my esteemed colleagues," stated the senator, standing tall, bearing the senatorial stripe upon his toga. "Some believe Sejanus may hath played a part in Drusus' death. What think thee, Tiberius Marcius? Thou knowest the Prefect better than most. Dost thou think he would commit treason?"

"I am of the mind that Sejanus is capable of anything…including treason. He doth possess great power…which he freely exercises for his own benefit. Most notably, he hath appointed himself as the Emperor's protector, controlling who may come before Caesar and who may not. It is nearly impossible to communicate with Caesar alone without Sejanus being present to monitor what is said. Remarkably, Caesar doth not seem to realize he is being guarded by the very one he ought to fear. No one is permitted an opportunity to tell him differently. Neither shall they be afforded the chance to accuse the Prefect of murdering Drusus. As it stands, there is very little anyone can say or do against the Prefect…and live."

"Thou knowest it doth not bode well for thee that Drusus' hath died," submitted Cassius, grim faced as he stood beside his father. "If the Prefect is bold enough to murder Drusus right underneath Caesar's nose…then he is certainly bold enough to come after thee, Tiberius Marcius. It is not a matter of if he will, but when."

"Cassius, I am aware of that."

"Now is not the time to let thy guard down," continued Cassius, meeting the steady gaze of his cousin. "I am hard pressed to believe thy servant can meet the formidable challenge of protecting thee from such a vicious enemy. Where is Quintus Atilius? Why is he not keeping watch at thy door?"

"Quintus Atilius was recalled yesterday morning by Macro," answered Tiberius, finding his cousin tedious to deal with as of late. "As for my servant, I hath confidence in him for I hath trained him in the ways of war. Anatole is as militarily sound as any soldier under my command."

"Tiberius Marcius, instead of relying on one servant with commendable ability, thou ought to hire several body guards," suggested Flavius, hoping his nephew would heed his advice. "Shall I hire some able bodied men and send them unto thee?"

"No," Tiberius responded flatly, feeling as though he was being mollycoddled and detesting it. "I am quite capable of handling my own affairs."

"Tiberius Marcius, I am not implying thou cannot handle thy affairs," retorted the senator, looking at him sternly. "I am concerned for thy safety and that of thy household. Thou art not yet fully recovered from thy grievous wounds. It would be difficult for thee to fight off another attack in thy weakened state."

Irritated with being seen as defenseless, Tiberius rose from his chair and said testily, "When I need a nursemaid, I will be sure to notify thee, Uncle."

Cassius laughed, finding his cousin's response amusing. However, Flavius did not appreciate his nephew's sarcasm in the least.

"Tiberius Marcius, thou art hard headed," Flavius fired back. "Do as thou wilt concerning thyself, but do not subject thy mother and sister to harm! As paterfamilias, thou art responsible for their safety! Lucius Servilius stands in thy atrium waiting, call him in and arrange thy sister's wedding. Once thy sister is married, send thy mother unto me for safekeeping. I will rest easier knowing Priscilla resides in her husband's house and Flavia is safe with me. As for thee, Tiberius Marcius…whatever evil befalls thee is on thy own obstinate head!"

"Pater, perhaps Lucius Servilius hath not come for Priscilla as thou dost suppose. What then?"

Turning to his son, Flavius snapped, "Cassius, I will not tolerate a repeat performance from thee. Priscilla is not thy concern."

"I hath heard enough," Tiberius interjected, deciding to usher his uncle and cousin out the door before tempers exploded. "I do not wish to revisit the subject of my sister with thee. I hath other pressing matters on my agenda that require attention. Be ye on thy way."

"The most pressing of which is safety," reiterated the senator, having the last word as he and Cassius were escorted to the door by Tiberius.

As his relatives exited, Tiberius called in Lucius Servilius, who strolled past Cassius without the slightest acknowledgment of him. Noticing there was no exchange of any kind between the men, Tiberius realized something had transpired between them, something neither man had discussed with him. Hoping the issue would be revealed in conversation, Tiberius invited Lucius Servilius into the tablinum.

"Tiberius Marcius, forgive the ill timing of my visit. I know thou dost mourn the loss of thy royal friend."

"Lucius Servilius, whatever the circumstances, thou art always welcome in my house."

"Friend, thou art gracious," said Lucius Servilius, seating himself in the comfortable client's chair, his eye on Tiberius, who also seated himself.

"Hast thou come on the matter of my sister?"

"I hath."

"Lucius Servilius, before I hear thy decision concerning my sister, I hath somewhat to say unto thee."

"Say on," replied Lucius Servilius, having an inkling of what Tiberius was about to say as he had long expected it.

"I am not going to mince words, Lucius Servilius. I hath violated thy trust. I knew of Priscilla's infatuation with Claudius and withheld the information from thee," confessed Tiberius, looking his friend squarely in the eye. "My reasons for concealing Priscilla's foolishness were largely self serving. I wanted nothing to interfere with our friendship or our business alliance. However, the communication from Claudius hath brought Priscilla's lack of wisdom to light as well as my attempt to hide it."

"I appreciate thy honesty, Tiberius Marcius…slow as it was in forthcoming," Lucius Servilius said coolly, meeting Tiberius' gaze. "Friend, since we are clearing the air, thou should know I knew of the matter. I hath my own reliable sources, which were only too eager to report such titillating news unto me."

"Then…Claudius' letter came as no surprise unto thee…" uttered Tiberius, visibly taken aback.

"The only surprise was thy sister's tearful plea to forgive her."

"The silly creature owed thee that much," remarked Tiberius bitterly, not bothering to mask his feelings. "Considering all the trouble Claudius hath caused, I should hath hired an assassin to put an end to his worthless life."

"Someone did exactly that. Claudius hath been dead for six months," said Lucius Servilius, his face and tone expressionless.

"By whose hand?"

"Suffice it to say, the deed is done. He shall not trouble either of us again."

"Well, that is a bit of good news in the midst of so much bad," quipped Tiberius, knowing Lucius Servilius had more reason to want Claudius dead than he. "Still, I am perplexed. How did a dead man write a letter unto Priscilla?"

"He did not write the letter…thy enemy penned it."

"Ye gods, I laid my belt to Priscilla and my steward on account of this deception," exclaimed Tiberius, remembering his heavy handedness.

"Thy enemy is wily. He doth not care what degree of mischief he causes…so long as he inflicts some measure of harm on thee."

"How dost thou know it was the Prefect who penned the letter?"

"I hath my sources," answered Lucius Servilius stiffly.

Disturbed, Tiberius shook his head.

"Tiberius Marcius, thy trouble hath not been for naught. The letter was useful in revealing Priscilla's heart. I hath decided to take her for my wife…though I do so with some stipulations."

"State thy stipulations, Lucius Servilius. I shall honor them."

"The wedding ceremony is to take place with as few in attendance as possible. I shall not reward Priscilla's errant behavior with a joyful celebration as if she hath committed no wrong. Her wedding day is to be solemn. The wedding meal shall be short in length and there shall be no merry procession to my home. I alone shall walk with her. It is my desire she enter my house with a healthy measure of fear and reverence. I intend to rule her with a firm hand."

"Lucius Servilius, I shall abide by thy stipulations. In addition, I hath a few of my own."

"I am listening."

"If my sister fails to please thee and thou dost give her a writ of divorcement, be it known, I shall not hold it against thee. What occurs between thee and Priscilla shall not hinder our friendship or our business. Should thou decide to divorce her, I make two requests of thee. One… if she displeases thee, do not send her back to me. I will not receive her in disgrace. Two…provide her with a generous allowance that she might live in the manner to which she is accustomed. I do not want her latter end to be so terrible that she should desire death."

"Tiberius Marcius, I agree to thy stipulations. The terms of the wedding are settled. I shall return for Priscilla in three days," announced Lucius Servilius, standing to his feet, his toga falling neatly about his robust frame.

"Thy wedding ceremony shall be conducted as thou hast said. I shall see to it myself," assured Tiberius, also rising from his chair. "Dost thou wish to inform Priscilla of thy decision?"

"No. I leave that to thee," replied Lucius Servilius and having said all he intended to say he exited the room abruptly, leaving Tiberius confounded.

Troubled by the restrained manner in which his friend had conducted himself, Tiberius sensed their friendship had been permanently altered and he was right for Lucius Servilius no longer fully trusted Tiberius Marcius, his sister or his cousin.

XXXII

Tiberius entered Priscilla's chamber and found his sister seated at her vanity, his mother standing directly behind her, her hands resting upon her daughter's shoulders. The women's conversation came to an abrupt end as the paterfamilias stepped inside and closed the door. "Hast thou any servants in attendance," he inquired, glancing about the room.

"No," answered Priscilla, fear gripping her as she vividly recalled their last encounter.

"What is it, son," asked Flavia, knowing why he had come, but feigning ignorance.

"Lucius Servilius hath informed me of his decision concerning Priscilla," stated Tiberius, fastening his dark eyes upon his sister.

Enduring her brother's scrutiny, Priscilla maintained her outward composure, though inwardly she was unsettled by his penetrating gaze. She felt her mother gently squeeze her shoulders, whether nervously or reassuringly, she could not discern.

"He hath decided to take thee for his wife, Priscilla."

"Thank the gods," declared Flavia, delighted with the news.

"Fortune hath smiled upon me," said Priscilla, sighing with relief.

"That remains to be seen," remarked Tiberius dryly, his gaze unwavering.

"What dost thou mean, son," questioned Flavia, not liking the sound of his words.

"Whether or not fortune hath smiled upon Priscilla is yet to be determined. The answer lies in her willingness to please Lucius Servilius. She hath angered her betrothed and he hath set forth stern stipulations pertaining to the marriage ceremony. He demands the wedding guests be few in number, the meal short in length and there is to be no joyful procession to his home. The ceremony is to take place in three days and is to be a solemn occasion in all respects."

Priscilla began to cry, her childhood dream of a beautiful wedding dashed, never to be realized.

Flavia swallowed hard, feeling her daughter's disappointment.

Unmoved by his sister's tears, Tiberius admonished, "If thy marriage doth end in divorce, Priscilla, I shall disown thee. Thou wilt not be welcome here. I wilt not receive thee in disgrace, neither shall I look upon thee again. Thou shalt be as a stranger unto me. Therefore, I do strongly advise thee to obey and reverence thy husband as is thy duty; lest he divorce thee. Thou would do well to spend thy days endeavoring to regain the favor of Lucius Servilius."

"Tiberius Marcius, why speak of divorce before there hast been a marriage," asked Flavia, perturbed.

"Mater, Priscilla hath lost the trust of Lucius Servilius. She must enter into the marriage at a disadvantage…one that may lead to divorce."

"What kind of a marriage begins with talk of a divorce," cried Priscilla, her large brown eyes brimming with tears. "I feel as though I am being punished!"

"Thou art," voiced Tiberius harshly, looking upon his sister with displeasure. "Thy misery is of thy own making."

"I wish I were dead!" wailed Priscilla.

"I am certain death is within the realm of possibility if thou doth cause Lucius Servilius any more trouble!"

Priscilla's tear filled eyes widened in horror.

"Woman, I counsel thee to obey thy husband and render unto him thy utmost respect for he hath the power to end thy pampered life," warned Tiberius, deliberately instilling fear in Priscilla.

Frightened by the thought of death at the hands of her husband, Priscilla turned to her mother, who threw her protective arms about her daughter, equally frightened.

Satisfied he had put the fear of the gods into his sister; Tiberius strolled out of her chamber, leaving his mother to handle Priscilla and the details of her impending marriage.

XXXIII

On the eve of her wedding ceremony, Priscilla left her room for the first time since being punished, Tiberius reluctantly granting her permission. Accompanied by her mother, she made her way to the altar in the atrium, to perform the customary offering to the household gods, having in her possession several cherished childhood toys and her gold bulla, a locket containing a protective amulet worn by children to ward off evil. With quiet reverence, she approached the altar, knelt down and laid her playthings on the marble floor beneath the shrine as her mother looked on. Then she rose to her feet and removed the bulla from around her neck, momentarily considering the last icon of her childhood before relinquishing it to the gods. Leaving her childhood at the altar, Priscilla stood on the threshold of womanhood. Tomorrow she would become the wife of Lucius Servilius, a man whose anger was kindled against her, whose favor she had foolishly forfeited. Afraid to face her betrothed and suffer under his hand the consequences of her actions, she earnestly sought the assistance of the divine deities, praying she might obtain his forgiveness and redeem herself in his sight.

Observing Priscilla as she stood before the family altar, Flavia felt a strong measure of concern for her daughter knowing her future happiness was very much in jeopardy. It did not bode well that Lucius Servilius had insisted on a solemn wedding ceremony thereby making public his displeasure with Priscilla. Flavia knew marrying under such circumstances was not ideal for any woman, let alone her strong willed daughter. Worried, Flavia bowed her head and uttered a heartfelt prayer to the gods, beseeching the powers that be with such intensity that she caught the attention of her son, who had just come into the main house from the garden courtyard.

Pausing, Tiberius regarded his mother, half wondering if her sincere petition would be answered in his presence. Certain she was offering up prayers for Priscilla, he then fixed a stern eye upon his sister and she being under his surveillance, endured his piercing gaze.

Upon finishing her prayer, Flavia lifted her head and saw Priscilla staring anxiously past her. Following her daughter's line of sight, she turned and found her son glaring at his sister. She was about to address him, hoping to ease the tension between her children, but Tiberius did not afford her the opportunity. Turning his back on the women, he strolled into his study and closed the door behind him, bringing relief to his sister, but distressing his mother. Flavia had grown concerned over her son's increased use of wine. His affliction was not only affecting him adversely, it was impacting the members of his household as well. No longer was he temperate in his drinking and in his disposition. He had become a man given to wine, a man of dark moods. No one was immune from his ill temper. Troubled by the disturbing change in her son, Flavia pondered what might be done to alter his grim mindset.

"Mater, will Tiberius ever look upon me with affection again?" asked Priscilla, interrupting her mother's thoughts.

Staring at the closed tablinum door, Flavia answered stiffly, "If thou please thy husband as a good wife ought...then thy brother shall regard thee kindly. Come. Let us return to thy chamber."

Beckoned by her mother, Priscilla followed her through the atrium, mulling over her words. Pleasing Lucius Servilius would not be easy. It would require great diligence on her part. Months, perhaps even years would be spent trying to undo the damage she had done to his dignitas. No man appreciated being made to look the fool and she knew he would not soon forget her trespass nor would her brother. Biting her bottom lip in contemplation of the matter, she entered her cubicle on the heels of her mother, who went directly to the closet and began looking through what was left of Priscilla's clothing.

"Mater, for what doth thou search?"

Emerging from the closet with a pale lavender stola thrown over her arm and a sizeable wicker basket in her hand, Flavia ordered, "Find Talia."

Perplexed, Priscilla looked at her mother, wondering why she had brought forth the stola. Her wedding clothes had already been prepared and her personal belongings packed. She had no need of this particular dress to complete her wedding ensemble. Why then had her mother chosen it?

"Find Talia," repeated Flavia impatiently.

"Yes, Mater," obliged Priscilla, dutifully leaving the room in search of the servant, having no inkling of what her mother was up to.

Carrying the basket and garment to Priscilla's vanity, Flavia set them down and rummaged through what remained of her daughter's jewelry. Coming across a dainty pearl choker, small pearl earrings and a shiny gold bracelet, she placed them in the basket. She then looked over a small collection of cosmetics and perfumes. Quickly sorting through the items, she selected creams and powders to beautify the complexion along with an alluring floral fragrance and finding some jeweled hair pins in an ivory box, she took a handful, putting the pins and everything else she had chosen into the basket. Pleased with her array of treasures, Flavia folded the stola neatly and laid it inside the wicker container.

Returning with Talia, Priscilla regarded her mother with curiosity.

"Close the door, Talia," commanded Flavia, her voice low. "What I am about to say is for thine ears only."

"Yes, Domina," answered the servant, obediently shutting the door behind her.

"Talia, prepare a bath for Tamar like unto the one thou didst prepare for Priscilla this evening. Anoint the maid with perfume and fine oils from the crown of her head to the soles of her feet. Spare no effort upon her beautification. Whatever thou didst for Priscilla, do also for the maid. When thou hast finished, adorn her with these," directed Flavia, handing the basket over to the trusted servant.

"Domina…what am I to say to the maid?" asked Talia, receiving the basket with hesitancy. "She shall surely question my efforts!"

"Tell her, I hath ordered it."

Perceiving her mother's intent, Priscilla's face colored as she listened in utter disbelief.

"When the maid hath been properly groomed, send her unto me and I shall instruct her further. I shall await her in my chamber. See that I am not disappointed with thy handiwork," charged Flavia, her eye keen upon the servant.

"Yes, Domina," breathed Talia, feeling apprehensive about the task ahead.

"Take care not to be seen," added Flavia as an afterthought. "If thou art questioned by anyone…lie and lie well. No one is to know my purpose."

"And what if I hath trouble convincing the maid to cooperate?" Talia questioned, almost certain that very thing would occur. "What then?"

"Apprise her of the consequences of disobedience…that shall befall her…and thee," came the matron's stern reply, leaving no room for failure. "Now go and do as I hath said."

Talia left the cubicle, her mind bombarded with anxious thoughts as she hurried through the dimly lit atrium. How would she ever convince the maid there was nothing to fear? She knew Tamar well enough to know she would resist what she feared and she knew Flavia well enough to know what she wanted done…she wanted done. No excuses.

Alone with her mother, Priscilla inquired, "What doth thou intend, Mater?"

"I intend to use the maid to put thy brother in a better frame of mind," replied Flavia in a matter of fact tone, turning to look at her offspring.

"Mater, could thou not hath chosen another?" Priscilla asked, feeling sympathy for the servant girl she had come to appreciate.

"No other would suffice."

"Could thou reconsider for my sake? I doth favor the maid and wish to take her to my new home. She shall be a comfort unto me," submitted Priscilla, attempting to save Tamar from dishonor. "I hath need of her."

"She is of more use to thy brother than thee, daughter. Choose another. She is to remain in thy brother's house and serve him," stated Flavia resolutely, walking away as she did not want to discuss the matter further.

"Mater, I beg thee…reconsider."

Reaching the door, Flavia looked back at her daughter and said, "Priscilla, fret not thyself on account of the maid. Rest now for thy wedding day draws nigh," and having spoken, she left the room, closing the door behind her.

Relieved Priscilla would depart from his house tomorrow morning after her marriage ceremony and he would finally be free of her; Tiberius drank the last of his wine and retired to his couch with minimal assistance from his steward, who noted his master had become adept at managing himself while intoxicated. Upon the servant's exit, Tiberius fell into a deep restful slumber and in that state he remained for several hours until a noise in the tablinum awakened him with a start.

Bolting upright upon his couch, bathed in darkness, Tiberius listened intently, thinking someone had entered his home with the intention of murdering him. His uncle had warned him of just such an occurrence and his prediction now appeared eerily accurate. Preparing to defend himself, Tiberius quickly rose from his couch and covered his nakedness. Laying hold of the knife he kept under his pillow, he quietly crept to one side of the doorway. Pressing his back against the wall, he fixed his eye on the door in anticipation of the intruder entering his bed chamber.

Straining to hear the light footsteps as they drew closer, Tiberius braced for the attack, his heart racing, his razor sharp knife held securely in his hand. He almost relished the thought of slitting the throat of the bold trespasser. He was in the mood for a little revenge for he had grown weary of his enemy. He welcomed the shedding of blood as long as it was not his own.

Then it happened…a shadowy figure came through the doorway. Sounding no warning, Tiberius attacked from behind, ambushing the intruder. Using his strong arm to encircle the throat, he violently seized the body, yanked it backward and cruelly tightened his chokehold about the neck. Wielding his knife in the other hand, he pressed it precariously to the intruder's throat, whose protests were muffled by the centurion's merciless vise. Breathing profanity and words of death, he threatened his victim, who struggled weakly against his mighty strength, scratching and tugging at the arm that rendered them powerless. Finding his victim perplexingly soft and defenseless, a heady fragrance filled his nostrils as a chorus of beads danced at his feet. Making sense of it, he suddenly realized the intruder was a woman. Stunned, he lowered his knife and released the female, who clutching her throat in fear, breathlessly cried out, "Domine, stay thy hand! Spare thy servant!"

Recognizing the voice of his maidservant, Tiberius chided angrily, adrenalin coursing through his veins, "Ye gods, woman! I nearly slit thy throat! What mean thee entering my bed chamber at such an hour as this? Explain thyself at once!"

Badly shaken, Tamar tried to speak again, but her breathing was so labored she could not.

His heart still pounding wildly within his chest, Tiberius left the maid where she stood, tossed his knife upon his couch and lit a lamp on the chamber wall. Having the aid of light, he turned to look at the intruder and was awestruck by her beauty.

Reeling from the assault, Tamar collected her wits and attempted to speak. "My lord…" she began and then sank to her knees, pleading, "be not angry with thy humble servant…"

Returning to the maid, Tiberius gazed down upon her and offered her his hand which she accepted and having her hand in his, he gently drew her to her feet. Coming face to face, the two stood; their hearts racing as they beheld one another in the soft flickering light.

"Woman, thou art altogether lovely," said Tiberius, the sight and scent of her igniting passion within him. Wanting to take possession of Tamar, he began removing the jeweled hair pins from her dark brown tresses, discarding them on the floor, one by one. Pleased she had not recoiled at his touch, he loosened her perfumed hair, letting it fall freely about her delicate shoulders. Looking earnestly into her large, dark eyes, he cupped her face tenderly and said, "Woman, I meant thee no harm. I knew not that it was thee."

"My lord…would thou ever harm thy maidservant?" Tamar asked in a small voice, meeting her master's steady gaze.

"I would not," said he, supposing she needed reassurance after their scuffle.

"Domine, would thou ever harm thy maidservant for pleasure?"

"I would not," Tiberius said, growing troubled. "Woman, why ask me this?"

"My lord, thou art well acquainted with violence. Thou art accustomed to taking that which doth not belong unto thee. I do well to fear thee."

"Woman, if thou dost fear me…why hast thou come to my bed chamber?"

"I came not of my own accord…I was sent unto thee…" replied Tamar, lowering her gaze, her heart accelerating in anticipation of his reaction.

Hearing her answer, Tiberius withdrew his hands from her face and asked gruffly, "Who sent thee?"

"Domine…I dare not say for I perceive thou art not pleased."

"What is it to thee if I am not pleased," he countered, becoming irritated.

"The one who sent me loves thee, my lord, and doth mean well," explained Tamar, lifting her eyes to his.

"When I ask thee a question, woman, I expect an answer. Who sent thee?"

"My lord, do not require me to say."

His temper rising, Tiberius walked away from his servant. He suspected the maid had been sent by his mother as she was the only one that fit the description given. Contemplating taking full advantage of the situation his mother had arranged, he poured some wine into a goblet and hastily downed it. Setting his empty cup on the table, he feasted his eyes upon Tamar as she stood in the midst of his chamber, her long, dark, wavy hair undone, her sweet countenance graced with the beauty of innocence, her comely form perfumed and adorned in appealing finery. She was very beautiful and she was his for the taking.

"Come hither," he demanded, his black eyes stormy and steadfastly pinned on her.

Slowly, Tamar approached her master; her bare feet encountering loose pearls as she made her way toward him, but she dared not let the discomfort she felt from stepping on the beads impede her from obeying his command. Her heart pounding rapidly within her chest, she meekly presented herself to him, fearing what was to come.

Burning with desire, Tiberius seized Tamar by the waist with one hand and with the other he lifted her face upward. Forcefully pressing her against his muscular body to restrain her, he leaned down and hungrily took her mouth with his, expecting her to fend off his advance, but she did not. Neither did she welcome it. Again, he kissed her. Still, she was passive and unresponsive. Losing his temper, Tiberius tightened his hold on her and whispered into her ear darkly, "Woman, defend thyself. Resist my advances…"

Every fiber of her being wanted to resist him, but Tamar knew if she tried to defend herself, he would only become more aggressive. Struggling to maintain her composure, she said timidly, "My lord…why art thou harming thy maidservant? Hast thou forgotten thy words?"

Unhanding her, Tiberius growled angrily, "Woman, I hath not forgotten my words…but thou hast forgotten why thou wert sent unto me!"

Fearing she would not escape unscathed if she remained a moment longer in his presence, Tamar fled from the bed chamber in tears, leaving Tiberius alone with his pricked conscience.

XXXIV

The next morning before sunrise, Priscilla was awakened by her mother leaning over her, saying, "Arise, daughter. It is thy wedding day."

Priscilla looked up at her mother and smiled weakly, feigning happiness. Gracefully stretching her long slender limbs, she lingered upon her comfortable couch a few moments longer as she was in no hurry to present herself to Lucius Servilius. Her first thoughts of the day were not of him, but of her maidservant. Interested in knowing what had transpired between Tamar and her brother the night before, Priscilla queried her mother, "Hast thou seen Tamar?"

"I hath not seen her," lied Flavia, irritated with Tamar for she knew the maid had not done as she had been told. Intending to deal with the servant later, Flavia kept her mind on the task at hand. "Up with thee, child, we hath much to do to prepare thee for thy wedding."

Complying with her mother's wishes, Priscilla sat up upon her couch aided by the gentle hand of Talia.

"Talia, hast thou seen Tamar?" asked Priscilla looking to her servant, expecting to hear a different answer than the one given by her mother.

Flavia shot Talia a sharp forbidding look which was not lost upon the wise servant, who heeded the matron's silent warning, answering, "No, Dominilla. I hath not seen her."

"If no one hath seen her, then she must be with Tiberius," said Priscilla aloud to herself, standing to her feet.

"Daughter, why trouble thyself with the maid's whereabouts? Thy mind should be on thyself and thy wedding," scolded her mother.

"Dominilla, thy breakfast awaits thee," announced Talia, running interference between the patricians for the sake of both. "I hath set the tray upon thy vanity."

"I shall miss thee, my dear, Talia," said Priscilla, regarding her servant with affection.

"And I thee, Dominilla…"

"Come, child, eat," beckoned her mother, keeping track of time.

After partaking of her morning meal, Priscilla was attended by several of her maids. They chattered excitedly as they anointed their mistress with expensive oils and perfume, arranged her long, brown silky hair in the fashion of the day and modestly enhanced her natural beauty with cosmetics that suited her flawless olive complexion. Finishing, the servants gave the bride over to her mother, who dressed her daughter in a wedding gown of pale yellow and fixed upon her coifed head, a veil of pale orange. Fully adorned in traditional wedding attire, Priscilla was shown her lovely image in a mirror, but she found her appearance of no consolation. Her spirit was cast down. Having foreseen her daughter's somber mood, Flavia brought forth a small, ornately carved wooden box and presented it to Priscilla.

"What is it, Mater?" inquired Priscilla, the unexpected gift sparking a flicker of excitement in her.

"Look inside," said her mother, smiling.

Opening the box, Priscilla gasped, the lovely emerald pendant taking her breath away. "Oh, Mater! It is gorgeous!"

"Priscilla, thy father wanted thee to wear the necklace on thy wedding day. He chose it for thee," said Flavia, wishing her husband had lived long enough to witness their daughter's marriage.

Priscilla looked at her mother, tears glistening in her brown eyes. "I do not deserve this beautiful necklace. I hath disgraced the family. I cannot accept it in good conscience, Mater," she said sadly, closing the box and returning it to her mother.

"Priscilla, it is thy wedding present," declared Flavia, surprised by her daughter's refusal.

"I hath brought disgrace to my betrothed…my brother…and my Pater. If he were alive…he would declare me a disgrace."

"Child, what is done is in the past…press forward…forgetting what lies behind thee. Today is a new beginning."

"How shall I press forward when my betrothed stands ready to publicly humiliate me for what I hath done in the past?"

"Thou art strong, Priscilla! Thou canst endure the ceremony with humility and patience! Wear the necklace. Let it serve as a reminder of our unfailing love for thee," said Flavia tenderly, offering the present once again to her daughter.

Tears slipped from Priscilla's eyes as she received the gift, her mother's benevolent words strengthening her.

"Oh, Mater," cried Priscilla, embracing her mother. "I miss Pater so much."

"As do I…child."

Moved by the scene before them, the maids in attendance wiped away their tears, but none was as touched as Talia, who hoped Flavia's words would sustain Priscilla through the trying times ahead. Brushing aside a stray tear, Talia said, "Dominilla, permit thy servants to look upon thy wedding gift."

Withdrawing from her mother's loving arms, Priscilla opened the wooden box and her maids flocked about her to admire the exquisite piece of jewelry. "Put it on," said one, joined by another, "Yes, do!"

Basking in the special moment, the bride obliged her maidservants with the assistance of her mother, who fastened the emerald necklace about her daughter's delicate neck, completing her wedding outfit.

In the garden, the guests had begun to gather in anticipation of the wedding ceremony. Tiberius stood with his uncle and cousin discussing the future of the bride and groom, neither of which had yet arrived. Turia and her mother were seated on a marble bench talking quietly with one another. Hoping to catch the eye of her betrothed, Turia smiled sweetly, but Cassius was too engrossed in conversation to pay her any mind.

"Upon my arrival, I noticed a woman standing under the cypress tree. I recognize her as the kinswoman of thy servant Tamar," said Cassius to Tiberius, his handsome face grim as he relayed the information. "I regret to hath to deliver this news on Priscilla's wedding day, but thou should be aware of her presence on thy property. It was so on the day thou wert attacked and left for dead. Her reappearance is not a good omen. Whether it bodes evil tidings for thee or for Priscilla…I cannot be certain. But if I were to venture a guess…I would say it doth not bode well for thee, Tiberius."

"Art thou certain, Cassius, it is the maid's kinswoman," asked Tiberius, finding it odd the woman had returned on his sister's wedding day.

"I am quite certain."

"Cassius, hast thou considered it could be a ploy to entrap my maidservant?"

"Ump…" grunted Cassius, not articulating his opinion, fearing discord between himself and Tiberius.

"Nephew, in light of all that hath befallen thee, I would not take the woman's reappearance lightly," Flavius cautioned. "Thou ought to rid thyself of the maid before any more trouble finds thee. It seems she draws trouble to thee."

Tiberius was on the verge of replying to his uncle when he noticed Lucius Servilius and his father standing at the entrance of the garden together. Excusing himself, he left his relatives and went to greet his soon to be in-laws, escorting them into the courtyard to await the bride. The father of Lucius Servilius was particularly adept at making small talk which came as a relief to Tiberius, who noted the groom seemed strangely uncomfortable in his company and had very little to say. Deciding not to take Lucius Servilius personally, Tiberius held his tongue and countenance in check.

After giving some last minute instructions to her servants, Flavia entered the garden accompanied by her sister-in-law, Calpurnia and together they warmly greeted the guests, beginning with the groom and his father and ending with the women, whom they made polite conversation with until Priscilla's entrance, at which point, everyone's attention shifted to the bride.

A vision of youthful beauty and promise, Priscilla stood tall and regal in her wedding clothes, bearing in her hands a single white flower given her by Talia. Stepping forward to claim his bride, Lucius Servilius approached Priscilla, viewing her with as much appreciation as he did animosity.

"Woman, did I not say thy wedding day was to be a solemn occasion?"

Disheartened by his stern greeting, Priscilla's gaze fell to the beautiful flower in her hands and she inquired meekly of her betrothed, "Pray tell, my lord, in what hath I offended thee?"

Snatching the flower from her, Lucius Servilius cast it to the ground and stepped upon it in the sight of all gathered, remarking bitterly in their hearing, "I said solemn…and solemn thy wedding shall be."

The women gasped, shocked by the groom's overt hostility.

"Forgive me…" breathed Priscilla, her voice barely audible, her eyes downcast, holding back the tears that threatened to spill forth.

Indignant that Priscilla should be so ill treated on her wedding day, Cassius started forward, intending to have a word with Lucius Servilius, but his father held him back, gripping his arm tightly.

"Pater, release me this instant," snarled Cassius under his breath, bent on having it out with Lucius Servilius.

"Thou hast no right to interfere," chided Flavius, maintaining a firm hold upon his son.

"Woman, why hast thou adorned thyself with this expensive ornament," the groom demanded, handling the emerald pendant about his betrothed's neck.

"It is a wedding present…from my parents…" the bride responded timidly, staring at the crushed flower at her feet. "If it displeases thee…I shall remove it, my lord."

Intervening, Lucius Servilius' father rushed forward, took his son aside and spoke to him privately, leaving Priscilla standing alone, humiliated in front of her guests.

Understanding why Lucius Servilius had treated Priscilla as he had, Tiberius restrained himself from interceding on his sister's behalf. She had made the situation what it was and she would have to endure it. He had little sympathy for her.

"Oh, Mater, how could Lucius Servilius be so mean to Priscilla on their wedding day," cried Turia, upset by her brother's behavior as she was quite fond of Priscilla.

"Thy brother is clearly very angry with her," replied her mother frowning, perplexed as to why her son was marrying a woman he obviously held in low regard.

"He ought not to marry her if he feels unkindly toward her," voiced Turia, glancing in the direction of her intended, who never seemed to be looking at her, much to her dismay.

Though she was close enough to hear Turia and her mother's verbal exchange, Flavia kept her thoughts to herself, quietly observing her daughter, who was bearing up under the public humiliation far better than she could have ever imagined possible. It seemed adversity had made a woman of her little girl.

"Flavia…dost thou think thy daughter should marry that dreadful man?" asked Calpurnia, whispering in Flavia's ear. "I should worry about her if I were thee. Good family or not…men are such awful brutes."

Flavia bore her sister-in-law's comments in silence, deeming them unworthy of a response.

Escorting his son back into the presence of all assembled, Lucius Servilius' father proclaimed to the guests, "Let the ceremony proceed."

The wedding couple was brought together and Priscilla managed a cheerful expression of consent to marry Lucius Servilius in spite of her heavy heart. A sacrifice was offered to the gods for the newlyweds, after which they signed a marriage contract and sat down to a wedding banquet, shortened in duration by decree of the groom, who wore an insufferable countenance the entire day. Never once did he smile, laugh or let down his guard in any way. To the guest's dismay, he merely tolerated his own wedding celebration and his dour attitude made it difficult for anyone else to enjoy the occasion, most especially his bride, who struggled to appear happy.

As the banquet drew to a close, Lucius Servilius took Priscilla from the arms of her mother and after bidding the guests farewell, he escorted his new wife from her home, dispensing with the joyful procession of guests that customarily followed the wedding couple. The groom spoke not a word to his bride as they made their way down the cobbled road alone, neither did he assist her when she caught her shoe and tripped, falling on the hard stones. Showing no empathy, Lucius Servilius continued on his way, leaving her where she fell.

Realizing her husband was not going to help her, Priscilla rose up from the dirty road with as much dignity as she could muster, dusted off her wedding dress and dutifully followed after him. Arriving at her new home, she stoically performed the marriage rituals, winding bands of wool around the doorposts and anointing the door with oil and fat, symbolizing prosperity and happiness. She was then unceremoniously swept her off her feet by her husband and carried over the threshold.

Setting her down inside the atrium, he offered fire and water and she lit a new fire in the hearth. His home was now her home. She belonged to him. And having observed all the marriage rites, but one, Lucius Servilius whisked Priscilla away to the wedding couch to claim what was rightfully his.

XXXV

After the wedding party disbanded, Tiberius acted on the information given him and informed his steward that Tamar was not permitted near the house exits. Charging him with the task of relaying the same to Anatole and the door servant, he walked back to the courtyard and set a watchman at the rear of the garden, giving the servant orders that no one was allowed near the back exit. Satisfied he had taken measures to keep the maid within the confines of his house, he leisurely strolled through the garden, contemplating the relentless tactics of his enemy. Coming upon Tamar unexpectedly, Tiberius stopped in his tracks and quietly observed the maid from his hidden vantage point, unbeknown to her.

Finding Priscilla's wedding flower lying upon the ground, Tamar knelt down and took the ruined bud in hand, sniffing the sweet fragrance exuding from its crushed white petals. Having seen with her own eyes the humiliation her mistress had suffered at the hands of her groom, Tamar said a silent prayer for Priscilla as she rose to her feet.

Puzzled by her seeming interest in the decimated bloom, Tiberius stepped forward and made his presence known, startling Tamar, who softly gasped at his appearing, remembering his aggressiveness the night before.

"Woman, why dost thou stare at a crushed blossom?"

Gazing thoughtfully at the flower in her possession, she responded to his question with one of her own, asking, "Why would a man destroy something so beautiful?"

Instantly, Tiberius' battle hardened conscience was pricked as the brutality of the previous night flashed in his memory. He had come close to destroying the beautiful maid and why he had, the gods only knew. Why had he treated her so shamefully? Why had he nearly violated her for his own gratification? Could he fault the wine? Was his mother to blame? Had violence led him down a dark slippery path? Was he no better than the others who had sought after her for their own pleasure? Confounded by his own contemptible behavior, Tiberius departed the garden without answering her.

Realizing she had unwittingly communicated with him on a deeper level, Tamar pondered the meaning of her master's silence. Tossing the flower into the fountain, she watched it float gracefully upon the water, her spirit troubled within her.

———

Lurking behind the large cypress tree located on Tiberius' property, Xenos kept a keen eye on the premises. Endeavoring to draw out the Jewess, he had positioned her kinswoman in a visible location where all who visited the centurion's home would notice her. The day was now drawing to an end and despite the old woman having been seen by a number of guests, her niece had made no attempt to reach her. Tired of playing cat and mouse, Xenos threw a coin at Ruth's feet and barked, "Go home, old woman. I hath no further need of thee."

"I do not want thy money," said Ruth, ignoring the Roman denarius lying in the grass. "Thou did swear on thy gods that I would see my niece. I shall not leave till I do."

"Suit thyself," growled the gladiator, peering menacingly at her from behind the tree. "Thy niece is in the hands of a shrewd master. It is clear he hath taken measures to prevent her from coming to thee."

"Then I shall go to her…" Ruth announced timidly, her heart pounding rapidly for she feared him.

"Suit thyself, old woman," hissed the gladiator.

Leaving the late afternoon shade of the tall cypress tree, Ruth headed toward the stately Roman dwelling, relieved to be out from under the thumb of the fierce gladiator. She suspected he intended to murder the centurion and it frightened her to think what he might do to her and her niece. She wanted to run and hide from him, but if she did, Tamar and the centurion would never know the danger he posed. Mustering courage, Ruth continued forward, the gladiator's calculating orbs marking her every step.

Approaching the house, Ruth noticed a short stocky man standing guard at the front entrance. As she came near, the sentry drew his sword and warned, "Halt, woman! Come no closer if thou dost value thy life! State thy business!"

"I seek my niece Tamar," Ruth answered nervously, meeting the guard's wary gaze.

"There is no one here by that name," lied Anatole. "Thou best turn thyself around and be gone from here, woman. The one thou dost seek doth not reside in this place."

"Inform thy lord of my petition…it may be that he will hear me," asserted Ruth. "I must warn him. He is in grave danger."

"Woman, I shall not trouble my lord on thy account! Depart from here!"

"I will not leave until I see my niece! I must warn her!"

Growing angry, Anatole took two steps forward and pointed his sharp sword a few inches from the woman's neck, commanding, "Get thee off my lord's property! And never return!"

"Please…I beg thee…" cried Ruth, giving way to despair. "I know Tamar is here! My heart aches to see her! Why art thou keeping me from her? Dost thou care nothing for thy master's safety?"

"Woman, heed my words," Anatole thundered, his eyes narrowing with purpose as he took another step closer to Ruth. "Get thee off my lord's property or else I will slice thy withered throat!"

Fearing he meant what he said, Ruth stepped back from his lethal blade, turned and ran away, bitter tears streaming down her time worn face.

Noting the old woman had failed to get past the guard; Xenos abandoned his hiding place, picked up the denarius, tucked it into his money bag and returned to Sejanus.

Waiting until the two would be troublemakers were completely out of sight; Anatole thumped the door with the back of his shoe, his alert eyes surveying the perimeter of his master's property.

The door servant opened the portal and stuck his head outside; uncertain of what he had heard.

"Tell the master, I need to speak with him," said Anatole, not bothering to look at him. "Be quick about it."

Hearing Anatole, the steward rushed forward. Nudging the door servant aside, he inquired, "Hast something happened?"

"It is important I speak with the master at once," replied Anatole.

Wasting no time, the steward hurried away in search of Tiberius, oblivious to the fact that he had annoyed the door attendant, who resented having lost his chance to leave his post and report to Tiberius.

The steward found his master in the tablinum sitting at his desk, considering a scroll. Upon his entrance into the room, Tiberius glanced up from the parchment and seeing the steward's worried expression, he questioned, "What is it, now?"

"Domine, Anatole requests to speak with thee at once."

Laying aside his scroll, Tiberius directed, "Assign Tamar a lengthy task…one that will keep her out of the atrium while I speak with Anatole. It is imperative she remain occupied. She must not find out her kinswoman is on the property. Her safety is at stake. Is that understood?"

"I understand, Domine," replied the steward, having been instructed earlier in the day concerning the maid's safety. "With thy permission, I shall assign her to the kitchen. The cook is complaining of weariness and is in need of some assistance."

"Very well, go and do as thou doth see fit."

The steward bowed and exited. He would have preferred to hear what Anatole had to say instead of tending to the maid, but having no choice in the matter, off he went to do as he was told.

After allotting the steward ample time to locate Tamar and busy her in the kitchen, Tiberius left his study.

Seeing his master approaching, the door attendant opened the front door, knowing his destination.

Slipping out of the exit, Tiberius looked about, checking for signs of trouble. Seeing none, he stood to the right of his body servant, listening attentively as Anatole told of Ruth's bold inquiry and how he had handled her.

Concluding his tale, Anatole said, "As the woman fled my drawn sword, I saw a strong man come out from behind the large cypress and depart. I believe he must hath been there the entire time. I was tempted to pursue the man, but I did not dare leave thee unprotected."

"Thou hast done well, Anatole," commended Tiberius, genuinely pleased with his servant.

"I think the woman may return," said the servant, turning to look at his master. "What would thou hath me do, Domine?"

"Do as thou hast done. The woman would not willingly endanger her niece. I suspect she is at the mercy of my enemy. I may hath to send Tamar away for her own protection. If her kinswoman returns, do her no harm; only threaten her as thou hast done today."

"Where shall thou send Tamar, Domine?"

"I hath not decided," replied Tiberius, remembering his servant had feelings for the maid.

"Domine, when thou dost decide…I ask thou make it known unto me," petitioned Anatole. "Perhaps Tamar will reconsider my proposal in light of the circumstances."

Perturbed by his servant's audacious request, Tiberius frowned and walked back into the house. He knew the day would come when he would have to confront Anatole about the maid and he did not relish the thought. He would leave that unpleasantness for another day. Spying his mother passing through the atrium, Tiberius went after her, catching her by the arm.

"What is it, son? Why dost thou hold me so?"

"Mater, I did not appreciate thee sending Tamar into my bed chamber last night," rebuked Tiberius, unleashing his anger. "I nearly slit the maid's throat…thinking she was an intruder! If I had murdered the defenseless maid, her innocent blood would be upon thy head!"

"I did not expect her entrance to alarm thee," explained Flavia, mortified by the strange turn of events. "I thought she had enough sense to announce herself."

"Never mind excuses! I hath no use for them," snapped Tiberius, tightening his vise about her arm. "Do not meddle in my personal affairs again, Mater! I am quite capable of procuring a woman for myself! I hath no need of thy assistance with such delicate matters!"

"Forgive me, Tiberius Marcius," Flavia apologized, patiently enduring her son's wrath.

"And if thou art of a mind to reprimand the maid…do not do so, Mater. What she hath suffered at my hands is punishment enough. I shall not hath thee adding to her misery."

"Son, I entreat thee to forgive my forwardness. I assure thee…my intentions were good."

"Nothing good came of thy intentions," Tiberius said crossly, walking away, his conscience weighing heavily upon him.

XXXVI

Retiring to her room for the evening, Tamar laid upon her couch reflecting on her life since coming into her master's house. All four seasons had come and gone. Not a day had passed she had not thought of Josiah and his parents. She remembered the loving kindness of Ruth and the goodness of Laham before the tragic death of his son had embittered him. Without Josiah, her aunt and uncle's survival was difficult at best. Daily, she prayed for God to meet their needs and provide for them in their old age for they had no one left but each other. All hope of a future generation had died with their son. They never knew Josiah had intended to take her as his wife. Tamar saw no point in disclosing the matter after Josiah's death, feeling the knowledge would have only added to their unbearable grief. She had loved Josiah very much and regretted they had not had time to marry. If they had, she might have been blessed with a child, who would have been a comfort to her and Josiah's parents in their time of sorrow. It saddened her that she had no husband or child and no foreseeable possibility that she ever would. She did not want to marry outside of her faith; neither did she want to birth a child in slavery. She longed for freedom, to once again live the life of faith, to observe the customs of her people and her God, but she did not dare approach Tiberius with her lofty request. Placing herself in his presence had become altogether hazardous to her virtue.

Greatly troubled by what had taken place between them, Tamar considered what manner of man her master was. From the very beginning, he had shielded her from all those who wanted to do her harm. Though it was hard to fathom, God had used the Roman to protect her from many evils, but why He had used a man of pagan beliefs still mystified her. The centurion had whisked her away from the Prefect and his lecherous men, rescuing her from their evil intent. He had bravely inserted himself between her and Drusus, staying the hand of Caesar's son when he would have struck her. He had even protected her from his sister's frightful temper and restrained Cassius, whom she knew would have treated her far worse than he had, if not for his reverential fear of Tiberius. The centurion had saved her from many dangers, but from himself, he could not save her.

Acutely aware of her vulnerability where Tiberius was concerned,

Tamar contemplated running away again, but she knew she would not get far before she would be found. She had nowhere to hide that the centurion did not know, no money to buy herself a passage on a ship and no one that could help her without fear of reprisal. To make matters worse, the Prefect might find her and do to her such things as she dared not even imagine. Dismissing the foolhardy idea, Tamar opted for the only safe avenue of escape, slumber. If the Lord God Almighty had sent the centurion to protect her, then surely, He would not permit him to harm her. Encouraging herself, she recited a verse from the Psalms, speaking aloud, "The Lord is my light and my salvation; whom shall I fear? The Lord is the strength of my life; of whom shall I be afraid?" And afterwards, she drifted into a peaceful sleep.

Down the hall, Tiberius lay upon his couch, his mind occupied with thoughts of Tamar. He recalled the first time he had ever laid eyes upon her, finding her beautiful beyond measure despite her grief stricken state and blood stained apparel. He could not help but to have mercy on the damsel. Aware of her dire circumstances, he had felt compelled to act on her behalf and call in Drusus' pledge, rescuing her from the royal heir's less than noble intentions. He had risked his own future to save her, incurring his commander's wrath, endangering both his life and friendship with Drusus in the process. Though Drusus was no longer a threat to her, Sejanus was still a very real threat. The maid had to be safeguarded from him. Tiberius had expended a great deal of energy shielding the maid from harm. It had even been necessary to protect her from his own family members, the most dangerous of whom was Cassius. Or was there another?

Did he actually pose more of a danger to the maid than anyone he had saved her from? Disturbing as the question was, Tiberius considered his own conduct. He knew he was not entirely blameless where she was concerned. He could not deny there was a part of him that wanted to take full advantage of the master, slave relationship and he had come very close to doing so. The maid had narrowly escaped being ravished and he no longer trusted himself to behave honorably toward her. And therein was his dilemma. How was he going to protect her from himself?

Mulling over his predicament, Tiberius tossed and turned, unable to fall asleep. Rising from his couch, he stepped upon something small and round. Feeling it under his bare foot, he did not need the light of a lamp to know it was another bead from the maid's necklace, broken in their physical confrontation. He had ordered the loose pearls to be cleared away, but to his annoyance, they continued to reappear and every time they did, his conscience suffered. Reaching down, his hand skimmed the floor in search of the pearl and finding it; he scooped it up and carried it into the study, tossing it into a bowl with the others found since that lamentable night. Taking up the wine flask, he drank from it deeply, medicating his conscience and dousing his thirst. Returning to his couch, he fell into a restless sleep, his subconscious at work.

Granted temporary leave of his post, Anatole entered the house at the dawn of the new day and headed for the kitchen as he was quite hungry. Talia had been expecting him and had prepared a meal.

"Greetings, my son," said Talia, smiling warmly as he stepped into the kitchen.

"Mother, thou dost spoil me," said Anatole, noticing the table she had set for him, the smell of freshly baked bread filling his nostrils.

"I could not hath done so without the cook's help," replied Talia, giving credit where credit was due.

"Thy mother hardly needs my assistance," bellowed the cook, a woman of large proportion. "She hath already baked two loaves of bread and I hath yet to begin."

Seating himself at the table, Anatole began eating, his hunger evident by his lack of conversation. Sitting down across from him, Talia watched her son devour the food set in front of him while the cook worked to prepare the morning meal for the patricians.

Finished eating, Anatole sat back in his chair, his belly full and revealed to his mother what was foremost on his mind, saying, "The master is thinking of sending Tamar away. It appears she is in harms way as long as she remains in this house."

The cook turned an attentive ear to his words, enjoying a juicy bit of gossip while she worked.

Talia's countenance fell as she was fond of Tamar and did not wish to see her sent away; neither did she want any harm to come to her.

"I hath asked the master to tell me where he shall send her. I want her for my wife if she will consent," said he, keeping back the fact that he had already proposed to Tamar and had been turned down.

Stunned by his declaration, the cook stopped what she was doing and stared at him.

His mother was rendered speechless and scarcely knew what she should say.

Seeing the women's reaction, Anatole remarked flippantly, "Is there a third eye upon my face? Why do ye look at me so?"

The cook turned away and began vigorously pounding and kneading the clump of dough in front of her. It was not her place to tell him.

Talia drew a deep breath and said gently, "Son, Tamar was sent into the master's bed chamber a mere night ago."

Angry, Anatole jumped to his feet, exclaiming hotly, "No one told me of this! The master said nothing of his desire for her!"

"Flavia sent Tamar unto him…the maid had no say in the matter. She had to do as she was told."

"I cannot believe it," said Anatole, digesting the shocking news. "Why did the master not tell me of this? I hath played the fool!"

"Anatole, be reasonable. The master owes thee no explanation."

"He hath no feelings for Tamar or else he would not send her away," voiced Anatole, thinking out loud. "It may be that I can yet persuade him to give her unto me for my wife. I care not that he hath known her."

"Son, I do not think it wise…" began Talia and then fell silent, beholding Tamar standing in the doorway, wearing a hurt expression, having overheard nearly all of their conversation.

The cook looked up from her dough and seeing the maid, her mouth dropped open, fearing the maid had heard an earful.

Realizing someone had entered the room, Anatole swung about. Seeing the object of his affection, he hastened toward her and tried to take her hand, but Tamar withdrew from him, tears standing in her gentle eyes.

"What is this thou hast said of me?" Tamar cried, addressing Anatole directly.

"Tamar, I hath feelings for thee…thou knowest this. I care not that the master hath known thee. I desire thy hand in marriage…if only thou wilt consent," replied Anatole, bearing his heart. "I would make thee a good husband. I would treat thee well…I swear upon all of my gods…great and small."

Blinking back tears, Tamar inquired in a small, trembling voice, "Why is my lord sending me away?"

"Tamar, I cannot answer thee…" said Anatole, his heart sinking. "If I tell thee…the master shall whip me sore. I hath already said too much for I see I hath upset thee and I am ashamed of myself."

"Tamar, pay no mind to our idle talk," said Talia, trying to diffuse the uncomfortable situation. "I do not believe the master would send thee away. Thou hast been a faithful servant unto him. Thou art highly favored. His eye is set upon thee and his heart is inclined unto thee."

Crushed by his mother's words and the distraught look on his beloved's face, Anatole stormed from the kitchen, his stomach churning with emotion.

Talia knew she had hurt her son's feelings, but the pain he felt was preferable to the sting of a whip across his back. She had said what was best for all involved.

"Come, Tamar...sit and eat," coaxed the cook, feeling genuinely sorry for the maid, whom she had found to be quite helpful in the kitchen the day before.

Talia came toward Tamar to escort her to the table, but Tamar turned and fled the kitchen. Worried, the two women ran after the maid, pleading with her to return.

Beside herself, Tamar ran to the back of the garden, ignoring their pleas. Seeing the freight gate, she frantically tried to escape through the door, but she could not open it for the door had been bolted closed. The guard who was sleeping nearby awakened with a start and shouted, "Stop, woman!" Scrambling quickly to his feet, he seized Tamar, who screamed as he yanked her away from the exit.

Witnessing the commotion, Talia and the cook tried to verbally intervene on Tamar's behalf, but to no avail. The guard was deaf to their appeals.

On his way to the kitchen in search of his morning meal, the steward heard a woman scream and hurrying forward; he came upon the guard struggling to subdue Tamar. Rushing towards them, the steward hollered at the guard, "Do not harm her!"

"Unhand me," demanded Tamar tearfully. "I hath done nothing!"

The guard looked to the steward for direction.

"Unhand her," said the steward, grimacing. "Woman, what hath happened here? Explain thyself."

"I took leave of my senses," said she in a strangely calm voice, wiping away her tears. "It will not happen again."

Finding her behavior odd, the steward said to her, "Come with me. I would speak with thee privately."

"I hath no more to say for myself," stated Tamar. "I became upset...that is all."

"Why art thou upset?"

"I cannot say," she answered.

Hearing her reply, Talia heaved a sigh of relief and returned to the kitchen with the cook at her side.

"Come with me, woman," ordered the steward taking her by the hand and leading her away, certain there was more to the story than he was hearing. With Tamar in tow, the steward walked briskly to his office. Escorting her inside, he shut the door behind them and turned to Tamar, who stood expressionless before him.

"Woman, tell me the truth. What happened?" asked the steward, his tone patient as he liked the maid.

"I hath already told thee. I became upset…that is all."

"Again, I ask thee. Why did thou become upset? Did someone offend thee in word or deed?"

"I cannot say," said Tamar meekly, bowing her head.

Considering her, the steward was moved with compassion and decided not to interrogate her aggressively. "Woman, I shall not press thee further… if thou wilt answer me this. Did thou try to escape thy master's house?"

Lifting her head, she met his inquiring gaze, confessing, "The thought entered my mind, but I repented of it."

"Whatever thy upset…it is not advisable to run away. It is better to face the problem than to run from it. Thy lord hath dealt with thee kindly. Thou hast no reason to run away…at least none that I am aware of…seeing thou wilt not reveal the cause of thy upset."

"I acted rashly," admitted Tamar apprehensively "Must thou inform the master of my transgression?"

"Woman, it is my duty."

"I fear punishment may follow thy report."

"Woman, it is I that doth fear punishment if I withhold from him this matter. I hath but once suffered the whip and do not ever intend to do so again…not for thee or anyone."

"May I leave," requested Tamar shakily.

"Thou may return to thy chamber and wait there for a time. If the master wishes to speak with thee, I shall come for thee. If after a time, I come not, then thou art at liberty to leave thy cubicle and perform thy duties in the kitchen. Wilt thou do as I hath asked of thee?"

"I will," said she, turning about and leaving the steward's office, resigned to her fate.

Standing in the doorway, the steward watched Tamar till he could see her no more, wondering what might have upset her. She had made no mention of her kinswoman and he felt it safe to assume she knew nothing of her aunt's appearance. Still, the situation was troublesome. Bypassing his breakfast, he immediately sought audience with Tiberius. He could not afford any passage of time, lest another make the report before he had the opportunity. As steward of the house, it was his rightful duty to inform Tiberius of all important matters and this time, he intended to do just that. Never again would he withhold information from the master. He had learned his lesson.

Tiberius was reclining in the dining room, awaiting the arrival of his meal which seemed to be taking longer than usual. He was just about to inquire of the delay, when the steward entered the triclinium.

"Ah, Steward…perhaps thou can tell me…what is the delay in the kitchen? I do hunger," snapped Tiberius irritably.

"Domine, the delay is due to a minor disruption that occurred just outside the kitchen. Many of thy household witnessed what I am about to tell thee, including thy cook…hence the delay."

"What kind of disruption," questioned Tiberius, sitting upright on the couch, his dark eyes fastened on the servant in anticipation of his response.

"Thy servant Tamar became greatly upset and tried to leave the premises through the freight gate. The guard restrained her, howbeit, he did so gently. I then took hold of her and questioned her privately in my office, but she would not reveal unto me the cause of her upset. I asked her if she had tried to escape…and she answered, saying thus… "the thought entered my mind, but I repented of it." Domine, I am of the opinion…the maid suffered a moment of weakness and succumbed to her emotions. She doth appear sincerely remorseful. I am of a mind to believe her."

"Hast thou any idea what distressed her?" Tiberius queried soberly, suspecting he was the reason she had tried to escape.

"No, my lord."

"Is it possible she found out about her kinswoman?"

"I do not think so, my lord."

"Where is she now?"

"I hath sent her to her cubicle. I told her to remain there for a time and I would come for her if thou wished to speak with her. Otherwise, she would be at liberty to perform her duties. Dost thou wish to speak with her, Domine?"

Not wanting his conversation with her to be heard by anyone, Tiberius stood to his feet, his toga falling neatly upon his tall frame and said, "Steward, I shall go to her and hear for myself her explanation."

The steward bowed and was about to depart the room when Tiberius spoke again.

"See thou dost not lean thy ear against her chamber door, neither let another do so."

The mild admonishment sparked the steward's interest, but he pretended indifference, promising, "None shall listen at her door, my lord. I give thee my word."

Tiberius laughed to himself, knowing he had outfoxed his steward. He was keenly aware his servants listened at doors and exchanged information with one another. This time, they would glean nothing. Skipping his meal which still had not arrived much to his irritation, he went to Tamar's cubicle and entered her room, shutting the door securely behind him.

Upon his entrance, Tamar arose from her couch where she had been sitting, lowered her gaze in respect and humbly entreated, "Domine, forgive thy maidservant and be kind unto me. Grant mercy to thy servant."

"For what trespass shall I forgive thee," asked Tiberius, testing her integrity.

"Domine, I seek thy forgiveness for I attempted to flee thy house."

"Woman, why did thou attempt to flee?"

"Domine, I…do not…know how to…to answer thee," she stammered, color sweeping over her lovely face.

"Didst thou try to escape on account of me," inquired Tiberius, studying her closely. "Woman, dost thou fear my affections?"

"Domine, my God will not permit thee to harm me…" stated Tamar, not daring to meet his piercing gaze.

Skeptical of her faith, Tiberius took Tamar by the arms and said sarcastically, "Tell me, woman, what thy God can do to protect thee…seeing thou art in my strong hand? How shall he protect thee from me? Shall a bolt of lightning come from the sky and strike me dead if I try to violate thee? Shall I now test thy God?"

"My lord, do not speak so! His thoughts are not our thoughts. His ways are not our ways. We must not test Him! We cannot know what He shall do," said she, trying to maintain her composure, her master's verbal intensity unnerving her. "I trust in my God."

"If thou dost trust thy God…then why did thou try to flee? Pray tell, what upset thee…if not I?"

"My lord, dost thou intend to send me away?"

"Who told thee this?" demanded Tiberius.

"I overheard it said. Is it true, my lord," asked Tamar, lifting her eyes upward, searching Tiberius' rigidly held aspect. "Hath I so displeased thee...that thou wouldst send me away in disgrace?"

A shadow fell over his countenance and he released her abruptly, declaring, "Perhaps, it is thy God's way of protecting thee. Thou dost trust in thy God...trust in me also." And having spoken, Tiberius departed from Tamar's chamber, leaving his maidservant perplexed by his strange response.

XXXVII

Since Tamar's thwarted escape, Tiberius had kept a close watch on her, checking on her whereabouts throughout the day. A month had passed and he was no less diligent despite having believed the steward's assessment of her questionable deed. Erring on the side of caution, Tiberius could not afford to be gullible where she was concerned. The maid had tried to escape once before. Who could say for certain, she had not tried again.

Making his rounds, Tiberius strolled through the courtyard, glancing into the kitchen as he passed, catching a glimpse of Tamar working beside the cook. Seeing her where she was supposed to be, he continued on toward the back gate and finding the guard at his post, he returned to the main house, satisfied all was well for the time being.

It had not escaped Tamar's notice that Tiberius was keeping tabs on her. Even the cook had made mention of the fact. Every day without fail, Tamar would see him pass outside the door at regular intervals. Sometimes he would simply glance inside and other times he would look at her directly, his gaze long and piercing. Disheartened by the daily occurrence, Tamar struggled to bear up under her master's intense scrutiny.

In spite of her circumstances, she refused to discuss the situation with the cook, Talia or Anatole, though each had tried in their own way to draw her into a conversation. They knew as well as she why the master was monitoring her and she saw no point in rehashing what had been said or done as she could do nothing to change it. Plagued by the thought she would soon be sent away, Tamar withdrew into herself.

Quintus Atilius stood in the atrium dressed in his military attire, a scroll held tightly in his hand as he waited on Tiberius to receive him. He knew instinctively what was written in the scroll was not good news for his friend. The missive had been penned by Caesar himself under the direction of the Prefect, who now exercised a great deal more influence over the Emperor than most knew. Retiring to the island of Capri after Drusus' death, Caesar had left the tedious affairs of Rome under Sejanus' control.

"It is good to see thee, Quintus Atilius," said Tiberius, laying a firm hand on his friend's shoulder in greeting. "I trust thou hast been well."

"As well as can be expected, my friend. And thee? Hast thou found relief from thy pain?"

"I hath…" answered Tiberius, hiding the truth. "Come; let us drink to good health."

"I must decline thy offer, Tiberius Marcius. My orders are to deliver this to thee…and not to tarry long in so doing," stated Quintus Atilius, handing the scroll to Tiberius.

Receiving the parchment, Tiberius noted the fine seal upon it, saying, "It bears the Emperor's seal."

"It may as well be the Prefect's seal," voiced Quintus Atilius darkly.

Breaking the imperial seal, Tiberius unfurled the scroll and silently read it. Finishing, he looked up at his friend and said plainly, "Caesar is displeased with the governor of Judea, a man by the name of Pontius Pilate. I am being sent to Judea to report on him and his province. Thou art to accompany me."

"It is Sejanus who hath persuaded Caesar to send us to Judea."

"Surely, Caesar doth not comply with the will of the Prefect," remarked Tiberius in disbelief.

"Friend, Caesar doth not know he is complying with the will of the Prefect as he now rules via correspondence from Capri. He hath isolated himself from virtually everyone save the Prefect, whom he refers to as his trusted advisor. Caesar hath granted him a free rein in public affairs and Sejanus is using his mighty power to eliminate his personal enemies, one by one. His cruel tactics are causing fear among the esteemed members of the Senate and countless others. I feel certain he intends to rid himself of us while we are in Judea. Why else would we hath been sent to that far country? There are plenty of capable soldiers already stationed in Judea who could easily report on Pilate. It is not necessary to send two centurions from the Praetorian Guard to accomplish this. If thou dost ask me…it is a thinly veiled trap and we are the prey, my friend."

"It doth appear so, Quintus Atilius," conceded Tiberius, his tone and expression serious.

"Thou did send Claudius to Judea…did thee not?"

"I did."

"Doth he yet live?"

"No."

"Friend, hast thou ever considered Sejanus may hath hired Claudius to woo thy sister?" asked the centurion, drawing a connection. "Perhaps, he now sends thee to the same god forsaken place thou sent Claudius…to suffer the same fate."

"I had not considered the possibility…till now," responded Tiberius gravely, his countenance hardening. "If what thou hast said is true, I hath further reason to want him dead."

"When are we to leave on this onerous journey, Tiberius Marcius?"

"I hath been given a week to set my affairs in order. I assume thou hast the same."

"Very well…I shall see thee in a week, my friend. Till then, rest well for after that…neither of us shall rest well for some time to come," predicted Quintus Atilius, taking his leave.

"May the gods preserve thee, Quintus Atilius."

"And thee," retorted the centurion, exiting the house.

Collecting his thoughts, Tiberius read the scroll again, but this time he read between the lines. The contents did not bode well for him or for Quintus Atilius. The Prefect had concocted the inane mission to take them out of Rome, leaving their lives and fortunes vulnerable. To preserve what was his, he would have to make provision for the safety of his family during his long absence.

"Steward," summoned Tiberius, walking toward the tablinum with purpose.

"Domine, thou called," said the steward, appearing quickly, seemingly out of nowhere.

"Fetch thy tablet and pen. We hath much work to do. I shall await thee in my study."

Interested in hearing what Tiberius would dictate, the steward hurried to his office and quickly collected his writing tablet, pen and ink pot.

Inside the tablinum, Tiberius poured himself just enough wine to dull the pain he felt in his side. Emptying the cup of its contents, he refrained from drinking any more for he needed to be sharp in his thinking. He had many things to attend to and too much wine might interfere with their remembrance. Strolling over to his desk, he seated himself and began to contemplate his course of action.

Entering the tablinum, his arms full, the steward set his things down on the opposite side of Tiberius' desk and sat down in the client's chair, making himself comfortable. Opening his tablet, he dipped his writing utensil into the ink pot and having the right amount of ink on his pen he eagerly awaited his master's words.

"Steward, I am being sent to Judea and I know not how long I shall be gone. Therefore, I must set my affairs in order should my absence be longer than expected. Some of what I am about to say shall require thy silence. I ask thee to keep these matters in confidence…if that be possible," grinned Tiberius, toying with his servant, who grew embarrassed, realizing the master knew he talked too much. "I ask thee to keep my words to thyself as they may needlessly worry those of my household. Can I count on thy silence?"

"Yes, my lord," answered the steward, finding it difficult to look his master in the eye. "I assure thee, I shall keep thy words to myself…even if it means cutting out my tongue."

"Let us hope it will not come to that," Tiberius responded good naturedly. "The first order of business is the purchase of three passages to Judea aboard a ship leaving seven days from now."

"Three, my lord," questioned the steward, looking up from his tablet, confused. "Dost thou mean two?"

"Three…" repeated Tiberius meeting his servant's gaze.

"Three passages…seven days…" said the steward aloud, recording his master's words, wondering who the third voyager was.

"Assign another to take over Anatole's duty that he may rest before our long journey. Hath him thoroughly inspect my military gear and begin packing it. Tell him he hath seven days in which to ready us. Steward, I want thee to begin closing up the house. Everyone is to be relocated to the country villa, everyone except my mother. Inform her she is to take up residence with her brother while I am away. He is expecting her. She may, however, remain here till the seven days be ended."

"Shall I summon Cassius?"

"No…that will not be necessary."

"Who then shall be in charge of thy household in thy absence?"

"Steward, I charge thee with the responsibility. I put my household in thy capable hands. I shall ask Cassius and Lucius Servilius to look in on thee periodically and they shall supply thee with the funds to run the house. If there be any trouble, contact one or the other for instruction. The rest of the time, my servants shall be accountable to thee in my absence. Do what seems right in thine eyes. I shall write thee when I am able to come home. If the gods be willing, I shall return in less than a year."

"Domine, art thou well enough to resume military service?" asked the steward, glancing up from his tablet, concern written on his face.

"I am," Tiberius answered tersely, disliking the question.

"My lord, forgive me…" uttered the steward contritely, perceiving he had offended his master. "I know thou dost still suffer…"

"Keep it to thyself, steward," said Tiberius sternly. "Let us continue. I want thee to invite my family to supper the day after tomorrow. Hath the cook prepare a fine meal for the occasion. No expense is to be spared…I shall not eat with them again for some time to come. I desire the occasion to be memorable and altogether pleasant."

"I shall see to it personally, my lord," assured the steward, scribbling his instructions.

"In addition, hath the cook pack two weeks' worth of provisions for the journey…enough to feed three."

"Enough to feed three…" repeated the steward.

"Steward, the rest of what I am about to say unto thee…thou must keep to thyself."

The servant laid down his pen and looked upon his master earnestly, anxiously anticipating his words.

"I am being sent on a dangerous assignment. Do not repeat this…particularly to my mother or sister. Such news would only distress them. Should I not return, but die in Judea, Cassius and Lucius Servilius will handle my estate. They shall carry out my wishes. In the event of my death, I hath granted thee thy freedom."

"May the gods preserve thee, Domine! I would gladly forfeit my freedom for thy life," exclaimed the steward, moved by his master's kindness.

"Upon my death, Anatole shall be granted liberty along with thee. Ye shall receive a generous inheritance for thy years of faithful service unto me," declared Tiberius, looking his servant in the eye. "Steward, I trust thou wilt not fail to do thy whole duty."

"I shall not disappoint thee, my lord," replied the steward, his voice emotional.

"There is one other matter which requires thy discretion and it concerns my maidservant, Tamar."

The steward's ears perked up at the mention of Tamar, asking, "What is thy will concerning her, Domine?"

"I intend to take her with me on my journey. I do so for her safety. I cannot leave her behind and burden thee or my family with her protection. My enemy wishes to harm the maid and will stop at nothing. For her own protection and those of my household, she must accompany me to Judea. Howbeit, she is not to know that she shall journey with Anatole and me until such time as we are ready to depart. She is to think she is going to the villa with the rest of the household. Instruct her to pack her things and take note of them for I shall call upon thee to fetch her baggage on the day of travel. Further, I ask thee to choose for her some comely raiment from Priscilla's closet. Take heed not to arouse suspicion. Pack such things that are pleasing and needful to a female and set them aside for the appointed time of departure. Provide also some bedding for her comfort. Can I trust thee to keep these matters to thyself, steward?"

"I shall cut out my own tongue if I utter a word of it to anyone," pledged the steward solemnly.

"I shall make certain of that…if thou dost betray my confidence."

"Is there anything else, my lord?"

Glancing at the bowl of loose pearls setting upon his desk, Tiberius leaned forward in his chair, took the bowl and handed it to his servant, saying, "Take these and hath them restrung. Add the necklace to the things thou wilt prepare for Tamar."

"Domine, these belong to thy sister," said the steward, looking at the contents of the bowl. "Surely, she shall accuse thy servants of stealing her pearl necklace when she doth return home."

"Fret not…do as I say. I shall inform Priscilla of her gift to the maid. Depart in peace. Thou hast much to do."

Feeling as though he had just heard Tiberius' last will and testament, the steward rose up from his chair and collected his writing utensils, along with the bowl of pearls; unable to dismiss the awful thought that his master did not expect to return from Judea.

And he was correct in his thinking.

XXXVIII

Inside of the triclinium, Tiberius was reclining comfortably on the middle couch, flanked on both ends by the male members of his family. The only man not in attendance was Lucius Servilius' father who had been called out of town. Representing his side of the family, Lucius Servilius occupied the couch to the right of Tiberius. Cassius and Flavius shared the couch to the left of their host. The table before them was beautifully set with a white linen cloth embroidered with gold and silver threads, imported dinnerware, silver goblets, pitchers and bowls. Contained in clear round glass vases were three colorful bouquets of fresh flowers, the fragrant scent of which filled the room. Two male servants stood nearby fanning the patricians as they dined on appetizers of fresh fish, an assortment of enticing fruits, steamed vegetables, olives, cheeses and breads; all nicely arranged and served on engraved silver platters. Everything was as Tiberius had envisioned when he instructed his steward concerning the family gathering. Nothing had been overlooked.

"Tell us, Tiberius Marcius…why hast thou called us to thy table," Flavius asked, sensing there was more to the invitation than a meal.

Sipping his wine, Lucius Servilius eyed his brother-in-law with interest having the same feeling.

Feigning disinterest, Cassius adjusted the bolster under his elbow.

"I hath called ye here for I hath an announcement which I am compelled to make…," declared Tiberius, looking at his guests. "Five days from today, I shall be sailing for Judea."

"Judea," exclaimed Cassius, coming to life. "Why in the name of Jupiter would anyone want to go there?"

"I do not want to go. I hath been sent there by the Prefect. I believe he plans to murder Quintus Atilius and myself while we serve in the capacity he hath ordered."

"This is an outrage," thundered Flavius, his face turning red with anger. "How can he get away with this?"

"The same way he gets away with everything," remarked Lucius Servilius dryly.

"Therefore, I hath set my affairs in order should the Prefect succeed in his endeavor. To protect those of my house, I hath instructed my steward to relocate everyone to the villa with the exception of my mother. Uncle, with thy permission, I shall send her unto thee for safekeeping," petitioned Tiberius, casting an eye on Flavius. "Permit her to remain with thee for the duration of my absence and should I not return, do what is best for her in thine estimation."

"I shall take good care of her, Tiberius Marcius," assured Flavius soberly, swallowing hard.

"While I am in Judea, my steward shall be left in charge of the household. I hath instructed him to notify either thee or Lucius Servilius in the event of trouble," Tiberius continued, directing his words to Cassius. "Ye shall disperse funds as needed to keep the house functioning. In addition, I ask ye to look in on the steward regularly. If thou dost rightly divide the duties between thee...neither of thee should be overly burdened."

"I shall diligently attend to thy household as I hath in times past," replied Cassius resolutely.

"And I shall do the same," promised Lucius Servilius, wondering if he and Cassius would be able to cooperate with one another.

"If I do not return from Judea, ye shall divide my estate according to these instructions," stated Tiberius, handing all three men a copy of his final wishes.

Gravely silent, each man received a sealed parchment, understanding the seriousness of the moment.

"I apologize for putting a damper on our meal, but it is important that I speak to ye concerning this matter that in the event of my death there may be no disputing what I hath said."

"Tiberius Marcius, is there anything more thou dost require of me," asked Lucius Servilius, carefully laying his scroll beside his plate.

"There is one thing...,"

"Name it."

"Forgive the personal nature of my inquiry, Lucius Servilius, but I greatly desire to ask thee a question...," confessed Tiberius, pausing as he hated to pry in others private lives.

"What is thy question," inquired Lucius Servilius patiently, meeting the eyes of his brother-in-law.

"Hast thou found Priscilla a willing and obedient wife?"

"Thy sister hath exceeded my expectations," answered Lucius Servilius, easing his brother-in-law's mind. "She hath almost caused me to regret my harsh treatment of her."

"I am pleased to hear Priscilla hath done well," Tiberius remarked, taking a chunk of yellow cheese and a slice of warm bread for himself.

"This is good news," voiced Flavius, relieved to hear his niece had redeemed herself in the sight of her husband.

"Tiberius Marcius, dost thou think the Jewess hast anything to do with thy being assigned to Judea," questioned Cassius, bypassing the subject of Priscilla.

Turning to look at his son, Flavius pondered his supposition as did Lucius Servilius.

Tiberius sighed, admitting wearily, "She hast somewhat to do with it… though she is not the sole reason for the Prefect wanting me dead. I hath been over this before with thee, Cassius. Must we revisit the issue?"

"I think it behooves us to revisit the issue for thou dost refuse to admit the Prefect wants thee dead because of the Jewess," argued Cassius, his dark eyes narrowing as he fixed blame on Tamar. "If thou had not interfered in Sejanus' plan and taken her from Drusus…thou would not be in the precarious position thou dost now find thyself. Neither would thou hath suffered all thou hast in thy body. I wish to the gods thou would rid thyself of this Hebrew woman. It would be preferable for thee to hurl her from the Tarpeian cliff than to go on enduring the strong hand of thine enemy. She hath been as a curse upon thy house. Do away with her that thou may live."

Cassius had barely finished speaking when a servant girl frightened out of her wits by his heartless suggestion, dropped a ceramic plate which shattered loudly on the marble floor, momentarily capturing the patrician's attention. She knew Cassius to be a hard taskmaster, but never did she imagine he would throw a servant off of the Tarpeian cliff to their death, a fate ordinarily reserved for criminals. Apologizing profusely, the nervous maid gathered up the broken fragments as quickly as she could and hurried from the room.

"Son, such talk benefits no one," rebuked Flavius, sensitive to his nephew's situation.

"I am well acquainted with thy sentiment, Cassius. Thou need not expand on it," said Tiberius sharply, not wanting to spend what could be his last meal with his family arguing. "Let us lay this matter to rest."

"Before we do so, nephew, I should like to know what thou dost intend to do with the Jewess. If she is the cause of so much trouble as my son hath pointed out, then she is a liability to thy household…and shall remain so even in thy absence," stated Flavius, matter of factly. "What would thou hath us to do concerning her?"

Before responding to his uncle's question, Tiberius dismissed his servants from the room to prevent his words from being repeated among his household. Upon their exit, he replied, "Ye need not concern thyselves with her. The maid shall accompany me on my journey."

"What!" exclaimed Cassius hotly, his dark eyebrows raised in consternation. "Hast thou lost thy mind, Tiberius Marcius?"

"I am pleased to say I hath not," said Tiberius calmly.

"Tiberius Marcius, dost thou think it wise to take her on thy journey? She shall be a burden unto thee at a time when thou dost need to be on guard for the wiles of thine adversary," asserted Flavius, taking care to maintain an even tone with his nephew.

"I must concur with thy uncle," voiced Lucius Servilius, equally concerned. "Taking her with thee would only serve thy enemy. It would be better for thee if one of us takes responsibility for her. Did she not serve Priscilla for a time? The maid could do so again till thy return."

"Why should we trouble ourselves on her account? Shove her off the cliff and be done with her," Cassius said nastily, lifting his goblet to his lips and drinking deeply.

"I would thank thee to keep a civil tongue in thy head," snapped Tiberius, eyeing his cousin sternly.

"Nephew, perhaps thou ought to consider the offer of Lucius Servilius," interjected Flavius, intentionally drawing Tiberius' attention away from his son. "The maid hath served thy sister in times past; let her do so again for a season."

"It is too dangerous to send her into the home of any of thee. Sejanus could learn of it and then thy own lives and fortunes would be jeopardized as mine hath been. I will not take that risk. I do not desire that ye should suffer on my account. I hath determined what is best for all concerned and my decision stands. Now, I must ask thee to keep this matter quiet as the maid hath not been told and shall not be…till the time of departure," explained Tiberius, looking from one man to the next. "I trust I hath thy silence."

Lucius Servilius and Flavius nodded in unison, but Cassius scowled at the request and Tiberius saw him. Angered, Tiberius bolted upright upon his couch, seized a sharp knife from off the table and menacingly pointed it at his cousin, warning, "Cassius, heed my words or I shall be forced to cut thy throat!"

Undaunted by his cousin's act of aggression, Cassius tendered a mild answer. "I shall heed thy words, Tiberius Marcius. There is no need to threaten me," he said nonchalantly, popping a grape into his mouth.

Half wishing Tiberius would make good on his threat, Lucius Servilius gloated, unable to hide his pleasure. The incident had made the visit most worthwhile.

Flavius could not fault Tiberius for he knew Cassius had been too vocal. Trying to restore some semblance of peace between the two, he suggested, "Call back thy servants and invite the women to join us. The conversation hath become too serious. We are in need of a diversion."

Obliging his uncle's request, Tiberius rose up from his couch, laid down his knife upon the table, staring hard at Cassius as he did. Shaking off his anger, he strolled to the dining room door to summon his servants and the women.

Cassius finished off his wine, eyeing Lucius Servilius, who met his steady gaze without wavering, each man feeling hostile toward the other.

Flavius filled his plate with food, doing his best to appear unaffected by the distressing occurrence between his son and nephew.

Returning to his couch, Tiberius announced, "Let us put the unpleasantness behind us and enjoy the meal."

Flavia, Priscilla, Turia, her mother and Calpurnia entered the triclinium, a collective vision of grace and beauty, but none more than Priscilla, who garnered the attention of every male at the table.

Lucius Servilius observed Priscilla appreciatively as a servant assisted her with her chair, finding his wife more beautiful than the day before.

Flavius and Tiberius admired not only Priscilla's beauty, but her grace under pressure as was evident on her wedding day.

Cassius on the other hand looked upon her hungrily, wanting what was not his.

Feeling all eyes upon her, Priscilla smiled sweetly as she glanced about the table and said cordially, "I am delighted to be in my brother's house again." As her gaze fell upon her cousin, she was taken aback by the brazen way he was eyeing her. Uncomfortable, she averted her eyes from him and stole a look at her husband, but he did not meet her gaze for he was watching Cassius, having seen the untoward manner in which he had regarded Priscilla.

Addressing Cassius, Lucius Servilius remarked caustically, "It would appear it is time for Cassius to take a wife of his own."

Grabbing hold of that notion, Flavius chimed in, oblivious to what was going on between Lucius Servilius and his son, saying, "I would agree. Another wedding would be good for the family."

Turia giggled and blushed, delighted with being the topic of conversation. Fixing her big brown eyes upon her intended, she eagerly waited for him to respond.

"Is not thy sister a little young to wed," replied Cassius sourly.

"I most certainly am not," declared Turia, rising to her own defense. "I am almost fifteen!"

Everyone at the table laughed except Cassius and Lucius Servilius who glared malevolently at one another.

"Since we are on the subject of marriage…," began Flavius, prepared to launch into a lengthy discourse. "Tiberius Marcius, thou art in need of a good wife and I know just the woman for thee. She is quite a lovely creature by the name of Antonia. Unfortunately, her father hath no money to provide her with a decent dowry due to a string of bad investments. Although her family lacks money and good business sense, they do not lack breeding. Antonia is a woman worth considering. She is a patrician, of marriageable age, well educated and I hear…she is very intelligent and quick witted. I think she would make thee a fine wife, Tiberius Marcius. She is worthy of thy consideration. Wilt thou permit me to make the introduction," queried Flavius, hopeful.

"I shall be gone for nearly a year, Uncle. Let the woman marry another. I do not think it advisable for her to wait on my return," replied Tiberius, motioning for the servants to bring forth the main meal, deliberately putting an end to the subject for he had no interest in marriage.

At his beckoning, hot enticing entrees were brought to the table and served to the patricians, a servant in attendance for each guest. Goblets were set before the women and the wine steward dutifully filled their cups with watered down wine, having first refilled the men's goblets with fresh undiluted wine. After performing their respective duties, the servants retreated to their corner of the dining room to wait till they were required to render their services again.

As everyone partook of their meal, Tiberius considered those around him, cognizant a rift existed between his cousin and brother-in-law. In spite of their dissension, they would be forced to work with one other in his absence and they would either settle their dispute or kill each another in the process. One way or the other, the problem between them would be settled, thought Tiberius, laughing to himself, having determined beforehand to enjoy his meal come what may. And that is precisely what he did.

Several hours later having had their fill of food and conversation, the guests gathered in the atrium to bid farewell to their host. Flavius and Calpurnia were the first to wish Tiberius a safe journey.

"May the gods protect thee and bring thee home safely," said Flavius, affectionately patting Tiberius on the shoulder, his wife standing beside him, smiling pleasantly. "Tiberius Marcius, before thou dost depart on thy journey…give some thought to Antonia. She is worthy of thee. Just say the word and I will arrange the introduction. I am certain her family would agree to wait on thy return."

Tiberius smiled, but said nothing. He did not dare give his uncle a shred of hope.

"Godspeed," wished Cassius grudgingly as he left with his parents, miffed at Tiberius for pulling a knife on him.

Lucius Servilius, Priscilla, Turia and her mother came forward together. The men spoke privately with one another while the women consoled Flavia concerning Tiberius' journey. When everything had been said between them, they filed out the door, each wondering if they would ever see Tiberius alive again. The last to exit, Priscilla glanced back at her brother and was surprised to find his eye upon her.

"Priscilla," beckoned Tiberius.

Returning to him, Priscilla gazed softly into his eyes, asking, "Dost thou wish to say something more unto me, Tiberius Marcius?"

Laying his hands upon Priscilla's arms, Tiberius gently drew her to himself, regarding her fondly as he spoke, saying, "Sister, I am pleased with thee…as is thy husband. Pater would be proud of thee for thou hast done thy duty well."

Priscilla's brown eyes filled with tears, his kind exhortation touching her very deeply. "May the gods go with thee on thy journey and may thou return unto those who love thee…," she cried and then hurried after her husband, her heart full for she had finally won the approval of her brother.

Moved by the intimate exchange between her son and daughter, Flavia joined Tiberius where he stood, looked up into his handsome countenance, her eyes filled admiration and said, "Thou art so like thy father. He would be very proud of thee."

At a loss for words, Tiberius embraced his mother warmly, her tender declaration strengthening him for what lie ahead.

XXXIX

The appointed day of Tiberius' departure had arrived and those remaining in the house congregated in the atrium to bid him farewell. Among them was the steward, two male servants, Anatole, Talia, Tamar and Flavia, the latter of whom, steadfastly refused to leave the premises before her son did. Fearing she might never see Tiberius again, Flavia was determined to continue in his presence as long as time permitted despite the prodding of the steward, who was anxious to send her on ahead to her brother's house, along with her maid Talia. He had relocated nearly all of the household servants to the villa, but the Roman matron would not heed his request to depart as the others had. Having no recourse but to alter his arrangements, the steward decided one manservant would escort her and Talia to their destination after Tiberius left, while the other manservant would assist him in closing up the master's residence. He had hoped to utilize both men to secure the house, but he would have to make do with one manservant for he dared not exert too much pressure on Flavia.

Resigned to waiting on the patrician to take her leave, the steward focused his attention on Tamar, finding her a great deal easier to manage than Flavia. Certain the maid would not pose any problem for him as she was unaware of her impending journey, he slipped out of the atrium and retrieved the bag he had prepared for her. Pulling from his tunic the strand of pearls that Tiberius had ordered restrung, the steward tucked them deep into the bag he had assembled, pleased with how well he had put together a feminine wardrobe. Smiling to himself, he collected two bags; one packed by Tamar, the other by him and carried them both into the atrium, setting them down with the other baggage at the entry.

Opening the front door, the steward spoke to the stable servant who stood outside tending to three horses, saddled and readied for the journey. "Load the baggage," he instructed. "It is all accounted for."

Wasting no time, the mute stable servant quickly did as he was told.

Catching sight of her bag, Tamar rushed to the steward thinking her belongings had mistakenly been taken. "He did load my bag," she exclaimed nervously, pointing out the door.

"Did he?" replied the steward, pretending not to know what had been done. "Fret not, woman. I shall correct the error. Return now unto thy place for the master cometh."

Hesitant to comply, Tamar considered the steward for a moment, wondering how the mistake had occurred, but having no reason to doubt him, she naively returned to her place beside Talia.

Sparing no look at the maid who had spurned him, Anatole approached his beloved mother. Beholding her son, Talia stretched out her arms and drew him into her tender embrace, weeping as he spoke to her in their native tongue, but her tearful farewell ended abruptly when Tiberius entered the atrium.

Clad from head to toe in his military attire, Tiberius wore the might of Rome upon his tall, formidable physique, commanding the respect of all who saw him. Finding his appearance daunting, a flood of painful memories swept over Tamar as she looked upon the centurion.

Meeting her offspring where he stood, Flavia said, "Son, I hath offered up prayers and sacrifices to the gods for thy safe travel. And I am happy to report…the augur I consulted, read the signs and assured me thy journey would go well," expressed his mother, her eyes bright as she studied her first born, committing every detail of his aspect to her memory, not knowing how long it would be till she would see him again. "Tiberius Marcius, I shall daily petition the gods and make sacrifices on thy behalf until the day of thy return."

"Mater, I covet thy prayers for thou art a devout woman. If the gods hear any mortal's prayers…it would surely be thine," said he, touching her cheek affectionately.

Laying hold of his hand as it brushed her face, Flavia reverently kissed his palm, tears uncharacteristically welling up in her eyes. Not wishing to make a spectacle of herself, she stepped aside, keeping her back to those around her as she discreetly wiped away her tears.

"Steward, hast thou any questions or concerns before I take my leave?" inquired Tiberius, resting the hand kissed by his mother upon the hilt of his fearsome sword.

"No, my lord. Everything hath been done according to thy instructions," answered the servant confidently.

"And the baggage…hath it been loaded?"

"All baggage hath been loaded, Domine."

"Art thou ready to depart, Anatole?" Tiberius asked, eyeing his faithful travel companion.

"As ready as I ever shall be," he replied, excited about the trip as he was eager for an adventure, hoping the time away would help him expunge Tamar from his mind.

Surveying those assembled in the atrium, Tiberius spoke to them, saying, "I admonish ye to do thy duty in my absence; obeying those I hath placed in authority over thee as if it were I. If ye shall do as I hath commanded, ye shall be recompensed when I return…for I would not hath ye labor in vain."

Heartened by their master's promise, his servants came to him and wished him a safe journey. The last to do so was Tamar.

"I shall ask the God of my fathers to protect thee from harm, my lord," she said, her gentle, dark eyes meeting the gaze of the centurion.

"Woman, petition thy God for thy own protection also for thou art accompanying me," announced Tiberius, looking at her intently.

"My lord…I fear thou dost intend to render thy servant into the hands of a stranger," voiced Tamar shaken, her knees weakening.

Not bothering to confirm or refute her assumption, Tiberius glanced past Tamar and directed, "Steward, fetch a cloak from Priscilla's closet. The maid shall hath need of it."

Disturbed, Anatole stepped forward, exclaiming, "Domine, no provisions hath been made for her and there is no time to do so. We must be on our way lest we be delayed and miss our ship."

"Provisions hath been made for her," Tiberius remarked stiffly.

Hearing his response, Tamar fell on her face before Tiberius, crying, "My lord, do not deliver thy servant into the hands of a stranger! I beg thee…do not deal treacherously with thy handmaid for I hath served thee faithfully! Be merciful unto me! I beseech thee…do not send me away!"

All eyes in the room watched the unfolding drama, but none dared to speak except Anatole, who was quite put out by the unexpected development.

"Domine…leave her," asserted Anatole angrily, looking flustered. "She is too much trouble!"

Disliking the manner in which his servant had addressed him, Tiberius' face grew hard and he scolded, "Anatole, I caution thee to remember to whom thou dost speak. If this thing displeases thee…it is not for thee to say. The maid is in my hand and I will do with her what I will. If it pleases thee not…what is that to me?"

Seething, Anatole stomped out of the house, shocking not only his mother, but everyone else in the room. They could not believe he had dared to challenge the master's will concerning Tamar.

Deeply troubled by the strange turn of events, Flavia pondered why Tiberius should want to take the servant girl with him. The augur had made no mention of an additional traveler and she worried that perhaps the priest had misread the signs.

Returning to the atrium with a woman's cloak neatly draped over one arm, the steward stoically regarded the maid huddled at the master's feet, pleading with him.

"Get up off the floor, woman," demanded Tiberius sternly, looking down on the distraught maid, his patience wearing thin.

Obeying his directive, Tamar stood up, her body trembling.

"Woman…put this on," barked the centurion, taking the cloak from his steward and handing it to Tamar, who donned it reluctantly, her teary eyes fixed upon her master.

"My lord, what evil hath I done…why dost thou want to send me away?"

"Woman…what I do…I do for thy sake," stated Tiberius, seizing her by the arm and escorting her out of the house.

Walking her to Anatole's horse, the centurion lifted Tamar up onto the animal, seating her behind his disgruntled body servant and having done so; he mounted his own familiar steed and signaled to begin the trek. Anatole and the stable servant, whose horses bore the excess baggage followed closely behind the soldier, both men finding Tamar's presence troublesome.

"Suddenly I am very much afraid for my son's safety…" Flavia admitted, feeling uneasy as she watched the trio ride down the cobbled road.

"Be not afraid, Domina," said Talia gently, turning to her mistress. "Tamar's God will not suffer harm to come their way."

XL

In route to the port of Ostia situated at the mouth of the river Tiber, the travelers were joined by Quintus Atilius, who rode up alongside of Tiberius.

"Greetings, my friend," said Quintus Atilius cheerfully, pulling back on the reins, slowing his horse.

"What kept thee?" inquired Tiberius, regarding him with interest.

"I was delayed by a beautiful woman."

"I take it the delay was pleasant."

"Indeed it was," grinned Quintus Atilius, recalling the romantic interlude.

Comprehending the nature of the hold up, Tiberius did not press the soldier for details.

"Since we are on the subject of women, my friend…why may I ask…hast thou brought thy fair maidservant with thee? She shall attract the attention of every man and boy from here to Judea. Even I shall hath a hard time keeping my eyes off of her," laughed Quintus Atilius.

Hearing the centurion, Anatole's ears perked up.

"Let us ride ahead and I shall answer thee, Quintus Atilius," suggested Tiberius, seeking privacy. Taking the lead, he lightly swatted his stallion on its hind quarters and trotted forward a comfortable distance.

Catching up with him, Quintus Atilius awaited his response, his ear attentive.

"As thou art aware…the Prefect's thirst for vengeance hath yet to be satisfied. In his ruthless determination to kill me, he hath now targeted the maidservant. For the sake of my household, she could not remain in my home during my absence…lest I should tempt fortune and jeopardize my family. It is best for my household that the maid accompanies me to Judea," explained Tiberius, his aspect grim. "I also believe it is best for the maid as well. A few weeks ago, Sejanus' hired man used her kinswoman in a clever attempt to lure her from the safety of my home. Fortunately, the maid never knew her relative stood outside for I was able to conceal the matter from her with my steward's assistance. I shudder to think what her fate might hath been if Sejanus' minion had been successful in his endeavor. The Prefect hath forced my hand. I must find the maid a place of refuge before he succeeds in destroying her."

"What a shame to relinquish such a beautiful creature. Is there not another alternative?"

"I think not. As long as I possess the maid, she shall draw the wrath of my relentless enemy. This is not a fate I would wish on anyone…much less her. I doth owe the maid my life. I am indebted to her for the benevolent care she rendered as I laid near death. Her gentle diligence kept me alive and by all accounts, I should hath died that day. The maid hath done well by me and I must do the same for her, even if it means…I must surrender her to another man."

"Ump…" grunted Quintus Atilius, pondering his friend's predicament. "Would to the gods…I were that man."

"The maid doth not know my thoughts concerning her," continued Tiberius solemnly, disregarding his friend's remark. "She believes I am displeased with her and she is fearful. She imagines I shall deliver her into the hands of some vile, wretched oaf."

"Women are such foolish creatures. Why should she think such a thing? Friend, she hast dwelt in thy house long enough to know thy ways. I would think by now she would hath learned to trust thee."

"It is not so with her…she is ever afraid."

"What hath she to fear from thee? Did thou not protect her from Drusus…from Sejanus…and from her conniving uncle…just to mention a few? No doubt there were others…known only to thee and the gods."

"In her defense, I did lay hold of her once or twice, but she resisted my advances and I permitted her to escape me. I take no pleasure in an unwilling woman."

Quintus Atilius burst into laughter, saying, "Friend, that makes two of us."

Anatole had been watching the centurions closely trying to figure out what was being said, but they were too far in front of him to catch even a single word of their conversation. Even so, that did not prevent him from trying.

"Anatole, dost thou know what the master intends to do with me?" Tamar inquired timidly, breaking the cold silence between them.

Ignoring her, he said nothing, his attention fixed on the soldiers ahead of him.

"Please…Anatole…speak unto me! Tell me, what thou dost know!"

Remaining silent, Anatole hardened his heart toward Tamar, refusing her a kind word.

The stable servant stole a look at Anatole, wondering why he would not answer the maid.

"Hath pity upon me…" entreated Tamar. "Why dost thou turn a deaf ear unto me?"

Still, he said nothing.

Pressing him for a response, Tamar inadvertently tightened her arms about his waist, imploring, "Anatole…speak unto me for thy silence frightens me!"

She received a response. However, it was not the one she had hoped for as Anatole in his anger, bellowed loudly, "Woman, do not hold me so! I loathe thy touch!"

Hearing Anatole's belligerence, Tiberius stopped dead in his tracks and stared back at his body servant, reading his angry countenance. "What troubles thee?" he asked impatiently, his own temper igniting.

"The woman troubles me!"

Perplexed by Anatole's strange behavior, Quintus Atilius glanced over his shoulder at the servant, shooting him a hard look.

Frowning upon Anatole's treatment of Tamar, the stable servant would have spoken on the maid's behalf if only he could speak, but alas, the gods had tied his tongue.

Tiring of his servant's antics, Tiberius circled back, his black eyes narrowed with purpose. Coming alongside of Anatole's steed, he regarded him with hostility. "Assist her onto my horse!" he demanded sharply.

Swallowing his anger along with his pride, Anatole did as he was instructed, not daring to withstand his master in word or deed.

Extending his strong hand to the bewildered maid, who feared to take hold of it, Tiberius coaxed, "Woman, come to me."

Caught between the two men and a healthy measure of fear, Tamar mustered up her courage and grabbed hold of Tiberius' hand in a moment of resolve. And no sooner had she done so than she found herself safely mounted upon her master's horse. Wrapping her arms about Tiberius' armored torso, she looked over at Anatole, her eyes filled with hurt for she did not understand why he had treated her with such disdain.

Meeting her wounded expression, Anatole instantly regretted his behavior and lowered his gaze in shame.

Having Tamar in his possession, Tiberius turned his steed about and trotted forward. Rejoining Quintus Atilius, he complained, "Never in all my days hath I experienced so much trouble on account of one woman!"

"Ah, but she is not just any woman, my friend," chuckled the centurion, eyeing Tamar appreciatively.

XLI

Tiberius and his entourage arrived at the Port of Ostia, passing through a throng of people, many of whom were waiting to be ferried to the large cargo ship anchored in the deeper waters of the Mediterranean Sea. Since the river Tiber was too shallow for the vessel to safely dock, smaller boats were used to load and off load cargo as well as transport passengers to and from the ship. Spotting one such boat ferrying travelers to the vessel, Quintus Atilius drew his horse to a halt. Hoping to catch the next available ferry, he dismounted and began unloading his bags. Anatole and the stable servant followed his lead. Tiberius, however, remained on his stallion. He was in no hurry to meet an uncertain fate. Facing the sun drenched sea; Tiberius observed the ship's main sail billowing in the morning breeze while contemplating the peril that lay ahead.

Seeing the ship looming on the horizon, Tamar realized she was to about to embark on a far journey and the prospect frightened her. She had never traveled on the sea, neither had she wanted to. Tales of violent storms, terrible shipwrecks and fierce pirates were enough to squash any desire she may have had to explore the seas. Feeling apprehensive, she leaned forward against the back of the centurion, her arms still wrapped about his waist and softly entreated, "My lord, I pray thee hath mercy upon thy handmaid. Do not send me across the waters into a foreign land…nor deliver me into the hand of strangers. I beseech thee to remember thy servant's faithfulness unto thee and send me not away from thy presence."

Hearing Tamar's plea, Tiberius looked over his shoulder at her and responded, "Woman, I hath remembered thy faithfulness. It is for this cause…that I send thee away."

"Domine, I do not understand," she said meekly, studying his strong profile.

"Woman, thou must trust me…but if thou cannot…then trust in thy God."

Pondering his advice, Tamar grew silent, finding it strange that a Roman would admonish a Jew to trust in their God.

"Friend, wilt thou allow me the pleasure of assisting thy fair maid," inquired Quintus Atilius, stepping up to Tiberius' horse.

"Suit thyself," replied Tiberius lightly, regarding his fellow officer.

Reaching up, Quintus Atilius took possession of the maid, pressing her near him as he removed her from her master's stallion. Feeling his physical closeness and his hot breath upon her neck, Tamar endured the discomfort in silence. Turning her face away from the soldier, her eyes encountered Anatole's.

Disliking the centurion's handling of Tamar, Anatole created a distraction to divert the soldier's attention from her. Pretending his foot had been stepped on by his horse, Anatole began cursing and hopping about on one leg, faking pain, but as he was not a very good actor, none of his male travel companions took him seriously. In fact, they found him quite funny to behold.

Laughing aloud, the centurions exchanged looks, highly suspicious of Anatole's foolishness. As for the stable servant, he thought the body servant had lost his mind and was no longer rational. Only Tamar was concerned for Anatole's well being as she did not know what the soldiers suspected; neither could she understand why they laughed.

"Ye gods, Anatole! What next? Wilt thou stand on thy head or juggle balls?" Tiberius asked, staring hard at his servant, his laughter giving way to displeasure. "Dost thou wish to leave my service and join the circus?"

Realizing no one except Tamar believed his charade; Anatole stopped jumping about and announced with a straight face, "Domine, I hath recovered."

Hearing his response, Quintus Atilius slapped his leg and howled with laughter. The stable servant just shook his head; convinced Anatole had indeed taken leave of his senses.

Objecting to the unruly behavior of the group, the herald who was nearby inserted himself in the midst of the centurions and loudly proclaimed the ship's imminent departure. The port was his arena and he was supposed to be the center of attention, not some fool hopping about while those around him laughed like hyenas. Frowning at Anatole, the herald made certain his disapproval registered with the offender.

Comprehending the herald's message, Anatole immediately busied himself with the baggage which appeased the herald, who then continued on through the crowd making his announcement.

Dismissing Anatole's bizarre behavior from his mind, Tiberius dismounted, unable to forestall the inevitable any longer. Surrendering his prized horse to the stable servant, who was not accompanying them on their voyage, Tiberius advised, "Be mindful of thy safety. Travel only the main roads. Do not stray from them, lest thou be ambushed by thieves. If thou dost not tarry, thou wilt make it safely to the villa before nightfall. Heed my words and it should go well with thee."

The mute servant nodded his head affirmatively. He had no intention of dilly dallying along the way or carving out an adventure for himself. He wanted no trouble or excitement of any sort. He was content to do his duty and return to the master's country residence. Eager to be on his way, the stable servant gathered the reins of each man's steed and whisked away the fine collection of horseflesh. As he disappeared from sight, the men hurriedly gathered up their baggage.

"Come, woman," beckoned Tiberius, casting an eye on his maidservant, who seemed altogether uncertain of what she ought to do.

"Must I accompany thee, my lord…" she asked hesitantly, meeting the centurion's gaze.

"Thou must," he replied patiently, handing her the bag she had packed.

Receiving her bag, Tamar submitted to her master's will and fell in step behind him as he led the small band of travelers down to the water's edge toward a waiting boat.

Watching from a hidden vantage point, Tiberius' wily enemy spied the young woman among them. Smiling wickedly, he devised how he might do her harm.

Once aboard the ship, the three men staked out an area large enough to house them all. Locating a suitable spot, each man set up their own accommodations on the main deck, erecting their tents side by side. Finishing, the men placed their personal belongings inside and for Tiberius that included his maidservant.

Standing outside of his tent, Tiberius held open the entrance flap and directed, "Woman, go in and rest thyself."

Desiring to escape the rising heat of the day, Tamar willingly complied.

Entering after her, Tiberius removed his helmet and laid it on top of the bag which held his military gear. After wiping the sweat from his brow, he sorted through the other bags. Finding the one he was searching for, he set it at Tamar's feet, saying, "This is thy bedding, woman. Lay it where thou wilt."

"Domine, where wilt thou sleep," she inquired nervously, anticipating the answer.

Looking her square in the face, he answered flatly, "Here…in my tent."

Given the answer she dreaded, Tamar blushed and glanced away, her mind fraught with worry.

Noting her distress, Tiberius assured, "Woman, fret not. Thou shalt slumber in safety. Thy virtue is in no jeopardy. I shall not lay a hand upon thee."

"Domine, I fear my modesty shall suffer in thy presence."

"Woman, I shall be mindful of thy modesty."

Resigning herself to the uncomfortable situation, Tamar took her bag and dragged it off into a small corner. There, she unpacked her bed, wondering how she would manage her personal grooming in light of the awkward circumstances she found herself in.

Deciding to give Tamar some time to adjust to her crude accommodations, Tiberius left his tent and entered the shelter of Quintus Atilius, who was thirstily downing wine upon his entrance.

"Mind if I join thee?" asked Tiberius, stepping inside.

Quintus Atilius lowered his flask from his mouth and grinned broadly, "I see the maid wasted no time in chasing thee from thy tent."

Tiberius grinned back at Quintus Atilius.

"Wine?" offered Quintus Atilius, putting forward his flask.

Taking the container, Tiberius swallowed two mouthfuls of the sweet wine, wiping the residue from his lips with the back of his hand. Returning the flask to its owner, he said, "The maid fears her modesty shall suffer."

"A reasonable assumption…given thy close quarters," chuckled the centurion. "Thy art welcome to bunk here, my friend…if thou art so inclined."

"I appreciate thy offer, but I intend to dwell in my own tent. The maid is easier on the eyes than thee, Quintus Atilius," remarked Tiberius light-heartedly, ribbing his friend.

Quintus Atilius laughed, appreciating the humor. "It appears Anatole hath found her easy on the eyes as well. I hath never seen him act as oddly as I hath this day."

"Nor hath I. I pray we hath seen the last of his peculiar behavior. I hath need of a body servant…not a circus performer."

"Still…Anatole doth seem to hath some theatrical ability."

"Quintus Atilius, I do believe thou hast enjoyed his ridiculous antics," commented Tiberius, watching the centurion open his flask again.

"Indeed, I hath for there shall be little to laugh about in Judea," stated Quintus Atilius, his countenance and tone suddenly becoming serious. "Tiberius Marcius, I would never tell anyone, save thee…what I am about to say…" admitted the soldier, pausing momentarily to take a swig of wine.

Tiberius braced himself for the coming confession.

"Friend, I fear this assignment may be our last. Sejanus fully intends to kill us both. Try as I may, I cannot shake the sick feeling in my gut that we shall never see Rome again…that we shall die at that stinking, god forsaken post in Judea," he said bitterly, raising the flask to his lips.

Tiberius drew a deep breath, feeling the need for a drink himself as he was quietly suffering a dull throbbing pain in his side.

"I sought an encouraging sign from the gods, but to my dismay, I received a bad omen, increasing my fear all the more," continued Quintus Atilius, looking Tiberius directly in the eye. "My courage doth almost fail me. Friend, I am afraid the gods are not on our side."

"Be strong, Quintus Atilius. Give no place to fear. We must not base our success on temperamental gods and superstitious omens as others do. We must trust in ourselves, in our military training and in one another. Together, we shall prevail over Sejanus and his assassins as well as any other enemy that dares to come against us. We shall defeat our enemies and destroy them all. They shall not conquer us. They shall find us formidable foes…men of courage. We are not dumb animals being led to the slaughter. We are battle hardened soldiers with wits sharper than a newly honed blade," declared Tiberius heatedly, extracting a knife from his belt, his black eyes blazing with fiery determination. "Let us now swear allegiance to one another and seal this oath with our warrior blood…that together we may defeat every enemy that rises up against us."

"Let us make this oath," agreed Quintus Atilius, feeling the resurgence of his courage.

Boldly, without flinching, Tiberius ran his knife across the palm of his own hand, cutting his flesh, blood appearing from the laceration.

"Tiberius Marcius, I offer the strength of my hand to thee," stated Quintus Atilius, presenting his open palm.

Grasping his friend's hand, Tiberius steadily cut it in the same manner as he had his own, drawing blood as Quintus Atilius looked on stoically.

Locking their bloody hands, the centurions regarded one another and swore a solemn oath in Latin, vowing nothing short of death would separate them. Strengthened by their blood covenant, the soldiers then passed the flask between them, drinking to their alliance.

In the next tent, Tamar was carefully ripping from the hem of her garment, two long slender strips of material.

A short while later, Tiberius returned to his tent and upon seeing him, Tamar rose to her feet, her countenance somber as she approached him. Beholding her with interest, Tiberius stood where he was, taking in every inch of his lovely servant, including the ragged hem of her dress. Coming to him, Tamar gently took hold of his bloodied hand. Turning it over, she examined his wounded palm.

"My lord, permit me to clean and wrap thy hand," she said tenderly, raising her eyes to his, which were steadfastly pinned on her.

"Woman, it is hardly worth the trouble," responded Tiberius, wondering at her.

"I desire to care for thee, Domine," insisted Tamar, guiding Tiberius to her corner, where she had laid out everything required to clean his self inflicted wound. Kneeling down, she looked up at the centurion, waiting on him.

Noting the proximity of her personal space to Quintus Atilius' tent, Tiberius stooped down in front of her and inquired, "Woman, how much did thou overhear?"

Reaching for his hand, Tamar rinsed it with warm water, answering, "Nearly everything, my lord. Thy conversation filled my ears as I prepared my bedding. Only thy Latin escaped my understanding."

Replaying in his mind what had been discussed, Tiberius was thankful he and Quintus Atilius had not said too much about the maid. He would have preferred she had not heard anything, but she had and he could do nothing about it.

"My lord, I shall pray to my God for thy protection," declared the maid, patting dry her master's hand and applying a healing ointment. "I shall ask Him to strengthen thee and thy friend in this battle against thy mutual enemy…Sejanus."

"I do not put my trust in gods."

"Domine, my God is not one of Rome's powerless deities," Tamar asserted, finding the inner strength to voice the truth. "He is Lord God Almighty. He is the one true God…the only God."

"Why should this one true God be concerned for Quintus Atilius and myself," questioned Tiberius, patronizing her for he doubted the validity of her words. "What can this one God do for me…that all the gods of Rome cannot?"

"Domine, my God is able to deliver thee from thy strong enemy because He is real…unlike thy gods who are but lifeless idols…mere statues of stone…having no power," explained Tamar, winding the bandage around Tiberius' hand.

"As I stated before…I do not put my trust in gods."

"Without God…there shall be no justice for thee or myself. Thy enemy is my enemy, Domine. Sejanus commanded his soldiers to murder my betrothed and I desire to see justice done."

"Woman, thou dost confuse me! Art thou saying thou wert betrothed to thine own brother?"

Gazing at her master with eyes thoughtful, Tamar voiced sadly, "Josiah was not my brother, Domine. He thought by saying this, he could protect me."

"Woman, nothing he could hath said would hath protected thee or saved his life. Sejanus had orders to kill him and I to bring thee back to the palace unharmed. Neither of us could disobey Drusus without penalty of death."

"That did not hinder thee from bravely staying the hand of Drusus when he would hath struck me," stated Tamar, tying a small knot to hold the bandage in place. "Domine, thou feared him not. I know now thou wert sent of God to snatch me from Caesar's son…and whether or not thou dost believe in my God…or trust in Him…His hand is upon thee."

Vexed by her strange words, Tiberius stood to his feet. Looking down on the maid, he queried, "Dost thou truly believe this of me?"

Meeting his eyes, she answered confidently, "I do, my lord."

"Dost thou trust me to do for thee what I deem best?"

"My lord, I stumble at thy question. I fear thou art sending me away for I hath failed to please thee."

Extending his good hand to Tamar, Tiberius assisted her to her feet, saying, "Woman, take heart. Thou hast not failed to please me. It is for thine own safety that I must send thee away. Perhaps, this is the will of thy God for thee."

"Why am I no longer safe with thee, my lord? What hath changed?"

"Woman, I shall not discuss the details with thee. Too much information shall only trouble thee."

Accepting his declaration, Tamar did not press him.

Looking at his bandaged hand, Tiberius remarked, "How could I be displeased with a maid who shows me such kindness?"

"Domine, wilt thou permit me to do likewise for thy friend? His hand must be strong to stand with thee against thy enemy."

"Come," bid Tiberius, impressed by her benevolence.

Gathering up a few items, Tamar followed her master out of their tent into the tent of Quintus Atilius, who was busy trying to wrap his own hand.

Glancing up from his endeavor, Quintus Atilius regarded his visitors with curiosity.

"Friend, the maid hath requested to help thee," said Tiberius, ushering Tamar forth.

Going to the soldier, Tamar loosed his untidy bandage and treated his hand as she had her master's, saying, "Centurion, I tend thee because thou art the trusted friend of my lord. Thou art a mighty man of valor and as such, I humbly entreat thee to let no harm befall him. Soldier, thou must not fear thy enemy. I shall pray for thee that The God of Abraham, Isaac and Jacob shall strengthen thee and grant thee courage. Only remember thy oath unto my lord...that it may be well with thee."

Considering her mild admonishment not to fear the enemy, Quintus Atilius realized she had overheard his private confession. If anyone else had heard what she had, he would have felt embarrassed and angry, but her words were gentle, spoken from a sincere heart and he could not help but receive them in the spirit they were intended.

"Maid, I thank thee," said Quintus Atilius, appreciating her act of charity. "Thou hast done me a good turn this day and I shall not forget thy words or thy kindness. Be assured, I shall do all in my power to see that no harm comes to Tiberius Marcius. I shall guard his life as I would my own. I give thee my word."

Pleased with the centurion's promise, Tamar knotted his bandage and returned to her master, who eyed her intensely, having heard her words to Quintus Atilius. "Leave us, woman," he commanded, mulling over in his mind what she had said.

Bowing humbly before Tiberius, Tamar obeyed his directive and left the centurions alone.

"Tiberius Marcius, I do believe thy maid doth care for thee."

Responding in Latin, for he had learned his lesson, Tiberius said simply, "She hath done her duty with kindness...nothing more."

"I disagree," voiced Quintus Atilius, also speaking in Latin, taking his cue from Tiberius. "She expresses concern for thee. This is more than duty, my friend. She doth regard thee with affection."

Scoffing at the premise, Tiberius shook his head in disbelief. "Thou art mistaken, Quintus Atilius. Thou hath read too much into her gentle nature."

"Friend, why not search out her heart?"

"It is best that I do not," stated Tiberius, seeing no wisdom in trifling with Tamar's affections. "No good can come of it."

"I suppose thou art right, my friend," conceded Quintus Atilius, dropping the subject for he respected Tiberius too much to meddle in his private life.

Taking his leave, Tiberius exited the tent and strolled to the bow of the ship for some fresh air. Finding no one about, he leaned on the handrail and stared at the vast open sea. He needed to clear his mind. He could not allow himself to be distracted by the lovely maid or her flowery talk of her God. He had a vicious enemy to fight and he had to be on his guard for her sake as well as his own. He did not intend to rely on the Roman gods for his protection, so why should he rely on the God of Jews?

Still, he was intrigued by the maid's statement that the hand of her God was upon him. But why would a God he did not worship be concerned with him? If only he had some proof, some indication that this God was truly with him. Maybe, he ought to ask for a sign. What could it hurt? No one would ever know he had uttered a prayer to the God of the Jews. What did he have to lose? If Tamar's God did not answer, then the matter would be laid to rest, but if He did, then so much the better. Gazing at a flock of sea gulls in the air, Tiberius uttered a simple prayer, requesting a sure sign, unaware of the approaching assassin, who was about to overtake him and push him overboard into a watery grave.

"Soldier, thy enemy is upon thee," came a thunderous voice, startling Tiberius, who whirled about, swiftly drawing his sword, prepared to defend himself, but to his amazement, the would be attacker turned and ran off. Stunned, the centurion looked around and seeing no one else, it dawned on him, the God of the Jews had granted him a sign unlike any other. He had spoken from the heavens and had saved his life.

XLII

"Well...is Tiberius Marcius at the bottom of the sea?" the gladiator questioned, his sinister black eyes searching the dull face of his lackey. "Is he fish food? Well...speak up! Is he or is he not?"

"He is not," answered the lackey nervously. "I was just about to jump him and push him overboard when suddenly he spun about...having his sword drawn...as if he had eyes in the back of his head. I do not know how he knew I was upon him. I made no sound...I swear unto thee! I swear on my life!"

"Stupid idiot! Thy botched attempt hath only served to put the centurion on high alert," exploded Xenos angrily, seizing his lackey by the neck with both hands and savagely choking him. "Incompetent fool...I shall feed thee to the sharks in his stead!"

Gasping for air, the lackey frantically struggled to extradite himself from Xeno's brutal hands, but he was no match for the gladiator's enormous physical strength.

Caught up in the violent frenzy, the gladiator maintained his strangling death grip, staring wildly at the lackey, whose eyes bulged and then rolled back into their sockets as life departed from his body. Releasing his victim, Xenos laughed callously as the lackey fell dead upon the dirty floor. Glaring down at his handiwork, he kicked the lifeless body, hissing coldly, "Serves thee right...stupid idiot!"

Later that same evening, under the cover of darkness, Xenos slipped out of his quarters and dumped the lackey's dead body into the sea. He had committed murder and it mattered not a whit to him that his evil deed could jeopardize the safety of the voyage he was on, for death aboard a ship was considered the worst omen of all. The gladiator, however, paid no mind to such things. He did not regard omens, especially not those of his own making. Neither feared he any god or man.

Being rid of the lackey, the gladiator peered about, making certain the coast was still clear of witnesses and finding it so, he crept across the deck to the spot where the centurions had set up their tents. Marking who dwelt in which tent, he fixed his sight on the one belonging to Tiberius Marcius. Lurking in the shadows, Xenos waited for an opportunity to do away with the centurion, plotting how he might kill him, not knowing Tiberius had settled in for the evening.

Having set up his sleeping accommodations in the opposite corner from where Tamar resided, Tiberius sat down upon his makeshift bed and made himself comfortable. Reaching into the provisions bag, he pulled out a container of wine, a loaf of bread, a hunk of hard cheese and a small knife, which he used to slice up some bread and cheese for himself and his servant. Spearing a chunk of cheese with the knife, he held it up and offered it to Tamar, beckoning, "Come and eat."

"I am not hungry, my lord," responded Tamar weakly, feeling nauseous.

"Woman, surely, thou must be hungry. I hath not seen thee eat this day."

"I do not feel well, my lord. I cannot eat for my insides are tossed as the waves of the sea. I feel as though I may die."

"Woman, thou shalt not die," he said, guessing her physical malady. "Thy sickness is caused by the sea. Thou wilt feel better if thou dost eat a little bread. Come hither and join me."

Obeying his directive, Tamar went to her master.

"Sit, woman," he bid, noting her pallid aspect.

Kneeling down, Tamar hesitantly received the bread given her, having no appetite.

"Eat some," coaxed Tiberius, observing her. "Thou wilt feel better."

At his word, she raised the bread to her mouth and bit off a small piece, hopeful her nausea would pass.

"Woman, thou must eat…especially when traveling upon the waters. If thou dost not, thou wilt find thy journey exceedingly difficult to endure."

"Domine, with thy permission…I wish to return to my bed."

"Thou may do so, but see thou dost finish thy morsel. It is for thine own good."

Taking the bread with her, Tamar rose to her feet and returned to her corner. Lying down upon her bed, she curled up into the fetal position and closed her eyes, praying sleep would overtake her and bring relief.

Regarding his maidservant with a measure of pity as she lay upon her bed, Tiberius ate his meal alone, washing it down with a considerable amount of wine, which he drank to ease the affliction in his side. Medicating himself with the fruit of the vine, he pondered the nearly fatal incident and the God that had saved him from certain death.

As far as he could surmise, everything the maid had said about her God seemed to be true. Still, he did not understand why the God of Jews would heed the prayer of a Roman centurion and grant a sign of His existence to a non Jew. Casting his eye upon Tamar, Tiberius suspected the reason had something to do with the Hebrew maidservant. Her God had intervened on his behalf, sparing his life, because she had asked Him to. And for that, he was extremely grateful, both to her and her God. Extinguishing his lamp, Tiberius laid down upon his bed and humbly offered gratitude to the God of the Jews.

Over the next several days, Tamar battled sea sickness off and on, but on the fourth day, she awoke feeling much better. Wanting to escape the confines of the tent, she ventured out unbeknown to Tiberius, who was with Anatole and Quintus Atilius, drawing fresh water from a wooden tank in the hold of the vessel.

Exploring the ship, Tamar inadvertently wandered down to the bottom of the ship and became disoriented, unable to find her way back to the main deck. Walking the dark, narrow passageways, she felt like someone was following her. Trying to remain calm, she turned around and looked about, but saw no one. Darting down another passage, she still could not shake the feeling that someone was behind her. Again, she turned to look and found no one. Growing alarmed, her heart began to beat faster and she picked up her pace, trying desperately to find her way out of the dark, dank maze. Spotting a doorway, she rushed through it only to stop dead in her tracks. Horrified by what she saw, Tamar nearly fainted.

There before her eyes were rows of male prisoners chained at the ankles, sitting on benches, stripped to the waist, their emaciated bodies dripping with sweat as they toiled in unison to move great oars through the mighty waters. The men were ill fed, weak and exhausted. Some had been abused by the foreman's whip and were slumped over their oar, hardly able to perform their labor.

Catching sight of the appealing female, a considerable number of the men slowed their work and gawked at the lovely creature. The more crude individuals among them began to hurl unsavory comments her way, while others were content to quietly gaze upon her. The rest of the prisoners were either too sick or on the verge of death to even care she was present.

Seeing the cause of the slowdown, the angry foreman stomped forward and grabbed Tamar roughly by the arm and snarled in her face, "This is no place for a woman! Get thee out of here!"

The foreman had barely finished speaking to her when an imposing man appeared out of nowhere, coming from behind the woman. Startled by his sudden appearance, the foreman let go of Tamar and as he did, the other man took hold of her and pulled her back toward him. Frightened out of her wits, Tamar screamed, not knowing who held her.

"Calm thyself, maid. It is I...thy master," declared Tiberius, drawing her to him.

Relieved to hear his familiar voice, Tamar turned around, fell against her master's armored chest and began to sob.

"Centurion, thou best keep thy woman out of here!" warned the foreman, eyeing the soldier with envy. "If I had such a one...I would never let her out of my sight!"

"She shall not trouble thee again," assured Tiberius, sheltering the distraught maid in his arms.

Having no more to say, the foreman walked off and cracked his whip across the bare backs of some unfortunate souls, hollering, "Get to work ye worthless bunch of dogs."

Hearing the snap of the whip, Tamar whimpered, "I do not understand the ways of thy people. They are cruel taskmasters."

"Woman, what is there to understand," Tiberius stated gently, looking upon the badly shaken maid he embraced. "Rome hath instituted law and order throughout the world. These men were condemned to die, but hath been spared to row the ship. What they suffer is their just punishment. Be not troubled over the likes of these."

Lifting her head, she gazed tearfully at the centurion, sniffling, "Domine, I am indebted to thee for thy protection."

Hearing her declaration, coupled with the fact, she had sought refuge in his arms, Tiberius came to the realization that Tamar no longer feared him. Somewhere along the way, her opinion of him had changed. Careful not to dwell too long on the revelation lest he succumb to fanciful thoughts of her, Tiberius dismissed the notion from his mind and guided his maidservant safely through the dimly lit passages.

Back on the main deck, Tiberius encountered Anatole and Quintus Atilius, who had been searching for the maid and had rejoined one another, both having been unsuccessful in locating her. Seeing Tamar with Tiberius, they heaved a collective sigh of relief that he had found her. Rushing toward him, the men questioned, "Where was she? We looked everywhere for her."

"Down below with the slaves," he responded, glancing at Tamar, who had recovered sufficiently from her fright. "She was lost and could not find her way back."

"Did they lay hold of her," asked Anatole, reading her tear streaked countenance.

"No. I found her before any harm could come to her. From this day forward, Anatole, thou must accompany her everywhere. She is not to be left on her own. Is that understood?"

"I shall be as her shadow, Domine."

"Woman, never leave thy tent without an escort again," admonished Tiberius, walking her past Anatole and Quintus Atilius. Opening the flap of his tent for her, he added, "It is unadvisable for thee to wander the ship alone."

"I shall not do so again, my lord," voiced Tamar meekly, looking about for she felt eyes upon her.

"For whom dost thou look?" inquired Tiberius, sensing something was troubling her.

"Domine, before thou found me…I felt as if someone was following me."

"And now?"

"I hath the same feeling."

"Go inside, woman. I shall keep watch over thee," said Tiberius, scanning the area, but seeing no one of concern.

Concealed from sight, the gladiator watched as Tamar entered the tent and Tiberius returned to the others. Disappointed the centurion had gotten to the maid before he could, Xenos murmured to himself, "I almost had thee my pretty little dove. Next time, thou shalt not be so fortunate."

XLIII

It was not yet daylight when Anatole and Tamar set out for the galley as they had done nearly every day of their two month journey, arriving before it was overrun with other servants vying for space to prepare the morning meal for themselves and their masters.

Carrying most of the provisions, a sack slung over each shoulder, Anatole trailed behind Tamar, weighed down by his heavy load. Trying to keep up with the light footed maid, he hurried forward, feeling as if someone were shadowing him. Concerned for himself and Tamar, who was no longer in view, Anatole was on the verge of calling out to her when suddenly, he suffered a blow to the back of his head and everything went black, his body slumping to the floor.

Thinking Anatole was coming along behind her, Tamar entered the ill lit galley. Seeing no one inside, she chose a preparation area and began to unpack a few cooking utensils, humming a cheerful melody as she worked.

Hearing the door creak as it closed, she looked up expecting to see Anatole, but instead, she saw an extremely large, muscular man bolting the galley door. Instantly alarmed, Tamar went weak in the knees and her chest tightened as fear gripped her. Grabbing a knife from among her utensils, she drew a ragged breath and uttered a prayer of distress in her native tongue.

Wearing a diabolical smile, the gladiator turned around, having secured the door and walked straight toward Tamar, eager to lay his hands on her.

"Do not come any closer…I hath a knife!" Tamar warned, trying not to sound afraid, though she was. Sensing he intended her harm, her heart beat faster with each step he took toward her.

Closing in on the maid, his eyes flashing dangerously, Xenos snarled, "Put it down, my little dove, for it will do thee no good."

"Whatever thy intent…thou shalt not get away with it!"

"Who shall stop me, little dove? There is no one to save thee now," he smiled malevolently, revealing several missing teeth.

Frantic, Tamar ran for the door, trying to escape him, but he cornered her and slammed her against a wall. Seizing her by the wrist, he unmercifully twisted it behind her back, nearly breaking her slender arm.

In excruciating pain and in fear of her life, Tamar screamed.

Maintaining his stronghold, Xenos plucked the knife out of her small hand and drew her to himself. Running the knife ever so lightly down her neck, he threatened savagely, "Do not scream, my little dove. I do not like screaming…it makes me angry…and if I get angry…I will cut thy beautiful throat."

Terrified, Tamar began to cry softly, but she would not plead with the evil man, knowing it would not benefit her.

"Shhh…shhhh…my pretty dove. Remember…no screaming," reminded the gladiator fiendishly, breathing heavily in her ear, drawing his knife slowly down her neck, deriving perverse pleasure from her trembling body.

Tiberius and Quintus Atilius were conversing when Anatole came staggering into his master's tent, blood dripping down the side of his face, declaring breathlessly, "Come quick! Tamar is in danger!"

"What happened?" asked Quintus Atilius, his aspect grave as he stared at the servant.

"I was struck from behind…" explained Anatole, laying his hand on his bleeding head. "I passed out…and when I came to…"

"Where is Tamar?" demanded Tiberius sharply, strapping on his sword. "I told thee not to let her out of thy sight!"

"She went ahead of me a little ways…I lost her…" confessed Anatole contritely. "Domine…if any harm befalls her…I will not be able to live with myself."

"Thou wilt not hath to," replied Tiberius darkly, furious with his body servant. Having no sympathy for him whatsoever, he pushed him aside and rushed from his tent to the galley with Quintus Atilius fast on his heels.

Supposing he had dealt Anatole a fatal blow, Xenos did not expect interference from the servant or the centurions while he terrorized the maid. Sejanus had directed him to assault the girl before he carried out her death sentence, an order that suited his depraved mind. Liking his sinister instructions, the gladiator intended to ravish the maid, strangle her and escape by way of a hidden passage before anyone ever missed her or her inept guardian. Once in Judea, he would deal with the centurions, but before he did, Tiberius would suffer the loss of the maid. Vengeance would be exacted on behalf of the Prefect, beginning with the girl.

Feasting his eyes on the frightened maid pinned underneath him, the gladiator cupped her mouth with his large hand and growled wickedly, "Sejanus hath sent me."

Reaching the galley portal, Tiberius leaned his ear against it, whispering, "I hear a man's voice," and turning to Anatole, he questioned impatiently, "Is there another way into the galley?"

"None, that I am aware of, Domine," answered Anatole, his head pounding with a dizzying headache.

"We hath no option but to throw our weight against the door and break it down," uttered Quintus Atilius, keeping his voice low.

"The door is thick," whispered Anatole, stating the obvious. "Can we bring it down by our strength?"

"Thou best pray we can," snapped Tiberius at his servant, giving him a hard look.

"We shall break down the door…if the gods be willing," said Quintus Atilius to Tiberius.

Mumbling to himself, Anatole evoked every god he could think of, calling for their divine assistance.

Desperately praying she would be rescued before the gladiator had his way with her; Tamar shut her tearful eyes, not wanting to see the evil that was coming upon her.

Ripping Tamar's dress from her shoulders, the gladiator ran his ravenous, callous hands over her soft flesh and then abruptly stopped, hearing pounding at the door.

"What a pity…I am forced to put a quick end to thee, my little dove. I had so desired to know thee," growled the gladiator, sadistically placing his large hands about her delicate throat and tightening them. "Be brave, my little dove…this shall not take long."

Feeling his strong hands about her neck, Tamar's eyes flew open and she clawed and scratched at her attacker, fighting to survive, but his strength was mighty and she was as nothing in his hands.

Suddenly, the door came crashing in and the centurions charged the oversized villain. Tiberius was the first to reach the gladiator, manifesting strength and speed he did not know he was capable of. Seizing Xenos by the hair, Tiberius violently yanked back his head and slit his throat from ear to ear, killing the gladiator before he could even defend himself.

Snatching Tamar up from where she lay, Anatole swiftly ushered her away from the mayhem, shielding her eyes so she would not witness the horrible, gory violence taking place.

Holding the giant by the hair of his head, blood gushing forth from his neck, Tiberius threw him down on the floor and Quintus Atilius drove his sword deep into the gladiator's black heart for good measure.

Staring at the gladiator's dead, bloodied body, Tiberius uttered, his chest heaving with exertion, "This was Sejanus' man. I recognize him."

"Is this the man that tried to push thee overboard?" inquired Quintus Atilius, stoically pulling his sword out of the gladiator's chest and wiping the bloody blade on the dead man's clothing.

"He is not the one."

Sliding his lethal sword back into its sheath, Quintus Atilius remarked, "Then, there is yet another to kill."

"Search him for anything of interest," barked Tiberius, his breathing labored, adrenalin still coursing through his body. "Perhaps, there shall be some useful piece of information on his person…something that points back to Sejanus."

Crouching down beside the dead body, Quintus Atilius went through the gladiator's personal effects, extracting all items of value, but he found nothing to connect the dead man to the Prefect.

Having fatally dealt with Sejanus' hired man, Tiberius slipped his bloodied knife back in its place, carefully sliding it snugly between his calf and the leather of his boot. With that done, he turned his attention to Tamar, who was in the arms of Anatole, coughing and weeping uncontrollably like a child, clutching her torn dress against her. Yanking his red cloak from his uniform, Tiberius walked over to his servants. Laying his cloak upon Tamar's shoulders, he took her from Anatole and tenderly enveloped her in his blood spattered arms. Pressing her close, he consoled his maidservant, stroking her dark brown hair and whispering words of comfort in her ear which only she heard.

Witnessing the intimate moment between his master and the maid, Anatole suddenly realized Tiberius had a deep affection for Tamar.

Quintus Atilius stole a look at the two, drawing the same conclusion.

Just then, three men came upon the sanguine scene. "What happened here?" asked the first. "This is a terrible omen," cried the second. "We must inform the ship captain," voiced the third man.

Thinking fast, Quintus Atilius threw the gladiator's money pouch at the men's sandaled feet, saying, "Nothing happened worthy of reporting…it was merely an argument over a woman. The loser is dead and if ye wilt dispose of his body discreetly, ye may divide his considerable riches among thyselves."

"Was the woman his?" inquired the first man, eyeing Tamar hungrily.

"No, the woman belongs to the centurion. If thou art wise thou wilt not demand what is not being offered to thee," warned Quintus Atilius, looking at him menacingly. "It is gold and silver or it is nothing. Take it or leave it."

"We shall take it," said the first man, picking up the money pouch. "May we search his body?"

"Suit thyself," replied Quintus Atilius, stepping aside and allowing the men access to the dead gladiator.

"What more shall ye render for our silence?" queried the third man, greedy for gain.

"I shall let thee live…" threatened Quintus Atilius in no mood for games.

"And I shall do the same," added Tiberius ominously, regarding them with suspicion.

"And I also," declared Anatole, throwing in with the centurions.

"Fair enough," said the greedy one, backing down.

"It is still a bad omen," said the second man nervously, watching the other two men rummage through the gladiator's clothing.

Trusting Quintus Atilius to handle the details, Tiberius whisked Tamar from the horrific scene, sweeping her off her feet and carrying her out of the galley. Returning to his tent, he went inside and gingerly laid his maidservant down upon her bed mat. Leaving her momentarily, he poured a little wine into a small cup and brought it to her. Lifting her head, he held it to her quivering lips, saying, "Drink some, Tamar. It will settle thy nerves."

Sipping from the cup, Tamar could not recall ever having heard her name spoken by her master, but as she was emotionally and physically spent, the thought slipped from her consciousness and she began to cry again, still feeling the grip of death upon her bruised throat.

Noticing the marks on her neck had already begun to turn black and blue, Tiberius laid her head down upon her pillow, spread a blanket over her trembling body and left her again. Locating a bowl, he filled it with water, slung a towel over his arm and returned with them to Tamar. Kneeling down beside her, Tiberius immersed the towel in the bowl, wrung it out and took the cool wet cloth and gently wiped Tamar's face and neck, reassuring, "Woman, thou art safe now. He shall never hurt thee again. I hath seen to that!"

"Domine…I was terrified…he tried to kill me!" she sobbed inconsolably. "I grabbed a knife, but he was too strong…he wrestled it from my hand…and put it to my throat. I was afraid…for my life…yet I pleaded not with him…I would not…give him the satisfaction…I would not…"

"Thou wert very brave," said the centurion soberly, sickened that his maidservant had been brutally attacked.

"Domine…he told me…Sejanus sent him…"

"I know," Tiberius said calmly, laying aside the bowl and towel.

"I prayed thou would come after me, Domine…and God…answered my prayer!"

Beholding the maid, his heart tender toward her, Tiberius verbalized the nagging question on his mind. "Did he violate thee, woman?"

"He had not the chance..," Tamar sniffled, turning her head to the wall of the tent, giving way to more tears.

Hearing her reply, Tiberius heaved a deep sigh of relief. Stroking her forehead, he said softly, "Rest. Thou hast been through a terrible ordeal, but thou art safe now."

"Domine, is it well with Tamar," inquired Anatole, peeking into his master's tent.

Glancing over his shoulder at his body servant, Tiberius stood to his feet, his temper reigniting at the sight of him. Going to Anatole, he physically backed him out of the tent, roughing him up as he shoved his servant into the tent of Quintus Atilius and unleashed upon him a severe tongue lashing.

"Anatole, how in the name of the gods did this happen? I counted on thee to watch over the maid! Thou should hath never let this happen! Thou should hath been on thy guard! Where wert thou when she needed thee?"

"Domine, forgive me! I failed in my duty to protect her!" admitted Anatole, hanging his bandaged head in disgrace, his conscience weighing heavily on him.

"Indeed, thou failed…thou failed miserably! Thou wert greatly remiss in thy duty! The maid almost lost her life, enduring unspeakable things at the hands of a vicious murderer and I hold thee responsible for her suffering! I told thee to watch over her! Thou should not hath let her out of thy sight even for a moment," fumed Tiberius, suppressing the strong urge to take a whip to his servant's back.

Apprehensive, Anatole backed away from his master, doing his best to appear remorseful which was not too difficult for he truly was.

"Thou art a worthless servant…good for nothing…" rebuked Tiberius hotly, his black eyes flinty.

"Hath mercy upon me, Domine!"

"Get out of my sight! I cannot bear to look upon thee!"

Bowing fearfully before his master, Anatole fled the tent, bumping headlong into Quintus Atilius, who was entering at the same moment he was fleeing.

Stepping inside, Quintus Atilius saw Tiberius' angry countenance and surmised what had transpired between master and servant, but he said nothing, as it was not his business.

"Did they dispose of Sejanus' man?" queried Tiberius gruffly.

"He is at the bottom of the sea, my friend," answered Quintus Atilius. "We hath only to be concerned with the three witnesses. I do not know if we can trust them to keep their mouths shut. We best keep a low profile…till this thing blows over. I for one do not trust them as far as I can throw them."

"Hath no fear. We shall be disembarking in a matter of days. They shall not trouble us again."

"There is still the little matter of the one who tried to push thee to thy death, my friend. We shall hath to keep a sharp eye out for him. I am puzzled as to why we hath not yet run across him."

"I suspect the gladiator took care of that problem for us."

Quintus Atilius grunted, "Ump…that would explain it. Tell me…how fares thy maidservant?"

"As well as can be expected…considering, she was very nearly strangled to death by a cold blooded assassin."

"Was that the full extent of her physical harm?"

"Fortunately, it was."

"Then we hath done valiantly, my friend. We hath destroyed the enemy before he could destroy thee or thy maidservant. Our oath hath not been in vain. Semper fidelis," exclaimed Quintus Atilius, lifting his scarred hand victoriously in the air.

"Semper fidelis," repeated Tiberius, firmly grasping Quintus Atilius' raised hand, appreciating his friendship far more than words could ever express.

XLIV

Traveling the last leg of the journey by foot, the oppressive heat taking its toll upon him and his band of travelers, Tiberius decided to rest at the city's edge before entering. Coming to a standstill, he surveyed the rough and hilly terrain of Judea.

"Just as I expected…Judea is miserably hot," remarked Quintus Atilius, who was standing beside Tiberius, also taking in the lay of the land.

Tiberius grinned, "Surely, thou did not think we were sent to a pleasant place."

"I suspect, we shall find the inhabitants miserable too," scowled Quintus Atilius, beads of sweat trickling down the sides of his face.

"Let us step aside," suggested Tiberius, removing his helmet and wiping his brow of perspiration. "I hath somewhat to ask of thee."

The centurions walked a few paces toward a patch of palm trees, seeking shade and privacy.

When they were out of the servant's hearing, Tiberius turned to his friend and said, "Quintus Atilius, I hath need of a favor."

"Whatever it is, Tiberius Marcius…consider it done."

"Hear me and then give thy answer."

"Very well. Make thy request."

"Quintus Atilius…what I am about to ask of thee is far more than I ought. Nevertheless, I am compelled to ask out of need. As thou art aware, we are expected to report to the garrison immediately, but I need some time to find a safe place for my maidservant. I wish to delay our arrival by a day. In essence, I am asking thee to disobey orders that I might attend to a matter of personal importance. If we are found out…our military careers and our lives will be at stake," stated Tiberius, his voice and aspect grave. "This is a risk I feel I must take. However, I cannot expect thee to do the same on my account."

"Tiberius Marcius, we hath been friends a long time. Risk or no risk, ask what thou will of me and I shall do it," declared Quintus Atilius resolutely, looking Tiberius squarely in the eye. "What is thy will?"

"Quintus Atilius, I want thee to take my servants and go find suitable accommodations. We may hath need of a place to sleep tonight. Lodge in the first clean, respectable inn thou doth come upon. I shall join thee as soon as I can. While I am gone, instruct the maid to bathe and dress in fresh apparel. I hath set apart a bag for this purpose. She is to use what she finds therein to clothe herself in a pleasing manner. If she is hesitant to obey thy instructions…tell her, it is my command. She is to be dressed and ready to leave upon my return. If all goes well this day, we shall escort her to a place of refuge and immediately thereafter, we will report for duty. If it doth not go well, then we shall make use of our accommodations for the night and I shall resume my efforts in the morning. Quintus Atilius, I ask of thee one full day and no more."

"May one day be enough, my friend. Tell me…which bag contains the apparel?"

"The one on Anatole's right shoulder," replied Tiberius, eyeing his body servant. "Inform the maid…everything inside is hers to keep."

Quintus Atilius turned to make note of the particular bag.

Anatole saw the centurions looking at him and was dismayed. He had not been in good standing with his master since the morning of the attack. He had done what he could to stay out of Tiberius' sight for his master had not yet forgiven him and he knew it. As long as Tamar's bruises were visible, there was absolutely no hope of receiving a pardon. Offering his water pouch to the fair maid, Anatole commented, "The master hates me because I failed to protect thee from the gladiator. Look how he stares at me. I may as well be dead."

"He doth not hate thee," voiced Tamar softly, feeling for Anatole.

"He blames me for what happened to thee and he shall not soon forget it."

"Give him time," said Tamar, returning the pouch, having sipped some water.

"Time is all I hath…" he replied sadly, raising the pouch to his lips and drinking.

"Thou wert not to blame, Anatole. I ran ahead of thee and the fault lies with me."

"The master doth not see it that way," he said, closing his water pouch and putting it away.

Tamar held her peace for she knew he was right. She had overheard the severe reprimand Anatole had received on her account and it grieved her, knowing she had been the cause of his trouble. She had tried to intercede on his behalf, but Tiberius would not hear her. He held Anatole responsible and he would not budge from his judgment.

"Quintus Atilius, I must go now," said Tiberius, leaving the cool shade of the tree. "The sooner I get started…the better it will be for all of us."

"Where art thou going, my friend?" Quintus Atilius called after him.

"To find Jews…"

Amused by Tiberius' answer, Quintus Atilius smirked, knowing the task would not be too hard to accomplish in Judea. Returning to Tiberius' servants, he led them in the opposite direction, committed to doing all that his friend had requested of him.

"Where goes my master?" inquired Anatole of the centurion, looking back over his shoulder at Tiberius, who had already faded into the distance.

"If he wanted thee to know…he would hath told thee," answered the centurion gruffly.

Navigating unfamiliar streets in a foreign land, Tiberius was mindful the Judeans did not like Romans, in particular, Roman soldiers. Rome had long dealt harshly with the providence believing the Jews treasonous in their attitude toward the Emperor because they rejected the notion that Caesar was divine and refused to worship him. They would worship none but the God of their fathers. Irritated by the Jew's stubborn beliefs, Rome had imposed higher taxes, which fomented greater resistance among the population, making Judea an extremely dangerous place. Soldiers had to be especially careful not to fall prey to roving bands of zealots, who protested Roman rule by ambushing as many soldiers as possible. Forewarned of the danger, Tiberius cautiously proceeded on his way, hoping Tamar's God would protect him and look favorably upon his endeavor.

Spotting an open marketplace, Tiberius joined the crowd of buyers, who picked over the wares, bartering as if their life depended on the price they paid for each item and for some it did. Hungry, the centurion approached a fruit vendor and chose a plump, juicy pear and two handfuls of figs. Fixing his eye on the vendor, he asked their price, wondering whether or not the Judean would inflate the cost. Much to his surprise, the vendor did not try to cheat him and because he did not, Tiberius thought he might be forthcoming with information.

Paying him, Tiberius inquired, "Can thou tell me where I can find an honorable Jew?"

The vendor chuckled. "I offer fruit and vegetables, soldier…not answers to strange riddles."

Taking out a denarius, the centurion held it in front of him, saying, "A day's wages will I give thee if thou wilt answer my question."

Regarding the soldier with suspicion, the vendor solemnly said, "God forbid, I should sell the life of an honorable man for any sum."

"Do not misunderstand my intentions. I mean no physical harm to the man. I need his assistance with a very pressing matter."

"What is thy pressing matter…that thou should seek the help of a Jew," asked the vendor, distrusting the soldier. "Since when doth a Roman centurion seek a Jew for any good purpose?"

"I hath a maidservant…a Jewess…and I want to set her at liberty. I seek a man of honor to assist in finding her a safe place among her people."

"If thy maidservant is a Jew…let her return to her own kin."

"She hath no kin in Judea unto whom I can send her. The maid is of marriageable age. It is my hope she can make a life for herself among her own kind. She hath served me faithfully and I wish to reward her, but I cannot unless there is a Jew willing to lend me a hand."

Pondering the centurion's unusual petition, the vendor grew silent, stroking his dark whiskers in contemplation.

Tiberius waited on him to speak again. He did not have to wait long.

"Soldier, I believe thou art sincere in thy quest. Therefore, I will help thee," announced the vendor, feeling a sense of peace that he was making the right decision. "Every day about this time, a man by the name of Joseph comes by my stall. He is held in high regard for he is a moral man, a wealthy man, having four sons and two daughters. He might be able to offer thee some assistance."

"I am indebted to thee," replied Tiberius, handing over the denarius, considering it money well spent. "I shall wait for this man. Wilt thou make the introduction on my behalf? I do not wish to unnecessarily alarm him."

"I will, soldier. Rest thyself in the shade. Joseph shall be along shortly."

Seating himself under a nearby palm tree, the centurion ate the pear as he observed the marketplace, thankful he had managed to find a reasonable man to speak to, a man willing to point him in the right direction.

Amazed at how well things had gone; Tiberius felt certain Tamar's God was with him.

Finding a roadside inn, Quintus Atilius entered, securing one small room to be shared with Tiberius and his servants. Paying the innkeeper, he was escorted to the room by the proprietor's daughter, who regarded the centurion with interest.

Throwing open the door of the room, she said to the soldier, "I hope thou wilt find the accommodations to thy liking."

Strolling into the room, Quintus Atilius glanced about, noting several sleeping mats, a bed stand with an oil lamp and a single chair. As he had not expected much, he was not disappointed. The room was clean and free of odor and that was enough.

"Ye may wash up at the well in the back. The outhouse is just beyond it a few yards," continued the innkeeper's daughter, shamelessly taking in the soldier with her eyes. "If thou art hungry, I invite thee to visit our dining room. We offer a variety of appetizing fare. Today, we hath fresh beef on the menu."

"I shall hath need of one more mat," stated Quintus Atilius, meeting the young woman's bold gaze. "Another shall join us later."

"I shall see to it that it is delivered before nightfall. Is there anything else?" asked the young woman, half hoping there was as she found the centurion quite handsome.

"No. Everything seems to be in order," replied Quintus Atilius.

"If there is anything…anything at all…" she smiled invitingly. "I am always available."

Not one to miss a woman's cue, Quintus Atilius knew exactly what the innkeeper's daughter had in mind, but he said nothing to encourage her, in part, because Tiberius' maidservant was watching him and in part, because he did not want to let down his guard in a strange land.

Turning to leave, the innkeeper's daughter stared at Tamar, thinking she was the reason the soldier had ignored her friendly invitation. Finding Tamar pretty, the innkeeper's daughter went away disappointed.

"Why stand ye there? Come in," ordered the centurion, addressing Tiberius' servants, who stood outside of the room.

Obeying, Anatole and Tamar entered the small room, set down their baggage and looked about the sparsely furnished space.

"Am I expected to dwell in such close quarters among three men?" asked Tamar, voicing her concern.

"Woman, take up the matter with thy master," responded the centurion lightly. Shifting his attention to the body servant, he directed, "Anatole, go to the well and refresh thyself. When thou dost return, I shall go and the maid afterwards."

Hesitating to obey the command, Anatole glanced at Tamar, wondering if he ought to leave her alone with the soldier. Uncertain, he spoke up, saying, "I fear to leave the maid. I hath already faltered in my duty and do not want to do so again…lest my master whip me unto death."

Understanding the servant's fear, the centurion assured, "Be not afraid to do as I say, Anatole. Thy master hath given me charge over ye."

"On thy word…I shall obey," submitted Anatole, taking his personal belongings and exiting the room, wanting very much to wash away the filth of the long journey.

"Where went my lord?" inquired Tamar, regarding the centurion nervously.

"Maid, I cannot say where he went, but I can tell thee what he expects of thee in his absence," answered Quintus Atilius, grabbing hold of a bag and setting it down on the chair in front of her. "Everything within this sack hath been given unto thee. Thou art to bathe and clothe thyself in a pleasing fashion using what thy master hath provided. When thou art dressed…thou art to wait for his return."

"And if I refuse to do this?"

"If thou doth disobey thy master's command…then I shall be forced to bathe and dress thee myself that his will may be done," asserted Quintus Atilius testily, sensing he had been intentionally provoked.

"That shall not be necessary," yielded Tamar, lowering her dark eyes in submission. "I only desired to know if it was my master's will thou spoke or thine."

"Woman, I hath no mind to act contrary to the wishes of Tiberius Marcius. I hath never done so and I am not about to do so now. It seems to me, thou dost think a little too highly of thyself," he said harshly, taking her down a notch for he did not appreciate his integrity being questioned.

Weary from the long trip, Tamar burst into tears at his mild rebuke.

Beholding her reaction, Quintus Atilius threw his hands up in exasperation, complaining, "Women! I shall never understand them!"

Noticing a well dressed man with a lad making their way through the marketplace crowd, Tiberius tossed aside the core of his fully eaten pear and rose to his feet for a better view. Watching the two closely, he waited for them to stop at the vendor's stall, correctly discerning the man was the one he had been waiting for.

Under the centurion's surveillance, Joseph and his son spoke with the vendor and the three discussed the soldier's unusual request. After hearing what the vendor had to say, Joseph turned and regarded Tiberius. It was not often a Roman made a civil request of a Jew. Intrigued by the occurrence, Joseph declared, "I shall speak to the centurion."

"Father, why should we help a Roman soldier? Rome does nothing for us, but kill our people and rob us blind. We owe the Romans nothing!"

"Son, what he asks, he asks for his servant. She is one of us. Would thou turn thy back on a daughter of Abraham?"

"What if it is a trick?"

"I do not think it is, my son."

"Nor do I," stated the vendor. "I am persuaded the soldier is sincere."

"Let us go and speak with him," said Joseph, leaving the vendor, his son following after him, praying his father was not walking into a trap.

Seeing their approach, Tiberius went forward to meet them.

"I am Joseph and this is my youngest son, Joshua," said the Jew, politely making introductions. "How art thou called, centurion?"

"I am Tiberius Marcius."

"I understand thou hath need of some assistance," said Joseph, sizing up the soldier.

"That is correct. Art thou willing to assist me?"

"I may be able to, centurion. Tell me about thy servant."

"She is young…of marriageable age…lovely to look upon and her ways are pleasing. I desire to find her a husband that she may dwell securely in this land."

Joseph laughed. "Centurion, thou hath need of a matchmaker. I am not qualified in matters of the heart."

"Father, thou hast three sons who hath not yet taken wives," reminded

Joshua, entering the conversation. "Perhaps, we ought to see this young woman for ourselves. It may be it is God's will that one of us should marry her."

Turning to look at his son, Joseph considered his words, finding them sensible.

Tiberius also looked at Joshua, judging whether or not he would make a suitable husband for Tamar. Deciding the youth was probably around fourteen years of age, Tiberius deemed him too young to take a wife.

"Tiberius Marcius, we should like to meet thy servant and judge for ourselves if she is all thou hast said," declared Joseph, studying the soldier's fine features. "If she is, then we shall assist thee in finding her a husband."

"Before I render her into thy hand…there are some requirements thou must agree to. I want her to live a good life…not one of mediocrity or servitude."

"I see thou hath her best interest at heart. What doth thou require of us?"

"The maid shall no longer serve another…save her husband. She is not to be betrothed unto an old man, but to a young man of courage. He must be worthy of one as lovely as she. He is to be well respected, intelligent, industrious and prosperous. He must not be a man given to vice or violence. I would not hath any man mistreat her. She is deserving of better."

"Clearly, thou hast given this matter much consideration, centurion. The maid must hath served thee well."

"She is the reason I stand before thee. I should by all accounts…be dead. It was her diligent care that saved my life. And life…a good life is what I want for her."

"Art thou prepared to grant her freedom and put it in writing?"

"I am."

"Art thou prepared to provide her a dowry befitting her?"

"I am."

"Very well, then. If this woman is all thou hast said…it should not be too difficult to find her a husband who fits thy description. I hath three eligible sons…all young men of character and means. We are highly blessed and favored of God. There is nothing that we lack."

Joshua pulled at his father's sleeve and whispered something into his ear.

"My son hath reminded me of one very important question…a most delicate question."

Knowing what he was referring to, Tiberius volunteered, "She hath known no man."

"When shall we meet this fair servant of thine?"

"I shall return with her this very day…if thou art agreeable."

"Centurion, I see no reason to delay meeting her. Go and do as thou hast said. Thou shalt find us at the vineyard which lies at the end of this road. Joshua shall watch for thy return."

In a gesture of good will, Tiberius extended his hand to the elder Jew.

Joseph regarded Tiberius' hand, noting the fresh scar across his palm. Realizing the soldier was in covenant with another, the Jew saw the Roman as a man of honor. Yet, it was not customary for a Jew to touch a Gentile and so Joseph did not take hold of the centurion's hand.

"I know not thy ways," confessed Tiberius, withdrawing his hand, choosing not to be offended. "I bid thee farewell."

"Shalom," responded Joseph, taking an uncommon liking to the centurion.

Waiting until the centurion was out of earshot, Joshua remarked, "Father, he is unlike the soldiers of Judea. The legion stationed here are the scum of the Roman army, but this centurion conducts himself quite differently. He speaks with a civil tongue and shows no outward contempt for us as the others do."

"I noted the same. He was forthright in his manner and speech. I hath never encountered the likes of him. Still, one thing doth trouble me…"

"What is it, Father?"

"I fear his words may hath betrayed his heart."

Traipsing the dusty road, Tiberius pondered the arrangements he had made for Tamar, knowing them to be sound, but instead of being satisfied that he had done as he intended to do, he was troubled. He knew what he felt had nothing to do with Joseph and his son, whom he had found to be a decent sort. The feeling stemmed from within for he did not want to relinquish Tamar to another man. Coming to a roadside inn, Tiberius shrugged off his contemplations and went inside to check if it was the place Quintus Atilius had chosen.

Delighted to see another tall, dark and handsome centurion, the innkeeper's daughter, mumbled under her breath, "The gods hath smiled upon me."

Drawing near the front counter, Tiberius noticed the woman gazed at him with dreamy eyes and he very nearly laughed aloud, finding her rather silly to behold. Stifling his urge to laugh, he said, "Woman, I seek my friend…a centurion. He came with two servants. Is he here?"

"He is," answered the woman. "Shall I show thee to his room?"

"I would appreciate it."

"If thou doth need anything…anything at all…I am always available," said she, seductively throwing her hips to and fro as she escorted him. "Things get mighty lonely around here at night, soldier…so if thou doth desire a little company, be sure to keep me in mind and that goes for thy friend too."

"Woman, I can not imagine how thou could be lonely…seeing there is a legion of soldiers stationed nearby," remarked Tiberius carelessly, immune to her feminine wiles.

Stopping in front of the room, the innkeeper's daughter glanced at the centurion, her expression one of hurt for she perceived he had insulted her.

Realizing he had offended her, Tiberius tendered a kinder response. "Woman, I thank thee for thy hospitality."

His words doing little to soothe her wounded ego, the innkeeper's daughter left Tiberius at the door. Hurrying away, she passed by Quintus Atilius, who was headed back toward the room, but she did not bother acknowledging him in any fashion. She knew when she was not wanted.

Seeing Tiberius, Quintus Atilius approached him, asking, "What in the world did thou say unto the woman? She looks as if thou did insult her."

"I am afraid I did," admitted Tiberius, none too proud of it.

"I take it she propositioned thee," grinned Quintus Atilius. "Hers will likely be the last friendly offer we get in this stinking part of the world."

"Where is Anatole?" questioned Tiberius, changing the subject.

"He is inside with the maid. I put him in charge of her while I went to get something to eat," said Quintus Atilius, having a small neatly wrapped bundle in his possession. "I hath in my hand fresh beef. Imagine that in a place like this."

"Take Anatole with thee and go eat. I want to speak with the maid alone."

"Did thou find a place for her?"

"I did. We shall be leaving here shortly. See if thou can find a few horses to make our journey easier."

"Consider it done," said Quintus Atilius, opening the door to the room and summoning Anatole forth.

"Go with Quintus Atilius," barked Tiberius, glaring at his body servant as he came out of the room.

Hanging his head, Anatole followed Quintus Atilius, wondering how long Tiberius would treat him with disdain.

Entering the small room, Tiberius closed the door behind him.

Beholding her lord, Tamar rose up from the chair in which she had been sitting, her heart quickening at the sight of him.

Facing his maidservant, the centurion marveled at her beauty, his keen eye pouring over her, committing every detail of the lovely girl to memory for soon she would no longer be his. Noticing the pearl necklace in her hand, he wondered why she was holding the jewelry, instead of wearing it.

Under her master's scrutiny, Tamar tried to manage a smile, though her heart was sorrowful.

Approaching her, Tiberius withdrew a small package from his uniform and handed it to Tamar, saying, "I gave thee figs when we met and I give thee the same at our parting."

Receiving the fruit, tears welled in Tamar's eyes finding the gift strangely sentimental. "Domine, I accept thy gift and render in return thy sister's pearls."

"Did not Quintus Atilius tell thee everything in the bag was thine to keep?"

"He did, my lord…but the necklace is Priscilla's."

"She hath given it unto thee."

"I shall treasure it always," said Tamar thoughtfully, setting the pearls and packaged fruit on the chair behind her.

Observing the maid, Tiberius announced, "Woman, I hath found a safe place for thee among thy people."

Hearing the dreaded declaration, emotion overwhelmed Tamar. Turning to face her master, she earnestly expressed her feelings, saying, "Domine, my heart is heavy. I do not want to leave thee. I beg thee to reconsider this matter."

"What I do…I do for thee, Tamar," he said, gazing upon her intently. "I send thee unto them with a writ of freedom and a generous dowry. Thou art no longer my servant, neither art thou poor. Thou shalt go forth from my house with thy head held high."

"No, my lord, I wilt not leave thee…send me not away lest my heart break," she pleaded, falling to her knees before him. "If I hath found favor in thy sight…let me remain with thee."

"Woman, stand to thy feet," directed Tiberius, looking upon the maid, deeply troubled by her reaction. "What manner of speech is this?"

"I wilt not leave thee…I wilt not," she cried, remaining on her knees, a picture of humility. "I should rather be a servant in thy house than be free in the house of another."

"Thou doth not know what thou art saying. Thou hath taken leave of thy senses."

"I know what is in my heart, Domine."

"Woman, again I say unto thee…stand to thy feet."

Tamar rose up before him, entreating, "My lord, send me not away."

Tiberius laid his hands upon her small shoulders, his dark eyes searching hers and said gently, "Woman, thou art a Jew and I a Roman…there is no common ground between us."

"My heart tells me different, Domine."

Stunned, Tiberius knew not what to say. He had not counted on her having feelings for him. His mind went into a momentary stir. Logic dictated he could not be entangled with her. He was a soldier and the military was enough for him. He did not need a woman complicating his life. Yet, his heart dictated otherwise. He longed to take her into his arms and love her as she was meant to be loved. He longed to wipe away her tears and protect her from every evil, but he could not. What he wanted was not best for her. Struggling to maintain his resolve, Tiberius turned away from his heart's desire and walked to the door. Pausing there, his back facing Tamar, he forced out the words, "Gather thy belongings. We leave shortly."

Quintus Atilius had borrowed three horses from the innkeeper, paying a hefty price for their use. Entering the hostile city on their loaned horseflesh, the soldiers rode side by side, presenting a united front. Anatole lagged behind so he might converse privately with Tamar, with whom he shared his steed.

"Woman, where is the master taking thee?"

"He hath found a place among my people," she answered, her heart heavy laden with sorrow.

"Tamar, may I ask thee a personal question?"

"I suppose…"

"Doth thou hath feelings for the master?"

"What doth it matter," she responded, her voice quivering as she fought back tears.

"Tamar, I hath seen the way he looks upon thee. His heart is tender toward thee."

Sensing he was being spoken of, Tiberius glanced back at his servants. "Anatole, join us," he summoned sharply, disliking the gulf between them.

Obeying, Anatole rode forward, abruptly ending his conversation with Tamar.

Arriving at the vineyard, Tiberius turned to Quintus Atilius and said, "Wait here with Anatole. I shall not be long."

Dismounting, Tiberius walked over to his servant's horse. "Give me her bags," he demanded of Anatole, who promptly complied, rendering them to his master.

"My lord, I beg thee…do not leave me here!" pleaded Tamar, fighting tears.

Reaching up, Tiberius removed Tamar from Anatole's horse and set her down in front of him. Slapping the hind quarters of the steed, he dismissed his body servant that he might be alone with her.

Withdrawing from his person, a leather money pouch and a sealed parchment, Tiberius took hold of Tamar's small hand and laid them within, closing her hand about them, saying, "Tamar, use these to secure a good life for thyself."

"My lord, please…do not leave me in this strange land!"

"Woman, thou art safe from Sejanus here. He will not persecute thee anymore."

"I do not want to leave thee, my lord," cried Tamar, tears glistening in her eyes.

"Woman, be of good courage," said Tiberius, wiping away her tears, a part of him wanting to draw her near, but he resisted the temptation to do so for more than one reason. "Thou art young and hath thy whole life ahead of thee. Thou wilt soon forget thou ever served in my house."

"I shall not forget thee…my heart is heavy…"

"Say not thy heart is heavy, neither let thy people see it be so. There is great hatred in this land between Romans and Jews. Thy people will not understand thy sentiment and I would not hath thee rejected by them. Do not mourn over one such as I. This is my final command to thee, Tamar. Heed my words for thy own sake that it may go well with thee in this place."

"I care not what they think…"

"Come," beckoned Tiberius, picking up her bags and leading her toward the house of Joseph.

Quintus Atilius and Anatole watched in silent disbelief as the moment of truth unfolded before them.

Joshua came forward, motioning to the centurion, "This way, Tiberius Marcius. We hath been expecting thee and the maid." Addressing Tamar cordially, Joshua spoke to her in Hebrew and she responded meekly in like tongue.

Hearing them, Tiberius felt uncomfortable as he did not know the language and it concerned him what Tamar might say. He did not want anything to jeopardize her future.

Entering the large, well furnished home, Tiberius encountered Joseph and the other two sons, who stood proudly beside their father. Joseph's two daughters stood quietly off to one side of the room.

"Welcome to our home, Tiberius Marcius," greeted Joseph graciously, his gaze drawn to Tamar, who humbly bowed her head and modestly drew her cloak about her. "Centurion, the maid is everything thou said. Thou art not only honest in thy estimation of a matter, but thou art accurate in thy stating."

"I am pleased thou hast found me thus," replied Tiberius to Joseph, studying the two men, wondering which of the two would marry Tamar.

"Ah, I hath forgotten my manners," said Joseph, seeing the soldier regarding his two grown sons. "These are my sons, Caleb and Joram."

Joseph's sons nodded in acknowledgement, neither being too thrilled about a Roman soldier standing inside their home. If not for the lovely girl he had brought with him, they would not hath tolerated his presence.

The young men's resentment was not lost on Tiberius, who was none too fond of them either.

"Caleb is next in line to marry, being the second eldest of my four sons. If he finds the maid to his liking, he shall marry her and if he doth not, then Joram shall consider her," explained the father. "And lastly...my youngest...Joshua."

"I assume the maid shall hath some say," remarked Tiberius stiffly.

"She shall."

"What is the maid's name?" spoke Caleb, his eyes fastened on the young girl.

"Tamar," answered Tiberius tersely, finding Caleb's scrutiny of her difficult to stomach.

"Tamar," repeated Caleb, liking the name and the girl.

Then Caleb spoke something to Tamar in Hebrew to which she responded in kind, irritating Tiberius for he did not know what was being said.

Deciding to hurry things along, he took control of the conversation, stating, "I hath given the maid a writ of freedom and a generous dowry, among other things. None of which, shall be taken from her. I hath kept my end of the agreement and I expect thee to do likewise. If I learn thou hast not kept thy word, then I shall return and forcibly take her from thee," warned Tiberius sternly. "She shall in no way be mistreated or taken advantage of."

Hearing her master's warning to the men, Tamar looked at Tiberius, suddenly realizing he cared for her much more than she ever dared to imagine.

"I assure thee, centurion, we are men of principle," said Joseph calmly, meeting the soldier's steady gaze. "We shall adhere to our agreement. She shall reside with my daughters until such a time, she is willing to marry."

"Then the matter is settled. I render the maid into thy hands. Treat her well," and having spoken, Tiberius swiftly departed from the house, leaving the girl standing before the three men, trying desperately to process all she had heard.

Coming to herself, Tamar addressed the elder man, "Permit me to bid my lord farewell…" and without waiting for his permission, she darted out of the house.

"Father, look how she runs after that Roman pig," voiced Caleb with disdain. "Let me go after her! No potential wife of mine shall behave in such a manner!"

Joseph took hold of his son's arm, saying, "Caleb, despise her not. The soldier hath done her much good. Thou must be mindful of this and judge her accordingly."

"Father, send Serah out to fetch her," suggested Joram, more sensitive in nature than his brother. "It may be the maid shall require consoling."

Liking his son's idea, Joseph dispatched his eldest daughter, Serah.

"Wait…my lord…" Tamar cried out, tears rolling down her cheeks as she ran toward Tiberius, her heart filled with unspoken words.

Just about to mount his horse, Tiberius saw Tamar coming. Acting quickly, he mounted his steed, shouting, "Quintus Atilius, I leave her to thee. Do not permit her to make a spectacle of herself."

"I shall see to her," assured Quintus Atilius, riding forward and blocking Tamar's path.

"Come, Anatole," ordered Tiberius, galloping off.

Stealing one last look at Tamar, Anatole reluctantly followed his master's lead.

Looking down from his horse at the maid, her sorrowful eyes pinned on Tiberius as he rode away, Quintus Atilius said, "Woman, forget him. He hath done for thee what he could."

"I never told him all that was in my heart…" she confessed tearfully. "I was afraid to say…"

"Woman, forget him!"

Looking up at the centurion, she sobbed, "How shall I forget him… when he takes with him…my heart!"

"Cursed be the gods!" swore Quintus Atilius. "Thou art in love with him!"

"How shall he know, unless thou wilt tell him…" appealed Tamar. "Please…thou must…speak for me…"

"Woman, it is too late! What is done is done," exclaimed Quintus Atilius, laying the whip to his horse and riding away. He could no more tell Tiberius that the maid loved him than the maid herself could. As far as he was concerned, he had never heard her confession.

Serah was of the same mind. She did not intend to tell her father or her brothers what she had heard. Some things were better left unsaid. Placing her arms about the weeping girl, Serah comforted her, recognizing a broken heart when she saw one.

XLV

Dismounting their steeds, the centurions unloaded their heavy bags of gear, preparing to walk the rest of the way to the garrison in Capernaum and report for duty. Charging his servant with the responsibility of the horses, Tiberius instructed, "Return them to the innkeeper."

"Better put some money in his hand," advised Quintus Atilius, glancing in Tiberius' direction. "The innkeeper was none too honest. It would not surprise me one bit if he accused us of stealing his horses."

Heeding the advice of his friend, Tiberius laid a fair sum of money in Anatole's hand, directing, "Rejoin us as soon as thou art able."

"I will, Domine," lied the servant, who had decided to run away, believing his master no longer cared about him. The goddess Fortuna had provided the funds to escape and escape he would.

"Anatole, thou would do well to return the horses and leave the premises quickly," urged Quintus Atilius, genuinely concerned they would be falsely accused. "If thou can do so without being seen by the proprietor or his saucy daughter…thou wilt avoid a heap of trouble."

Looking to his master, Anatole waited for his word on the matter.

"Do as Quintus Atilius hath said," concurred Tiberius, masking his physical affliction behind a sober aspect. He had not medicated himself since arriving in Judea and was in need of strong wine to dull the pain in his side, but he denied himself the luxury of relief. He could not afford to exhibit any sign of weakness while serving militarily.

Seated on his steed, Anatole leaned down, grabbed hold of the reins of the centurion's horses and hastily led them away without bidding farewell to either soldier.

Observing his servant's departure, Tiberius sensed something was amiss.

"What troubles thee, my friend?" inquired Quintus Atilius, noticing Tiberius' gaze fixed on the servant as he rode off.

Turning to his friend, Tiberius said stoically, "Anatole doth not intend to return."

"Shall I go after him?" questioned Quintus Atilius.

"No. Let him go."

Astounded by his answer, Quintus Atilius did not know what to think. His friend had lost two valuable servants in the brief span of one hour and appeared strangely accepting of the fact, but underneath the calm outward appearance, he suspected Tiberius Marcius was distressed over their loss. Eyeing their gear laying on the ground, Quintus Atilius pushed through the awkward moment, suggesting, "Let us find a strong Jew to carry these for us."

As if on cue, a robust adult male dressed in traditional Jewish garb passed by the centurions. Recognizing the man was a Jew; Quintus Atilius swiftly withdrew his lethal sword from its sheath. Employing the blunt side of his weapon, he tapped the man on the shoulder, commanding with bridled ferocity, "Carry our bags, Jew!"

Feeling the weight of the sword upon him, the man stopped dead in his tracks, knowing the centurion had the right under Roman law to press him into service. He was obligated to carry the soldier's load one mile and no further. Obeying without protest, the Jew turned around, picked up the heavy bags and followed the centurions down the road.

Encountering others along the way, the soldiers were the recipients of many a sneer as the people of Judea expressed their contempt for all things Roman.

Reaching a mile marker, the centurions came to a halt, expecting the Jew to drop their gear and hurry away because he had fulfilled his duty.

In need of another able bodied man to take his place, Quintus Atilius scanned both sides of the road in search of a suitable candidate, but found no one in sight.

"Know thee not; thou art compelled to go but one mile?" asked Tiberius, looking at the man, surprised to find him still carrying their load.

"I know the law," replied the man mildly, retaining possession of the centurion's bags.

"If thou dost know the law, why then dost thou yet stand before us?" questioned Tiberius, puzzled. "Why hast thou not thrown down our bags and run off?"

"There is a prophet in Judea, who teaches that we ought to love our enemies and do good to those that hate us," answered the man, looking thoughtful.

"Fascinating," said Quintus Atilius dryly, half wondering if the heat had affected the man's ability to reason.

"He also said, "Whosoever shall compel thee to go a mile, go with him two."* I shall do as the prophet taught. I shall go with ye another mile."

Astonished at his willingness to be of service, the centurions glanced at one another, judging the man's attitude most unusual.

"Suit thyself," said Quintus Atilius, satisfied to take advantage of the Jew's offer.

Regarding the man favorably, Tiberius queried, "What is thy name?"

"I am Aaron bar Jethro," responded the man proudly.

"And the prophet's name?"

"Jesus of Nazareth."

"This Jesus must be a man of peace," remarked Tiberius, finding the prophet's words thought provoking.

"Let us be going," interjected Quintus Atilius impatiently, having no interest whatsoever in the people of Judea or their prophets.

Resuming their hot and dusty journey, the three men traveled slightly less than a mile before finally arriving at the Roman outpost. Seeing the garrison straight ahead, Tiberius stopped and addressed Aaron, saying, "Thou may leave us. We hath no more need of thy service."

Aaron wearily shed the soldier's gear from off his shoulders, setting it upon the ground with intentional care which did not go unnoticed by Tiberius.

Withdrawing a denarius, Tiberius offered it to Aaron, who upon seeing the coin, declared, "No payment is necessary, centurion. What I did...I did of my own free will."

"Precisely...that is why I want to reward thee."

"I expect no payment...neither do I wish to take any from thee," stated Aaron, refusing the denarius. "God himself shall reward me. The prophet said, "Love ye your enemies and do good and lend, hoping for nothing again and your reward shall be great."** Centurion, I desire this great reward of which he spoke. Keep thy money that I may attain the greater reward."

"May thou receive it," replied Tiberius, respecting the man's ethics.

"Shalom," bid Aaron, leaving the centurions contemplating the words of Jesus.

Watching his departure, Quintus Atilius quipped, "Strange land... strange people."

Taking their military gear upon themselves, the centurions headed toward the Roman camp. Upon their arrival, they were escorted by a guard to the commanding officer in charge of the outpost.

Ushered inside a nicely appointed room, the centurions saw three soldiers and an officer seated about a table playing a lively game of dice. Upon their entrance, the game ceased as all eyes surveyed the newcomers in their midst.

Quintus Atilius and Tiberius respectfully saluted the high ranking officer in near unison as did the guard, who then took up position at the door.

"Hast thou any papers of introduction?" barked the Tribune, studying the centurions, who stood before him, their aspects and posture displaying soldierly reserve.

"We do, Tribune," answered Tiberius, producing a scroll.

The Tribune motioned to the guard, who heeding the unspoken command, went to Tiberius, took the scroll from him and delivered it to the officer.

Breaking the wax seal, the Tribune unfurled the parchment and read it. Finishing, he rolled it back up, asking grimly, "Which one of ye art Tiberius Marcius?"

"I am he," declared Tiberius.

"Tiberius Marcius, it appears thou hast incurred the wrath of the Prefect. Any man Sejanus sends here…he fully intends to destroy. I assume this comes as no surprise to thee."

"Thou doth assume rightly, Tribune," stated Tiberius unruffled.

"Mind telling me, centurion, what thou did to deserve such a punishment?"

"If I should say…thou would laugh me to scorn."

"Try me."

"I am here because of a woman."

The three soldiers at the table snickered, but stopped abruptly when the Tribune shot them a stern look.

"Go on…" urged the officer, having restored order in the room.

"I interfered in the Prefect's plan for this woman."

"How did thou interfere?" pressed the Tribune, finding the tale rather intriguing.

"Prior to his death, Drusus, son of Caesar desired a certain woman. The Prefect brought her to him. However, she managed to escape the palace and the Prefect went after her again. He tracked her down and was about to escort her back to the palace when I arrived on the scene and took her from his hand. The Prefect did not know Drusus had given me the same orders as he, neither did he appreciate it. Thus, I am here."

"Where is this woman now?"

"She was set at liberty," said Tiberius, careful not to reveal more than was necessary. The less he said about Tamar the better.

Turning his attention to Quintus Atilius, the Tribune questioned, "And what was thy part in all of this?"

"I and Tiberius Marcius are friends, Tribune."

"I see…guilt by association. How unfortunate for thee, centurion."

"With all due respect, Tribune, I do not see it that way," asserted Quintus Atilius boldly.

"Oh…and how dost thou see it, centurion?" queried the Tribune testily, staring hard at Quintus Atilius, trying to ascertain whether the soldier was being insolent or simply stating his perspective.

"If I am to suffer the same fate as Tiberius Marcius, I consider it an honor, Tribune."

"Let us see if thou wilt consider it an honor when I put thee both in charge of the worst century of soldiers on the premises," declared the Tribune gruffly, carrying out the Prefect's written orders to humble the centurions. "These soldiers are grossly undisciplined and dangerously insubordinate. They are the worst of the worst and they art now under thy shared command."

Hearing the officer, the men at the table chuckled, but this time the Tribune did nothing to silence them.

"Tribune, I request permission to speak," voiced Tiberius, maintaining his composure under physical and mental duress.

"Permission to speak…granted."

"Was there any mention of Pontius Pilate in the missive?"

"There was not."

Swallowing hard, Tiberius said no more for the Tribune's answer confirmed what he had suspected all along. Sejanus had sent him and Quintus Atilius on a spurious mission. In all probability, they would never even lay eyes on the governor of Judea.

"Guard, show these men to their quarters," bellowed the Tribune, troubled by Tiberius' question.

Realizing their audience with the Tribune had ended; the centurions saluted the officer, picked up their gear and fell in step behind the guard.

Eyeing the centurions as they exited the room, the Tribune growled, his tone riddled with sarcasm, "Welcome to Judea!"

Appreciating the Tribune's sardonic salutation, laughter erupted from the soldiers at his table, who knew there was absolutely nothing in Judea that made a Roman feel welcomed.

---

*   *Matthew 5:41*
** *Luke 6:35*

XLVI

Tamar had been in Judea two months, dwelling securely in the house of Joseph, who being true to his word treated her as he would one of his daughters. Serah and her younger sister Rachel adored Tamar and did everything possible to make her feel welcome in their home. The sons of Joseph also did their part, but of all Joseph's children, Serah was Tamar's closest ally. From the day they met, Serah had been by Tamar's side, supporting her as she struggled to make the transition from one home to another.

"Come with us, Tamar," coaxed Serah, smiling sweetly. "It will do thee good to go into the city and shop. Abba hath generously bestowed upon us funds with which to purchase something pretty for ourselves."

"Please come…please…" little Rachel pleaded, her long, dark curls framing her pretty face, her enormous black eyes wide with excitement. "I will not go without thee!"

"I fear I would not be very good company," replied Tamar apologetically, feeling downcast. "Perhaps, another time."

"Please come…" begged Rachel, gently tugging at Tamar's hand, refusing to take no for an answer.

"Tamar, it will be good for thee," insisted Serah.

"Please…please," whined Rachel, accustomed to having her way.

Fond of the sisters and grateful for their kindness to her, Tamar reluctantly yielded to their pleas, sighing, "I will go."

Elated, Rachel released her hold on Tamar's hand and flitted about the bedroom like a butterfly, singing a loud, cheerful ditty. Serah and Tamar laughed at the young girl's childish antics, finding her delightfully entertaining.

"What is all the commotion about?" asked a matronly female servant, poking her head inside of Serah's room. "Is everything alright in here?"

Serah and Rachel giggled when they saw the old woman, who had cared for them since their mother's death several years earlier.

"Everything is fine, Miriam," assured Serah, trying to stifle her laughter. "We are celebrating."

"Celebrating…what?"

"We are celebrating because Abba hath given us money that we might buy ourselves something pretty."

"Thou art pretty enough…" said Miriam gruffly, hiding her deep love for the girls behind a stern aspect. "Thou hast no need of frivolous things to enhance thy beauty."

"Nonsense," sassed the little girl, defiantly putting her hands on her hips. "Those frivolous things shall help us catch the eye of some young man."

"Rachel, thou art but nine years of age! Thou art much too young to catch the eye of a man, but not too young to catch a switch on thy backside," scolded Miriam, frowning.

"Do not pay her any mind, Miriam. Rachel is just teasing," voiced Serah, coming to her sister's rescue.

"Hath thy father assigned a guardian to escort thee into Jerusalem?"

"He hath not," answered Serah, knowing what was coming next.

"Then, I shall be thy guardian," volunteered the servant, eyeing Rachel who was her favorite. "I shall inform thy father of my intent. In the meantime, ready thyselves…we shall leave shortly."

The sisters exchanged looks and burst into laughter upon Miriam's departure.

Having familiarized themselves with their surroundings, Tiberius and Quintus Atilius tackled their daunting assignment and began the task of assessing every soldier under their shared command. After careful consideration of each soldier's ability or lack thereof, the centurions divided equally between them, the ill trained the cowardly and the insubordinate. Noting they were four soldiers shy of a full century, they looked into the whereabouts of the missing men. Learning they were incarcerated, the centurions went to the military prison in search of them. Entering the dark, dank holding cell, they discovered the four had been severely beaten and were in dire need of medical attention. They tried to ascertain why the men had been flogged, but their inquiry was met with startling silence. The penalized soldiers would not confess what they had done and neither did any other man volunteer the information. Having nothing to go on, Tiberius granted the four the benefit of the doubt and made arrangements for them to be seen by the military physician, promising him an enticing sum of money if he could get the soldiers back on their feet quickly. Having duly accounted for all one hundred men, the centurions instructed their soldiers in warfare tactics, conducting strenuous military maneuvers daily from dawn to dusk, determined to make of them skilled warriors.

One morning, Tiberius was drilling his men, marching them about to and fro in the hot sun when a guard approached him, bearing a verbal summons from the Tribune. Placing his soldiers under the supervision of Quintus Atilius, he accompanied the guard to the commander's quarters, having no inkling why his superior should want to see him. Stepping inside of the room, Tiberius dutifully saluted the officer, who was seated comfortably behind a large desk, perusing a stack of parchments.

Glancing up from his work, the Tribune dismissed the guard with a cursory wave of his hand, desiring to converse with Tiberius privately.

"At ease, centurion," spoke the Tribune, fixing his narrow, brown eyes upon the soldier before him. "It hath come to my attention that thou hast whipped thy wretched century of men into respectable Roman soldiers...and hath done so in record time. Quite a commendable feat, I must admit."

"I can not take all the credit. I had assistance, Tribune."

"Yes...yes...I know...thy friend, Quintus Atilius," said the officer impatiently, regarding the soldier closely. "I am aware of his part in thy success, but I did not summon thee to discuss the merits of thy friend. Thou art here because I wish to discuss thee, Tiberius Marcius."

Tiberius braced himself, wondering if the Tribune had found out he had not reported for duty as promptly as he should have upon his arrival in Judea.

"Centurion, I hath just finished re-reading the letter Sejanus sent along with thee. Frankly, it troubles me that a soldier of thy fine caliber hath been assigned to this remote outpost. A man of thy considerable ability deserves better. Sejanus gave no explanation as to why thou wert sent here...and thine own account doth not make the matter any clearer. Centurion, I find it difficult to believe a woman is the sole cause of thy fall from grace. Is there something more thou would care to reveal?"

"No, Tribune."

"Then answer me this, centurion. Was the woman desired by Caesar's son...also desired by Sejanus?"

Meeting his superior's penetrating gaze, Tiberius responded, "I know not if he desired her."

"Did thou desire her," queried the Tribune, still staring intently at Tiberius.

"Tribune, surely, thou did not call me away from my duties to inquire about a woman," retorted Tiberius stiffly, disliking the line of questioning.

Making no headway with his interrogation for the centurion was predictably tight lipped, the Tribune switched subjects, saying, "Tiberius Marcius, I summoned thee because Rome shall soon hath need of thy service. A week from now there shall be a large influx of Jews into Jerusalem to celebrate a religious observance they call Passover. Every year at this time there is talk of a Messiah and trouble flairs up. Bloodshed during Passover is so commonplace that troop reinforcement is automatically carried out in anticipation of it."

"Messiah?" repeated Tiberius, unfamiliar with the term.

"The Jews believe a savior…a Messiah…will come and destroy their enemies…that would be us," sneered the Tribune. "Violence erupts too easily in this part of the world and we must be ever vigilant if we are to retain control of this turbulent territory. Thou may hath heard some of our soldiers were murdered last week. This latest uprising was led by a man called Barabbas, who we now hath in custody, but lest we grow complacent, there is always another ready to take his place. The Jews greatly resent Roman occupation and challenge the government whenever possible. Pontius Pilate hath tried for years to subdue this region, but to no avail. He is, in my opinion, partly to blame for the ongoing problem. He seems to pleasure in provoking the people, especially their esteemed religious leaders. He hath erected imperial images about the city and robbed the temple treasury of funds in order to build the aqueduct. He hast done nothing to win the hearts and minds of those he rules. It is his prerogative as governor to do as he sees fit…but I often wonder if he hath considered the consequences of his actions."

"Tribune, why art thou telling me all this…seeing I serve here in Capernaum."

"Centurion, I am sending thee into Jerusalem, in the midst of mayhem and treachery, but lest thou think, I am doing thee a disservice, think again. Thou shalt stand before Pontius Pilate and serve him. Thy assignment shall hath its challenges, but it is not without honor."

"Tribune, it was my understanding that no mention of the governor was made in Sejanus' letter."

"None was, centurion. What I do for thee, I do because thou hast shown mercy unto my nephew. One good turn deserves another."

"Tribune, forgive my ignorance...but I know not thy nephew."

"Thou released him from prison," stated the Tribune solemnly. "The one called Marcus is my nephew. He hath not measured up as a soldier. I fear he doth not hath the stomach for it. He hath tried everything short of murder to escape military duty."

"I know not what to say, Tribune," voiced Tiberius, stunned by the revelation.

"There is no need for thee to say anything, centurion. Thy deed speaks for itself. Thou hast done for him what I would not do. I did not intercede on his behalf for reasons that I shall not state. Suffice it to say, I am indebted to thee."

Tiberius stood amazed at his good fortune. Never did he imagine any degree of favor would come his way in Judea.

"Tiberius Marcius, it is within my power to transfer thee and thy friend back to Rome or wherever thou dost wish to go...and I shall...if thou wilt do my bidding and perform it to my complete satisfaction. Art thou interested in hearing my proposal?"

"I am interested, Tribune."

"My proposal is this...make a decent soldier of my spoiled nephew and I shall transfer thee and thy friend out of Judea. Be warned, Tiberius Marcius, I expect a great deal of thee. Training my nephew shall not be an easy undertaking. Do not be fooled by him. He is capable of more than he lets on. My sister mollycoddled the boy to the point of ruination. She did nothing to make a man of him. That is thy task. Art thou willing to take him on?"

"I am willing, Tribune," replied Tiberius, still reeling from his good fortune.

"I thought thou would accept my proposal...so I took the liberty of penning this," said the Tribune, handing Tiberius a sealed parchment. "Take it and Marcus with thee and report to Pilate."

"And Quintus Atilius...shall he go also?"

"Quintus Atilius shall remain at his post. There is a company of soldiers stationed at the Praetorium. No more are needed. I send thee and my nephew only. Attach thyselves to the company. Thy friend and thee shall fair as well or as poorly as my nephew doth under thy instruction. Is that clear, centurion?"

"Perfectly clear, Tribune."

"Do not fail me, Tiberius Marcius. My neck is on the line. If Sejanus learns of this, we shall both be dead men," warned the Tribune.

"I shall not fail thee, Tribune."

"Go thy way, centurion, and see that thy words come to pass."

Saluting the Tribune, Tiberius left his presence and promptly sought out Quintus Atilius, apprising him of the development.

Grinning ear to ear, Quintus Atilius slapped his friend on the back after hearing the news and declared enthusiastically, "The gods are with thee, Tiberius Marcius! Even thy ill fortune turns to good! Truly, thou art favored!"

"We are favored," corrected Tiberius. "We shall soon return to Rome for I am confident Marcus shall fare well under my instruction."

"As am I, my friend. I ask only that thou train him quickly. I am eager to leave this miserable land. I miss Rome and a few other things which I wilt not mention," winked Quintus Atilius in a jovial mood.

Tiberius nodded, knowing what things he was referring to.

"To Rome, to Marcus and thy success," said Quintus Atilius, extending his covenant hand to his blood brother.

Grasping the hand of Quintus Atilius, Tiberius responded, "To Rome, to Marcus and our success."

And with that, the centurions parted ways; both encouraged there were better times ahead.

Later that afternoon, Tiberius and Marcus were passing through the city on the way to the Praetorium when they came upon a very large assembly of people gathered about the Temple.

"What did the teacher say?" asked one man of another within the hearing of Tiberius and his charge.

"I heard the teacher say we ought to feed the hungry, give drink to the thirsty, clothe the naked, care for the sick and visit those in prisons," the other man replied, repeating with remarkable accuracy what he had heard. "He said whatever thou dost for the least of these, thou hast done for me."*

"Dost thou think he is the Messiah?"

"It is said he hath raised the dead and healed the sick. I myself hath not witnessed these things, but I hath heard it told among the people. Some doth call him…the Son of David."

"What is the name of this teacher of whom ye speak?" asked Marcus, intruding in the conversation.

"Jesus of Galilee," answered the first man, nervously.

"I hath witnessed this same Jesus restore sight to a blind man," stated Marcus, jolting Tiberius and the two men with his declaration. Sensing they did not believe him, Marcus vehemently asserted, "I tell the truth! Ye may believe my report or not. It is of no importance to me. I know what I saw!"

Wary of soldiers, the two men faded into the mass of people, fearing to speak any further with the young cadet.

"I suppose thou doth think I am crazy," said Marcus, turning to Tiberius, who was studying him with quiet interest.

"Cadet, I hath no reason to believe thee…or to doubt thee. I know not what manner of man thou art. Perhaps, if I knew why thou wert disciplined and thrown into prison…I could better discern the truth of thy words," responded Tiberius diplomatically, not wanting to alienate Marcus.

The centurion had taken the long route to the Praetorium on purpose in order to get acquainted with the young soldier and gain valuable insight into his character. He had heard the Tribune's less than glowing assessment of his nephew, but Tiberius preferred to make his own judgment. And to do that, he had to keep the lines of communication open.

"Why did thou shorten my incarceration? Was it by my uncle's command?"

"What I did, I did of my own free will. The Tribune issued no command concerning thy welfare…one way or the other. Neither did I know of thy kinship…until today."

"Mean to tell me…my own flesh and blood did absolutely nothing to expedite my release from prison!"

"Nothing."

"I certainly know he did nothing to save me from the whip! I hath the scars on my back to prove it," uttered Marcus bitterly, remembering the terrible pain and humiliation of his flogging. "Thou hast done more on my behalf than my uncle! I despise him!"

"He is not as uncaring as he doth appear," said Tiberius, laying a reassuring hand on the cadet's shoulder.

"He is worse," countered Marcus angrily.

"Not so, soldier. He believes in thee. He hath asked me to come along side of thee and train thee. If he did not care about thee…he would hath left thee to thy own devices. He would hath disavowed he knew thee."

Moved by the centurion's words, Marcus choked back his emotion, saying, "I find it hard to believe that he cares a whit about me."

"A man must stand alone sometime in his life, soldier. Thy uncle understood it was thy appointed time."

Pondering the centurion's sobering wisdom, Marcus fell silent as he and Tiberius resumed their trek.

"Tamar…Tamar! Wait, Tamar," shouted Anatole, chasing after the maid, frantically pushing his way through the throng of people. "Tamar!"

Hearing her name, Tamar turned around and saw Anatole coming toward her, his beggarly appearance so heart-rending that she felt as if she could not breathe and laid her hands against her chest, overcome with great emotion.

"Tamar…please help me," pleaded Anatole, falling to his knees in front of her as Miriam and the girls looked on in sheer horror.

"Anatole…what evil hath befallen thee," cried Tamar, beholding the servant, who was dirty from head to foot, his clothes tattered and his body emaciated. "Where is thy lord? Surely, if it is not well with thee…then it is not well with him. Speak quickly, Anatole…lest I faint."

"I ran away from the master. Tamar…hath mercy upon me. Give me something to eat. I am hungry and do thirst terribly," said he, lowering his head in shame. "Hath mercy, Tamar! I ask for mercy!"

Seeing his plight, silent tears streamed down Tamar's cheeks. Wanting to relieve his suffering, she opened her small purse and withdrew the money given her by Serah's father. Kneeling down, she took Anatole's soiled hand and laid two denarii therein, promising him, "When this is gone, come to the house of Joseph and I shall give thee more. All that I hath is yours. Thou wilt not go hungry as long as there is breath in my body."

Touched by her kindness, Anatole began to cry and so did little Rachel, who being frightened of the beggar, buried her face in the folds of Miriam's dress.

Sheltering the sobbing child within her protective arms, Miriam was about to usher the girls away from the beggar when Serah opened her purse, took out her money and gave her coins to Anatole, saying kindly, "There is an abundance of food in my father's house. Thou need not go hungry. Come to the house of Joseph and we shall give thee bread and wine."

"Serah!" gasped Miriam mortified, scarcely believing her ears. "I do not think…"

"Hush, Miriam. I hath given my word," said Serah. "He shall be fed from my father's table."

"Return to thy master…he wilt show thee mercy," urged Tamar, rising to her feet and helping Anatole to his.

"May thy God bless thee…" uttered Anatole humbly. Turning away from the women, he wiped his eyes and ambled into the sea of people.

Putting her arm about Tamar's waist, Serah consoled her, saying, "Thou hast done what thou could for him. Thou hast heard and obeyed the words of Yeshua. It is well with thee."

"And with thee also, dear Serah," said Tamar affectionately, losing sight of Anatole in the crowd.

"Instead of following the teachings of this Yeshua…thou ought to follow the teaching of thy father. He taught thee not to speak to strangers…nor to touch them," Miriam rebuked sharply, staring at the girls with great displeasure.

"Miriam, it is not right to turn away from those in need," countered Serah, emboldened to speak the truth. "Father also taught us to consider the poor."

"I gave nothing to the beggar," wailed Rachel, crying afresh, under conviction for her selfishness.

Hearing little Rachel, Serah left Tamar's side to comfort her sister. Stroking the child's hair, she said tenderly, "There, there, little one. Fret not. There art many poor whom thou may bless."

"Come, let us go home," prompted Miriam, seizing control of the situation. Without protest, all the girls meekly followed after their guardian, each having been affected by the teachings of Jesus and the subsequent appearance of the beggar, but none more than Tamar.

Trailing behind them, mulling over what it all meant, Tamar mindlessly looked about and to her amazement; a familiar countenance distinguished itself from among the crowd. Blinking her dark eyes in disbelief, her heart leapt for joy. It was him and he was looking straight at her.

"Dost thou know her?" queried Marcus, noticing the centurion's attention was keenly fixed on a lovely damsel.

"I do not," lied Tiberius, yearning for the maid who had captured his heart.

"Shall I fetch her for thee?" offered the cadet.

"No. Leave her be."

Tamar took a step in Tiberius' direction on the verge of running to him, when suddenly from behind her came the familiar voice of Caleb, announcing as he laid hold of her, "I hath been searching for thee, my pretty flower."

Tamar froze as Caleb swung her about, severing the visual contact between her and the centurion. Her heart sank in despair.

"Ah, she hath a husband," said Marcus, watchfully.

Tiberius turned away, showing no outward sign of emotion, his feelings for the maid pent deep within his heart. "Come…" he commanded stoically. "Pilate awaits our arrival."

---

* *Matthew 25:37-40*

XLVII

"Father…Father…Yeshua hath been arrested," declared Joram breathlessly, bolting through the front door of the family residence, his older brother Caleb close behind him.

"Arrested? Joram, art thou certain?" asked Joseph in disbelief, ushering his sons into the main room of their home, anxious to hear what they had to say.

"We went into the city to buy what was needed for the Passover preparation. Everywhere, people were talking about Yeshua," explained Joram, speaking so fast, he hardly stopped to draw a breath. "We were told the temple guards arrested him last night. Yeshua was tried by the council of religious leaders and condemned to death!"

"Why? What hast he done?" Joseph questioned, visibly distressed. "He taught daily in the temple courts…if the chief priests wanted to arrest him, they could hath done so on any day. Why…at night? Why…now? Why…death?"

"The elders and chief priests dared not move against Yeshua by day for fear of the people," answered Caleb soberly. "His following was growing and the religious leaders felt threatened by him. It is reported they paid one of his disciples to betray him."

"He is being brought before Pilate as we speak," continued Joram. "I fear for his life!"

"Ye must do something to help Yeshua," entreated Serah, making her presence in the room known.

Turning to look at Serah, Joseph voiced sadly, "Daughter, what would thee hath us do? We are but three against so many."

"Abba, thou dost know some of the religious leaders…thou hast a measure of influence…" cried Serah, giving way to tears. "Please…Abba…try…"

Softened by his daughter's emotional plea, Joseph gave in, saying, "My child, I can not promise it will do any good…but I will go and speak to the elders."

Grateful, Serah rushed forward and threw her arms lovingly about her father.

"I shall go with thee," announced Caleb, looking on as his father affectionately kissed Serah upon her forehead.

"And I shall go too," said Joram, grim faced.

"May I go, Abba?" requested Serah, gazing up at her father with tears in her eyes.

"No, my daughter. There will almost certainly be trouble. Thy brothers and I shall go. We shall do what we can. Now, let us be on our way…while there is yet time to save Yeshua," said Joseph, extracting himself from Serah's embrace.

"What can I do, Abba? I must do something."

"Pray, my daughter. Pray this innocent man is not put to death by the authorities," instructed Joseph, hurrying out of the house with Caleb and Joram.

Tiberius and his charge had been assigned to guard the governor's palace and had served in that capacity for a week, when they found themselves in the midst of a potential riot. At their posts, dutifully safeguarding the premises, they were astonished when a large multitude of people assembled early one morning in front of the judgment hall, demanding to see Pontius Pilate.

Stepping outside of the palace, his body fitly draped in Roman attire, Pilate beheld Jesus, who was in the custody of the temple guards. "What charges bring ye against this man?" he asked.

"If he were not a malefactor, we would not hath delivered him unto thee."

Loathing the chief priests and their religious nonsense, Pilate thundered, "Take ye him and judge him according to your law."

"It is not lawful for us to put any man to death," answered a chief priest, glancing side to side, signaling for some assistance from the crowd.

"He is a criminal," hollered one man, followed by other voices.

"He opposes paying taxes to Caesar!" yelled the individuals that had been coached what to say by the religious leaders, who hated Jesus.

"He incites riots! He is no friend of Caesar!"

"He claims to be the Christ…a king!" shouted others. "We hath no king, but Caesar!"

Hearing the latter charge, Pilate went back inside of his palace and summoned Jesus, who was promptly brought before the governor, bound hand and foot. He had clearly been abused by the temple guards.

Considering the man who stood before him, Pilate inquired, "Art thou the king of the Jews?"

Jesus answered him, "Sayest thou this thing of thyself or did others tell it thee of me?"

"Am I a Jew?" Pilate sneered. "Thine own nation and the chief priests hath delivered thee unto me. What hast thou done?"

"My kingdom is not of this world."

"Thou art a king then!"

"For this cause I was born and for this cause I came into the world, to testify of the truth. Everyone that is of the truth heareth my voice."

"What is truth?" Pilate asked, believing truth was a relative matter. "Hast thou heard how many things of which they accuse thee? Wilt thou not answer their accusations?"

Jesus answered not a word.

Marveling that Jesus made no attempt to defend himself from the charges levied against him, Pilate returned to the chief priests, the rulers and the people and said, "I hath examined him and hath found no fault in him. Neither did Herod find fault in him. He hast done nothing deserving of death. But it is thy custom that I release one prisoner at Passover. Shall I release unto ye…the king of the Jews?"

The crowd shouted in unison, "Give us Barabbas!"

Sensing the chief priests had delivered Jesus out of envy, Pilate sought to release him and appealed to the crowd, asking, "What shall I do then, with the one ye call the king of the Jews?"

"Crucify him! Crucify him!"

"Why? What evil hath he done?" questioned Pilate, noticing the crowd was becoming increasingly hostile. "I hath found no cause for death in him. I will, therefore, chastise him and let him go."

"Crucify him! Caesar is our king!"

"Release Barabbas!"

"Crucify Jesus!"

Concerned a riot was about to erupt, Pilate gave into public demand. Calling for a basin of water and a towel, he washed his hands in front of the multitude, declaring loudly that all might hear his words, "I am innocent of the blood of this righteous man. See ye to it."

"Let his blood be on us and on our children!" cried the people.

Yielding to the will of the people, Pilate ordered Barabbas released from prison and Jesus flogged and crucified.

Stunned by the pronouncement, Tiberius had never witnessed anything like this in Rome. An innocent man was being condemned to death while a known murderer was given amnesty. How could such a travesty of justice take place?

Staring at the centurion, Pilate barked, "Why stand thee there? Take Jesus away!"

Coming to himself, Tiberius stepped forth and did as he was ordered; leading Jesus to the common hall of the Praetorium, where a segment of callous, blood thirsty soldiers ruthlessly administered the floggings.

Handling the prisoner with brute force, several soldiers stripped Jesus to the waist, laying bare his back and tied his hands tightly to a pillar.

Two particularly menacing looking fellows stepped forward, who had been chosen to administer the strokes, each in possession of a three pronged whip called a flagrum. The thongs of the flagrum held tiny lead balls and sharp bits of sheep bone designed to rip the flesh and cause so much blood loss that its victim would suffer bodily shock and teeter on the brink of death. Smiling callously, the soldiers made quite a spectacle of themselves, getting a rise of laughter from those who were standing about, waiting expectantly for the violence to begin.

Tiberius withdrew a little ways from the fray, bewildered by the unfolding events.

Taking turns, the two soldiers hurled their flagrums against the back of Jesus, counting out the lashes, while the onlookers cheered their violent performance. With each stroke, the flesh of Jesus was savagely ripped and torn, his sacred blood spattering on the marble floor and on his Roman tormentors. Noticing their victim did not plead for mercy like the others they had whipped, neither did he curse them, the two soldiers held a contest to see who could bring Jesus to the point of begging for mercy. Competing, each man tried to outdo the other, laying brutal stroke after brutal stroke upon Jesus, but to their great astonishment, he endured the stripes laid upon him.

"Thirty-eight," announced the first soldier, lashing Jesus as hard as he physically could, fatigued from the barbaric exercise.

"Thirty-nine," counted the second soldier, barely having the strength in his own body to administer the blow.

"That will do," bellowed the officer in charge, putting an end to the gory sport. "We do not want him to die before we can crucify him."

Finished with the flogging, the two exhausted soldiers stepped aside while others untied Jesus from the whipping post and dragged his near lifeless body off to a corner where the entire company of soldiers gathered about him. Indifferent to his great physical suffering, they laid upon Jesus a scarlet robe and placed a circlet of spiky thorns upon his head, cruelly pressing it into his flesh. Spitting upon Jesus, they mocked him, saying, "Hail, King of the Jews!"

"A king needs a scepter," hissed one soldier, shoving a reed into Jesus' right hand. Bowing his knee before the bloodied king, the Roman soldier ridiculed, "Hail, King of the Jews!"

Peels of hysterical laughter arose from the hardened soldiers.

Another soldier came forth from the company, grabbed the reed from the king's hand and struck him on the head with it over and over again, evoking more laughter from his fellow comrades.

When the soldiers finally grew tired of mocking his kingship, they escorted Jesus back to Pilate, who presented the bloodied king, robed in scarlet, to the multitude gathered, saying, "Behold the man!"

The governor hoped the crowd would be appeased when they laid eyes upon the battered and bloodied Jesus. But it was not so.

"Crucify him! Crucify him!" screamed the people when they saw Jesus.

"Take ye him and crucify him! I find no fault in him!" declared Pilate perplexed, seeing the people were not satisfied merely to have Jesus scourged. They demanded his death.

"We hath a law and by our law he ought to die, because he hath made himself the Son of God!" said a religious ruler whose self righteousness was unrivaled among his peers.

Hearing that, Pilate became afraid. He had suspected there was something unearthly about Jesus; something about the man had defied explanation. Returning to the judgment hall, Pilate asked Jesus, "From where art thou from?"

Jesus gave no reply.

"Speakest thou not unto me? Knowest thou not that I hath the power to crucify thee and I hath the power to release thee?"

Jesus answered, "Thou could hath no power at all against me, except it were given unto thee from above; therefore; he that delivered me unto thee hath the greater sin."

Pilate wanted to release Jesus for he knew he was innocent of the charges brought against him, but instead, he harkened to the people, who cried out, "If thou let this man go, thou art no friend of Caesar!"

Fearing the religious leaders would report him to Caesar and thereby end his political career; Pilate brought Jesus forth and sat down in the judgment seat, making one last appeal on behalf of Jesus. "Shall I crucify your King?"

"We hath no king but Caesar," answered the chief priests and religious leaders.

"Do as they hath required," Pilate commanded reluctantly. "Crucify their king."

Tiberius, along with five of the governor's soldiers stepped forward and led Jesus away to be crucified.

Preparing Him for crucifixion, the soldiers stripped Him of the scarlet robe and dressed Him in his own clothing. Afterwards, they tied the heavy, cumbersome, wood crossbar to the lacerated shoulders of Jesus. Wishing to humiliate and make a public example of Him, they paraded Jesus through the streets, escorting him to the sight of execution, which was located outside the city walls of Jerusalem. However, Jesus was too weak from scourging to carry his cross any measurable distance and the soldiers found it necessary to compel a bystander to assist Him.

"Carry his cross," demanded a Roman soldier, singling out from the crowd a man called Simon of Cyrene, who was visiting Jerusalem for the Passover.

Facing the fierce Roman soldier, Simon knew he had no choice but to do as he was told. Approaching the weak and bleeding figure of Jesus, he looked upon the condemned man and was startled by the compassion that emanated from his eyes. Lifting the weighty crossbar off of Jesus' shoulders, Simon took it upon himself, following in the footsteps of the suffering king.

Two other men, who had been condemned to death as they were guilty of their crimes, bore their own crossbars.

Jesus stumbled and fell to the pavement.

"Get up…we do not hath all day," yelled a soldier, anxious to get the whole nasty business over with.

A sympathetic bystander rushed to help Jesus to his feet.

"Get back," shouted the same soldier, snapping his whip in the direction of the offender.

A vast multitude followed the condemned men along the execution route, but most had come out to mourn Jesus. Wailing with great sorrow, women reached out to Jesus as he passed, lamenting the injustice done to Him, while others in the crowd looked on with confusion and some with contempt. Still, others looked upon Jesus with love.

"Father, we are too late," said Joram as Jesus passed before him.

"Son, I know not what to say," said Joseph in despair, his gaze fixed on the one he had believed was the Messiah.

"If he were the Messiah…this would not be happening," stated Caleb, reading his father's thoughts.

Jesus fell again.

A woman rushed forward to wipe the face of Jesus, kneeling near Him and tenderly laying a cloth upon his bloodied visage.

"Get away from Him," snarled a soldier, coming toward the young woman. Reaching her, he stopped dead in his tracks, seeing she was oddly unafraid of him. Rising to her feet of her own accord, the woman retreated, her eyes never leaving Jesus.

On foot, assisting with crowd control, Marcus was in a state of shock that the teacher, whom he had seen restore sight to the blind was to be crucified. Glancing up at the centurion, whose aspect was set like flint, he desperately wanted to speak to him, but Tiberius did not look his way.

Seated on a horse, overseeing the grim procession, Tiberius was lost in his own cogitations, deeply troubled by all he had seen and heard. Reading the sign carried by a soldier proclaiming the crime of Jesus, the centurion pondered its inscription. Pilate had not written upon it any charge worthy of death. So why was this man sentenced to die?

Jesus fell a third time.

Simon of Cyrene came forward, laid down the cumbersome crossbar and gingerly assisted Jesus to his feet.

"I said…keep moving," bellowed a soldier, who then began cursing.

Reaching the summit of Golgotha, the place of crucifixion, four soldiers stripped Jesus of his garments, adding nakedness to the countless indignities He suffered. Knocking Him to the ground, they stretched out his arms over the crossbar and callously drove long, iron nails between the bones of his wrists, affixing Jesus to the crossbar. The four soldiers then combined their physical strength and hoisted up the crossbar, fixing it onto the upright sturdy wooden post that had been permanently positioned to serve as the perpendicular beam of the cross. Finishing their gruesome task, they drove nails into the ankles of the condemned king. Lastly, the sign was placed above the head of Jesus, written in Greek, Latin and Aramaic, stating, "Jesus of Nazareth, The King of the Jews."

Jesus was crucified between the two criminals, one on each side of Him.

Standing nearby, keeping watch, the centurion surveyed the three crosses, knowing the condemned men were in excruciating pain, especially the one called Jesus, who had refused the wine mixed with gall to deaden his pain. As Tiberius stood there, Marcus came to him and asked, "Why was there no justice for this innocent man?"

Sighing heavily, the centurion regarded the young cadet, understanding his confusion. "Marcus, I know not why these things hath happened to this man, neither do I know why we hath witnessed them."

Suddenly, their attention was drawn to Jesus, who said, "Father, forgive them, for they know not what they do."

"He forgives us for what we hath done..." said Marcus, his gaze falling on the four soldiers casting lots for the garments of Jesus. "How can he forgive us for killing him?"

"Marcus, He is not like other men. I watched Him as the soldiers flogged Him unmercifully...mocked and spat upon Him, smote Him...stripped and crucified Him, yet...through it all...He endured the grave injustice done unto Him with a strength and a dignity that is beyond human comprehension," stated Tiberius solemnly, looking at Jesus upon the cross.

Contemplating the centurion's assessment of Jesus, the cadet fell silent.

"Give it to me," demanded one of the four soldiers, grabbing the coat of Jesus. "It is mine! I won it fair and square!"

"Thou won it...but whether it was fair...I hath my doubts," growled another soldier angrily as he was a sore loser.

Amused, the other two soldiers swallowed a little more cheap wine and laughed at the loser.

A small crowd remained at the cross of Jesus. Some wept for Him and some derided Him. Among the latter, was one of the malefactors, crucified along with Jesus.

"If thou be the Christ, save thyself and us," said the criminal.

The other malefactor rebuked him, saying, "Dost thou not fear God? We hath received the due reward of our deeds, but this man hath done nothing amiss." Turning to Jesus, he then said, "Lord, remember me when thou comest into thy kingdom."

And Jesus said unto him, "Verily, I say unto thee, today, shalt thou be with me in paradise."

"He saved others, himself he cannot save," scoffed the chief priests, talking among themselves. "Let Christ, the King of Israel descend now from the cross that we may see and believe."

Observing Jesus, the centurion heard him address his grieving mother and the disciple that stood beside her, tenderly supporting her in his arms. Standing with them, were two women, weeping at the foot of the cross.

Suddenly, the sky grew black and darkness descended over the land from noon to three.

One of the four soldiers exclaimed, "Strange weather for this time of the year."

"For any time of the year…" said another, looking up at the ominous sky, feeling uneasy.

Surrounded by the eerie darkness, Tiberius and Marcus passed the time in quiet, sporadic conversation, most of which pertained to Jesus.

At three in the afternoon, Jesus cried out, "My God, my God, why hast thou forsaken me?"

"Behold, He calls for Elijah," said an onlooker.

Another man ran and filled a sponge full of vinegar and put it on a reed, offering it to Jesus.

"Leave Him be," rebuked the others. "Let us see whether Elijah will come."

Then Jesus cried with a loud voice, "It is finished," and gave up his spirit.

At that very moment, an earthquake occurred, splitting rocks in two and opening the tombs of the dead. Terrified, all those who stood near the cross of Jesus looked upon the Righteous One, whom they had crucified.

Moved by all he had witnessed, Tiberius declared as he beheld the crucified king, "Truly, this man was the Son of God!"

The account of Jesus' crucifixion was taken from the King James Version and the New International Version of the Holy Bible, according to the Gospels of Matthew, Mark, Luke and John.

XLVIII

Two days had passed since the crucifixion of Yeshua, the long awaited Messiah, spoken of by the prophets. Many, including Joseph's sons, thought the Messiah would be a military figure, who would free them from their Roman oppressors, while others, like Joseph, looked for a holy priest. In either case, the men's hopes were shattered with the death of Jesus, who though he had not fit Joseph or his son's expectations, yet, they had believed he was the one. Never once did it enter into their minds that the Messiah would come into the world and be rejected by those he came to save.

Lingering over their evening meal, Joseph and his sons remained at the table, conversing with one another.

"Did ye notice the centurion was among those who crucified Yeshua," Caleb asked, his gaze wandering from Joram to his father.

Preferring to forget the centurion was one of Yeshua's executioners, Joseph threw Caleb a sharp look. He did not wish to revisit the unpleasant subject which had marred their Passover.

Joshua, however, was very interested in hearing what Caleb had to say. It was the first he had heard of the matter for he had not been with his father and brothers on that terrible day.

"I saw him…" Joram responded dryly, leaning back in his chair, his stomach full.

"Evidently, the centurion is not the honorable man we took him to be," continued Caleb, not in the least bit dissuaded by his father's reprimanding glance. "He is Roman through and through. Like the rest of his barbaric ilk, he murders our people without regard…without mercy. We should hath laid hold of the centurion and done to him…what the Romans do to us."

"And what would that hath accomplished," Joseph questioned, suddenly feeling very old.

"There would hath been one less Roman dog in Judea," growled Caleb, pushing away from the table.

"If we had harmed the centurion…the Roman authorities would hath retaliated by killing us," remarked Joshua, though younger than his brothers, he understood the tense state of affairs between the Romans and the Jews. "I for one…prefer to live and let live."

"Well said, Joshua," commended his father, appreciating the voice of reason.

"Caleb, hast thou forgotten, the centurion brought thee Tamar, thy future wife," said Joram, staring intently at his older brother.

"He brought me nothing…for she shows no interest in me," said Caleb bitterly, his aspect sullen. "She doth pine for the centurion."

"Be patient, my son. Give her time."

Hearing the approach of his sisters, who were laughing amongst themselves, Caleb fixed his eye on the entrance of the room in expectation of their entry.

Playing with Rachel, Tamar and Serah chased the little girl into the dining area, but the game of pursuit ended abruptly upon seeing the men's grim faces.

"What is the matter, Abba?" inquired Serah, feeling little Rachel's hand slip into hers.

"Nothing is the matter, my child."

"Why keep it from her?" voiced Caleb gruffly.

"Keep what?" asked Serah, looking at her father.

"The centurion was among those who crucified Yeshua!" Caleb declared, eyeing Tamar coldly, measuring her reaction.

Mortified by what she heard, the color drained from Tamar's face.

Realizing this was not a conversation for young ears, Serah instructed her little sister to go to Miriam, who was standing nearby, eavesdropping.

Taking her youngest charge in hand, Miriam was forced to leave the room, much to her chagrin for she wanted to hear the outcome of what was proving to be a most interesting discussion.

"Speak thou of Tiberius Marcius?" Tamar asked, her voice shaky, unable to believe the evil report.

"I do," Caleb replied curtly.

"Caleb, why art thou speaking against the centurion?" Serah questioned, sensing her brother had a motive for doing so in front of Tamar.

"He speaks the truth, Serah," voiced Joram, coming to the defense of Caleb. "Why should we hide what the centurion hath done?"

"Enough said," intervened Joseph, disliking family squabbles. "We are all upset. There is no need to bicker among ourselves; such talk serves no good purpose."

Feeling physically ill, Tamar walked out of the dining room. The revelation was too much for her to bear.

"Thou hast intentionally hurt her," exclaimed Serah, glaring at Caleb. "Whether this thing is true or not, there was no need to speak of it in her presence!"

Resenting his sister's reprimand, Caleb sprang to his feet and went after Tamar with a vengeance.

Worried, Serah turned to follow him, but her father's words stopped her.

"Daughter, thou wilt stay here with us! Let us mind our own business and leave them to work out theirs!"

Overtaking Tamar in the hallway, Caleb grabbed her by the arm and forcibly walked her into her room, slamming the door behind them. Alone with Tamar, Caleb unleashed his verbal fury.

"Woman, thy loyalty to the centurion hath clouded thy judgment! It is time thou did face the truth! Tiberius Marcius is a murderer of Jews! An oppressor of our people! Consider how he dealt with thee…he pawned thee off on my family as if thou wert nothing more than livestock to be bought and sold! If he truly cared for thee…he would hath treated thee with dignity! Instead, he treated thee like a dumb animal!"

Feeling as if a knife had been plunged into her heart, Tamar tried to maintain her composure as Caleb's words assaulted her ears. Yanking her arm from his vise, she attempted to get away from him, but he seized her, taking custody of her once again.

"The man is a barbarian…a cold blooded murderer," spewed Caleb angrily, holding Tamar by both arms, forcing her to acknowledge him. "Woman, why dost thou desire him over me? Dost thou think so little of thyself?"

"Unhand me, Caleb," implored Tamar, becoming frightened as she stared into his angry eyes.

"I will not let thee go…till thou dost answer me! Why dost thou desire him over me?"

"Caleb, thou dost not know the man! Thou ought not pass judgment upon him!"

"He murdered Yeshua!"

"I do not believe he would do such an evil deed," cried Tamar, crumbling emotionally. "Thou must be mistaken…"

"Tamar, I saw him with my own eyes," insisted Caleb, perturbed she had begun to weep. "He was one of them."

"No…it is not true!"

"I tell thee the truth! Why wilt thou not believe me?"
"Thou dost not know him…"
"He is a soldier…they murder the innocent."
"He is not like the others…"

Unable to convince her of the centurion's guilt, Caleb stormed out of the room, his mind made up concerning her.

Upon his departure, Tamar threw herself on the couch and wept bitterly.

Returning to his family, who were still seated at the table, Caleb announced stoically, "I could not persuade Tamar of the truth. Her heart belongs to the centurion. I shall never find favor in her eyes…or she in mine. I shall no longer pursue her for my wife. I defer to thee, Joram, but I must warn thee…thou wilt hath no more success in winning her affection than I. Her heart belongs to the centurion…of that, I am quite certain." And having spoken, Caleb left the room, handing his brother the opportunity Joram had secretly longed for.

Digesting Caleb's words, Joseph began to question whether it had been wise to take in the young girl after all. He had not expected things to turn out like this.

The gravity of Caleb's declaration weighing upon her, Serah exited the room in search of Tamar, mulling over in her heart what her brother had said. Coming to the bedroom she shared with Tamar, she tapped lightly on the door and then entered, finding Tamar sprawled upon the couch weeping. Drawing near, Serah knelt down beside the couch and stroked Tamar's long, dark brown hair, voicing tenderly, "Do not cry, Tamar. My brothers did not mean to upset thee."

Lifting her head, her eyes swollen and her face wet with tears, Tamar sobbed, "Serah, is it true…what they said of my lord?"

"Tamar…the truth is very painful…for all of us."

"Then, it is true?"

"My brothers do not lie," said Serah softly, her heart aching.

"Why would my lord do such an evil thing to the Messiah?"

"Is not the centurion a man under authority?"

Deriving no consolation from Serah's words, Tamar buried her head in the couch and cried afresh.

"Tamar, I must ask thee some hard questions. I pray thou wilt answer them honestly."

"What are they?" sniffled Tamar, finding it difficult to stem the flow of her tears.

"Can thou forgive the centurion for murdering Yeshua?"

"Would not Yeshua hath done so? Did he not teach us to love our enemies?"

"Dost thou love the centurion?"

"I do," affirmed Tamar tearfully, raising her head and meeting Serah's gaze.

"Tamar, I had hoped thou would marry one of my brothers," confessed Serah sadly, her eyes clouding with tears. "I know now, thou dost belong with the centurion and not with us. Thou must return to him."

"Serah…how can I return unto him? I know not where he is…or if he would even permit me to return."

"We must pray and ask Jehovah to make a way of return," Serah said, brushing the tears from her cheeks. "If thou art meant to be reunited…The Lord shall make a way for thee."

"Oh, Serah…thou hast given me cause for hope," cried Tamar as she sat up on the couch. "Thou art dear unto me…like a sister."

Rising to her feet, Serah joined Tamar on the couch, saying, "Whatever happens…we shall always be sisters." Teary eyed, the girls embraced, vowing sisterly fidelity to one another as evening fell upon the house of Joseph.

Tiberius was bunked down for the night in the soldier's quarters, sleeping upon his mat when suddenly he bolted upright, awakened by a startling dream. Breathing rapidly, he glanced around the dark barracks, finding all was as it ought to be at such a late hour. The only disturbance was the cacophony of snoring soldiers. Heaving a heavy sigh, he laid back down upon his mat, finding a comfortable position on his less than comfortable bedding. Shutting his eyes, Tiberius contemplated his strange dream, replaying it in his mind.

The dream had begun with the cross of Jesus silhouetted against the dark ominous sky…the violent earthquake rumbling beneath his feet, followed by the blood of Jesus descending as lightly as a spring rain upon himself and those around him. Perplexed by the strange occurrence, Tiberius tried to wipe the blood from his person, but he could not remove the crimson stain. Then suddenly, he found himself engulfed by a glorious light and in the midst of the illumination, stood Jesus. Overcome by the glorious vision, Tiberius fell to his knees at the feet of the one he had crucified. Bowing his face to the ground, he worshipped the Son of God.

Convinced the dream signified the deity of Jesus, Tiberius tried to decipher the full meaning of what he had dreamt. He knew he was guilty in the death of Jesus and there was blood on his hands, innocent blood. Yet, there were those present at the cross which had not lifted a finger against him. Why then did the blood of Jesus fall upon them? What was the significance of His blood? And why could he not remove it from himself? He had proclaimed at the cross that Jesus was the Son of God, but now what? What did this Son of God…this Jesus expect of him? Failing to come up with intelligent answers to his profound questions, the centurion fell into a deep slumber.

The next morning being the third day since the crucifixion, Tiberius awoke, feeling better than he had since the brutal attack by Sejanus' assassins which had left him in constant pain. Then, it dawned on him. Unable to believe it, Tiberius laid his hand against his left side and to his amazement, not only was the pain gone, but even the unsightly scars had vanished. Surely, this was the work of God! Exuberant, Tiberius jumped to his feet and ran his hand up and down his once lacerated flesh. Overwhelmed by his healing, he was oblivious to the fact that he was being observed by several of his soldiers, neither did he notice that Marcus had entered the barracks.

"Tiberius, thou dost look as if thou hast been granted a furlough," said Marcus, approaching the centurion, who upon hearing him, looked up at the cadet. "I hath never seen thee look so pleased. Thou art usually of grave aspect."

"Marcus…in a manner of speaking…I hath been granted a furlough," declared Tiberius, his countenance beaming. "I hath awakened this morning feeling like a new man…the chronic pain I suffered is completely gone… even the scars I once bore upon my side are no longer visible! Come…see for thyself!"

Marcus drew near to take a look for he had seen the centurion's unsightly scars. They were hard to miss. Having permission of his superior, the cadet examined Tiberius' left side for himself. Marcus could not believe it. The terrible scars were gone! They had disappeared from his body! Astonished, Marcus asked, "Tiberius Marcius, what hath happened unto thee? How is this possible?"

"Last night, I had a dream about Jesus...He appeared to me in a great light! This morning, I awoke...free of pain and scars! Marcus, I am greatly persuaded Jesus was who He said He was! Who but the Son of God could do such a miracle?"

"Jesus performed many miracles. I myself witnessed one of them... make that two," amended Marcus, his expression serious. "But why would Jesus perform this miracle for thee? Thou art not blameless in his death. Thou did oversee his crucifixion."

"Marcus, I am as astounded as thou art...I know I am altogether unworthy and undeserving to merit such a wonderful miracle, but I hath received...and my heart is full of gratitude. I can scarce contain myself. If this barracks were not full of soldiers and I was not an officer, I would whoop and holler at the top of my lungs for I am exceedingly overjoyed!"

"Then, let me not rob thee of thy joy, Tiberius Marcius."

"My joy cannot be so easily stolen," grinned the centurion.

"Hearing thy good news, I nearly forgot my duty," stated Marcus, remembering why he had come after Tiberius in the first place. "Pilate hath sent for thee. Thou art to report to him as soon as possible."

His countenance sobering, Tiberius questioned, "Dost thou know why he hath summoned me?"

"I do not, Tiberius Marcius."

"Wait outside. I shall join thee as soon as I am fully dressed."

Heeding the centurion's orders, the cadet left Tiberius, who quickly donned his uniform, his step lighter than it had been in a very long time.

Meeting up with one another, the soldiers dutifully headed to Pilate's residence and upon reaching their destination, they separated. The cadet reported for guard duty and Tiberius presented himself to the governor.

"Thou did send for me, thy Excellency?"

"I did," said Pilate, staring hard at the centurion, who stood ram rod straight before him, having his helmet tucked under his arm. "I hath somewhat to ask of thee concerning the King of the Jews, whom thou crucified three days ago."

Accustomed to being interrogated by those in authority, Tiberius maintained a calm outward appearance, though he felt rather unsettled at being called before the governor and doubly so, considering the subject.

"Centurion, it was told unto me by the chief priests that the King of the Jews said he would rise from the dead on the third day. The only way humanly possible for this to occur is that he never died in the first place."

Motivated by self preservation, soldiers made absolutely certain their crucifixion victims were truly dead, knowing if they failed to perform a crucifixion properly, they would suffer the same brutal fate.

"Centurion…I ask thee…art thou certain he died on the cross?"

"I am quite certain, governor," answered Tiberius steadily, wondering why Pilate was questioning him again on the death as he had already so inquired of him on the day of the crucifixion. "One of my soldiers confirmed the death of Jesus by taking his spear and piercing his side," stated the centurion, his response bringing to remembrance his own pierced side that was now healed.

Pondering the centurion's reply, Pilate grunted and turned away.

Tiberius sensed the governor was troubled. His conscience was clearly bothering him and rightly so for he had bowed to the will of the people and had ordered the execution of an innocent man.

"Centurion, thou art dismissed," uttered Pilate with an imperious wave of his ring clad hand. "I hath no further need of thee. Return to thy post."

"Hail, Caesar," said Tiberius, striking his breast in deference to the name of the Emperor and then departed, breathing a deep sigh of relief.

"Why did the governor summon thee?" asked Marcus, upon the centurion's return.

"He wanted to be sure Jesus had died upon the cross."

"Why?"

"The chief priests reported unto Pilate that Jesus said he would rise from the dead on the third day."

"This is the third day…" stated Marcus, wondering if such a thing were even possible. "Dost thou think he will rise from the dead?"

"It stands to reason he could," said Tiberius, lowering his voice as he and Marcus were under the surveillance of a soldier. "Let us resume this discussion later. We are being watched."

Just as Tiberius and Marcus finished speaking together, the soldier approached them and addressed the centurion directly, saying, "Art thou Tiberius Marcius?"

"I am he."

"Quintus Atilius hath sent me to deliver this," said the soldier, handing a parchment to the centurion, who unfurled it and read its contents.

Looking up from the parchment, Tiberius spoke to the soldier, saying, "Tell Quintus Atilius, I welcome the return of my body servant and I request he provide for his needs in my absence."

"I will relay thy message as stated," replied the soldier and then disappeared as suddenly as he had arrived.

"This is a memorable day indeed!" exclaimed Tiberius, delighted to learn Anatole had returned to his service. "My servant who ran away hath come back of his own free will!"

"Truly, this is a day of good tidings," said the cadet, genuinely happy for the centurion. "The day is young. Perhaps, there is more good news in store for thee."

"Perhaps," said Tiberius, basking in his good fortune.

XLIX

It had been four months since Tamar had seen Tiberius in the crowd and though he had not sought after her, she believed in her heart that he would return for her. Longing for that day, she tried to make the best of her life, which was relatively uneventful with one notable exception. Tamar was now faced with a new candidate since Caleb had voluntarily relinquished his right to her. Joram had begun wooing her with gifts and compliments. Determined to win her heart, he showered her with attention, but she felt no more for him than she did his elder brother. Finding it increasingly difficult to put off Joram, who sought a commitment from her, Tamar threw herself on the mercy of God.

She prayed and fasted, beseeching God to deliver her out of the delicate predicament she found herself in for she did not want to hurt Joram as she had Caleb. The situation had become strained as the family had come to the stark realization that Tamar did not want to be a part of their clan. Even Serah was not herself. Miriam, however, was the most disagreeable of all. She voiced her displeasure as often as she could and this day was no exception.

"Thou art a foolish woman," scoffed Miriam, verbally attacking Tamar in front of Serah and Rachel. "Any young woman would be fortunate to hath either Caleb or Joram for their husband. Yet, thou hast steadfastly refused both of these fine, young Jewish men! Instead, thou dost pine for that immoral pagan soldier! I am beginning to wonder if thou art even a child of Abraham! Thou dost behave thyself more like a Gentile! Since when doth a Jew fall in love with a Gentile?"

"Miriam, hold thy tongue," reprimanded Serah, appalled at the blatant hostility manifested by Miriam toward Tamar.

"I am only stating what everyone in this house is thinking!" argued Miriam, giving Tamar a nasty look. "If thou dost ask me…she is a poor excuse for a Jewess!"

"Stop it…I love her…" Rachel cried out, running to Tamar and throwing her arms about her waist, not understanding what the fuss was about. "I love Tamar! Do not talk about her that way!"

Encircling Rachel within her arms, Tamar blinked back her tears, not wanting to further upset the little girl.

Eyeing Miriam sternly, Serah scolded, "Thou wilt never speak to Tamar in that manner again! Leave us!"

Heeding Serah's command, Miriam left the room, grumbling under her breath.

"Serah, how doth Miriam know for whom I long?" Tamar asked timidly, mindlessly stroking Rachel's hair. "Did thou tell her?"

"I told her nothing, Tamar. What Miriam knows...she knows because she heard Caleb discussing the matter."

"What I am I to do, Serah? It hath been six months since I came to thy house...and my lord hath not yet returned."

"Tamar, hast thou considered...he may not return for thee," said Serah gently.

"I am praying...fasting...believing! Wilt God not answer me?"

"It may be that He hath already answered thy prayer, but His answer was not the one thou did desire," Serah reproved softly. "We do not always recognize the sovereign hand of Jehovah God."

Growing bored with the conversation; Rachel slipped from Tamar's arms and ran off to play.

"Tamar, perhaps thou art not meant to return to the centurion. God may intend for thee to remain in this house and marry either Caleb or Joram. I know things are uncomfortable between thee and my brothers, but if thou would simply choose one of them for thy husband...all would be well again."

"Serah...I cannot deny what is in my heart. It would not be fair to thy brothers."

"Do then what seems right unto thee," replied Serah and having no more to say on the subject, she walked out of the room, leaving Tamar to consider what she had said.

"Marcus, where wert thou?" demanded Tiberius, his aspect rigid. "I hath been searching for thee. Dost thou not know thou art to seek permission of thy superior before taking leave?"

"My apologies, Tiberius Marcius," said Marcus humbly, knowing he had erred in proper military procedure. "I failed to notify thee of my whereabouts. It was stupid of me."

"That is putting it mildly! I could severely reprimand thee for this infraction," threatened the centurion, greatly displeased with the cadet's conduct. "What was so important that thou did risk taking unauthorized leave? Where wert thou?"

"I was summoned by my uncle…the Tribune. There was no time to seek thy permission. He bade me come immediately."

"Even so, thou should hath sent word through another!" admonished Tiberius, not letting the cadet off easily.

"I stand corrected," uttered Marcus, appearing contrite.

"Why did the Tribune summon thee?"

"So that I might personally deliver this…" answered Marcus, producing a scroll. "Tiberius Marcius, thou hast been recalled to Rome."

Stunned, Tiberius snatched the scroll from the cadet's hand, unrolled it and read it, hardly able to believe his eyes. The Prefect requested that he return at once to Rome by order of Caesar. No further details were given.

"I am to return to Rome immediately," announced Tiberius, his mind reeling.

"I am going with thee, Tiberius Marcius."

"Thy uncle is here and thy military future would be better served under his watchful eye."

"My uncle sees it differently. He believes I shall fare better if I go with thee to Rome."

"If the Tribune hath granted thee permission to go with me…then I shall not stand in thy way."

"I am pleased to hear that, Tiberius Marcius."

"I must notify Pilate of our departure," remarked the centurion, rolling up the parchment tightly.

"That will not be necessary. The Tribune hath already done so on our behalf," voiced Marcus. "We art officially relieved of our duties."

"Wait," exclaimed the centurion, grabbing hold of Marcus' arm. "What of Quintus Atilius? Hath he been recalled also?"

"He was not recalled by Sejanus…but the Tribune hath granted him permission to return to Rome with us. He told me to tell thee…he is a man of his word."

Relieved to hear the good news, Tiberius let go of the cadet's arm, ordering, "Go pack thy gear. When thou hast done so, we shall return to the garrison and join Quintus Atilius. Go…be quick about it for I am anxious to leave Judea."

A short time later, Marcus and Tiberius arrived at the military outpost and sought Quintus Atilius among the company of soldiers, finding him and Anatole busy packing their personal belongings.

Seeing his master, Anatole dropped what he was doing, sank to his knees and pleaded, "Domine, hath mercy upon thy servant for I hath repented of my unfaithfulness."

Walking over to his servant, Tiberius put his hand on Anatole's shoulder and looking upon him, he said sincerely, "I hath missed thee sorely, Anatole. I am pleased thou hast returned unto me."

"Domine, I do not deserve so kind a greeting," conceded the body servant meekly, surprised by his master's gracious reception.

"Arise, Anatole. All is well between us," assured Tiberius, regarding his servant favorably.

Standing to his feet, Anatole said, his voice choked with emotion, "My lord, behold thy humble servant."

Taking it all in, Marcus stood by quietly.

"Tiberius Marcius, thou dost look remarkably well," declared Quintus Atilius, noticing his friend appeared not only healthy, but happy. "Serving Pilate evidently suited thee."

"Quintus Atilius, I am a changed man. The hand of God hath touched my circumstances. I shall explain everything on our journey home."

"I look forward to thy tale, Tiberius Marcius," said Quintus Atilius, tossing gear into his bag.

"The ship leaves in two hours," Marcus reminded his superior. "We hath not much time. With thy permission, I wish to say a proper farewell to my uncle."

Granting his request, Tiberius said, "Go…but do not tarry long."

"Is he accompanying us back to Rome?" queried Quintus Atilius, upon the cadet's departure.

"He is."

"Should we be concerned?"

"The Tribune wishes him to remain under my supervision. I hath no qualms about his coming with us, nor should thee. In fact, I believe it bodes well for us."

"I assume we are leaving this place because the Tribune is pleased with thy training of his nephew."

"Quintus Atilius, we are returning to Rome sooner than we imagined, but we are returning by different mandates," explained Tiberius, his voice dispassionate. "I hath been recalled to Rome by Sejanus and thou art returning with me…because the Tribune hath kept his word."

"Friend, I find it troubling that Sejanus hath recalled thee," expressed Quintus Atilius, somber faced. "Dost thou hath any idea why he hath done so?"

"I do not and I am not overly concerned. I believe a power greater than I is at work in my life and whatever will be is in His hands. My enemy hath not been able to destroy me thus far and I trust he never shall."

Digesting the peculiar statement, Quintus Atilius sensed Tiberius was altogether a different man than the one he had known only a short time ago. Something had indeed changed him. He seemed at peace with himself. Even his countenance was more relaxed. Quintus Atilius could see whatever had impacted his friend so profoundly had clearly been beneficial to him. Wondering if it had anything at all to do with Tamar, Quintus Atilius probed, "Tiberius Marcius, hast thou any word on thy maidservant?"

"I saw her once in a crowd, but we spoke not," answered the centurion, his eyes thoughtful as he recalled the day. "It appeared well with her."

"I too saw her…" interjected Anatole, remembering the dire circumstances of that day. "I had need of assistance and she provided for me."

Turning to look at his servant, his interest peaked, Tiberius inquired, "What kind of assistance, pray tell?"

"Domine, I am ashamed to admit it, but I was begging…for I was hungry."

Tiberius and Quintus Atilius were visibly shocked by the servant's admission.

"I am indebted unto Tamar for not only did she give me money, but she bid me return unto thee…saying thou would forgive me. If I had not encountered her that day…I would be lying by the side of the road…dead from starvation."

"Did she say anything else?"

"Domine, the first words she spoke were of thee. Seeing my pitiful condition, she feared for thy welfare…supposing ill had befallen thee also."

"Anatole, before we leave Judea, we must make certain it is well with

Tamar," said Tiberius, moved by the maid's concern for him and his servant. "It is the least we can do for her…after what she hath done for thee."

Quintus Atilius and Anatole exchanged glances, each man knowing the centurion had a soft place in his heart for the woman.

Upon Marcus' return, the three soldiers and Anatole left the outpost and rode out to Joseph's residence. Wasting no time for time was of the essence; Tiberius directed his servant and Marcus to maintain a reasonable distance from the house, while he and Quintus Atilius went ahead of them a little ways and conferred privately.

"Quintus Atilius, my conscience will not rest till I know how she hath fared," said Tiberius. "I ask thee to go and inquire on my behalf. The inquiry shall not be unexpected. I warned those of the house, I would return, vowing if they had mistreated her, I would reclaim her. Wilt thou go in my stead?"

"Tiberius Marcius, I would rather not," stated Quintus Atilius honestly.

"Why?" questioned Tiberius, frankly surprised as his friend had never before denied him a request.

"The day thou left her, she tearfully pleaded with me…to tell thee…"

"Tell me what?" Tiberius demanded impatiently.

"She begged me to tell thee…that she loved thee."

"Why then, did thou not tell me?"

"Tiberius Marcius, thou art no fool. Thou knew she loved thee, yet thou left her here. What difference would it hath made to relay unto thee what thou did already know?" contended Quintus Atilius stiffly, his face expressionless. "My words would hath availed her naught."

Staring off in the distance, Tiberius fought to discipline his emotions, acknowledging, "I hath deceived myself…but not thee, my friend."

"Tiberius Marcius, she shall surely come unto thee and it shall not be due to any mistreatment. She shall come to thee…because she loves thee. Friend, if thou hast no affection for the maid…trifle not with her tender feelings. For her sake, I urge thee to leave this place if thou dost feel nothing for her. There is no sense in trampling upon her heart."

Considering the tactful rebuke of Quintus Atilius, Tiberius' heart sank, realizing it was he who had mistreated Tamar. Falling silent, he turned his steed about and trotted back toward Marcus and Anatole.

Wondering if he had overstepped himself, Quintus Atilius turned in his saddle and watched Tiberius ride off.

Alarmed by the presence of soldiers on the property, a field servant came running inside of the dwelling, shouting, "There are four men on horseback standing at the end of the road. Three of them are Roman soldiers! What shall we do, my lord?"

Caleb ran quickly to the door and peered out; having a notion the centurion was among the unwanted guests.

"What is it, my son?" asked Joseph coming into the main room, his mature face etched with worry, having heard the commotion.

Closing the door, Caleb answered soberly, "Father, the centurion hath come for Tamar."

"There is no need to be concerned. We will not hath to relinquish her unto him," Joram said confidently. "When he is satisfied that she hath been well cared for, he will depart…never to return."

"Caleb, fetch Tamar and bring her here quickly," ordered Joseph. "Make no delay!"

Caleb left to do his father's bidding.

Turning to face Joram, Joseph said, "Son, we hath provided for Tamar's physical needs, but thou dost know as well as I, she suffers emotionally. It would be better for all involved, if we allow her to return unto her Gentile master."

"Father, do not send her away. I want her for my wife," stated Joram earnestly.

"Son, she doth not belong among us. It was a mistake to hath thought differently. I fault myself for this grave error in judgment. I should not hath brought her into our home."

Swallowing his disappointment, Joram held his tongue, realizing he would never wed Tamar.

Having Tamar by the arm, Caleb briskly escorted her into the room, arriving just as there was a knock at the door.

Joseph motioned to the field servant to open the portal, which he did reluctantly.

Standing at the entrance was a young Roman soldier, his visage calm and stoic.

"I come in peace," said Marcus, cautiously surveying the men of the house. "I hath been sent by Tiberius Marcius. He wishes to inquire on the welfare of the one…called Tamar. May I speak with her?"

Tamar's heart swelled with joy and she boldly stepped forth declaring, "I am Tamar."

Beholding her, Marcus instantly recognized her as the maid who had held Tiberius' attention that day in the crowd. "Tiberius Marcius wants to know if thou hath been treated well."

"I hath," replied Tamar, her heart pounding with expectation.

"Hast thou any message for Tiberius Marcius?"

Glancing nervously at Joseph, Tamar hesitated to answer, her words lodged in her throat.

Marcus waited for her reply.

"Go in peace, my child," Joseph said kindly, blessing her departure for he knew her heart was not aligned with his house nor would it ever be.

Tight lipped, Caleb and Joram spoke not a word, respecting their father's decision.

Serah came into the room, having packed Tamar's belongings and set the bag at her feet.

Turning to Serah, Tamar warmly embraced her and bid her farewell.

"God hath answered thy prayer, Tamar. Go in peace," cried Serah, giving way to tears.

"May the Lord bless thee and keep thee; the Lord make His face to shine upon thee, and be gracious unto thee; the Lord lift up His countenance upon thee and give thee peace," voiced Joseph, reciting the Aaronic blessing over Tamar. *

Withdrawing from Serah's arms, Tamar responded, her voice wrought with emotion, "May the God of Abraham, keep thee in all thy ways and reward thee abundantly for thy kindness unto me."

Entering the room with Joshua, Rachel quickly surmised what was happening and ran to Tamar. Wrapping her small arms around the object of her affection, Rachel clung to her and tearfully entreated, "Do not leave us, Tamar! I wilt not let thee go!"

Regarding the child with tenderness, Tamar stooped down to the little girl's level and kissed her on the forehead. Wiping her tears, Tamar tried to comfort the child, but Rachel would not be comforted and began to wail.

Coming to the aid of Tamar, Serah lovingly took Rachel in her arms and consoled her.

Finding the child's tears heart wrenching, Tamar slowly rose to her feet. Collecting herself, she took one last look at those around her, picked up her bag and walked out the front door, eager to be reunited with the one she loved.

Escorting the maid down the road, the cadet studied her with great interest as he was taken in by her uncommon beauty. It was quite apparent to him why the centurion desired her.

Beholding Tamar, Tiberius swiftly dismounted his steed and went out to meet her, his heart quickening at the mere sight of her.

Quintus Atilius and Anatole remained upon their horses, intently monitoring what was to be.

Seeing Tiberius coming toward her, Tamar dropped her bag and ran to him, her heart overjoyed.

Picking up the discarded bag, Marcus headed back to his horse, mindful not to interfere in the reunion.

Coming face to face with the centurion, Tamar saw as if for the first time, his physical handsomeness and her heart fluttered at the sight of him. Catching her breath, she said with tenderness, "My lord…it is good to look upon thee."

"Woman, hast thou willingly returned unto me?" inquired Tiberius, his tone and expression guarded as he took in the lovely maid.

"Yes, my lord," answered Tamar, smiling serenely.

Reading the love in her dark, luminous eyes, Tiberius asked, somewhat nervously, "Woman, dost thou love me?"

"Yes, my lord…I love thee," professed Tamar, overwhelmed by the moment. "I prayed thou would return…that I might declare my love for thee. I hath dreamed of this day."

Touched by her ardent declaration, Tiberius took Tamar by the hands and drew her to himself. Lifting her soft hands to his lips, he gently kissed them and looking into her soul, he declared passionately, "Tamar…my beloved, I hath desired thee from the moment I laid eyes upon thee. There is none that compares unto thee. Thou art beautiful in every way. I cannot tell thee how often I yearned for thee…how I longed to confess what was in my heart. Tamar…I hath always loved thee."

Tears gathered in Tamar's eyes, her heart melting at her lover's confession.

"Tamar, my love, I hath much to tell thee. So much hath happened since we parted. Thy God hath made Himself known unto me and hath done me good. It is because of His goodness that I wish to serve Him. My love, thou must teach me of thy God."

"My lord, truly He hath made a way for us where there was none before!"

"Return to Rome with me, Tamar, and if thou art willing…I shall make thee my wife. Together, we shall serve this great God of thy people."

"I would be honored…to be thy wife…my lord," cried Tamar, tears of happiness glistening in her dark eyes.

Taking possession of her, Tiberius swept Tamar into a blissful embrace and tilting her beautiful face upward, he lowered his lips to hers and kissed her tenderly, their hearts merging in sweet union. God had granted them the secret desire of their hearts and to this day…there is no greater love than His.

THE END

* Numbers 6:24-26

About the Author

Hopeless romantic and lover of all things beautiful, Dara Viane resides in South Florida with her husband of twenty-two glorious years, their two energetic teenagers and one very spoiled dog. *NO GREATER LOVE* is Dara's first published novel and she is currently working on the sequel, tentatively titled, *THE CENTURION'S WOMAN*.